PRAISE FOR
WILLIAM S. SLUSHER AND

SHEPHERD OF THE WOLVES

Books by William S. Slusher

Butcher of the Noble
Shepherd of the Wolves

Published by POCKET BOOKS

BUTCHER OF THE NOBLE

William S. Slusher

POCKET BOOKS

New York   London   Toronto   Sydney   Tokyo   Singapore

An *Original* Publication of POCKET BOOKS

POCKET BOOKS, a division of Simon & Schuster Inc.
1230 Avenue of the Americas, New York, NY 10020

ISBN: 0-671-89545-1

First Pocket Books printing September 1996

10 9 8 7 6 5 4 3 2 1

POCKET and colophon are registered trademarks of
Simon & Schuster Inc.

Cover photo by Steven Weinberg/Photonica

Printed in the U.S.A.

Butcher of the Noble is dedicated with deep gratitude:

To my fellow rider, Ms. Liz Casazza, for telling me such things as: "Little girl riders wear paddock boots when hunting, not knee boots!"

To my dear friend Dr. Lee Elliott, a consummate connoisseur of books, for doggedly insisting that I can write.

To my former police aviation partner, Paramedic J. J. Greeves, for making such wry editorial observations as: "Although it creates a very interesting image, I'm sure you meant to say *formally* dressed pianist and violinist, not *formerly* dressed. . . ."

To my true love, Dr. Linda Shields, for being my medical advisor, but so much more for being my love.

And to my oldest, Jason Slusher, struggling so valiantly to complete a searing metamorphosis in an unforgiving land. Hang tough, son. Keep the faith. Success is the sweetest revenge.

William Slusher
March 1996

BUTCHER OF THE NOBLE

PROLOGUE

•••••••••

My name is Lewis Cody.

I am a six-foot-two-inch, 190-pound Caucasian male born the year of the atomic bomb. My gods all died in Vietnam, and my politics lean gently to the right on most issues. I love women, well-raised children, cold Norwegian beer, and the Mother Blue Ridge, not necessarily in that order. I despise arrogance, cruelty, bleeding-heart liberals, and smokers, not necessarily in *that* order. I believe capital punishment is woefully underutilized in America, yet I was "sensitive" decades before it became trendy in heterosexual American men. I speak my mind and I don't much give a damn if it comes out "politically correct" or not.

I am sheriff of Hunter County, Virginia.

They were still wailing when I got there, the cold night the butcher came to Hunter County. I had the windows and the volume up on my unmarked car, and majestic Handel filled it; still, I heard the young girl's screams.

Blood was everywhere: gleaming wet puddles on the ground, smearing and flecking the walls. It was everywhere, but it wasn't what you think, believe me.

Jesus, I thought. *Here we go again.*

1

●●●●●●●●

A Bad Day

In a macabre way, it was fitting that my day, which had degraded steadily from getting shot at to the tragic and senseless killing of a young woman and her baby, should end with the coming of the butcher. Twice I would think the day could not get worse. I was 0 for 2.

It was a sunny Wednesday in early November when the creature called on Hunter County. I'd gotten to bed at three that morning, after pulling duty officer so one of my men could attend a concert in Roanoke with his girlfriend. My chief deputy now had the duty, so I was as "off" as any rural sheriff ever is.

I awoke a little after noon in a bed that seemed empty and cold without Lucia's sweet brown body to snuggle drowsily against, without being able to grow hard against the silken warmth of her, to slide atop her, to delight in that sleepy smile on her face, and to slip into her delicious wet heat. You might think I'd have gotten used to it in the four months since we separated. I guess parts of me had gotten more used to it than others. My heart and my dick were a little slow to adjust.

I reside on the estate of my late friend, Dr. Coleby Butler, as trustee and surrogate father to his daughters, Elizabeth and Anne, until Anne turns twenty-five, when it will all revert to them. Elizabeth, eleven, was in the Hunter County

Elementary School, and Anne, eighteen, was a freshman at UVA in Charlottesville, which suited me at the moment. Solitude both pained and sheltered me now.

I switched on the TV to get the news, and of course, it had to be a plane crash. Some airliner in Oregon down. My daughter, Tess, would've been nineteen this year were it not for the crash of an airliner eight days after her ninth birthday. Every time another aircraft went down, I had to fight off a batstorm of horrid memories and the resulting depression. I slapped the TV off.

I washed my face, staring glumly at the stranger in the mirror, and I put on jeans, riding boots, a turtle-neck sweater, and a bomber jacket. I wore my weathered old Jones hat and reflexively stuck my 9mm automatic and my handcuffs on my belt. I had Arthur, the ancient stablehand, saddle my huge Belgian mare for a ride along the Blue Ridge in hope of collecting myself.

Before mounting, I donned a pair of deerhide chaps over my jeans, a garment to protect the legs against briars and branches and stirrup straps. Chaps never failed to evoke a vivid memory, but I'll get to that later.

I rode my horse north from home, or what is temporarily home for me, a twelve-thousand-square-foot mansion called Mountain Harbor on a high-plateau horse farm overlooking the serene Shenandoah Valley.

The Belgian mare was unglamorously named Moose, partially by virtue of her phenomenal size. A few years ago, I attended an auction of the property of a Hunter County farmer crippled by a tractor accident. I wanted to help the farmer and his family, by way of buying something, and the pretty little filly with white fetlocks (horse ankles) captured my heart. I knew less then than I know now about horses, which is pitifully little. I didn't even know the animal was of a pulling breed descended from medieval warhorses, let alone that she was still a kid by horse standards. A horse was a horse, I thought, but feed bills the size of O. J. Simpson's lawyer fees would teach me better, quick. It was like buying a Saint Bernard puppy, thinking that was as big as it would ever get. Belgian monsters are not bred for riding, but I never plowed anything in my life and didn't intend to start. Furthermore, if I owned a horse, I was going to ride it, so I started riding her early on. She took to it, even if her gaits were a bit rigid.

Moose loped up the high rocky pastures to the edge of the plateau, blowing big puffs of steam, and we moved into the woods. Frigid air bit my face. Even the lower altitudes of Hunter County are mountainous, nestled as it is in the western face of the Blue Ridge. It was cold, and a deep carpet of brittle brown leaves covered the forest floor. It was cathartic to sway with Moose's rhythmic gait for nearly an hour, her huge hooves splitting the rustling leaves.

The high Blue Ridge is still relatively isolated, in defiance of the general crowding of the eastern United States. Here in these hazy mountains, "traditional" values are alive and well. Up here, traditional values aren't the politically darling sort that condemn unwed mothers, of which we have several; homosexuals, of which we have a few; or sex before marriage, of which we have mucho. This is not to say such social elements are embraced by the traditional values of mountain Virginia; rather, the values mean being able to go on a month's vacation and leave your house unlocked, knowing that your neighbors would be insulted if you locked it and would promptly blast the legs out from under anybody they caught burglarizing it. These traditional values mean that if you forget your checkbook at the Piggly Wiggly, the clerk just laughs and says, "You're good fer it," and you are.

I halted the big mare and dismounted her on a rock outcropping that afforded a forever view of the serene Shenandoah Valley. Moose seemed happy to be out in the brisk, clean, highland air. I was glad one of us was happy.

I was miserable. Lucia and I were to have been married the previous summer, but at some point prior, she began to have misgivings. She wanted to postpone the marriage until October, to give us time to know more of each other, she said. She meant more than we had learned of each other during the trying time of her grandfather's murder, when we met and fell in love. But by August, it had become clear that whatever was wrong with us wasn't going away. The break-up was bittersweet and, as broken love affairs go, it was civilized, but oh how it hurt. We held each other, we cried, and we ached, for the truth was now unavoidable for us both.

On a rainy night in August, to a gloomy dirge of rolling summer thunder, we faced it and agreed to separate. Lucia said she was afraid marriage would destroy us, bind us rather than bond us. I knew she was probably right for the long run, but, as I stared through the haze at the distant, winding Shenandoah River the day the butcher came, I still felt like a bleeding filet of my soul had been torn out. A man does not get so close to so trophy a woman and not leave a part of himself forever with her.

I'd get over it, I supposed, remounting Moose and heading back through the woods toward Mountain Harbor. I had gotten over worse, or at least I had come to terms with the death of my daughter and the later death of a child I was . . . responsible for.

Still, I was haunted by a seemingly mundane incident years ago when I was a D.C. cop. Some hapless dump-truck driver had inadvertently triggered the dump-bed lever as he was rolling down Pennsylvania Avenue near the National Archives. Unbeknownst to the driver, the empty bed was rising as he drove. At Seventh Street, the upright dump bed on the heavy truck snagged an entire intersection of vital overhead wiring, tearing out stoplights and pulling down utility poles for blocks in two directions. Worse, telephone communications and electricity for most of downtown Washington was wrecked for hours. When I wailed on to the scene in my D.C. police cruiser, the stooped and weathered old dump-truck driver was sitting on the running board of the truck. He smoked a cigarette with wrinkled, trembling hands, and with squinted eyes, he surveyed the sparking wires, screaming people, and flashing fire trucks that lay in his wake. As I approached him, he raised a scarred, *Grapes of Wrath* face that had seen many hard decades. I remember he seemed so unsurprised, so resigned that life was just a string of disasters. As I loaded him into my cruiser, his foreman ran up and screamed: "You're *fired,* you dumb old son of a bitch!" I pushed the enraged foreman back, got in, and drove away. "It don't mean nothin', son," the old man said with a sigh. "Hell, everything turns to shit in the end."

He said it with such tired, total resignation that I was depressed for hours. His words are with me to this day.

Was that the best that could be said of life? Everything turns to shit in the end?

This was my frame of mind when the bullet, tearing through brush at three times the speed of sound, ripped through the loose back of my coat just above my waistline. Its blast echoed down the mountainsides.

As a career police officer, I have made a lot of people do a lot things they did not want to do; I have killed three men and sent many more to prison. Although I enjoy a reputation for being fair, you still don't have a career like mine without making a few enemies, some of whom are inevitably going to be a bit more motivated by revenge than others. I wouldn't have been the first cop somebody tried to even a perceived score with. My heart was pounding before my boots pounded the forest floor.

I have been shot at before, on both sides of the Pacific. I unassed my horse and scurried ungracefully like a panicked crab to a leafy crevice among the big roots of two huge, close trees and hid. Moose is gunshot trained; at the initial shot, mostly because of my unconventional dismount, she started and ran several yards away, but now she stood peering through the brush at me. I whipped the Stetson from my head, drew my pistol, and peeked carefully over the low mound in the forest floor between the two giant oaks. I also felt desperately about the small of my back with my unarmed hand, but it came out with no blood on it, to my considerable relief.

Soon, however, it became apparent that this was to be nothing so dramatic as a revenge hit.

"Ernie!" I heard a man's tense, excited voice shout in the cold autumn air. "Ernie! Over here! I got one! I got one, Ernie!" I peered from cover to see a large, overweight white man, about 35 or so, run partially into view, panting, wearing expensive mail-order hunting duds covered with the requisite safety-orange vest and cap. He was carrying a beautiful scoped deer rifle. He stopped, heaving for breath, and cranked off two more thundering rounds in my general direction. I ducked but I knew he wasn't shooting at me, he was firing signal rounds to "Ernie." I whirled about to look for Moose, but she was downslope beyond his view, only a section of her golden hide showing through the brush.

"Er*neeee!*" the man shouted, his voice high with excitement. "Over here! I got one, Ernie! I got one! A big buck, Ernie!" The man was breathless now, and he was ambling my way with great effort, his feet swishing through the leaves.

"I hear you, Chuck!" Another man's voice called from farther away. "I'm comin'!"

"It's a big one, Ernie!" Chuck shouted. "Biggest goddamn buck I ever saw! I'll make the Boone and Crockett record books with this beauty! Wait 'til the guys back in Richmond see this monster! Over here!"

"I'm comin', Chuck! I'll be right there!"

Chuck came lumbering up the mound, about to have a stroke, from the looks of his beet-red, bloated face. He galumphed several feet past me, facing away toward Moose. He apparently saw what little of her rump that now showed through the forest brush, because he grunted suddenly, shouldered his rifle, and sighted it her way. I took two quick strides and I hit him in the back of the head with the palm of my hand, delivered with a lot of weight behind it. I was a little tense. Truth is, I hit him so hard his head snapped forward, cracking his nose against the stock of the rifle. The gun went off, but the muzzle was pointed at the ground and he promptly dropped the weapon. I swiped the Day-Glo hat from his head, grabbed his hair in my left fist, and yanked him flat on his back. Dry leaves blew from his impact. Still holding a handful of his hair, I landed with a knee on his chest and stuck the big black Sig-Sauer muzzle on the end of his fat nose. His eyes crossed and grew very wide.

"Guess what, Chuckie," I whispered hotly, "you are in some deep shit. You make a sound, and I will compost your whole goddamn *head!* You hear me?"

He nodded with vigor, whimpering and farting at the same time.

He was heavy, but he slid easily over the blanket of leaves to the depression between the two trees.

"Chuck?" the other voice called again, closer now.

I turned Chuckie's hair loose and held a finger to my lips. Gaping up the bore of the automatic pistol in his face,

8

Chuckie became a model of cooperation. He was fairly choking to keep quiet. I rolled him over on his ample belly, patted him down, and handcuffed him.

"Chuck!" Ernie shouted, staggering into view, gasping and looking around. He, too, wore expensive and fashionable hunting togs with the orange safety garb, and he carried a fancy deer blaster. "Where are—*holy shit!*"

"County sheriff!" I shouted at him, sighting my pistol on his chest. "You point that rifle at me and I'll kill you where you stand. Drop it!"

"Hey! Wait a minute!" Ernie said with a trace of anger, still holding his rifle pointed at the ground. His fingers were opening and closing nervously on the grips of the weapon. "What the hell is this all—"

"Drop that rifle!" I demanded.

"Hey, wait a damn minute, buddy!" Ernie snapped. "You don't look like no cop to me! Where's your badge?"

"Mister, you are looking up the barrel of the only badge you're going to get to see while you're holding that weapon. In fact, it is going to be the last thing you ever see if you don't *drop that fucking rifle! Now!*" I shouted the last few words; restraint is not what I do best.

Ernie jumped, pitched the rifle down, and raised his hands.

"Turn around," I said, walking toward him with my gun still aimed at him. "On your knees; hands behind your head. *Do* it!" I searched him and yanked him up. "All right," I said, displaying my silver star and ID folder, "stand easy. But you get within ten feet of me without being told to and I'll shoot you. You understand me?"

"Okay. Sure. Hey, what's this all about, Sheriff? We're hunting legal here!"

"He just *jumped* me, Ernie!" Chuckie whined.

I stuck my gun in my belt, walked back to Chuck, and heaved him to his feet. "What this is all about," I said, "is Daniel fucking Boone, here, is the kind of stupid, tenderfoot city boy who shoots wild at noises in the bushes!"

"Bullshit, mister!" Chuck said. "I shot a deer, man! The biggest goddamn buck you ever saw! Get these handcuffs offa me!"

I whistled loudly through my teeth and yelled, "Apples,

Moose!" Moose will come out in a blizzard for apples. She loped through the trees and up the grade toward us, snorting. Ernie got a slightly sick look on his face as he began to put two and two together. Chuckie stepped back nervously and gawked at Moose as she pounded to a stop and snorted again. I gave Moose an apple from the saddlebag. She peered curiously at the two Great White Hunters.

I took off my perforated bomber jacket and stuck my fingers through the entry and exit bullet holes in the lower back of my coat. "That look like a *deer* to you, Davy Crockett?" I shouted, on the edge of my control. I looked at Chuckie. "You almost killed a cop today, genius! All because you didn't wait for a good enough look at your target to tell a hundred-pound deer from a *ton* of *horse* with a rider on it!"

"Aw, man." Ernie was sweating now. "Hey, Sheriff, I . . . I'm sorry man, I—"

"Sorry, my ass! You almost killed me, you dumb bar-stool woodsman! Hunters and hikers and livestock are killed every year by incompetent assholes like you! You trigger-happy fools give *real* hunters a bad name. You're goddamned lucky I didn't blow your face off in self-defense." Chuck nervously eyed the Sig 9-mm in my belt.

"Hey, hey, Sheriff," Ernie said with a supercilious smile on his face, white teeth flashing beneath his mustache. He withdrew a hundred-dollar bill from his wallet and waved it like a flag at a fourth-of-July parade. "I don't blame you for being a little worked up, man. Chuck did a stupid thing—"

"Aw, thanks a lot, Ernie!"

"Shut up, Chuck, I'll handle this. Look . . . Sheriff . . . I'm sure we can . . . well . . . let's just say we can sort of pay for the damage to your jacket." He continued to wag the hundred conspicuously. "There's . . . nine . . . others just like this one back in my car. Man could buy a damn fine new leather jacket. Know what I mean, Sheriff?" His eyebrows arched.

"Ernie," I said, walking toward him and staring him in the eyes, "you listen real carefully. You tear that bill up and put it in your mouth."

Ernie's eyebrows drooped to a frown. He looked at the hundred. "What?"

"You heard me. Tear it up. Put it in your mouth. Chew it up . . . and swallow it."

"What? Are you nuts? That's a hunnerd-goddamn-dollar bill!"

"Attempting to bribe a police officer in the performance of his duty is a *felony!*" I shouted, a tad overwrought. "Unless you eat the evidence! Get the *fucking* picture?"

Ernie started to look like a preacher who begins his sermon and an attack of diarrhea at the same time. He took one fond last look at the bill in his hand, tore it slowly, and tucked the pieces into his mouth.

I uncuffed Chuckie. He looked at me sheepishly, rubbing his wrists. "Uh, Sheriff," he mumbled, "I don't, ah, I don't suppose there's any evidence I could eat, is there?"

I went to the two huge trees, retrieved Chuck's gorgeous rifle, and swung the barrel down hard into the crotch of one of the trees, where it wedged with a crunch. Chuckie winced. I removed the stout lead rope that was looped about Moose's neck and hooked to her bridle. I tied one end around the polished stock of the rifle and hooked the other to the roping ring on Moose's saddle.

Chuck figured it out. "Aw . . . shit, Sheriff. That's a forty-eight-hundred-dollar Weatherby rifle; I had it custom built!"

"Looks like evidence to me," I said, tersely.

"Yeah," Ernie said in confirmation, spitting little pieces of U.S. currency onto the leaves, "me too."

"Aw, you're a big help!"

"What *dumbass* got us into this?" Ernie snapped.

I offered Moose another apple from three feet away. The rope went taut, but then, Moose really likes apples. Chuck squinted at the creak of the rifle barrel bending and the glass in the scope shattering. He flinched when the stock broke with a loud crack that echoed in the cold mountain air.

I snatched up the other guy's rifle, removed the bolt from it, and pitched it at him hard. Ernie juggled it in surprise and dropped it, then picked it up.

I drew my pistol, turned, and sighted on Chuckie's horrified face. His eyes blinked rapidly and his lips twitched. "No! Please, *no!*" His voice broke.

I altered aim minutely to the huge tree eight feet behind

Chuck and pulled the trigger. The big black automatic whipped in recoil, flashed, and roared. The bullet passed Chuckie's ear a carefully measured six inches away. "Oh . . . Jesus," he whispered, quivering all over. He began to cry.

"That's what it feels like to be *shot* at, you *asshole!"* I roared, now pretty much out of control. I decocked and holstered the pistol. "If I ever see you idiots again, I'll charge *you* with reckless discharge of a firearm and *you* with bribery! Now get the fuck out of here!" I was nearly screaming, breathing heavily.

The two men tromped smartly away through the swishing leaves as Chuck stared morosely at his ruined rifle. Ernie hissed vehement remarks that suggested an appalling lack of concern for Chuck's self-esteem.

I sat down weakly on a log, propped my arms on my knees, and hung my head, waiting for my respiratory rate to subside. "Christ," I whispered. "What a day."

I didn't know it then, but my day hadn't even begun.

2

•••••••••

A Bad Day Worse

I crossed the footbridge over the creek between the stable and the grand old mansion. My official car was parked in a two-story, six-car garage by the creek, alongside a big Ford four-wheel-drive dually pickup truck for pulling gooseneck horse trailers and the old blue Plymouth Horizon that belonged to Polly, the housekeeper and cook who lived over the big garage.

My sheriff's cruiser was a new silver Chevrolet Caprice. It was "unmarked," as we say in the business, which was a bit silly. Who else but a cop would drive a monocolored sedan with blackwall, high-performance tires, blue lights in the grill and rear-window tray, and enough antennas on it to make a guided-missile frigate jealous? Every hot-rod kid in Hunter County could spot it half a mile away in a rain-storm. In the trunk, among the road flares, radio receivers, and tire chains was a sheepskin case containing my sweet old M-14 rifle. The M-14 was an antique by modern weaponry standards, but I could still drop a running man at fifty yards with it. If he was courteous enough to stand still for a few seconds, I could send him to hell from two hundred yards. Not bad for a thirty-year-old iron-sight rifle, let alone for a middle-aged lawman who'd fought one war and a marriage and lost both.

I climbed the spiral staircase from the foyer to the second floor, which had six bedrooms. The door to Elizabeth's room was open. I paused to look in at her high-canopied bed and the required-issue, alphabet-described equipment of the modern American preteen: her TV, VCR, CD, and her 486SX IBM. At eleven, Elizabeth had discovered horses, as if she had not been raised in Virginia riding country. She had thrown herself into equitation lessons and "pony club," and she had read scores of books, ranging from *Horses Throughout History* to a nauseatingly illustrated veterinary text entitled *Diseases of the Equine Digestive Tract*. The walls of her bedroom were covered in pictures of horses, some of which were photographs of her in her little boots, coat, jodhpurs, and velvet-covered helmet, mounted on the sturdy little Irish jumper I bought her with estate money. She named the little mare Dublin since its papered name, Golden Juniper's Fair Niece Of Dublin, was a tad awkward. I was proud of how well she had applied herself and was glad that she had such devotion, but I could not avoid remembering that part of it was that she had been so desperate for a diversion from the deaths of her parents last year. The equestrian pursuit had been very good for her recovery. Old friends of the family from Charlottesville had come by on Tuesday and had taken Elizabeth and Dublin to a hunt near Middleburg. Her grades remained good enough that she could afford the occasional day or so out of school.

I stripped down and collapsed in the huge, hot-tub/shower arrangement off the master bedroom. I soaked for twenty minutes, reflecting that I should have handled the Great White Hunters more professionally. What was happening to me? Was it Lucia? Was it the job? Was I just getting too old?

By the time I descended the curving staircase in moccasins and a maroon sweatsuit, the marvelous smells of prime burritos were making me even more grateful that I had Polly to fuss after me.

My dog, Gruesome, a crippled English Bulldog ugly as a syphilitic warthog, charged in from the den to greet me. I rolled him over on the foyer tiles and he growled and nipped gently at my hands in an old ritual. His breath smelled suspiciously of beer.

I sat down at a walnut dining room table the 187th Tactical Fighter Squadron could have landed on, and Polly brought me a steaming plate of cheese-smothered, jalapeno-peppered burritos that could give Julia Childs an erection. I cut a generous chunk from one, savored its aroma, lifted it, and froze with my mouth open, as that most dreadful of dinnertime sounds, the telephone, jangled the evening peace.

"Hello. *What?*" I heard Polly demand in the kitchen. Polly was the self-appointed sheriff of the sheriff. She hated it when people called me at mealtimes and she didn't strain herself to conceal it. I prayed the call was for Elizabeth, even though she had her own phone. "Yeah, I reckon he is, but he *eatin'!*" Polly continued, dashing my hopes. "Well . . . okay, Captain Arroe, I'll git him, but . . . he eatin'!" Uh oh. Percy Pierce Arroe was my chief deputy, a giant and utterly reliable man who would not disturb me when he had the duty except to inform me of something I needed to be aware of.

"Hi, Pierce," I said, when Polly brought me the phone. Pierce tears the heads off people who call him Percy. "What's up?"

"Hey, Sheriff," Pierce's deep bass voice rumbled. "Sorry to interrupt your dinner, but I thought you'd want to know, Roanoke County sent a message through on the computer about two assholes who roughed up a girl and took her purse outside a mall in Roanoke. Description's for two standard-issue redneck maggots in a dark-green pickup truck, tags unknown. Roanoke County thinks they could be comin' our way. Lewis, it appears the victim was the daughter of Roanoke County Councilman Arnold Dreyfuss, and of course he's jumping up and down and screaming at the Roanoke County boys like it was the crime of the century, even though the girl ain't hurt and she only had about twenty bucks. They said they'd really appreciate if we can help 'em out on this one. Just thought I'd let you know, since it's the daughter of a fat cat and all."

I knew Arnie Dreyfuss. He was a corrupt jerk, but then,

if two punks assaulted my daughter, I'd be hopping mad, too.

"Okay, Pierce, thanks. Get the description out to the men on duty, but don't call anyone in on their off time."

"Okay, Sheriff. Say, Lewis, if it's okay with you, I need to run by the house for an hour. I just called Brenda, and she says Bryant's science project is due tomorrow and he can't get the damn thing to work right."

"Sure, Pierce. I'm not doing anything heavy, so I'll get dressed and help look for Roanoke County's little problem. Take the evening if you need it."

"Naw, thanks anyway, Sheriff. If I can't get Bryant's principles of hydraulic displacement gadget working in an hour, he may have to change his project to principles of decaying hotdogs, or something. I'll be back on the road in a hour. Turn in around oh-three-hundred."

"Good enough. I'll take the duty 'til I hear from you. See you on the road in an hour or so."

"Ten-four, Sheriff."

I finished dinner and put on my uniform. When I was elected sheriff, I scrapped the old departmental uniform that made us look like the doorman at the Waldorf. The former sheriff, Oscar Wheeler, another corrupt jerk like Arnie Dreyfuss, seemed to feel that he had to dress like an Argentine field marshal, and that was only one of the reasons I didn't want to look anything like him. I ordered new uniforms of simple tan, with departmental patches on the shoulders, discreet rank insignia on the collars, and badges and name tags on the fronts. We wore brown boots and leather gear, with narrow-brimmed Stetson hats and brown leather bomber jackets in cold weather. It was a simpler, more dignified, and less expensive uniform, and we no longer looked like Starfleet commanders.

By the time I rolled down Mountain Harbor's long winding drive, which was bordered by tall old pines, and out onto the highway, the sun was well below the surrounding mountaintops. It was downright dark between the steep hillsides. I turned on my headlights.

I was reaching for the microphone to mark myself on the air when my dispatcher spoke. "Sheriff Six, assist State with an accident with injury, hit-and-run, Highway 665, one mile south of Bram's Ridge Road. Sheriff Six?"

"Sheriff Six," Haskel Beale replied. "Reassign that, please, Cindy, I'm jist fixin' to make me a traffic stop."

I held the mike to my mouth. "Sheriff One; I'm in service, Cindy. You can hold me on that accident until the trooper arrives."

"Ten-four, Sheriff One. Thank you, sir. The area state trooper is en route."

"Very good, Cindy. Rescue on the way? And is there a description and last-seen on the runner's vehicle?"

"Sheriff One, Rescue is notified. The caller could provide no description other than a pickup truck last seen south on 665. No further. The call came in from a car phone. We're ringing back for more information, but there is no answer. Ten-four?"

"Ten-four. I'm about five minutes away."

"Seventeen twenty-four." Cindy said, logging the time on the tapes.

I turned on the blue strobe lights in the grill and rear-window tray, stuck a magnetic "Kojak" blue light on the dash, and stepped on the powerful, police interceptor-model Chevy. As it cornered flatly through the mountain turns, I briefly wondered if the pickup in which the striker had fled this accident could possibly be the truck Roanoke County was seeking. It had to be considered, but it was a long shot. There were more pickup trucks than cars in any agricultural jurisdiction like mine.

Ahead, I could see a car stopped on the roadside, flashers blinking, a new Buick Roadmaster with a car-phone antenna on its rear deck. A hundred yards beyond it, a cloud of steam was rising from wreckage off the road in the evergreens by Spoon Creek, which paralleled the highway.

As I got out on the shoulder at the scene, a hysterical older woman I didn't recognize ran from the wreckage toward me, waving her hands in the air. "Oh, Officer! Thank God you're here! She's dying! Get an ambulance! Get an ambulance!" The woman was about one nerve fiber short of a heart attack.

I glanced at the wreck, about fifty feet down a shallow

embankment into the woods near the creek. It looked bad. You learn to recognize the signs of high-speed impact when you see them, and they were all there now. It was too dark to see any more.

In the old days, it was usually disease that accounted for the gravestones of those under 60 or so. Nowadays, the plague that can rise up out of nowhere and smite any of us is car accidents. They've become the modern metaphor for the chance cruelty in life. The risk of the road can get any of us, anytime.

"Get an ambulance, quick!" the woman screamed. "She's dying! Get an am—"

I put my hands on the woman's shoulders. "Listen to me, ma'am," I told her. She heaved for breath. "Rescue is on the way. Are you hurt?" She shook her head, struggling to bring herself under control. "Okay, good. Now listen to me, ma'am. Did you see the accident?"

She now nodded her head, her lower lip trembling. "Y-yes, Sheriff. Well, I just saw some headlights passing her, coming right at me in my lane! He was passing over the double yellow line, Sheriff! He was coming right at me! He just swerved back into his own lane to miss me and he hit that poor woman and ran her right off—right off the road!"

"What kind of vehicle, ma'am?"

"I don't know, Sheriff . . . uh . . . it was . . . it was some kind of pickup truck! I just saw headlights!"

"Did you see a license plate?"

"No! No, I—"

"Did you see who was driving?" I asked quickly, glancing again at the wreck.

"No! I just saw these headlights, Sheriff! He stopped! He stopped and—and—and he ran down to that lady's car, but then he saw me, and he ran back to his truck and left! He drove off real fast! I said, 'Stop, stop!' but he just drove off real fast!"

"Then you must have seen him, ma'am. What did he look like?"

"No! I couldn't see him—I mean, not real good! It took me a long ways to get my car stopped after I saw the woman go off the road! By the time I got out, he was standing down by the wrecked car looking in it. When he saw me walking back, that was when he ran to his truck and drove away! I mean, I could see it was a man, but it was dark, Sheriff. My eyes are not so good and I just couldn't see, Sheriff! I just couldn't—"

"It's all right, ma'am, you move over here out of the road and try to relax for me, okay? You've done real good. You're going to be a big help to us, I know. Now, you just sit down in your car and stay there for me." She nodded, her breathing coming in gasps. "There'll be an ambulance and some more police here soon."

I hurried back to my car for my flashlight, speaking into my portable radio with its stubby little antenna. "Sheriff One. Cindy, tell Rescue to expedite, this is a bad one. Driver's trapped." As I was running to the wreck, I heard Cindy's reply on the little radio, which I returned to my jacket pocket. "Ten-four, Sheriff One. Seventeen thirty-one."

Wrecks are never fun, but this one was a real mess. The car was blue, but I couldn't even tell what make it was. Steam rose from the distorted metal, there was the pungent smell of gasoline, and thousands of little diamonds of shattered glass lay everywhere. There was a scorched rubber smear and traces of dark paint flakes on what remained of the left front quarter panel and wheel and the left door skin. The little car had hit a thirty-inch poplar that hadn't budged since before the *Titanic* went down. The front end was severely compressed, and the engine was jammed back alongside the driver, who was also hard to recognize. Her head lay back on the bloody headrest of the collapsed seat. The door lay open; my face tightened when the flashlight beam fell on her. She had probably been a very pretty young woman, but she now looked like the loser in a machete fight. The steering wheel was warped in a way experience told me had probably caused major internal injuries. I switched the ignition off and removed the keys.

The woman moaned and opened her eyes, but I doubted she could see through the blood in them. "Don't let him—*cuh!*—see us," she said, choking and coughing. "Help him! Help my—*gah!*" Her lips were split and most of her front teeth were missing. She lisped wetly, trying to pronounce words with an *s* in them. Her lower body was

19

pinned to the seat and the buckled floor by the dashboard and steering column and I doubted she could last the time it would take to cut her out. I'm no doctor, but I've seen a lot of wrecks. I wondered what first aid I might render, but I knew that with this poor woman I wouldn't know where to start.

"Ma'am," I said, kneeling in the pine needles by the door. Something sharp stuck me in the knee. "Did you get a license number of the vehicle that hit you?"

"Noooo! Noooo! Pickup truck. He looked at me!" When she spoke, her voice gurgled in a way that made my skin crawl. "He looked at me. *Cuh! Cahg!* Don't let him see us! Help him. Please!"

People in shock say strange things. I was glad to hear the sirens of the volunteer fire department's ambulance and rescue truck growing nearer. I saw the woman's purse on the floor by what was left of her feet. I pulled it out and went through it, looking for her identification. Her driver's license photo showed a smiling, lovely young woman in her early twenties. Catherine Lynn Calder. I thought for a moment that the name rang a bell, but then a lot of names did. I tucked the license in my belt.

"Ma'am, did you see who was driving? Man or woman?"

"Man! Don't let him—"

"White or black?"

"White man! Smelled like whiskey! Don't—"

"Did he have a beard or mustache? Tell me what he looked like, ma'am." I struggled to understand her bubbly, distorted speech.

"No!" she said, gasping. "Older man! He looked at me. He looked at me."

"Long hair or short hair?"

"Short . . . he looked at me. He tried to pass me. Hit me. Pushed me off the road! He—aach!" She choked on her own blood, coughed agonizingly, and gave me that awful look, that please-tell-me-I'm-not-dying look. I hate when they do that. "He came and looked at me. Don't let him see us. He looked at me. Then he ran away . . . away." Her bloody hand suddenly seized my wrist and I jerked, but I recovered and took her hand in mine. "Don't let him see us," she

20

gurgled in agony, then, hideously, her eyes rolled back. I realized I was fighting to get my breath, too.

I felt another sharp stick in my knee when I stood, and I groped the surface of my uniform trousers. A thin, twisted piece of metal about two inches long was imbedded in the fabric. It was part of the wreckage, I supposed. I absently stuck it in my pocket. Then I raised my eyes and my heart clutched.

I almost dropped the flashlight. Spotlighted among the glass particles in the back seat was one of those yellow Fisher-Price toy steering wheels. A toy. Like you put on a baby seat. Don't let him see *us!*

"Oh *shit!*" I cursed, and I scrambled frantically around to the downslope door of the car. *Help him,* she had said.

I wrenched at the passenger door, but it wouldn't budge. Sucking hard breaths through my nose, I shined the flashlight into the dark hole beneath the dislocated dashboard and saw it. A tiny leg, maybe six inches long, with a blue knit bootie on the foot protruded from beneath an upturned gray plastic baby seat crammed between the distorted dash and the buckled floor. The little leg wasn't moving. "Shit!" I spat, yanking furiously on the jammed door, my hat flying from my head, "Shit! Shit! *Shit!*" I heaved with futility several more times on the door. Furious with myself, I bashed the car roof with my flashlight, shattering the light and flinging batteries.

A boxy med unit and a large fire truck screamed up and stopped in the road, their plethora of white and red lights blazing. Yellow-coated firefighters scurried down the slope. The first one was the chief volunteer paramedic, Andy Harmon, a capable veteran who pulled rubber surgical gloves on to his hands as he drew near. The almost imperceptible squint in his eyes when he viewed the driver was telling.

"Andy!" I yelled, "Andy, there's a kid in here!"

"Charlie!" Andy Harmon called loudly with the forced slow calm of a disaster pro. "You and Jasper get that door off. Now! Alice May, get over here and help me with this woman. Move!" The fire personnel scrambled, dragging power tools that could cut cars like paper.

Andy knelt by the driver, probing with rubber-gloved fingers in a slash on her neck. He looked over the roof and made eye contact with me. He shook his head, grimly.

Charlie Hullett spread his feet, lifted a heavy device that looked like two thick, parallel crowbars with a motor on one end, and jammed it into the door seam. The tool emitted an angry howl. Jasper Meriweather pushed me out of the way just as the car door sprang open. Charlie dropped the tool and he and Jasper dived into the car. "Awww. Awww, my God," I heard Charlie say, his helmet banging against the door frame. Jasper stepped back, whirled, and angrily slammed his helmet on the ground. In Charlie's light, I saw the gleaming red mush under the baby seat.

Heaving on that car door moments ago, I had prayed the child was alive. Now I prayed it was dead. It was. Ain't prayer a wonderful thing?

I tried to get my face to relax. Accident, hit-and-run, double fatal. Wonderful. Just *fucking* wonderful! I walked up to the road.

I picked the radio from the pocket of my brown leather bomber jacket with the star pinned to it. "Sheriff One. Updated lookout," I said into the little device. Half a mile away, I could see the single rotating blue roof-light of a Virginia State Police cruiser responding.

"All units, stand by for a hit-and-run lookout," Cindy said on the radio. "Sheriff One, go ahead."

"Sheriff One. This will now be a hit-and-run, fatal. The only additional information will be a white, older male with shorter hair, no facial hair, in a pickup truck, last seen south on 665. The victim was apparently forced off the road, and the fleeing vehicle probably has damage including blue paint transfer to the right front quarter or side. Clear."

Cindy rebroadcast the lookout on her more powerful transmitter as the state police officer pulled up and stepped from his blue-and-gray cruiser. The trooper waved at me and smiled. I waved back. I knew him; he was a sharp, amiable, professional young trooper. He put on his gray hat and strolled toward me.

Suddenly I felt like I'd been kicked in the chest. I snatched the license from my belt and stared at it in horror.

Catherine Lynn Calder. *Don't let him see me.* Oh, dear God. Not this, please.

"Evenin', Sheriff Cody!" the young trooper said brightly, extending his hand.

I shook his hand, reflexively, but I was staring at his nickel-plated name tag with its black letters.

Corporal Boyce Calder.

3

•••••••••

And Worse

I looked around, struggling to order my thoughts. The woman witness was standing by the ambulance, being comforted by a firefighter. The rotating lights of the ambulance and rescue truck threw slashing beams of red light across the nearby trees. The woman's distressed expression pulsed blue in cadence with the alternating flashes of the grill lights in my cruiser. Corporal Boyce Calder looked like all Virginia state troopers on duty looked: he stood ramrod straight in an immaculate blue-and-gray uniform with trooper hat and black patent-leather dress shoes, equipment belt, and holster. Additionally, Boyce had the carefree unconcern of youth and the emotional detachment of a professional road officer who worked a dozen hideous wrecks every month.

"Whadda we got here, Sheriff?" Boyce said, smiling again at me and glancing at the floodlighted, steaming wreck surrounded by laboring firefighters in yellow coats with iridescent striping. "Looks like an ugly one from here. Understand it's hit-and-run?"

"Ah, yeah, Boyce, it is. It's . . . it's a fatal," I said, loudly enough to be heard over the roar of the rescue truck's engine powering the bleaching floodlights on tripods and the screeching cutting equipment.

"Damn. Anybody we know?"

"Boyce," I said, struggling to find my tongue, "listen to me, son." Boyce picked up on my tone immediately, and jerked his gaze from the crowd of firefighters to engage my eyes. His eyes narrowed, but a remnant of smile remained on his face. It was the last smile he would know for a long time.

I sighed. "Boyce, I—" I said, struggling for the right words—as if there were any—but he saw it in my eyes.

The smile on Boyce Calder's face vanished. I could see the realization hit him like a bullet. He had become a player in every road cop's worst nightmare, and now he knew it. He backed up a step. "Oh, God," he whispered. "Cathy. Stevie!"

"Boyce, you don't want go down there. We'll handle this. Just let me drive you—"

"Cathy!" the young man cried, looking toward the wreck. He gathered himself to sprint.

I grabbed his arm. "Boyce, please, son. You don't want—" He threw my hand off and ran wildly down the slope.

Don't let him see us, she had said.

The name hadn't fully registered at first, but I had met Cathy Lynn Calder once before. Fourteen months prior, Boyce Calder and I happened to be involved together in the vehicle pursuit of a pair of notorious brothers who had abducted . . . someone . . . from my custody in front of the Hunter County courthouse. Shots were fired and the infamous Sloan brothers fled with their captive. Boyce happened to be driving through town, on duty. He heard the shots, picked me up, and the chase was on. The abduction both was and was not successful, but I'm not up to explaining that now. In the course of that day's terrible events, Boyce took a bullet. He wasn't too seriously injured, as gunshot wounds go, but he did a couple of weeks in Roanoke Memorial Hospital, recovering. It was there, on a visit, that I met his wife, Cathy, briefly. She was a cute cheerleader sort who obviously adored Boyce.

I could not help but contrast the charming, pretty face I saw that day with the ghastly mess in the steaming wreck.

* * *

"Boyce! Wait!" I shouted, and I went after him, hoping to keep that mangled face in the crash from becoming his last vision of his wife, and, oh, Lord, to keep him away from that baby. But the days I could catch a twenty-five-year-old fit kid on the run were long over. Boyce bounded down to the wreck and exploded through the surprised firefighters. I arrived too late to stop him from pulling the red-stained sheet off the body in the mangled car.

His lips pulled back from gritted teeth and he staggered rearward a few steps, staring at the horror before him. I elbowed through the confused firefighters and quickly drew the sheet back over the vacant-eyed remains of Cathy Calder.

I turned to Boyce, taking him by the shoulders, pushing him gently away. "Come on, Boyce," I said. "Come on, son. Let's go back to the car. My people will handle this."

"Where's Stevie?" Boyce asked softly, pitifully. "Where's my little boy?"

"He's gone, son," I answered, "I am so sorry, but he's—"

Boyce suddenly raised both hands, and I released him. His face was tight and his eyes were wide and fixed. He was pulling sharp breaths through his nose. "I'm okay," he said tersely, fighting hard to do as he had been trained, as he had been taught that his kind of man always did, to hold his composure and self-control even in the face of catastrophe. "I'm okay, Sheriff Cody," he said, gasping, "I . . . I . . . I can handle this. I can *handle* this."

"You don't have to handle it, son." I placed my hand lightly on his upper arm. "I'll handle it for you. You just—"

Boyce shook with the strain he was under, yet he was mechanical, like a robot. "No. No sir. I'm okay. I'm okay. I can *handle* this. I can handle—"

"Come on, Boyce, I'm going to drive you home. I'll notify your sergeant and your relatives. I'll take care of everything. Come—"

The controlled but excited voice of one of my deputies, Haskel Beale, suddenly burst from the radio in my coat pocket. "Sheriff Six. I'm in pursuit!"

"All units hold your traffic," Cindy replied. "Sheriff Six, go ahead."

We could hear the siren yelping in the background of

Haskel's transmission. "Sheriff Six. I'm in pursuit of a dark-green Dodge pickup truck occupied two times. Virginia tag beginning with Adam-William and ending with three-eight. Cain't see the rest of the tag for a trailer hitch. We're east on the Perry Hollow Road about two miles before the school. This truck's got right front-quarter damage, people; I think it's the one in that fatal hit-and-run!"

"Ten-four," Cindy answered with professional calm. "Units responding; acknowledge."

Boyce Calder's eyes suddenly focused and he looked at the radio I was pulling from my pocket.

"Sheriff Seven. I'm en route!" the radio blared.

"Sheriff Five responding!"

"Ten-four, Sheriffs Seven and Five. Sheriff One?"

I saw Boyce's glassy gaze boil instantly into molten rage. He yanked away from me and bolted for his idling blue-and-gray cruiser at a dead run.

"Boyce! No!" I shouted, but he was slamming the big Chevy's door. I ran toward the cruiser. "Boyce! Don't—"

He clapped the car in gear and stood on the pedal. The machine roared and spewed streams of gravel from its rear wheels. Then the tires screamed and smoked as they took purchase on pavement. The siren began to whoop, and the car faded down the road fast, its blue roof-light sweeping the trees. He was headed toward the Perry Hollow school.

"Damn!" I said, and I scrambled past astonished fire-fighters to my own car. The tires of my silver cruiser howled as I stormed after Boyce, clicking my seat belt into place and grabbing the microphone. "Sheriff One. I'm responding on that pursuit. Ah . . . so is Trooper Calder."

"Ten-four, Sheriff. Seventeen forty-three."

"Where are you, Haskel?" I asked on the radio.

His yelping siren made it hard to hear him. "We're still east on Perry Hollow Road, Sheriff! Almost to the school. These guys are driving like they're drunk. They're fast, but I'm stayin' with 'em. It's got to be them people in that hit-and-run, Sheriff. I had 'em stopped for speedin', and when I found the right front fender banged up, they run. Almost run over *me!*"

I was trying to keep Boyce Calder's taillights in sight, which was getting harder to do. I hoped I didn't hit a deer, or anything else, at this speed. "Ten-four, Haskel. Don't get yourself hurt."

"Ten-four, Sheriff!"

Ahead, the red brake lights on Boyce's state police cruiser glowed, and blue smoke rose from skidding tires. For only a moment, I feared he was crashing, but then I knew what was happening. Boyce was turning onto the old Saddle Mountain logging road. It was a brutally rough dirt trail that would come out on Perry Hollow Road about four miles east of the Perry Hollow Middle School. Boyce could get ahead of the chase if he was fast enough, and he knew it.

I braked hard and turned onto the rocky logging road, but was forced to follow at a distance because of the thick cloud of gravel dust Boyce's car was leaving. The beams from my headlights refracted in the gray dust and it was like trying to drive in thick fog.

"Sheriff Five. I'm on the pursuit!" the radio sputtered. "We're now east of the school, near the farmers' co-op." Otis Clark, Sheriff Five, was now behind Haskel in the chase. Per procedure, Otis was doing the radio work, leaving Haskel to concentrate on keeping the suspect vehicle in view.

"Ten-four, Sheriff Five," Cindy answered, still soothingly cool. "All units, the pursuit is now east on Perry Hollow Road near the farmers' co-op. Seventeen forty-five."

The logging trail wound up the mountain, crested in a small gap, and wound down the other side, switching back like a hairpin in places. When I crested the ridge I could see Boyce's headlights and blue roof-light bounding down the mountain trail below me. To the west, I could make out the blue flashing lights of Haskel's and Otis's cars approaching on Perry Hollow Road. I couldn't see the lights of the fleeing truck.

At the bottom of the little mountain, I came upon Boyce, stopped, his car idling with its lights off by the edge of Perry Hollow Road. Immediately, leaving all lights off, he pulled the car left into the road so that the chase would come from behind him. He rolled slowly east in the left lane. I looked to my right and saw headlights approaching, jerky and fast, which could only be the chased truck. Then behind those headlights appeared the flashing lights of the two pursuing sheriff's cruisers. The truck swished by me with two figures briefly distinguishable inside it, the driver's elbows high and flying, the passenger looking through the rear window. In the quick glimpse of the truck afforded me when it zipped through my headlight beams, I made out an abused old dark-green Dodge, three-quarter ton. Haskel and Otis whipped past me, blue light-bars blinking and sirens yelping. I spurred the Chevy and charged after them. When I caught up to them, I could see the pickup truck's brake lights gleam, a quarter-mile ahead, probably because the driver had just spotted a Virginia State Police cruiser moving parallel in the other lane with no lights on. The truck slowed sharply, but then its brake lights went off and it accelerated to pass Boyce on the right.

Boyce's lights and blue flasher came on and the back of his cruiser squatted under acceleration as it ran alongside the truck.

"Watch it! Keep back!" I said on the radio, and the brake lights of both sheriff's cars shone brightly.

I suspected Boyce would ram the truck if it attempted to pass him, and I was right. The big police cruiser swerved hard to the right and then everything in my view became obscured in glowing brake lights, blue tire smoke, and clouds of gray gravel dust churned up from the shoulder. When my car penetrated the dust cloud, Haskel and Otis were swerving to miss Boyce's car, which was sliding sideways on the road. Chunks of sod and pieces of wooden split-rail fence littered the road, and the pickup truck lay on its roof in a bordering pasture, its hood and one door open, its wheels still spinning.

As I slid to a halt, I saw something else I was afraid I would see. Boyce abandoned his car in the middle of the road, leaving its door open, and sprinted for the wrecked truck, cocking his shotgun as he ran.

Boyce's car, as well as Haskel's cruiser, had slid to a stop with their headlights deployed on the overturned pickup truck. The two occupants crawled from it and ran toward a nearby woodline, each in a different direction, like experienced criminals do. On foot, I jumped the ditch closely behind Otis and Haskel, all of us with our guns drawn. As well as I could see in the shadow-split headlight beams, the two fleeing suspects appeared to be garden-variety white-trash punks with Yassir Arafat beards, and long, greasy-looking hair under ball caps worn backward. They were dressed in dirty jeans, unlaced basketball shoes, and flapping shirt tails, and did not appear to be armed. The passenger was limping and holding his head; the driver was sprinting like he was uninjured and quite disinterested in jail. Boyce, of course, angled after the driver, but then he stopped and took aim with his shotgun.

"Boyce, no!" I shouted. "Don't!"

I personally would have loved to shoot the fleeing suspect in the back. I once heard Pierce Arroe tell fourteen-year-old Bryant Arroe that if he ever caught the boy wearing a ball cap backward he would turn his head until the cap was on straight. Pierce was probably kidding, but then, I never saw one of his four sons wear their caps backward. Ever. Anyway, aside from the morality of the issue, the rules in America say you can't shoot assholes for looking like assholes. Besides, Cathy Calder's last words were that she only saw one man, and that man was "older" and had short hair.

I still don't know if Boyce responded to my shout or if he simply couldn't get a good sight picture. As Boyce could shoot like Polly could cook burritos, I bet on the former. Whichever, the driver disappeared into the woods without a terminal case of twelve-gauge lead poisoning.

"Get the other little shit!" I bellowed at Haskel and Otis, pointing toward the gimpy passenger. "I'll back Boyce!" My deputies charged after the passenger, and I ran for where Boyce and the driver had gone into the woods.

When I penetrated the woodline, there was still enough light from the cars to barely make out what was happening. Basically, Boyce was cleaning the forest up with the driver of the pickup truck. Boyce's shotgun and hat lay in the leaves, and he had a fistful of the driver's shirt. With his other fist he was beating the man witless. If it continued, Boyce would kill him.

"Boyce, Boyce, knock it off! That's enough!" I grabbed his arm, but he whirled and shoved me backward. The prisoner dropped to his knees, his eyes half closed. I tripped on a root and fell on my back in the leaves, losing my own hat and reflecting that I was too old for this Hollywood bullshit. Boyce yanked the driver, who now didn't even know where he was, to his knees and continued to beat him in a mindless, blind rage. I regained my feet, rushed Boyce, and seized him from behind, pinning his elbows to his waist. He cried out in anger and thrashed wildly, but I held him for a moment before we fell rolling in the leaves. We both leaped to our feet, Boyce still consumed by his fury. He tried to get past me at the suspect, who was now on his hands and knees, his head hanging. I was able to push Boyce back only because he slipped in the leaves. He tried to run by me again and we grappled.

"Boyce!" I shouted, struggling to hold him. "Listen to me! It's not them! These guys didn't kill Cathy and your boy, Boyce. *Listen* to me, goddamn it!" I finally made eye contact with the driven young trooper. He was heaving for breath, and he made a whimpering sound each time he exhaled. He was losing it, I knew. "Boyce, she got a good look at the driver! He came to her car on foot after the crash! Listen to me, Boyce, I swear to God she said the guy that hit her had short hair! Short hair and no beard, Boyce; *look* at this son of a bitch! It's not him! This is not the guy!"

Boyce Calder stood with his hands on my shoulders, breathing fast and deep. He looked fiercely from me to the man on his hands and knees, and then back to me. When his eyes met mine, I could see them change. Rage was washed from them by a flood of crippling despair. His face began to quiver and his mouth opened. Agony had arrived.

The young man's wail of grief carried long and high in the cold night air. He sank to his knees before me, seized me around my waist, and he wept wretchedly. I held his head to my chest. The boy shook with deep, racking sobs.

Flashlight beams from the pasture began to cast spidery, moving shadows about us.

"Sheriff Cody?" I heard Billy Vaughn, another of my deputies, call.

"Over here!" I shouted.

Billy and Otis Clark crunched through the leaves and ran onto the scene, each with a flashlight in one hand and a gun in the other. They jerked to a halt and gaped at us. I still held Boyce, and he still cried like a man whose life has caved in.

I nodded at the hapless pickup truck driver. "Get him out of here," I ordered. "Get an ambulance out here to check both those clowns, and then lock 'em up."

"Sir?" Billy said, still gawking at us. To be fair, he was shocked, and he probably didn't hear me over Boyce's sobs.

"Get that asshole out of here!" I said, sharply. "Get out of here and leave us alone! Don't let anybody come up here until I bring Boyce down to the road! *Nobody!* Especially no news people! You hear me?"

"Yes sir!" both deputies replied, scrambling for the prisoner. They hauled him to his feet, searched him quickly, and handcuffed him. As they were hustling him away, I said, "Hey, guys."

They stopped and looked back at us.

"The victims in the fatal hit-and-run were Boyce's wife and baby. But these crime lords are not the hitters. Have Cindy get hold of the state police and let them know. And I don't want us disturbed until we come down."

"Count on it, Sheriff," Billy said, and they took the prisoner toward the road.

Boyce sagged. I released him, and he collapsed on his back in the leaves, wrecked. It is truly awful when a man surrenders his dignity because nothing matters anymore. Boyce screamed in abject misery, his cries echoing in the cold, black air.

I am not a religious man. I have nothing to protect me when I ache like this.

I cried a few tears of my own.

4

•••••••

Diplomacy

State police officers arrived. I briefed them and they shepherded Boyce away while one remained to make a report and remove Boyce's damaged cruiser.

I thought to have Cindy urge all my people to double their efforts at locating the running vehicle and driver. I thought to have her tell them to stake every road out of the county, to notify every auto body shop, to put out feelers, call in markers, promise whatever was legal, and turn over every rock in Hunter County for a pickup truck with right front-quarter damage. I thought to order Cindy to transmit the lookout statewide and to the peripheral states. I thought about all these things and more but I did none of them. The wife and child of one of our own had been grievously wronged and the perp was still at large. For me to issue all those instructions would be to insult my people by suggesting they were not already doing their dead-level best at carrying them out. My people were pros. I knew nothing I could suggest was not being tried, and nothing I could say would motivate them more than they already were.

Instead, I assigned deputies to handle the accident scene at Spoon Creek. I ordered Cathy Calder's car be left where it was after her body was removed, and that the scene be guarded by a deputy until state police forensic investigators could examine the car at first light. As Haskel and Otis left with the two punks from the pickup truck, I told Haskel to get me the story on them as soon as he could. It was pretty clear they had not killed Cathy Calder and her son, but we needed to investigate and document and move forward against whoever did. A wrecker from Stout's Texaco showed up, and Billy Vaughn stood by while the wrecked pickup truck was righted and hooked off to the impound yard.

In the meantime, since the state police budget can afford car phones, I used one of theirs to call the VSP commander, Colonel Able Clair, at his home in Richmond, and bring him up to speed on the night's events where he was concerned. He thanked me for the courtesy. I asked him to send a team of VSP accident reconstruction experts to examine Cathy Calder's car. Colonel Clair assured me in no uncertain terms that his best people would be on the scene by helicopter at dawn, and I would have their completed report on my desk by noon.

I elected not to elaborate to Clair on Boyce's—shall we say—spirited arrest of the pickup truck driver. The driver had been too drunk to remember it, and the truth is he deserved everything he got for driving drunk, and for putting my people and the citizens of Hunter County through the danger of a high-speed pursuit. Further, he might even be one of the guys who robbed Roanoke Councilman Arnie Dreyfuss's daughter. There should be a price to pay for being an inconsiderate asshole.

I was halfway to the county seat town of Hunter, trying to order the events of the day in my head, when, in the mirror, I noticed a set of four lights closing on me from the rear. The headlights were on blinding high beam and were compounded by a bumper mounted pair of brilliant "driving" lights, so it was hard to miss. The lights came rapidly up behind me, swerved into the opposite lane and swept right by my unmarked car a good thirty miles an hour faster than the fifty I was already doing. It was one of those hellaciously expensive new Porsche 911s, I noticed before all I could see was taillights.

"Damn," I whispered, and I stood on the cruiser. I didn't need this now, but chances were good this driver was drunk, too, and needed to be off my roads before Andy Harmon got to pronounce anybody else dead tonight.

It took a full minute to close on the red Porsche, which cut expertly through the mountain turns, way above the speed limit, but not recklessly. In fact, the driving was so smooth and calculated I began to doubt the driver was drunk. I got a legit clock at eighty-five. I flipped on the grill and dash flashers and the woods on both sides of the road pulsed blue in rhythm with the high electric squeal and pop of the strobes. I high-beamed my headlights and trained the spotlight into the driver's door mirror. He didn't stop.

The heavier Chevy squealed and leaned to stay with him. I gave him a five-second blast with the electronic siren, but it was almost like he was racing me, neatly steering the capable car in a way that was very hard to keep up with. Just as we reached a brief, straight stretch where I could free a hand for a microphone and call on pursuit, the Porsche's brake lights shone brightly, and the car slowed and pulled over.

"Damn," I muttered to myself pulling to a stop. The license plate has horizontal blue, white, and red stripes. Oh, just fucking marvelous. A goddamned diplomat.

One of the more disgusting examples of classist arrogance is something called diplomatic immunity, which the world-wide diplomatic community generously grants itself and its family members and employees, placing them all neatly above the law. A diplomat cannot be arrested anywhere, for anything, because of this immunity. Years previous, when I was a D.C. street cop, they were the scourge of the town. Diplomats routinely illegally parked anywhere they wanted, habitually ignored parking tickets by the thousands, and frequently drove drunk and recklessly. Many of them arrogantly flaunted their status, shrugging off hit-and-run accidents in which they were at fault, laughing when caught shoplifting, and behaving belligerently in public, all with total impunity. The most a police officer could do once confronted with diplomatic ID was forward a complaint to the state department, which went right in the trash can with all the unpaid tickets.

I hate diplomats, I reminded myself, jamming the cruiser

into park. Promptly, however, I knew this one was going to be hard to hate. A woman kicked open the driver's door, got out, and slammed it so hard the car rocked. She lowered her head and glared at me, a strand of her reddish blond hair draped across one eye and her hands propped defiantly on the flares of her hips where they swelled outward from a slender waist. She was the kind of take-no-prisoners beautiful that a man knows from twenty feet away did not come out of any bottle and will never go away.

I couldn't help staring at the Porsche driver standing with her hip cocked, wearing well-fitted forest-green pants and a thin green cashmere turtle-neck sweater. With her green leather heels and gold earrings, watch, and necklace, her outfit was feminine and sensual but wholly appropriate to a woman of breeding and style.

Her reddish blond, thick hair flowed to her shoulders. Perfect eyebrows arched over gray-blue eyes framed in long, curling lashes. She had lines to her face that models pray for, and lines to her breasts that men pray to. Soft, unspoiled skin. A straight nose and last, but no, no, no, not least, a soft, full, plump mouth that utterly compels a man to want to cover it with his own. As she stalked toward me, squinting into the cruiser lights, she opened her mouth slightly and the clincher sank its hooks in me; it was there, the tiny imperfection that makes a beautiful woman believably human and thus infinitely more sexy. Her teeth were white and pretty but not perfect, the front two uppers overlapping just slightly at the tips, just enough to rocket her from the impossible distance of fantasy to only inches from me.

I know, I know. Men get silly over beautiful women, there's no denying it. I'm no exception. And as I watched the lady in emerald green approach, I felt myself getting truly, abba-dabba stupid. In this day of feminist McCarthyism, it has become politically incorrect for a man to perceive, let alone describe, a woman in sexual terms, as though doing so somehow demeans her. It's lunacy, of course. Women *want* to be seen as sex objects; they just don't want to be seen *solely* as sex objects, justifiably. The concept of the asexual woman will pass in time to take its place in history among similar jewels of brilliance like the flat-earth theory and the notion that washing removes life-sustaining bodily oils. This woman's refined but commanding sexual attractiveness was a welcome diversion from an otherwise damned dreary day. A rabid fox in a chicken house couldn't have caused more commotion than that woman stirred in me, and when that no longer happens, you may shoot me—with my gratitude. I'll even pay for the ammunition.

Watching her walk, furious, placing each foot neatly in front of the other, two things were readily apparent: she was positively not carrying any concealed weapons, and she was not drunk.

I hustled out of the cruiser to meet her charge. "Uh," I said, eruditely. I am such a stupid fuck around women like this.

"Oh, *fantastic!*" she said in a throaty voice with a very slight German accent. I always did love Ingrid Bergman. The woman snapped to a halt before me and jammed her fists on those fabulous hips again. "Oh, I *really* needed *you* tonight!" She rolled the *r* in *really*. "What the *hell* do you want?"

"Uh, Lew . . . ah . . . uh *hum!* Cody. Sheriff . . . Cody," I said, mercifully remembering half my name, at least. *Jeez,* I hated what women like her did to me. "Let me see your license and registration, please."

"Oooooh!" she snarled, whirling about and causing her hair to spin out from her head. She stamped back to the Porsche and leaned inside. I followed her, flashlight in hand, partly because it is professionally wise to ensure people don't come out of the car with a gun, and partly because when she bent over to reach into the car I could have died on the spot and considered my life fulfilled.

While she stood with her arms folded, tapping her toe, I took her documents and stumbled back to my cruiser to write her up for eighty-five in a fifty-five. As a diplomat, she would almost certainly ignore it, but I'd go through the motions just for my own sake. The international driver's license said the woman was Karin Reinholdt Steiger, Embassy of the Federal Republic of Germany, 4645 Reservoir

Rd., NW, Washington D.C.; a DOB making her thirty-seven years old, WF, 5'7", 122, BLD, BLU. I wondered what she was doing in Hunter County, which wasn't on the way to anywhere but Hunter County.

As I wrote, Miss Steiger strolled briskly to my passenger door. I hit the electric door lock. When she got into the cruiser and closed the door, a gentle but penetrating perfume made its way to me, and what little concentration I had left cratered. I looked at her. She possessed the oddest eyes; they were intense, delving eyes, like those of a surgeon peering into an open heart.

"Are you taking me to jail?" she asked sourly.

"Nuts," I answered, pulling my eyes back to my citation book. "You know better than that. Even up here on the frontier of civilization we serfs know what diplomatic ID means. You'll forget this ticket before I'm out of sight, but you're getting it anyway."

"Nuts," Karin Steiger repeated, sighing. From her, the word sounded more like *noots*. "Isn't that what one of your generals said to one of ours at the . . . Battle of the Bulge, I think you call it? You Americans are so fond of your colloquialisms." I said nothing while I scribbled. "Mmmm," she continued, agitated. "I don't suppose you would consider not giving me this, um, warrant?"

"It isn't a warrant. It's a common speeding ticket, and what do you care? We both know you won't pay it and there's nothing I can do about—"

"You don't know my father."

"Pardon me?"

"I am a cultural attaché with the German embassy," Karin Steiger said with clear irritation. "Ambassador Goss Steiger is my father, and I assure you he will be most unpleasant when he learns of this."

The ole I'm-gonna-tell-my-daddy-on-you line. "An unpleasant diplomat," I muttered, still writing. "Fancy that."

"I mean he will be unpleasant to me, not to you. Father is very concerned about German public image, and he castigates embassy employees for infractions of American law. Especially me."

"That's dreadful beyond words, but—"

"In my country, we drive very fast, and our accident rate

38

is lower than yours! Your stupid American motorway laws are laughable!"

I sighed and handed her the ticket book for a signature. "Well, this ought to be a real scream, then."

She scratched the ticket with her name, thrust the book back at me, and tossed my pen on the dash, glowering.

Wearily, I retrieved the pen. "Look, in Germany they make drivers earn their licenses. Over here, a blind, drunk, paraplegic monkey who can't speak English can get a driver's license at fifteen and not have to requalify for it until he's a hundred and ninety years old. This isn't the Autobahn, it's a stupid American motorway. So slow down, before you wind up in a stupid American hospital."

Karin Steiger lowered her face to one hand and rubbed her eyes. I barely detected enough of a sniff to realize she was on the verge of crying. I can't stand it when women cry. "Look, Miss Steiger," I said gently, handing her the top copy of the ticket, "we both know you'll trash this. The important thing is to slow down and not get hurt, okay?"

She lowered her hand and fixed me with lovely damp eyes. Her chin trembled, and at that moment I wanted to hold her and pet her and shoot anything that got near her. She fixed that, though.

Karin Steiger glanced at my badge and name tag. *"Sheriff* Cody," she said, snatching the ticket from my hand and opening the car door. She slid out, turned, and bent to look at me, a tear running down her cheek, "it is a great comfort to me to know that if I were ever to have a retarded son . . . he could always make a good living as a *policeman!"* She slammed my door and stalked back to the red Porsche. She cranked the high-performance sports car, and I expected her to blaze away, but she drove off modestly.

I sighed still again. I had to think about another line of work.

The Hunter County Jail and Sheriff's Department offices are housed in a hundred-and-twelve-year-old stone building, which I adore and refer to as "the dungeon," in the tiny mountain county seat town of Hunter. The building was once the county courthouse, but was replaced by the "new" courthouse on the town square about fifty years ago.

As I parked my car in the space marked SHERIFF OF HUNTER COUNTY, I heard Pierce mark back into service on the radio: "Sheriff Two; in service." I knew he would have been monitoring his portable radio, since it was his duty night, and he would have known he was needed on the road.

Immediately, Cindy answered him: "Ten-four, Sheriff Two. Sheriff Two, we just received . . . uh . . . an animal complaint, I guess, at the Gordon Huckaby farm out on Route 8, first right after the Trace Creek bridge, right at the first fork. Can you handle it, Captain Arroe? Everybody else in the sector is tied up on accidents and pursuit arrests."

I heard the last of a sigh as Pierce keyed his microphone. As duty officer, he was supposed to supervise and oversee, not do the paperwork on petty calls, and I knew he was not exactly bubbling over with enthusiasm. An *animal complaint* didn't mean a dog or cat had a gripe; it was a generic term used to refer to any call we got that involved an animal, like a dog bite, a dead deer blocking the road, or a raccoon getting into somebody's garbage. There was generally nothing practical that could be done to satisfy the complainant. It's hard to arrest raccoons; handcuffs don't fit them, and it's tough to get convictions in court. Animal complaints were usually an exercise in futility that could only be recorded on a report form. "Ten-four, Cindy," Pierce answered, vastly underwhelmed. "Hold me en route." I knew what he was thinking; he'd much rather be scouring the county for a dented pickup truck with blue paint smears on its right front fender.

I walked into what was once the main courtroom of the two-story stone dungeon, a room that had long since been converted to a reception/administration/booking area. It still had a twenty-foot ceiling and was impossible to heat comfortably in the fall, let alone winter. Enough space heaters were plugged in around the big room to brown out Chicago. Haskel and Otis were in a distant corner questioning the two sullen nitwits from the pursuit, who were handcuffed to steel rings pinioned through large solid walnut desks that were over a hundred years old. My facility was furnished throughout with antiques the county board had used for over a century as an excuse not to allocate the sheriff's department any redecorating money. So be it. The furniture was part of the smoky, worn, historic character of the place.

My office was the original judge's chambers and had a broad, blackened stone fireplace in the outer wall; one of the staff had thoughtfully started a warming fire in it. I sank into the maternal embrace of the cracked-leather judge's chair behind my massive walnut desk and ran my hands over my face. What a day.

There came a knock on my door, followed, without acknowledgment, by the entry of a squat, bosomy black woman in her forties wearing a fluffy purple sweater under voluminous denim bib-overalls. On her feet were ankle-high basketball shoes with no laces; the tongues drooped forward. The overall cuffs were bunched in rolls at the tops of her shoes. She was not likely to be seen wearing that outfit at a Tokyo fashion show, but I knew she wore what she felt comfortable in and didn't give a happy damn who liked it. If it had been a weekday, the woman would've been dressed differently; she'd have been neatly wearing the tan uniform of a Hunter County Sheriff's Department sergeant. Her name was Milly Stanford and she was the best desk sergeant any sheriff could ask for.

"Evenin', Sheriff," Milly Stanford mumbled, looking at documents she carried as she waddled into the office.

"Hi, Milly. Thanks for coming in," I said.

"It a cast-iron bitch about Trooper Calder's wife and baby, ain't it, Sheriff?" Milly grumbled. She continued without waiting for any reply. "Sorry sonnabitch done it prob'ly drunk on his ass. Hope the boys catch the mother-fuckah what done it—soon—and I hope they kill him dead doin' it." Milly isn't big on turning the other cheek.

"My Lord," Milly went on. "Ain't no justice in this damn world. Speakin' of justice, Sheriff, them two little hunky turds Haskel caught is the same two boys Roanoke County's after for that robbery. They both drunk, too. Driver done blowed a two-eight."

"They confess to the robbery?"

"Hell, naw. The lyin' little shits keep sayin' they didn't do it, but Haskel done give they names to Roanoke, and Roanoke got sheets on 'em. Showed they mug shots to the little victim girl, and she done identified 'em. 'Sides, Sheriff, they a dumb pair. They throwed the girl's purse away after they emptied it, o' course, but Otis found this in the crack in the seat when he searched they truck."

Milly handed me a small plastic card that proved to be a driver's license bearing the name and photograph of Audrey M. Dreyfuss. Bingo. Do da word *penitentiary* mean anything to ya, boys?

"Anything else? I asked.

"Billy called from the impound lot. Say he done looked at the truck them two was drivin', and he say that in a good light you can tell the damage Haskel saw when he stopped them is old damage, and it ain't got no odd paint on it nowhere."

I sighed for the umpteenth time. "Well, tell Billy thanks, but all that means is we are totally clueless on who hit Cathy Calder. Incidentally, make sure the department sends flowers to the funeral home, and let me know where and when the services are. I think they'll bury them in Christiansburg."

"I'll take care of it, Sheriff."

"Is that it?"

Milly nodded, heading for the door. "Hell, tha's enough for one day, I reckon. I'm gon' go lock up Haskel's prisoners."

"Thanks for coming in, Milly."

Milly stopped at the door. She smiled that huge smile like a Cheshire cat. "Shit, Sheriff. Wadn't for you, I'd still be the maid and cook at this jail, 'stead of runnin' it. Ain't gon' be no day when you need me that I ain't here." She closed the door behind her.

I was reading the interrogation reports by Otis and Haskel when I heard one of the criminal masterminds from the Roanoke caper make a dreadful faux pas.

"Git yer fuckin' hands *off* me, you fat negger!" he shouted.

Uh-oh. That was not the wisest thing one could say to a jailhouse sergeant on her own turf with years of experience handling uncooperative prisoners. I got up and went to my office door to keep an eye on the lesson in etiquette I suspected was nigh. Across the booking room, Milly stood before one of the prisoners whom she had uncuffed from the table and invited to her cellblock. As he could stand unassisted, he was clearly not the one Boyce Calder caught up with. I imagined Milly had put a hand on his arm as he got up, which is part of controlling prisoners, and she probably thought it was a courtesy to keep the drunk cracker from falling on his ass. Now he stood a foot taller and thinner than Milly, eyeing her with a contemptuous sneer, his brow high and his nose wrinkled.

"Sir," Milly said courteously, putting her hand out, "procedure requires that I maintain contact with you while—"

"Bullshit!" the prisoner spat, yanking his arm back. "Ain't no negger gonna handle Eddie Potts!"

Eddie was conveniently ignoring the fact that Otis Clark, one of the deputies who "handled" him in from Perry Hollow Road, was as black as Clifton Forge coal. But I supposed that was a reach of logic for a mind too ignorant to pronounce a slur correctly. Haskel and Otis stood and positioned themselves behind Eddie, who was still glaring at Milly. My deputies glanced at me, and I shook my head ever so slightly. Milly didn't need any help.

Milly had her back to me, but I knew she was trying her big smile as a last resort. "Look, Mr. Potts, I don't want no trouble. Let's you and me just take a little walk down the hall and—"

"Hey, *fuck* you, bitch!"

Strike three.

Einstein postulated that nothing could move faster than the speed of light, but, then, ole Albert never saw Sergeant Milly Stanford slap anybody. This was not one of those little ceremonial cheek-wobblers a high-school debutante gives a fresh beau. A slap from Milly Stanford was more like a semilethal open-handed right cross designed to brain damage a Cape buffalo without leaving any marks a trial lawyer could buy a new Mercedes with. Potts's dirty backward ball cap sort of maintained its stationary inertia in space while his head was jet-propelled out from underneath it. His eyes got a little fixed and dilated, and he staggered back two steps. "Wuh," he said. By the time both his eyes were again seeing the same thing, he was sitting behind bars in suite number four, the Longstreet Room, we call it.

The other prisoner could not wait to get into his cell.

I looked at my watch, returning to my desk—6:56 P.M.

What a day, I thought for the umpteenth time. The Great White Hunters, Boyce Calder's poor blitzed family, and this hairy pursuit. *At least it can't get any worse,* I thought.

Then the phone rang.

"Sheriff," Milly said, "Broken Arroe on line one. Say he need to talk to you right now."

I stabbed a blinking button. "Pierce?"

"Sheriff, you better get out here, pronto."

"What? Where?"

"The Huckaby farm. First right after the Trace Creek bridge on Route 8. First right fork. Better get out here quick, Lewis. We got a hell of a mess on our hands. Goddamndest thing I ever saw."

5
• • • • • • • •

The Creature Comes to Call

A stately something called Handel's *Water Music Suite* played loudly on the CD as my blue-flashing cruiser bounced past Gordon Huckaby's big farmhouse, down the dirt drive to his huge barn. Lest you think I pretend to be musically elitist, I must confess that I had just removed Hank Williams, Jr.'s great "Women I've Never Had." I was still wondering how an "animal complaint" had turned into "the goddamndest thing" Pierce had ever seen. I would find out soon enough.

There were a dozen pickup trucks and cars clustered around the expansive four-story gray-wood barn. Several men, most in boots, hunting coveralls, and ball caps, stood off to one side in a group, conversing, which I found especially interesting since they were all holding shotguns or rifles. Cigarettes glowed in the dark. The men glanced up at me as I rolled in, then went back to mumbling among themselves. The big barn doors were slid open on their tracks, and light shone into the barnyard from the brightly illuminated interior center aisle of the big barn. I rolled in by Pierce's tan, marked sheriff's-department cruiser. It was then I heard the kind of shrill, hysterical screaming that makes shivers go up the spine. Unlike Boyce Calder's howls of agony, these were female.

45

Pierce trotted briskly out of the barn and hurried to meet me. "Hey, Sheriff, glad to see you," Pierce said, a worried look on his face. "Things is gettin' ugly here."

"What's going on?" I asked, looking over Pierce's shoulder at the barn. I could hear what sounded like a younger girl wailing and at least two older women crying loudly.

Pierce drew a deep breath, held it, and let it out slowly, looking at the ground. "I reckon you better see for yourself, Lewis," he said, and he turned and walked back toward the barn entryway. I followed him.

I squinted at the fluorescent brightness of the barn lighting while I strode down the broad dirt aisle past open stalls containing a farm tractor, an old pickup truck, and stacked hay bales. At the far end of the long barn, by what appeared to be several closed horse stalls, western saddles sat on posts extending from the walls, and bridles hung from hangers. On the walls, there were numerous dusty framed photographs of a young cowgirl on horseback and several large blue or red ribbons of the kind riders win at barrel-racing competitions. Halfway there, five women of varying ages knelt, huddled around a pale, honey-haired girl of about fourteen who lay splayed on her back, emotionally wrecked. Steam rose into the night air from her sweaty forehead. She was wailing wildly and being restrained or comforted by the other women, one I knew to be her mother, Charlotte Huckaby, a local schoolteacher. Pierce passed them without a glance. Stepping past them, I heard the girl let rip another chilling scream and be gently shushed by the older women. Charlotte Huckaby cried, sharing her daughter's distress. Mindflashes of a sobbing young police officer sparked in my head.

Gordon Huckaby stood with his hands jammed in his jeans pockets, a western hat tilted back on his head and a grim look on his face. Four other men stood with him, also holding weapons. You'd have thought an invasion by the Iraqi Republican Guard was imminent. I glanced at the photos on the walls, which were all variations of the girl, smiling, in western clothing, mounted on a pretty silver-gray quarter-horse mare.

"Gordon," I said, offering my hand. He shook it briefly

46

and dropped it. "Evenin', Sheriff Cody," he said. His eyes were those of a man who wanted to kill somebody.

"Gordon," Pierce said, "you want to tell the sheriff what you told me?"

"Well, Sheriff, my girl Darlene come down here to do the evenin' feedin' fer her little mare and"—Gordon's face twisted, and he continued with razor-edged bitterness—"well, looka here at what my baby girl had to find." He walked slowly, apprehensively, toward the last stall on the left, an enclosure of about fifteen feet on each side, the heavy oak half-door of which stood open. The stall was brightly lighted by an overhead quad-fluorescent fixture. Pierce and the other men remained where they were and looked at the ground or the ceiling. I walked to the open stall and looked in.

It didn't take Columbo to figure out that whatever was in the stall was probably going to be the horse, but even my years as a cop hadn't prepared me for what I saw.

In retrospect, I suppose it shouldn't have surprised me that a thousand-pound horse could lose that much blood. Maybe it was the vivid lighting that made it seem so copious and brutally red. Maybe it was the fact that the mess was smeared on the lower plank walls, lay puddled by the quarts in the low areas of the straw-covered dirt floor, and was flecked along the upper walls in patterns that could only have been made by streams of blood propelled through the air.

More shocking than the blood, though, was the grotesque manner in which the animal had been left by whatever had killed it. The horse lay partly on its left side, but its neck and extended head sloped steeply upward, bound in an elevated position by a green nylon halter about the horse's head and two heavy, snap-hook ropes securing it to posts on either side of the stall. Another rope, secured to a left side-post, was knotted to the animal's tail, stretching it taughtly upward toward that post. The rear legs were bound together by twisted coathanger wire. One foreleg lay sharply and unnaturally angled, broken probably as the poor animal thrashed in its agony. Worse, the mare had been extensively and mercilessly sliced by some kind of large, sharp instrument throughout its hindquarters, vagina, and belly. The flesh lay open in long, wet, gaping pink gashes and a section of bluish bowel lay eviscerated upon the bloody straw.

There were two finishing touches, which left no doubt that something vicious and evil had visited here. The business end of a pitchfork was impaled in the mare's side, its handle broken jaggedly off just aft of the tines. About two feet of what was probably a five-foot broken pitchfork handle protruded from the quarter horse's lacerated vagina.

Something that created agony and symbolic debasement for pleasure had been here. The scene shook me, and I was a Vietnam veteran, career cop. I could only guess what it must have done to a fourteen-year-old girl raised gently on a farm, a child who, I judged from the photos in the aisle, had loved and fussed over the mare since it was a spindly filly wet with the membranes of its mother. I could picture the girl going happily to feed her beloved pet, flipping on the bright lights of the stall, and beholding a sight she could not forget in seven lifetimes. It wasn't hard to understand why there was murder in Gordon Huckaby's eyes.

My nose wrinkled at the rank odor of horse manure and the sickly sweet smell of immense quantities of congealing blood. Being careful not to affect anything that might become evidence, I stepped into the stall and looked closer, though it took effort. Something possessed of utterly pitiless savagery had been here, and the horror still hung in the air.

I felt that contracting-testicle sensation that sweeps over you when you're walking alone in the dark and a twig snaps behind you. Whoever did this was big, very strong, and very, very bad.

I had seen enough for the moment. I backed cautiously into the aisle where Gordon stood, his jaw muscles twitching. The armed men who had been near the stall had gone to join the crowd outside. Pierce stood by Gordon.

"I was up at the house," Gordon said in a low, intense, barely controlled tone. "Charlotte run in from the garage, said, 'My God, Gordy, I think I hear Darlene screamin'.' I looked out the kitchen winder and I seen Darlene a-standin' in the barn doorway a-jumpin' and wavin' her arms. I run down here and . . . I couldn't believe . . . I couldn't believe this, Sheriff Cody. What kind of . . . of . . . person could *do* somethin' like this, Sheriff?" I couldn't quite tell if Gordon was furious or scared. He had reason to be both. There was one sick son of a bitch loose in my county.

At still another wail of misery, we both turned to look up the barn aisle, where the women were lifting the devastated Darlene to her feet. Her head lay back and she wept uncontrollably. They helped her down the aisle toward the house.

"That girl will never be the same again," Gordon whispered, choking with the strain, his jaw muscles rippling.

"All right, first things first," I said. "Gordon, your daughter should go to the hospital in Roanoke. She's probably going to need sedatives to sleep for several nights, and they have trauma counselors there who are trained to help her cope with the shock and her grief. I recommend sending her there right away. Charlotte can go with her. My people are going to need to investigate for a while, and then the horse is going to have to be removed and buried, and the mess cleaned up. Darlene doesn't need to be here for any of that."

Gordon sighed, thinking over my suggestion. He nodded.

"Pierce, tell Cindy to get some help over here, even if she has to pull it from north quad. I want this scene investigated carefully. You know what we need."

"You got it, Sheriff."

"Now," I said, "Gordon, what's with all the gun-toting neighbors?"

"You know how bad news travels in these hills, Sheriff. Charlotte called her sister; I called my brother. Next thing I know, all the men start showin' up. They . . . well, Sheriff Cody, we all figure Roadkill done this. Couldn'ta been nobody else in Hunter County. We're ready to go after him."

"Roadkill Rudesill?" I said. "Did Darlene see him? Did anybody see him, Gordon?"

"No, Sheriff, nobody seen him, but it *had* to be him!"

"Did anybody see *anything* to connect Roadkill with this event?" I glanced at Pierce, who shook his head.

"Nobody saw nothin', Sheriff Cody," Gordon answered, hotly, "but who else *could* it 'a' been?"

I put my hand on Gordon's shoulder. "Gordon, we're going to do everything possible to arrest whoever did this, but we can't just round up every weirdo in the county on no evidence. Even if we could, we would never get past an arraignment, let alone a conviction. They'd walk in twenty-four hours."

Gordon's eyes fastened on mine. "I don't know nothin' about all that legal bullshit, Sheriff. That's your problem. All I know is whoever done this is got to be caught! Who *else* coulda done this, Sheriff Cody? Who else but Roadkill?"

Gordon was approaching the limits of his restraint, that was pretty clear. I spoke softly, trying to calm him. "Gordon, we will investigate this thoroughly, and if a shred of evidence turns up linking Roadkill, I'll go get him myself, but—"

"Well, I don't need no goddamn *eva-day-ence,* Sheriff Cody! I lived in these hills since I was born, and I know they ain't a soul in Hunter County could do a terrible thing like this 'cept Roadkill! If you won't go get him, goddamn it, we will!" Gordon stepped back, looking at me with contempt. He spun on his heel and stormed down the aisle after the women. Another satisfied customer.

Pierce and I walked up the aisle, watching Gordon stalk off. Then, into the light, hurrying toward us, I saw a highly respected local veterinarian and old friend of mine, Hap Morgan, and a pleasant-looking oriental woman in her thirties I'd never seen. Hap was rotund and bald and had a gray walrus mustache. He was about sixty-five and tonight he wore his trademark granny glasses, jeans, and a brown canvas hunting jacket. He carried a satchel of his gear, and the woman carried one of those thick, expensive aluminum briefcases. The woman got prettier the closer she came. She strode resolutely, head high, on hips and legs that make it very hard for a man to concentrate. She was correctly dressed to attend to a horse mutilation, having donned an insulated one-piece coverall over whatever feminine duds were underneath. On her feet she wore rubber barnyard boots. Her hair was shining Chinese black, falling loose and straight in a short, modern cut that covered her head like a bathing cap. Hap and the woman stopped to speak to Gordon. Pierce and I couldn't hear clearly, but we could see Gordon gesticulating angrily, and he ended exclaiming something about "goddamned evidence!" It was pretty clear that he was underwhelmed by Hunter County's long arm of the law. The woman looked at me soberly, then she tilted her head, her pretty oriental eyes gleamed, and her face burst into a charming white-toothed smile. I got that terrible feeling I first got when I looked at Patsy Nolan in the sixth grade and something in me realized that maybe girls weren't so yucky after all. Hap said something to Gordon, who shook his head vehemently before striding toward the gun club standing outside.

"Here comes Doc Morgan," Pierce said in a low voice. "Look, Lewis, Gordon's pretty pissed. So is that bunch out there. They been talking about taking dogs and going after Roadkill. They're gonna be hard to hold."

"I'll handle them," I answered, walking toward the approaching old vet and the pretty Chinese woman. I wanted to prepare them to view the last stall on the left. "Roadkill Rudesill didn't do this," I told Pierce, "and you and I both know it."

"Maybe not, Lewis, but I'm with Gordon. Who the hell else could have done it?"

"That's what we get paid to find out. Look, Pierce, I have a bad feeling about this. It has all the earmarks of a sex nut, and if it is, this probably won't be the last time he tries to do it. Worse, he's obviously very violent. If some horse owner happens in on him when he's pursuing his perversion, somebody could get killed. Let's bear down on this thing. Pull the manpower you need—pay overtime if you have to—and let's get this guy quick, before it turns from dead horses to dead people. Keep me informed, and let me know what you need. Questions?"

"No sir. I'm on it."

"*I* have a question. Who's the woman with Hap?"

"Don't know her, but if I had to guess, I'd say she's the new vet that's thinking about partnering in with ole Doc Morgan, taking over his practice when he retires. S'posed to be a gook fox, I hear, so I bet that's her. I'm gonna get busy, Lewis. I'll talk to you outside."

I slapped Pierce on his massive back as he walked away. He nodded politely at Hap and tipped his Stetson to the woman.

"Hi, Hap," I said as the pair walked up, still out of view

of the horrible scene in the last stall. Over Hap's shoulder, at the end of the long barn aisle, I could see Gordon Huckaby gesticulating at the neighbor men. One man with a Washington Redskins ball cap on his head and a scoped rifle in his hand put an arm on Gordon's shoulder while he frowned at me. I'd seen him somewhere before.

"Lewis," Hap said in his gravelly twang, shaking my hand, "I'd like you to meet Dr. Julianne Chu. I'm tryin' to git Julianne to come in with me at the clinic." Hap's smile was buried beneath his shaggy gray mustache, but the Santa Claus twinkle in his eyes was unmistakable. "I'm a-gittin' too old to cut it!"

"Sure, Hap," I answered with a slight smile of my own. "Like George Burns was too old to tell a joke."

The woman's perfume eased into me, doing to me exactly what good perfumes are supposed to do. Looking at her, I could see she was disgustingly wholesome, and I wouldn't have bet fallen leaves that she'd stay with Hap Morgan two weeks. She was too . . . sweet . . . for a country vet in Hunter County. I couldn't see her on her knees in some shit-stained barnyard in the dark, rainy February cold with blood up to her elbows, trying to save one of Horace Peale's newborn calves. Especially not for the kind of money Hap Morgan had to charge in Hunter County. I could much more readily see Dr. Julianne Chu patting rich little suburban Chicago kids on the head while she gave painless rabies shots to their kittens at a hundred bucks a pop. I hoped she had a strong stomach.

Julianne Chu offered her hand, and looked me square in the eyes. Her grip was firm, but, I was relieved to note, not that of a chip-on-the-shoulder feminazi. Deliver me from defensive causists. "Hello, Sheriff Cody," she said. "I'm pleased to meet you at last. Dr. Morgan has told me so much about you."

"Yeah, well the old geet hasn't told me a damn thing about you, Dr. Chu, and I think I'll choke him to death for that."

"Please, Sheriff, do give the old geet a second chance. He had so many lovely things to say about you."

"He'll say anything to lure you into buying his worthless

practice. He probably even told you Hunter County is a nice place to live."

"He certainly did."

"He's a pathological liar. I gotta warn you, Hap makes Bob Packwood look like a priest; and did I mention his rampant alcoholism?"

"I don't git no respect," Hap mumbled. "Look, Barney Fife, you kin try to charm your lame way into Dr. Chu's pants some other time."

Dr. Chu gave Hap a look of exaggerated false astonishment before looking at me and smiling that fabulous smile again. That was good, I reflected. Hap knew Julianne Chu well or he wouldn't be looking to partner his practice with her. That, together with her genuine amusement at his remark, told me this was a woman who was comfortable with herself and with men. She wasn't the insecure, whiny excusist sort who screamed sexual harassment every time men neglected to act like women.

"What's goin' on here, Lewis?" Hap asked. "Gordy Huckaby's brother called while me and Bev was havin' Julianne to dinner. Said somethin' about one o' Gordon's horses a-gittin' hurt. Now ole Gordy won't say nothin' 'cept yellin' about he don't need no evidence."

I sighed and looked over my shoulder toward the last stall on the left. "Hap, I'm afraid what we have here tonight isn't likely to motivate Dr. Chu to buy a cup of coffee, let alone a veterinary practice, in Hunter County. Somebody has . . . mutilated Darlene Huckaby's little mare. It's . . . well, it's something you'll have to see for yourself, but you'd better know it's bad."

"Is the animal dead, Sheriff?" Julianne Chu asked.

"Very. Look, Hap, I'd appreciate it if you'd look the horse over for me and give me your impressions, but please be careful not to disturb the scene."

"Sure, Lewis. Down this way?"

I led the two vets to the death stall.

Hap stopped. His massive mustache bobbed up and down but he said nothing. I watched Dr. Chu in case she was inclined to faint, my Southern chauvinism showing, but she stepped delicately into the stall without hesitation. She wore a look of immense sadness, of empathy for the poor animal's suffering, I suspect. "Charming . . ." she whispered.

"I'll let you two look around," I said. "I'll be outside trying to calm some hot farmers down. Remember, don't change anything you see."

I walked out of the barn to the cluster of mumbling, armed men gathered around Gordon Huckaby. For the first time, I noticed the hollow barking of coon hounds coming from one of the trucks in the dark.

"Evenin', men," I said firmly. Most of them mumbled some reply. I looked at each individual to see whom I knew, which was most of them. The man I'd seen talking to Gordon earlier peered down his beaky nose at me. He was a local I had seen in Hunter on occasion, but I didn't know him.

Gordon Huckaby raised his head and frowned at me. "Sheriff Cody, me and the boys have done talked it over and, well, we *know* it had to be Roadkill. We . . . uh . . . we'll help you go git him." Gordon's last sentence was more a demand than an offer.

"We brung the dogs, Sheriff!" one man shouted from the rear.

"Yeah!" another said. "We'll help you bring him in, Sheriff!"

"Yeah!" several others echoed.

Wonderful. An old-fashioned Wild West posse with a chic touch of Southern lynch mob.

"Thanks, gentlemen," I replied. "I appreciate your concerns, and I'm grateful for the offer of support, but nobody's going after Roadkill Rudesill tonight. This situation will be thoroughly investigated, and if any indication that Roadkill was involved is found, we will arrest him promptly."

"*Come* on, Sheriff!" Gordon snarled. "You seen what that son of bitch done to my little girl's horse! You know what it done to her! Let's go *git* the bastard 'fore he gits away!"

There was a supporting chorus of yeahs and damn-rights.

"I can guess how you feel, Gordon, and I sympathize. But all you men need to understand that, in Gordon's own words, nobody saw anything here tonight to indicate that Roadkill had anything to do with this awful act. Even strange numbers like Roadkill have rights, guys, and one of them is not to be arrested unless there is reasonable cause to believe they committed a crime. Now what I need you men to do is put all these guns away before somebody triggers an accidental round, then I need you to help out the Huckaby family the best way you can. For most of you, that's going to be to go on home and let me and my people handle this. I promise you, every effort will be—"

"*Look,* Sheriff," the beaky man finally spoke, stepping forward and tipping his Redskins ball cap back on his head. He had a wad of chewing tobacco wedged in one cheek and he swung a scoped Remington 742 easily from one hand. I noticed Pierce unobtrusively shift to where he could get at the man if he needed to. I knew he was concerned about the man's belligerent tone, not to mention his rifle. "Let's put this another way, Sheriff Cody," the Redskin continued with confidence. "We don't give a fuck about all that rights bullshit. We all know ain't nobody coulda done this but Roadkill, and we want him locked up." He spat a brown stream onto the straw near my feet, pointed a finger at me, and spoke slowly. "Now, either you go git that crazy nigger right now"—he looked right at me with mean eyes—"or by God, we will."

A silence ensued, and all eyes were on me. This was not a time to blink.

6

•••••••••

He Who Blinks First

I maintained eye contact with the sneering man while I stepped squarely before him.

He also didn't blink.

"What's your name, sir?" I asked.

"Roscoe Lee Byner. What's it to you?"

I might've known. Half the people in these hills were named after Robert E. Lee in some fashion.

"Well, Roscoe Lee Byner," I said, "you have any idea where Roadkill is?"

"Hell, yes. We run him to ground about five years ago down on Emmitt Cutter's farm in Trout Run Gap, but he got away. By God, I reckon with all these men and dogs, we'll git him this time. Don't you worry about that."

I remembered the incident. Now I knew where I'd seen the man. "Okay," I said. "You can go get him."

Roscoe Lee Byner took on a satisfied smirk and beamed at the group of men. "All right, boys, let's go!"

"Hold it." I said.

Everybody froze.

"I said *you* can go get him. Just you . . . Roscoe Lee Byner."

Now he blinked.

"Uh . . . say what, Sheriff?"

I aimed *my* finger at Roscoe Lee's nose. "I said you can go get Roadkill, but you're going by yourself. I'm not having some armed mob running around."

Roscoe Lee broke eye contact with me, which was a good thing. I was getting a migraine. He looked nervously at his friends, who were watching him carefully.

"Well, uh, shit, Sheriff. I . . . hell, I ain't goin' up there alone."

"Why not, Roscoe Lee Byner?"

"Well, I won't be able to find him without dogs and help!"

"You won't have to find him, Roscoe Lee Byner. Trust me. He'll find you."

Roscoe Lee was beginning to look like the captain of a munitions ship who has just sighted mines. He had dealt himself in; the entire assembly was waiting to see his cards, and he knew it. "Well . . . I . . . uh . . . hell, I still cain't go git him alone, Sheriff!"

"Why not, Roscoe Lee Byner?" I asked, softly. "You don't have to arrest him, just tell him Sheriff Lewis Cody wants to see him. You can even take your big bad rifle with you, because you'll never lay eyes on him. But don't worry. He'll be there."

"Well, I . . . I still ain't goin'!" Roscoe Lee said, angrily.

"Why not, Roscoe Lee Byner?" I asked again, stepping a little closer to him, drilling his eyes with my own.

"Well, because . . ."

"Because *what?*" I snapped.

"Because it ain't my goddamn job!"

"Yeah!" I shouted close in Roscoe Lee's face, causing him to step back with a startled look. I snatched the rifle from his grip, dropped its magazine, racked the round out of it, and tossed the weapon into the muddy manure. "You finally got something right, you dumb fuck! It's *not your goddamn job!*" I poked him stoutly in the chest with the knuckles of my first two fingers, causing him to back up another step. "It's *my* goddamn job!" I poked him again, backing him up farther. The other men parted to make way. "And I don't need some monkey-breath smart ass telling me how to do it! You understand me, *Roscoe Lee Byner?*" It occurred to me that I should calm down. What the hell was happening to me these days?

"Well, yeah, Sheriff. I just meant—"

I sighed and brought myself under control. "Shut up, Byner. You had your say, and now I'm having mine." I addressed the group. "You fucking heroes go up in those mountains after Roadkill Rudesill tonight and he'll put broadheads in every one of you and eat your goddamn dogs for breakfast. He's healthy now, men; he's not crippled like he was the year your bunch ran him down. But the bottom line is there is *no* evidence to connect Roadkill with this crime! If and when there is, I *will* go get him. In the meantime, no *fucking* vigilante gang is going to violate his rights or anybody else's in Hunter County!" Damn! I was bubbling over again.

I walked about the little crowd, eyeing each individual in turn, giving the rage in me time to subside. "Now. If there is any man here who has any further dispute on this subject, let him sound off right now. He can spend the night in my jail, and tomorrow morning he can find out how Judge Holman Lemon feels about vigilantes." I looked about, waiting for any takers. Pierce's huge bulk floated about in the rear. I knew anyone who piped off now would be handcuffed and locked in the back of Pierce's cruiser faster than Carl Lewis could run the forty-yard dash.

Nobody said anything for several seconds. Finally, Gordon Huckaby cleared his throat. "You . . . uh . . . you're right, Sheriff. We're all pretty worked up, I guess. Maybe some of us is too worked up."

"I know you're upset, men. So am I. This is a disgusting crime, and I can't wait to get my hands on whoever did it. We'll do everything we can possibly do, I promise you. Now go on home. Keep your eyes and ears open, and phone me right away if you learn anything that bears on this case. For that matter, I'm also looking for a pickup truck with fresh damage on the right front quarter. You may as well watch out for that while you're at it. Whoever was driving it this evening hit Trooper Calder's wife and baby and killed them both." A startled mumble ran through the group. I looked at Pierce and jerked my head toward the parked vehicles. He got the message and went to check the trucks for damage. "Gordon, go on up to the house and take care of your wife and daughter. The rest of you guys get out of here and let my people do their job. Go on."

Gordon glanced at me, only pain in his eyes now, the anger past. A few of the men mumbled, "G'night sheriff," and all walked away to their cars and pickups.

I turned around to find Drs. Morgan and Chu standing behind me. I didn't know how long they'd been there, but Julianne Chu looked at me strangely for a moment. Of course, after what she'd just seen in the end stall, anyone could have appeared strange.

Pierce came back, shook his head at me, and carried his cameras into the barn. As the trucks filed out of the Huckaby farm, I noticed two of my departmental cruisers coming in. Behind them, I saw a car that I could have guessed would show up, but one I could have done without. It was the only Volvo in Hunter County, a battered old station wagon, and it was driven by Pete Floyd, editor of the local weekly newspaper, the *Hunter Press*. Stupendous. Pete clambered out of his car, waving at me. Two cameras hung around his neck, and his beloved red press pass was clipped to his coat. He seemed unsure of whether he wanted to interview me or rush inside for photos. He went inside, but I doubted he was going to publish any photos he would take in Gordon Huckaby's barn tonight.

I turned back to Hap and Dr. Chu. "Lewis," Hap said in his raspy grumble, "in all my years, I ain't seen nobody abuse an animal like that."

"Yeah, Hap. I'm worried about this. Whoever did it is sick and dangerous."

I noticed Dr. Chu seemed to be trembling slightly. Her lips were tightly pursed. "Are you okay?" I asked her, and then she confirmed what I feared.

"You don't know how sick he is," she said, intensely. She fixed me with her lovely brown eyes. "This creep is going to make Jeffery Dahmer seem cuddly. The horse was repeatedly stabbed and lacerated with an instrument having a blade dimension of approximately one hundred forty millimeters by thirty millimeters. There was no tearing of the hide or uprooting of hair particles at either the points where the blade entered or where it was at its full depth, indicating that the blade was quite sharp along its entire length. The wounds were randomly and, from a physiological standpoint, ineffectively placed and demonstrate no intent to either prolong or shorten the animal's misery, indicating, in my opinion, that the assault was rendered with savagery rather than skill. I believe he bound the horse with the ropes and wire, impaled it with the pitchfork, raped it with the broken handle, and then slashed it, probably in that order."

"Can you pinpoint the time of death?" I asked her.

She nodded. "I assumed you would need to know. I took the heart temperature—don't worry, I used a probe and marked the hole with a piece of tape—I'd have to consult pathology tables to be more accurate, but in this ambient temperature I'd guess a horse of that weight has been dead about four hours." Dr. Chu looked hard at me. "Unfortunately, Sheriff Cody, the pitchfork handle was possibly the second rape of the animal. I found traces of what I'm pretty sure will test out to be human semen near the mare's vagina. I think he ejaculated on or in the horse before he butchered her. You have a big problem, Sheriff." Julianne Chu's beautiful lower lip trembled as she exhaled long and slowly. "He gets off on this. He will do it again, somewhere, and probably soon."

I nodded. I'd suspected as much. I also looked at the woman with new respect.

Behind Julianne Chu, I saw Pete Floyd walk slowly out of the barn with a stricken look on his face. He looked around desperately, then hurried off into the darkness beyond the side of the barn.

Briefly, I wondered if the . . . person . . . who butchered Darlene Huckaby's horse was still out there in the darkness, watching us all.

"Thank you, Dr. Chu," I replied, hearing retching sounds from where Pete had disappeared. I looked at Doctor Morgan. "Hap, anything to add?"

"Ain't much to add to that. I can tell you he's probably done this before. He knew how to secure a half-ton animal so it couldn't escape or injure him. Also, Lewis, they's a feed bucket in the corner of the stall that's been took off its eyebolt. Couldn'ta fell off. And it's got muddy footprints on the bottom of it, like maybe he turned it up and stood on it when he . . . when he done it."

"Thanks. Listen, both of you. I want to keep the sexual aspect of all this strictly between us. This thing is going to turn into a big enough horror story anyway; let's not magnify it unnecessarily. I don't want Hunter County shooting at every stranger they see." Both vets nodded soberly.

"This Roadkill person, Sheriff—why does everyone think he did it?" Dr. Chu said.

I looked up and saw a full moon coming into view over the trees. Great. Pete was probably working on a werewolf theme for the story, even as he was chucking his dinner in Gordy Huckaby's barnyard. Next thing you knew, I would have a mob of villagers carrying torches, pitchforks, wooden stakes, and silver bullets.

"Roadkill Rudesill," I said to Julianne Chu. "is sort of Hunter County's answer to the Sasquatch. He's a Vietnam veteran—one of several who discovered after their return that they could no longer function in mainstream American society—who went off to live alone in the woods. He scares the hell out of people, but I don't think he did this. For one thing, he's been skulking around these mountains for at least nine years that I know of, and this is the first thing like this we've ever had in the county. For another, I know him, in a way, and it's just not his style. I never rule anybody out, and we'll look at all the evidence with the notion that it could be Roadkill, but I'll be very surprised if it is."

Pete reappeared near the barn door, wiping his mouth. He looked sheepishly at me, and started ambling in our direction. He already knew Hap, and I introduced him to Dr. Chu.

"Lewis," Pete said, a little hoarsely, "I have never seen anything . . . anything like that. What happened?"

"All we know right now, Pete, is that Darlene Huckaby came down about five P.M. to feed her horse and found what you saw."

"And you think Roadkill did it?" Pete said offhandedly. It was an old tactic of his, to fish with a leading statement, but I was surprised that he still thought I'd ever go for it after all these years.

"Really?" I answered. "What do you know that connects Roadkill with this event, Pete?"

"Well . . . uh . . . nothing. I just heard—"

"Bullshit is what you heard, Pete. Nobody saw anybody,

let alone Roadkill, and nothing we have found so far indicates any specific individual. I'd appreciate it if you'd not mention Roadkill when you go to press, Pete. There is no evidence so far that he's been within ten miles of here. I have too many people now who are itching to witch-hunt themselves a scapegoat for this thing. If we get everybody whipped up over Roadkill Rudesill, it's just going to muddy up the water, aside from pinning a target on Roadkill."

Pete thought for a moment. This sort of negotiation was old hat with us. "Okay," he said, "but the instant you learn that any individual, Roadkill or otherwise, is suspect, I want to be the first to know about it."

"Deal. Did you get the word on Boyce Calder's family?"

"No. You mean that young Virginia state trooper assigned to this area? What about—oh no! Lewis, was that his wife and baby in that hit-and-run-fatal I heard about on my scanner?"

I nodded.

"Oh no," Hap Morgan echoed. He leaned close to Julianne Chu's ear to explain to her.

"What was her name?" Pete scribbled furiously in his little notebook.

"Catherine Calder. Baby's name was Steven, I think. Somebody tried to pass her and ran her off the road into a tree. Both died on the scene. I need the story to say we're looking for an older white male with short hair and a pickup truck, probably with alien blue paint and damage on the right side."

"Done."

"Thanks, Pete. I have people working both incidents. I'll let you know as soon as we turn anything."

Pete's pen slashed to a halt on his pad, and he suddenly looked up at Julianne Chu.

"Dr. Chu!" Pete exclaimed. "I just realized who you are! You're that young veterinarian who's going to take over Hap's practice!"

"That ain't a done deal yet, Pete," Hap Morgan groused.

"Let's just say the matter is under consideration, Mr. Floyd," Dr. Chu said. "I am considering two other possibilities."

"Oh well, Dr. Chu, I'm sure that you'll find Hunter County is the most delightful little place in the world to make a home and career!"

"So I see," she said dryly.

Dr. Chu looked at me with what my lonesome and horny bones interpreted as a glimmer of interest. Yet from years of having to read people's faces to tell if they were about to try to kill me, my eyes saw something in hers less practiced observers might have overlooked. There was a taste of pain in her face, somewhere behind her eyes, that seemed out of place with her otherwise delightfully pleasant personality. I knew that look. I saw it in the mirror each morning. She smiled again, no less lovely, but shyly this time, and she went to Hap's veterinary truck with her aluminum equipment case.

Pete asked a few more questions, then he excused himself and left in the smoking, faded old Volvo. I was about to thank Hap Morgan when Hap beat me to the punch.

"Say, Lewis," Hap said, his walrus mustache bobbing again, Hap himself bobbing up and down on his heels. "How long you gonna be here?"

"Uh, well . . . not long, I guess, Hap. Pierce can handle the scene. I need to follow up on Cathy Calder's death, though. I—"

"Ain't nothing you can do for her 'til mornin', right?"

"Well, yeah. I got everybody looking for the suspect vehicle, but—"

"I need your help, Lewis."

Hap Morgan had saved Gruesome's life two times and had refused to take a cent for it. More than that, he was a friend and a man of character. He was someone I owed many times over.

"Sure, Hap. What's wrong?"

"I . . . um . . . I really need you to help me talk Dr. Chu into buying in with me. She's a damn good vet and a fine young woman. I need an equine specialist and besides, when I retire in a few years, you know I don't want to turn my practice over to just some New Age kid with the money, I want—"

"Jeez, Hap," I said, "I'd be glad to help any way I could, but I don't know anything about—"

"Good. Drinks at my place in half an hour. Be there."
Hap started for his truck.

"What? Whoa, Hap! Tonight?"

"Ain't no time like the present, I always say," Hap mumbled, still walking. "Julianne ain't gonna be here but a couple a days. No time to waste."

"Yeah, but, Hap, I—"

"See ya in half an hour, Lewis," Hap answered without breaking stride. "I ain't got any of that Norwegian shit you drink, but the Bud'll be cold."

7

•••••••

The Perverse and
the Pretty

Hap and Bev Morgan lived in a house listed in the National Registry of Historic Structures, a two-story, pre–Civil War home built of the heavy gray stone borne up from Virginia highland soil for centuries. The stately, rugged old place was called Fox Haven, and was set among towering poplars with limbs you could hang a bus from. One of the histories of Hunter County allowed that a young United States Army captain named Robert E. Lee visited Fox Haven when it belonged to the Schlosser family, who were among the German immigrants that settled the area. There was no record of Lee having visited the area during the war, but one of Jackson's cavaliers, Turner Ashby, was known to have slept at Fox Haven in passing. It was a home of dignity, strength, and understated character, wholly befitting Hap and Bev Morgan.

The dogs barked at my arrival, but when gently scolded by Hap, they wagged and sniffed and went back to their business.

Bev Morgan rose when I entered the high-ceilinged living room floored with a thick hooked rug, and bordered on one end by a blackened stone fireplace radiating heat from a blazing fire. She gave me a hug, took my jacket, and directed me to a chair near a sofa on which sat the charming Julianne

Chu, in yellow silky blouse and dark-brown pants. She hit me with that puppy-cute smile again. I looked for the pain, but it was better hidden now.

I was about to sit in the chair when Hap came back into the warm room carrying a cold beer. "Hold it!" he commanded. I froze with my butt stuck out. "That ole chair's got a loose leg, Lewis! Here, you sit on the sofa there by Julianne!"

I took the beer and sat a cushion away from Julianne Chu. Perplexed, Bev Morgan said, "Why, I didn't know there was a loose leg on that—"

"Well, they is!" Hap groaned, sinking into the embrace of an easy chair he had also been married to for forty years. One of the cats instantly launched itself into Hap's lap and lay down.

We accomplished the obligatory recount of the evening's horrors for Bev Morgan's sake. After expressing her sorrow over the Calders' untimely demise, Bev asked, "Lewis . . . why would . . . a violent sexual deviate who preys on horses suddenly show up in Hunter County, of all places?"

"That's among several questions I could sure use some answers to," I sighed, rubbing my forehead. I sipped on my beer.

Hap pulled at one corner of his bushy mustache. "Human sexual deviancy involving animals ain't as rare as a lot of people think, I'm afraid. 'Course, that still don't explain what the crazy son of a bitch is doin' up here."

Julianne Chu was staring into the fire. "We touched on a few cases of it in veterinary school, while studying animal abuse in general. What worries me most about the atrocity to Miss Huckaby's mare was the savage violence. Dr. Morgan—"

"Hap, dammit," Hap mumbled absently.

Julianne smiled, but it vanished quickly. "Hap is right. Bestiality occurs on a limited scale, but almost never is it accompanied by violence. From what little I've read, unlike what is typical in the rape of human females, the rapist of an animal isn't typically anger driven. The animal sexual abuser seems to be exclusively motivated by misplaced sexual desires. Psychiatry isn't my field, of course, but what data I've seen showed not one case of violence together with

66

bestiality. It is theorized by some scholars that when human sexuality dawns in an adolescent, they usually are directed to the opposite human sex by the programming of thought and deed that habitually occurs during childhood. In short, boys are commonly drawn to girls and vice versa because all their lives they've seen and heard and been taught that this is the correct thing to do and that there are no alternatives. Occasionally, however, an adolescent may by chance or some psychological peculiarity be close to a nonconventional object or nonconventional action at the precise time their sexuality is awakening. Such objects might include animals or human members of the same sex. Such actions might include sexual abuse or exposure to death or humiliation. But when these nonconventional objects or actions occur as the adolescent is entering puberty—more exactly, at the moment they make critical associations of action or object with their sexuality—then a sexual deviancy may occur. This theme is thought to be a possible reason why homosexuality may not be a choice but something programmed into certain people by forces beyond their control. Taken to a bizarre extreme, the theme is also offered as a possible explanation for the Jeffery Dahmer types that we see. Perhaps something they were exposed to at pivotal moments of adolescent sexual association influenced their sexual preference in some way they could not help."

"Julianne, I can understand all that," Bev Morgan said, leaning forward in her chair, drink in hand. "But doesn't it account only for the object in the case of this . . . person . . . who killed the Huckaby horse. Why is he so horridly violent?"

Julianne smiled wanly again. "Well, let's keep in mind I'm a vet, not a shrink, but as I understand the research, he could have been exposed to violence, either upon him or just in his observation, at the time he was making critical adolescent sexual associations. He could have unknowingly put violence together in his mind with sexual pleasure, and it might have stuck as a fetish. Dahmer was exposed to the death of animals in his dawning adolescence, and it is theorized that he associated death, and by extension, killing, with sexual fulfillment. No one has any clear answers, I'm afraid."

"Humph!" Hap grunted. "But why Hunter County, Virginia?"

"Why not?" Julianne said. She slipped her feet from her boots and drew them beneath her on the sofa.

We sat in silence for a minute, fixed on the crackling fire in the soot-blackened stone hearth.

"I don't care about his reasons," I said at last. "At least not beyond the point where they help me pull him down. How he got that way is not my problem. Stopping him is."

"I'm with you, Lewis!" Hap said springing out of his chair. "I don't care if a horse kicked him on his first hard-on—"

"Hap Morgan!" Bev scolded.

"—that still don't give him no right to brutalize one o' God's gentlest creatures! Come on, Lewis, I wanta show you my new truck. Ladies, me and Lewis will be back in a minute."

With that, Hap marched out of the room toward the garage. I had seen Hap's new truck before and had already had the male ritualistic discussion with him about it, and he knew it, but dutifully, I shrugged at Bev and Julianne and followed Hap down the hall.

In the frigid vehicle shed, Hap busied himself checking the heat/refrigeration unit many farm vets have mounted on their trucks to keep their medicines from freezing or spoiling.

"Awright, Lewis," Hap said as though he were confessing a crime, "here's the story on Miss Julie. She was married for eleven years to a computer executive up in Loudoun County. Two years ago, he died. Tough on a sweet kid like her, you know? She told Bev all that, of course. You know how easy folks talk to Bev. She ain't had no man in her . . . life, since. Know what I mean?"

"Uh, Hap, what—"

"'Course, none o' that's got nothin' to do with nothin'," Hap said, forging on. "Bottom line is, single and beautiful or not, she's a natural vet, highly experienced, and she's a expert on horses. And I want her for a partner, but I cain't offer her the kinda money she can make at the other two places she's considering."

"Ooookay," I said, baffled. "So what do you want me—"

"Well, just show her a little kindness! That too much to ask?" Hap growled, like I was dense. Maybe I was. "Tell her what a swell place to live we got up here in these mountains! Tell her what nice folks we are! Hell, tell her the Gettysburg Address, just get her to buy in with me!"

"Sure, Hap, I'll try, but—"

"She ain't too hard to look at, is she? I ain't too old to see that. You ain't either, I already seen."

"That's the God's honest truth," I had to agree, "but—"

"Good! Glad we got a plan, Lewis. I'm grateful. Now let's go back inside. It's past my bedtime!"

I stood in Hap Morgan's garage considering that one didn't get to finish many sentences around Hap.

As soon as I walked back in the living room, Hap yawned like a sleepy coon dog. "Awright, Beverly," he said, taking a confused Bev by the hand. "Let's you and me turn in. It's late."

Good-nights were exchanged and the Morgans exited, stage right. "Remember the bad leg on that chair, Lewis!" Hap called.

Still standing, I looked at Julianne Chu, who was looking at me, I found. She averted her gaze, swirling the drink and ice that remained in her glass. "Dr. Morgan practically has our wedding invitations printed up," she said softly.

"He is a character," I agreed. "I'm sorry. I don't know what gives him the notion—"

"Oh, I'm used to it," Julianne said with another smile. "Everybody thinks a woman in her thirties should be married. Besides, Dr. Morgan is so sweet. His heart is in the right place." An awkward pause ensued. I filled it by stoking the fire with two pieces of firewood. When I turned, she was looking at me again. "Maybe we'd both be more comfortable if you sat down, sher—Lewis. There's nothing at all wrong with that chair, of course—I sat in it all last evening—but there's room for both of us on the couch."

I laughed a little, in spite of the day I'd had. "Hap made it plain to me he's very taken with you, Julianne," I told her as I sat down.

Julianne twisted to her left, toward me on the sofa,

placing her arm on the back. "Not half as taken as he is with you. Bev told me how you saved their son's career with the FBI. Hap and Bev both think you hung the moon."

"I stopped Hap's boy for DWI one night years ago, when I was first hired as a deputy. He was just out of law school, a good kid who rarely drank, but his fiancée had just canned him and he took it hard. I just brought him home to Hap and Bev, that's all."

"Yes. Still, the Morgans and I both know he had applied to the FBI, and an arrest would've destroyed his chances of being hired."

"Well, maybe. But I know how he felt. Anyway, we were talking about how much Hap thinks of you, not me."

Julianne sipped her drink and watched the fire. "I know how he felt, too," she said. Another silence hung in the air.

Desperate for conversation, I said, "I've been given firm instructions to talk you into buying in with Hap. He'll kill me if you don't."

"Isn't that strange?" Julie replied. "All day, while we've been touring, meeting some of Doctor Morgan's clients, he's been regaling me with what a sterling—and single—man you are."

"He's a conniving old cuss, but I love him. I'm flattered that he thinks a young beauty like you could be sold an old goat like me."

Julianne laughed a rich, sexy woman's laugh for the first time since I'd known her. "Aren't you the charmer? Phoo. Even if you fooled me, Dr. Morgan has already explained to me that you're 'only a few years older'—"

"Old enough to be your daddy."

"At fourteen, I doubt it. Besides, Dr. Morgan says that at our ages, 'a few years' difference don't matter a hoot.'"

"My Lord. He's probably already booked a church," I said, shaking my head. "Anyway, if you're only fourteen years younger than me, then time and gravity have been exceedingly kind to you."

Julianne fixed me with that killer smile once more. "You silver-tongued devil, you," she said, looking right at me. Another pause ensued, but this one was not so awkward.

"Speaking of silver," I said, retrieving from my pocket the little piece of twisted metal I found stuck to my knee at the Calder crash site. "What do you make of this? All I know is I think it really is silver."

It was about two inches long, was thin and light in color, and was clearly twisted from its originally designed shape. It seemed to be composed of a fairly substantial metal quite unlike any item of trash or automobile part I could imagine. Looking at it more closely, I could tell it was decoratively tooled, in a tiny floral pattern, with considerable precision and craftsmanship. Puzzling.

Julianne Chu leaned close to me to take the piece. The upper surfaces of her breasts were the kind of warm-soft smooth that Nature invented to reward men for having eyes.

"Where did you find it?" she asked.

"By the wreckage in that fatal hit-and-run tonight. The point where I knelt on it was too far off the road for the item to have been thrown there from a passing car, and the crash site was not a place where people normally passed. I have no idea what it is or where it came from, but I can't help feeling it's connected to the wreck in some way."

"Hmm," Julianne said. "I've never seen anything like it. It's silver?"

"What do I know? Seems too heavy for aluminum and too soft for steel."

Julianne bent the piece slightly. "Soft enough to be silver." She handed it back to me.

"It's a mystery," I said, "one of several I'm blessed with right now." I stowed the metal away.

"Well!" Julianne said brightly. "Dr. Morgan says you're very smart—"

"Oh, Jeez."

"—so I know you'll solve the mystery!"

"Like I said earlier tonight, Hap will tell you anything to make you buy in with him."

"Phoo. Dr. Morgan doesn't know how to lie. Besides, he said you were a very nice man, and that certainly seems to be true." Julianne looked me heavily in the eyes again.

"Hmm, now who's silver-tongued?" I asked her.

"Maybe you'd like to hold me," Julianne Chu suddenly said to me.

"Excuse me?" I said, not sure I'd heard her right.

"Don't panic," Julianne said, looking up at me from but inches away. "I'm not going to get all teary-eyed on you."

"I'm not water-soluble. If crying is what you need, help yourself. I've had my crying times."

"Thanks. I'll take a rain check. Right now, what I need is just to be held." She turned away from me on the couch and leaned back on my chest. I draped an arm around her, and I drew in the fragrance of her as slowly as I could.

"I'll try to suffer through it a little while longer," I said.

Julianne's soft red lips parted in another slight smile. Her teeth were white as porcelain. "Thank you. I . . . I lost my husband twenty-eight months ago. For a long time, I couldn't imagine being held by anyone but him, then there seemed to be no one I cared to be held by."

"Ooh. I think I was just complimented very sweetly, thank you."

"I get so tired of being alone, sometimes . . . Lewis. I can do it, but I get so weary of it, you know?"

I thought of the last four months since Lucia, and the years before that after my daughter was killed.

I pulled her to me tightly, looking up at the high ceiling of Fox Haven. "Yes," I said to her. "I know."

She nestled against my chest for a while. I held her quietly without speaking. What she was purging or even if she *was* purging, I didn't know. It just felt so very fine to hold a beautiful woman, to mean something to her, to fill a need in her, if only for an evening.

A grandfather clock in the hallway bonged as we covered all the where-from, what-school questions that usually ensue at times like this. Julianne was third-generation American, raised in San Francisco, where her parents ran an insurance business. As we talked, her pretty brown eyes began to close and her speech slowed. In a time, the fire turned to coals, and Julianne Chu fell into the deep, evenly spaced inhalations of sound sleep. Her mouth was parted slightly.

For a long time, I just sat and enjoyed the female warmth and heat and scent. Then, painstakingly, I eased from beneath her, but she was too exhausted, physically and emotionally, I suspected, to wake. I covered her with Bev

Morgan's knitted afghan, kissed her beneath her delicate ear, sucking lightly on the little fuzz. Then I walked out into the cold, clear mountain Virginia night, a night that somewhere was hearing the cries of young man robbed of his woman and baby, a night in which crept a creature that tortured and debased for fun.

8

•••••••••

Curious Silver

Prior to coming downstairs before dawn, Gruesome, my hideous English Bulldog, and I looked in on Elizabeth, still asleep in her room. She'd returned from the Middleburg hunt the previous night before I'd come home from Fox Haven. Elizabeth was such a pretty child, with the Brahmin beauty of her late mother, but without, I fervently hoped, the vitriol and bitterness of her mother, which had destroyed her parents' marriage and ultimately both of them. I covered Elizabeth again, as she constantly kicked her quilt onto the floor and lay shivering on the bed in her U.S. Equestrian Team dream shirt.

Gruesome and I walked out in the dark onto the big brick veranda between the rear of the house and the cedar-sided garage structure with Polly's apartment on the second floor. Both of us were suffering a severe enthusiasm crisis, and this was not improved by the thick, cold fog that surrounded Mountain Harbor on the morning of the second day of the butcher. All that sustained the two of us on our morning runs around the estate was the knowledge that every calorie we burned made more room for the cholesterol-nightmare breakfasts we would eat later at Lady Maude's, with the Gentry.

Gruesome and I staggered beneath the massive pines behind the mansion and crossed the footbridge over the bubbling little creek between the house and the stable. Arthur, the old man who lived in an apartment over the stable, was still asleep. I made a mental note to advise Arthur to arm the alarm system on the stable when he was away from it or asleep. I went to Moose's stall, where she snuffled, extended her massive head over the half-door, and nosed me. I petted her and fed her a couple of apples. Looking at the stall blew mindflashes in me of the Huckaby barn the night before. Involuntarily, I tried to picture a human being doing what was done in that place of horror. I pondered how I'd feel if I found Moose sadistically slaughtered in the way poor Darlene Huckaby found her mare. My horse was gentle and giving and trusting, yet possessed of a certain dignified nobility. She was easily a more worthy living being than many humans I could think of. I knew damn well how I'd feel if somebody tortured her to death; I'd want to kill them.

On the way out, I noted Elizabeth's little mare, Dublin, was back in her stall, wearing what horse folks called a sheet. I called it a horse blanket, but you learned early on that it is a big thing to horse folks to use all the correct terms. The little Irish mare had been perfect for Elizabeth—perky, enthusiastic, and affectionate. She was meticulously groomed, as it was her blessing to be the obsession of Elizabeth Butler. She came to me, but seeing that I bore no grain bucket, she looked down the aisle for Arthur, who wouldn't feed them for another hour.

On the morning run, I was tempted to wallow in self-pity for my star-crossed love life with Lucia Dodd, but we Southern boys are supposed to be above that sort of thing. Besides, at the moment, I could still smell Julianne Chu's perfume, which took a little of the sting out. Still, the realism, or pessimism if you prefer, of a lifelong cop reminded me that last night Julianne had been made lonely, tired, shocked, and insecure by the horrors of the evening, and she'd had a couple of stiff drinks. I might well find upon seeing her next that she was embarrassed and regretful about our minor intimacy. Then, too, she might be feeling guilt at "betraying" her late husband. Hell, like a thoroughly modern American woman, she'd probably sue me for date rape. *No matter,* I thought, jogging down the Mountain

Harbor drive. I had the tender memory of last night, and even a cop's sour cynicism couldn't take that from me.

Images of Julianne dissolved quickly into ghastly mind-flashes of a once-lovely young Cathy Calder choking in her own blood. Running back up the Mountain Harbor drive, thirty minutes later, I felt guilt for having felt so good last night when a fine young man was knowing the worst night of his life.

Why me? I pondered, shifting my self-pity around a little. *Why here?* Most of the time, Hunter County was a sleepy, isolated mountain community where the biggest news in months would be the wreck of a chicken manure truck. It ought to be against the law to transport chicken manure through Hunter County! The paper would quote local outraged citizens, as though the crash were a nuclear haz-mat incident. In Hunter County, a fire in the courthouse Dumpster was a major breaking event.

Why, then, in this delightfully mundane county, did I suddenly have one guy who kills a woman and baby with his truck and evades the music, and, oh joy, an industrial-grade psycho who has sex with horses before he sadistically butchers them? Why Hunter County? Why me?

I deposited Gruesome on the den rug and lit off the gas fireplace. He lay down on the warm, elevated stone hearth to let the heat soak his sore bones, while I went up to shower. When I came back down the winding staircase in my uniform, Elizabeth was in the kitchen with Polly, eating her breakfast.

"Uncle Lewis!" the beautiful, dark-haired child cried, and she rushed to give me a hug. "I had a wonderful time riding with the Albertsons! Dublin ran like the wind! Thanks for letting me go!"

I squeezed her and hurried her back to breakfast. "I'm glad you enjoyed it, darlin' girl. I hope you thanked the Albertsons properly, and by the way, I expect to see a thank-you letter to them ready to go out in tomorrow's mail."

"I've already written it!" Elizabeth announced with obvious glee at having trumped me.

I kissed her on the top of her head. "That's my girl," I told her. "I'm proud of you." Polly smiled at both of us.

Gruesome limped out to my cruiser with us and I helped him into the front seat, where Elizabeth cuddled him. We dropped Elizabeth at the bottom of the drive to await her school bus. Knowing the butcher was about, I elected to wait with her the five minutes it took the bus to arrive. It was a paranoid overcaution, I chided myself; statistically, deviates like the butcher almost never changed the objects of their fetish, and the Huckaby farm was over ten miles away. Yet I had failed to adequately protect two young girls in my charge before. Although my daughter Tess was killed in an airliner crash three hundred miles from me, I will always wonder if I could somehow have prevented her being on the plane. And the Sloan brothers killed fifteen-year-old Peggy Sloan not two years ago, about twenty minutes after I promised her I would never let them hurt her again. Such experiences give whole new depth to words like *failure* and *nightmare.* I had promised Elizabeth's father in his dying moments that no harm would ever come to Elizabeth and Anne. If anything happened to another child I was responsible for, I would have neither the courage nor the right to live.

Elizabeth waved cheerfully as the old yellow bus ground away. It was a thrill to see her so happy. There was a time when I feared she might never recover from the terrible deaths of her parents. What an incredible blessing to love a child so much her laughter renders pale all other joys.

The heater in my cruiser felt good. I headed out 665 toward the Calder accident scene. Gruesome propped his knobby front feet on the armrest of the passenger door and streaked the window with steamy noseprints.

At the accident site, one of my deputies, Charles Harmon, was handling traffic while the destroyed Calder car was winched onto a flatbed wrecker from the local Exxon station. Three VSP accident investigators, wearing blue coveralls and ball caps, stood conferring with each other and examining Polaroid photographs. The road was streaked with lines of safety-pink spray paint that marked skid streaks and other points of measurement. One investigator held a large set of bolt cutters and the entire speedometer assembly from the Calder car. My deputy halted the traffic and waved me to a parking spot on the shoulder. The three VSP accident reconstruction specialists shook my hand and introduced themselves.

One trooper held up the speedometer assembly. "We'll put it under the ultraviolet to see where the needle hit the backplate when the car impacted the tree, of course. But, Sheriff Cody, I've already done the friction coefficient and crush depth calculations based on the estimated surface and ambient air temperatures at the incident time, and I'd say she was doing about forty-five or fifty when she hit that tree. We examined her body in the Roanoke morgue early this morning. Her right ankle was broken, and the brake pedal on the car is bent, so I'd say she saw it coming."

These guys were as much detectives as any homicide investigator. They could arrive at an accident scene of incredible devastation, and eventually they could tell you who was seated in which car going how fast in what direction. They could tell what, if anything, broke on a destroyed car and caused a crash. They could examine a corpse and tell you where the deceased was seated in the car he was ejected from, whether he was aware the crash was coming, and where his body traveled in the nanoseconds following impact. They were good, but they loved to talk about their science. If you asked one of them what time it was, he would tell you how to build a watch, and he'd be right. Sometimes I wished they'd get to the point and skip the background detail, but then, they had their way of doing things, and it got results.

"Sheriff Cody," a second trooper began, "the deceased's vehicle was struck at a codirectional twenty-two-degree angle by a taller, heavier vehicle moving about thirty miles an hour faster. We'll know more when we've analyzed the data and the lab reports, but right now my best guess is it was a Ford F-350 truck. Ford's dark red is a little more maroon than GM's or Chrysler's or any of the foreign makes. The lab will pin it down when they've done the paint samples, but I'd say it's gonna turn out being Ford Dusk Red, not more than three years old."

"Why the F-350?"

"Well, Sheriff, the F-350 is Ford's ton-rated pickup truck and the only one of their F-series pickup truck models that has extruded front hub lugs. They's signs on the deceased's vehicle that the fender was ground into by the spinning lugs of an extruded hub. Again, we'll know more—"

"When the lab replies. Right."

The third Wise Man spoke. "The debris pattern and surface irregularities bear out what your witness said, Sheriff. Looks like he tried to pass her, realized he was about to have a time-space dispute with a head-on vehicle, and he steered suddenly back to his own lane, colliding side-on with the deceased's vehicle, forcing it from the road, down the slope toward Spoon Creek, and into the tree. Oh, and this'll come as no shock to you, but it looks like he was drunk. The intermittent skid and residue patterns down course of the vehicle contact site are indicative of somebody grossly overcontrolling the vehicle, consistent with an intoxicated operator. Also, we found busted fragments of a Jack Daniel's bottle with some of the whisky still unevaporated. Getting prints off a busted bottle will be about as likely as the Democrats lowering taxes, though. We'll have the whole report to you late today, Sheriff."

"Guys, what do y'all know about Trooper Calder?" I asked. "How's he doing?"

"We're from the Richmond accident reconstruction division, Sheriff Cody, so we didn't know the boy. But I'm told he's taking it hard. Seems he's obsessed with finding out who did this. Cain't blame him, I reckon."

I sighed and stared at the disturbed earth where I had knelt only a few hours earlier, where the mysterious little piece of silver had stuck me in the knee. "That's natural enough, I guess," I said. "Thanks for your help, men. I appreciate the quick response."

"Sheriff, we got the word from Colonel Clair himself. He said to see to it you got whatever you need. He wants this one, Sheriff Cody. So do we."

I looked again toward the big poplar with the bark disturbed on one side. I remembered a toothless, cut-up Cathy Calder trying to tell me not to let her husband see her. She'd been thinking of him, loving him, even in her last moments alive.

I wanted this one, too. Bad.

I drove into the little county seat town of Hunter to have breakfast with the Gentry. I parked in a police-only spot by the courthouse. Gruesome whizzed on the hedges to let every dog know whose courthouse it was.

Across the square, I saw Cynthia Haas, a woman in her early forties to whom life had not been kind. She walked slowly on the cracked, gray sidewalk, wearing the same old mink coat with the holes in the lining that I had known her to wear every winter since I had been Sheriff of Hunter County. She was a slender, reasonably attractive woman who always seemed mildly depressed, or she used to, at least. Today she seemed perkier than usual.

Cynthia Haas spent fourteen long, miserable years spoon-feeding and ass-wiping her husband after the Marines brought what was left of him home from Vietnam. The husband had mercifully died, but not before reforging Cynthia Haas into a woman who never smiled, a woman with the hollow eyes of someone who has awakened to five thousand mornings of hope only to see that hope die five thousand and one times.

Some secrets just don't get kept in little communities like Hunter County, so if Cynthia Haas had ever cheated on her invalid husband in all those years, it would have gotten out. She never did. For fourteen agonizing years, she kept the faith with a brain-dead husband, right on past the morning he finally quit breathing. She never remarried, but she took up the family jewelry shop on the square after her father also died. I knew from a certain local plumber that Cynthia grew a couple of marijuana plants in her greenhouse, among her flowers and vegetables, but the pope would spear Madonna on the fifty-yard line of the Super Bowl at halftime before I arrested Cynthia Haas.

Seeing Cynthia fitting a key to the door of her little jewelry store put me in mind of something, and Gruesome and I crossed the square to her shop. Little bells chimed when I opened the door.

"Good morning, Mrs. Haas," I said as she appeared from the room in the back were she had hung the frayed mink.

Cynthia actually smiled at me; it was only a slight, worried smile, but it was the first I could ever remember seeing on her face.

"Cynthia, please, Sheriff Cody. Good morning, sir. How can I help you?"

I couldn't put my finger on why, but Cynthia Haas seemed younger and healthier than I remembered her being before. I removed from my pocket the mysterious little piece of metal that had stuck me in the knee at the scene of Cathy Calder's fatal accident the night before. I slid it across the glass. "Cynthia, what can you tell me about this?"

Cynthia stared impassively at the little two-inch sliver of metal for several seconds. She picked it up, carried it to her little work table, and weighed it on a tiny digital scale. Then she held it under a small, lighted magnifying glass and examined it, digging at it with what looked like a dental pick. After two minutes of examination, she placed the item in a small white envelope and slid it back across her counter to me.

"Interesting," she said. "What is it?"

"I was hoping you could tell me."

"I am sorry, Sheriff, but I cannot. The item is quite bent from whatever its original form was. Aside from the obvious cosmetic distortion, the metal shows clear indications of having been stressed in several places. I can tell you only that it is a very high quality of sterling silver—"

"I thought so."

"—and it has the residue of an epoxy adhered to its underside, as though it was once bonded to something. Also, it bears intricately hand-tooled engraving, probably by a good European craftsman."

"Engravings of what?"

"Nothing definitive. Only the sort of decorative curved lines commonly engraved on silverware and metal jewelry."

"Is that all you can tell me about the piece?"

"Yes, Sheriff. I'm sorry."

"Not at all. I just wish I knew what to make of it. Thanks. What do I owe you?"

"Not a cent, of course, Sheriff. I am happy to assist. I can offer you one last observation."

"Please."

"Whatever the little item of silver came off of, it was probably quite expensive. Such excellent engraving and high silver content are costly."

Watching her, it began to occur to me what was so different about Cynthia Haas. She no longer wore her hair in a dowdy bun with stray strands; her hair was trimmed short, worn loose, and was combed neatly. Further, I noted she had applied some slight make-up, which radically altered the vaguely sick look she had always projected. She looked downright attractive, I was surprised to realize.

I thanked her again as Gruesome and I strode to the door. Before exiting, I turned back to her. "Whatever it is you're doing to yourself recently, Cynthia," I said, "it's working. You look like a new woman."

Her eyes widened as though she was shocked, but then she blushed, smiled again, and looked at the floor. "Why . . . uh . . . thank you, Sheriff Cody," she said softly.

I felt a welcome burst of cheer as I stepped out onto the square, my breath steaming in the air. Cynthia Haas was a woman who had richly earned some happiness and now it seemed she was getting a little from somewhere. Happiness, I mean.

Sudden mindflashes of an unrecognizably mutilated Stevie Calder and his mother, of fourteen-year-old Darlene Huckaby screaming, and of a hideously tortured little quarter-horse mare put a fast end to my cheer.

9

•••••••••

Merlin the Magician

Crossing the town square before the courthouse, I casually saluted the noble Captain Jedidiah Hunter, a Confederate son of the county and a cavalry officer who rode with distinction with Jackson in the Valley. Stonewall, kiddies, not Michael. Captain Hunter stood implacably rigid in birdshit-spotted granite on the courthouse lawn, leaning on his saber, but he always seemed to wink at me. If I were a believer in anything supernatural, especially reincarnation, I might believe that in another life I was Captain Jedidiah Hunter. He was a champion of his day, but one who had mastered the fine art of not taking life too seriously. Thus it was that, unbeknownst to most Hunter Countians and studiously ignored by others, Captain Hunter was killed in a horseback riding accident, naked, drunk, and in the company of a Richmond whore. My kind of hero.

Gruesome and I crossed the street, waving back at the dawn locals calling, "Mornin', Sheriff!" We walked into Lady Maude's Café, hands down the best restaurant anywhere in the Federation of Planets.

The grand dame of food herself, somewhere in her seventies and still working every day of her life, slid a large crockery mug of hot chocolate across the counter at me, which I scooped up as I walked by, smiling at the sweet old woman. She also flipped a sausage over the counter. Gruesome plotted a target-intercept solution and nailed it like a Patriot missile. It was a sign of my stature in Lady Maude's eyes that she allowed me to bring Gruesome into the place, a gross violation of the Virginia restaurant codes, of course.

In the rear, by the blazing stone fireplace, was the long table where The Gentry gathered each weekday morning. Gruesome and I were treated to a chorus of greetings from Burt Willis, the barber; Arnold Webb, the fire chief; Amos Cotter, the postmaster; Pete Floyd of the *Hunter Press*; and Merlin Sowers, the county board chairman and closest thing to a banking/real estate tycoon Hunter County had to offer.

One chair always remained vacant at the table in the rear, in memory of the late Dr. Coleby Butler, Elizabeth's and Anne's father. Mountain Harbor was his family home. Lady Maude had not removed the chair after Coleby died, and no one ever sat in it.

Lady Maude's geriatric crew of waitresses automatically placed huge, steaming platters of scrambled and fried eggs, sausages, biscuits, bacon, pancakes, and gravy on the table. There were pitchers of orange juice, coffee, and, especially for me, hot chocolate, since I am the only cop in the galaxy who'd rather drink yak piss than coffee.

Pete Floyd, the *Hunter Press* editor, offered the morning prayer. Vietnam had scoured all the religion from me, but I respected the believers by bowing my own head; besides, vocally godless sheriffs didn't endear themselves to many voters in rural Virginia, so I stayed pretty much in the closet on that issue. Pete thanked his God for the food—as Lady Maude's cooking was good enough to seed doubt in the most hardened atheist. He ended the prayer thusly: ". . . and Lord, we beg Thee to embrace a flower of Southern womanhood and a child of innocence snatched from this earth way before their time. Lord, please welcome into your bosom the soul of Miss Cathy Calder, and little Steven Calder. And dear God, be with the grieving young husband and father, and help him through his time of trial. And Lord, please lead Lewis to the poor misguided soul who killed the Calders, so he can lock the sorry, rotten, drunk *son of a bitch up! Soon!* Amen. Let's eat." Pete grabbed his napkin with a grim set to his jaw.

I don't know if Pete's God got the message, but it wasn't lost on me.

Everyone dug in. There would be time for talk later.

When the time came, it was Burt Willis the barber who opened things up with his usual sophistication. "Hey! Ya'll hear some little gook twat is gonna buy ole Doc Morgan's veterinary practice?"

I rolled my eyes.

"You're shittin' me!" Arnold Webb the fire chief sputtered through a mouthful of scrambled eggs. "A *female* vet? A *gook woman vet?* Naw!"

"It's true!" Burt replied. "Ain't it, Pete?"

Pete Floyd stared at Burt and Arnold with disgust. "If you two diplomats are referring to Dr. Julianne Chu, a lady who happens to be a highly qualified and experienced veterinarian, then yes. There is a possibility she may buy into Hap's practice. We'll be lucky to get her if she does. She comes highly recommended, according to Dr. Harper over at Tech veterinary school."

"Damn!" Arnold said with his mouth full. "A woman vet. Hell, next thing you know, we'll be havin' a woman *people* doctor!"

"Oh, perish the thought," Pete muttered.

"Well," Merlin Sowers the banker groused, "I tell you I wish we'd get *some* kinda new doctor in Hunter. Every time Arlette sneezes, I have to carry her all the way to Roanoke."

"Hell, I sure wish Doc Butler hadn'ta . . . died," Arnold said between chomps, glancing at the empty chair. "Now I gotta traipse clean down to Christiansburg to get my prostate checked."

"Maybe we'll git *us* a lady doctor, Arnold!" Burt the barber said, winking at me.

"Yeah," I said, cutting sausage, "I'm sure there are scads of women doctors lining up to practice cutting-edge medicine in an enlightened, progressive, deep-pocket community like ours."

"Shit," Arnold grunted. "*I* ain't goin' to no woman doctor!"

Burt made a hobby of baiting Arnold. "Why not, Arnie?" he said, smirking at me. "Then you wouldn't have to go all the way to C-burg for your pros—"

Arnold sat up with indignation. "Humph! I tell you true: ain't no *female* doctor *ever* gonna do the prostate ramma-jamma on Arnold Webb!"

"You really know how to hurt a girl, Arnold," I said. "You're brutal."

Amos Cotter the postmaster sighed and peered over his glasses. "Can we talk about something besides Arnold's prostate, for Christ's sake? I'm tryin' to eat my breakfast!"

"Second the motion," Merlin Sowers said.

"Hey, Lewis!" Burt said helpfully, while he gulped down a sausage. "I hear somebody cut the guts outta one a Gordy Huckaby's horses last night. Is that—"

"Burt!"

"Aw, Jesus, Burt! We're tryin' to eat here!"

"Come on, Burt!"

Burt looked puzzled. "Well, it's true! Ain't it, Lewis? Blood all over the goddamn place! Roadkill done it, I hear."

"Wait a minute," I said.

"Roadkill cut up a horse?" Merlin asked with sudden concern. Merlin was an avid horseman who had a small stable of his own. He fancied himself to be some sort of high-plains cowboy trapped in a fat banker's body. Every year, in the fourth of July parade, Merlin rode one of his horses with an elaborate silver-laden Mexican saddle, as if any horse carrying Merlin Sowers wasn't already over maximum gross load weight. To top it off, on parade, Merlin always wore a colossal western hat that would've branded him a dude a good five hundred yards from any respectable ranch.

"Somebody attacked one of Gordon's horses," I said testily. "There are no suspects at all, right now. And there is no indication whatever that Roadkill Rudesill was involved. Don't spread rumors, Burt. I got half the farmers in the county looking to shoot Roadkill already."

Merlin looked pained. "Lewis, are ya'll saying somebody killed a horse in Hunter County?"

"Cut the guts right out of it!" Burt exclaimed, wide-eyed.

"Goddamn it, Burt," I said, "I'm gonna cut the guts outta you in minute."

Amos Cotter sighed again and pushed his plate back.

"Well, Lewis, that's what I heard!" Burt whined.

"Lewis," Merlin went on, concerned, "what did happen?"

"One of Gordon Huckaby's mares was killed—all right, Burt—the animal was basically hacked to death last night. My people are working on—"

"Oh, that's just *awful,* Lewis!" Merlin said, looking even more pained.

"Yeah, it was ugly. Poor Darlene Huckaby had to find it, and it was a mess, trust me."

Pete Floyd now pushed *his* plate back.

"No, that ain't what I mean, Lewis! I was gonna tell you this morning. Hunter County finally has a wonderful opportunity to get on the map in the horse world!"

"Why, pray tell, were you going to tell me that, Merlin?"

"Because, Lewis, this could be very important to the county, to us all! If we can establish Hunter County as a desirable place for serious horse people to set up homes and stables, we can draw some big-money folks into the county!"

"Fuck 'em," Arnold slurped, graciously. "Who needs 'em?"

"We do, Arnold!" Merlin continued, distressed. "You do! If we could attract some prominent wealthy horse people to locate in Hunter County, especially a movie star like Robert Duvall or somebody, then we'd have the muscle to demand more political advantages and state funds out of Richmond. Like for new fire trucks, for instance!"

"No shit?"

"It's true! Shoot, right now, the governor thinks we're about as important as a tribe of pygmies. *Republican* pygmies! Nobody ever heard of us!"

"Some of us like it that way," Amos the postmaster said.

"Well!" Merlin huffed, "others of us would like to see better roads and schools and libraries in Hunter County! A chance to help get some real influential people to move here has come along, and now there's this . . . this . . . horse murder! This could screw everything up!"

"Merlin," I said, "you want to tell me exactly what you're talking about?"

"Lewis, you know who Meriah Reinholdt is?"

"Never heard of her."

"Lewis! She is only the daughter of the late Carlton Reinholdt, of the Reinholdt paper fortune! She is *only* the most successful woman in the American equestrian industry! Three times an Olympic dressage medalist! She's in her sixties now, so she's no longer competitive, of course—"

"The old bag's over the hill," Pete, sixty-one, said acidly.

"—but she is a prominent breeder of several show-jumping and dressage champions!"

"Merlin, get serious," I answered. "I'm sheriff of an obscure Republican pygmy tribe; how the hell would I know Meriah of the Reinholdt paper fortune?"

"Well . . . you . . . ah . . . you're gonna know her. Soon."

"What?" I said suspiciously. "Merlin, what have you gotten me into?"

"You're gonna like her, Lewis. I mean, she's filthy rich and all, but she's still a nice lady and—"

"Merlin!"

"All right! Here it is. Meriah Reinholdt runs a huge stable in Loudoun County, up by Washington. Breeds and trains horses and gives instruction to some of the most promising competitors in the horse world. Her animals and her students are consistent winners. Very, *very* successful. She's got people coming from Europe and Japan to study with her. In fact, in the last two years she's become so successful, she's outgrown her holdings in Loudoun County and she's got the place sold. She . . . well, she's thinking of locating her entire operation here in Hunter County."

"Merlin," I said, putting a nefarious two and two together, "I don't suppose this would have anything to do with that huge piece of land over near the Weymouth County border that you've been trying to sell for six years?"

"It's *perfect* for her, Lewis!"

"I knew it."

"It's *perfect!* It's more than big enough, good water, and it's within reasonable driving distance of the Roanoke airport, the railhead, I-64 and I-81. It's centrally located for the entire eastern U.S. horse establishment. It's—"

"And she's made you an offer for it that gives you a hard-on you could cut diamonds with," I added.

"Uh, well, I wouldn't have phrased it quite like that."

"Um-hmm. I'm faint with excitement to learn what all this has to do with me."

"Well, uh, there's a contingency to Meriah Reinholdt's offer, Lewis."

"I'll bet."

"Lewis, horses and equestrian competition are big business on her level. The sport—hell, it's more than a sport, it's an obsession to some folks—the sport draws some powerful people with world-class money and, like most people with world-class money, they play to win."

"So?"

"So security can be a problem. According to Ms. Reinholdt, it is not unheard of to have attempts made against winning animals, even against star dressage, show-jumping, and eventing riders."

"Eventing?" Pete Floyd said, jotting notes on a napkin.

"It's a kind of riding contest, Pete," I answered. "Eventing is a three-day competition that involves dressage, stadium jumping, and cross-country obstacles. It's done worldwide, but the great events are in England. Elizabeth wants to get into it, but I don't know; it's a lot more demanding and dangerous than it looks from the outside."

"Anyway," Merlin went on, "Meriah Reinholdt is very concerned with security, since she breeds and trains some key horses as well as hosting some of the most important competitors in the equestrian world. She's been very emphatic, Lewis. Before she will close on this deal, she's got to be satisfied that we can provide her operation adequate security."

"We? *We,* Merlin? What are 'we' going to do to convince the horse queen she'll be all snug and comfy in Hunter County? Oh, I know. I'll let her see my forty-man SWAT team in action. I'll give her a tour of my bomb squad and arrange a fly-by of my helicopter division—"

"Aw, Lewis—"

"Aw, Lewis, my ass. Merlin, I police nearly eight hundred square miles of remote mountain terrain with a total road force of sixteen men, of whom—given time off, sick leave, and the need to staff three shifts—maybe four of us might be on duty at any one time! I can't secure Gordon

Huckaby's *barn!* How am I going to support the security needs of a world-class stable twenty miles from here on the edge of the county?"

"Well, Lewis, Ms. Reinholdt is aware that this isn't New York City—"

"That astute, is she?"

"After all, while her offer is substantial by Hunter County land values, she's still not paying near what she'd have to pay for that much quality acreage in northern Virginia. So she's aware of . . . of our limitations. But she still insists on . . . well, Lewis, she wants to meet you."

"*Me?* Jesus, Merlin, I hope you didn't set this whole deal up to swing on the impression she gets of me."

"Well, *she* did. Sort of. She's one tough business lady. Look Lewis, all she wants to do is meet with you and see what kind of . . . law enforcement person you are, what your attitude towards horses and horse people is. Actually, as she put it, she wants to know that she can work with you."

"Merlin, you'd do damn well not to spend any of that money yet."

"Aw, Lewis, I know she'll like you if you'll just—"

"Oh yeah. All the wealthy socialite heiresses east of the Mississippi are throwing their panties at Sheriff Lewis Cody. Wait a minute. I don't like the sound of that. If I'll just what?"

"Ride with her. I told her you'd ride with her."

"What?"

"Well, Lewis, she said she'd never locate where the law-enforcement authorities didn't understand riding and horses, and, well, she said if you didn't ride horses, there was no way you could appreciate the horse world enough to understand her security needs and work with her. And of course you ride your horse, so I thought it would be a great idea if you sort of . . . well, you know, rode with her."

"A great idea? Merlin, she rides hyperbred competition stock. I ride an organic farm tractor! She's an Olympic equestrian medalist; I am a guy for whom any ride is a smashing success if the dismount is voluntary on my part! Doesn't that tell you something?"

"So I told her you would. Today."

"*Today!* Are you nuts, Merlin? Some hit-and-run fool killed Trooper Calder's wife and boy last night, and it might surprise you to learn he'd actually be interested to know who did it! Not only that, I have to catch the 'horse murderer,' as you call him! I got things to do, Merlin, and they don't include sucking up to some prima donna of the horse society!"

Merlin was beginning to sweat. "Aw, come on, Lewis. It's important. Hell, it's critical. She ain't gonna buy if she—"

"Merlin, look at this," I said, pointing to my star. "See this? This means I am a *cop*, not a real-estate agent!"

"Yeah, but it's important to the whole county, too, Lewis!"

"Yeah," Burt Willis said, "I can hardly wait for all the haircuts that're gonna come my way outta this deal."

Merlin fired a scalding look at Burt, who shrugged.

"It's doubly important now, Lewis," Merlin pleaded, "since the Huckaby horse was . . . well, butchered!"

Pete jotted like a maniac on that one. I winced.

"When Meriah Reinholdt finds about that, she'll back out for sure if you can't convince her, Lewis! The whole county is depending on you!"

"Save the bullshit, Merlin."

"Okay, *I'm* depending on you, too, but damn it, Lewis, can't you see where the county would benefit from all this, too? If Meriah Reinholdt locates her operation here, Hunter County will become a prominent landmark in the horse world. Some powerful people will want to visit and even move here—"

"And some poor, suffering soul will have to sell them real estate."

"—and it'll mean more political clout for the county, Lewis! The kind we can use to get attention to our roads and our schools and sheriff's department staffing and—"

"Oh, pullease, Merlin. You're gonna start singing the national anthem any minute now."

"Gee, I'd like to hear that," Arnold said, enjoying Merlin's distress immensely.

"It's important to us all, Lewis!"

"Where am I supposed to ride with this woman?" I asked, sourly.

"Oh, thank you, Lewis! Thank—"

"Can it, Merlin. I haven't said I would yet. And even if I do, I doubt you're going to net much to thank me for."

"You'll like Ms. Reinholdt, Lewis—"

"Where and when, damn it?"

"They're expecting you at eleven; you'll ride with them after lunch."

"Them? Who's them?"

"Well, you know where Laurel Ridge Farm is?

"Sure. The Whitley estate. What does Professor Whitley have to do with this?" I had a mindflash of a beautiful German woman, suddenly. Reinholdt. Karin Reinholdt Steiger. Uh-oh.

"The Whitleys are big-time horse folks. Helen Whitley runs a stable of her own at Laurel Ridge Farm, mostly for kids."

"I know. That's where Elizabeth takes riding lessons and they run the summer pony camps."

"That's the place. Anyway, it turns out Helen and Professor Mitchell Whitley are close friends of Meriah Reinholdt—that's how she got wind of Hunter County— and she's staying with them. He is, too."

"He who?"

"Dr. Eicher Dietrich. He'll be riding with you—"

"Who? Merlin, did you have a program printed up?"

"Eicher Dietrich, Lewis. My God, don't you know anything about the horse world? He's the famous New York surgeon and horseman who dominates the eventing scene. Long-time star of the U.S. Equestrian Team! He's also a dressage master."

Eternally in the dark, Burt asked, "Is he one a them frog fags that wears black shiny leather underpants and designs them funny dresses that New York broads pay ten grand for?"

"No!" Merlin snapped. "Lewis, Dr. Dietrich must travel with his own bodyguard, which only underscores the security—"

"*Dressage* doesn't mean dresses, Burt," I said. "Think of

it as horse dancing. What's the Kraut doctor buying from you, Merlin?"

"Nothing! He's an old friend of Meriah Reinholdt; four times an Olympic medalist, including the last three golds in eventing; and still the dominant competitor in the sport. Dietrich is disgustingly rich from his practice, his riding endorsements, and old family money, yet the guy insists on trailering his own horses! He competes with a magnificent horse named Grand Teuton; yet he's so eccentric, he won't let anybody groom it but him. He's here to help Meriah select a site for her new stable. Plus, he's gonna be the featured speaker at the Whitleys' annual Laurel Ridge Charity Hunt, this weekend."

Pete piped up. "The annual Whitley charity hunt draws horsy types from all over the eastern U.S. Almost a hundred prominent riders at a thousand dollars a head coming for the dinner dance on Saturday night and the big ride on Sunday. The first Laurel Ridge Charity Hunt got written up in a number of equestrian journals last year. Ole Mitch and Helen Whitley doll up their indoor riding ring into a dance hall, complete with an orchestra up from Roanoke. They lay on a hell of a dinner and then dance 'til the wee hours. Next afternoon, they hold the big ride. Horses and riders and fancy trucks and trailers everywhere. Book up half the hotel and motel space in Roanoke. I covered it last year. I tell you, it's something to see."

I remembered the traffic headaches of last year's charity event. "I wasn't invited," I quipped. "An oversight, I'm sure."

"Well, Lewis," Merlin said, still very worried about his land deal, "it ain't your kind of affair. You know, these are some of the wealthiest folks in the horse world; some of 'em trailer their horses in from as far away as Florida and Connecticut. The dance is black tie and all—"

"Shucks," I said. "And to think I bought that green-sequin leisure suit for nothing."

Burt spoke, shaking his head. "Well, why the hell would you even *want* to dance with a horse?"

"Never mind!" Merlin groused. "Lewis, they'll be expecting you about eleven. You're a life-saver, Lewis!"

"Just hold it a minute, Merlin," I said. "I haven't agreed to a damn thing yet."

Merlin eyed me carefully. Like most businessmen, he was a trader at heart and he sensed there would be a price for my key cooperation. "Okay, Lewis, what's it going to cost me?"

"Oh, this is gettin' good," Arnold said.

"Merlin, you know Paul Gaines, of course."

Merlin's eyes narrowed as he sought the meaning in this question. "Why, yes. Damned unfortunate, his cancer."

"Oh yeah, Merlin, it's goddamned unfortunate. Your bank foreclosing on his farm is even more unfortunate."

Merlin became wary. "Well, yeah, Lewis. Hell, we've carried that mortgage on just the interest for almost a year now. I'm afraid foreclosure is impossible to avoid at this point. It ain't like we're enjoying it, for Christ's sake. Paul Gaines can't work anymore. He never will. I've got a board of directors and a state banking commission to answer to."

"Fuck the board *and* the commission. Paul's oldest boy, Furman, will graduate with honors from UVA law school next year and step into an seventy-thousand-dollar-a-year job. He's already got the offer from a Richmond law firm. Then he'll be able to pick up the payments. Until then, they're just another hard-scratch farm family trying to squeak a kid through college. You shut 'em down now and the kid'll have to drop out to help support the family. I want the Hunter County Farmer's and Merchant's Bank to extend the Gaines mortgage for another year until the boy gets a shingle."

Merlin looked very uncomfortable. "Aw, Lewis. Look, if I made an exception like that for everybody who falls behind on a mortgage, why, we'd go out of business. I can't do that."

"Not everybody who falls behind on their mortgage is dying of colon cancer and has a kid who'll pay the bank every cent owed it, with interest, in due time, Merlin."

"Be reasonable, Lewis. You're meddling in bank affairs here. I just can't do what you ask. I've got people to answer to."

"You can't or you won't, Merlin?"

"Damn it, Lewis! This is a bank matter! It doesn't involve you. All right! I won't, then."

"Yaaaaaaannnh! Wrong answer!" Burt said.

"Well, okay, Merlin, I understand," I replied calmly. "There is one other thing you can do for me."

"Anything, Lewis, just name it."

"You take that Reinholdt stable deal, roll it into a neat little tube, and shove it up your ass. Come on, Gruesome, we're outta here." I stood and kicked my chair back.

"Wait a minute, Lewis! Don't be so damned hasty! I'll try to convince the board. That's the best—"

"Not good enough. It's a done deal or no deal. Give the horse queen my love, hear?" I turned to leave.

"All right! All right, damn it."

"A done deal? No excuses? Whether Reinholdt buys or not?"

Merlin sighed, like he was very tired at seven-thirty in the morning. "Yes. Okay. I'll guarantee the extension with my own money if the board won't go for it."

"You're a gentleman and a scholar, Merlin. Tell the Gaines family it was your idea. Moose and I will be at Laurel Ridge Farm at eleven, and I'll do the best I can to convince the old gal that buying your land would be like purchasing her own little piece of heaven. When I'm done with her, she'll think she couldn't be any more secure with the Army Delta Force camped at her gate."

"Hey, Merlin," Arnold inquired, "ever wonder what they mean when they say 'slam-dunk'?"

"Um, there may be a small problem, though," I added.

"What?"

"Does the name Karin Steiger mean anything to you?"

"Christ, Lewis, you really are out of touch with the horse world! Karin Steiger is *only* the daughter of the German ambassador and the fiancée of Dr. Eicher Dietrich! She's *only* the top German Equestrian Team competitor in eventing! She's *only* the first eventing rider in twelve years favored to finally unseat Dietrich at the Atlanta games! Their rivalry and engagement make them the hottest couple in the equestrian media. Uh-oh. Why?"

"You don't want to know."

"Lewis!"

"Well, you could say the Steiger woman has already made a contribution to the county economy."

"What do you—"

"I wrote her a speeding ticket last night. Right now, she thinks tapeworms are charming compared to me."

Merlin cradled his head in his hands. "Oh my god."

I zipped my brown leather jacket against the nippy air as Gruesome and I walked out of Lady Maude's Café.

10

● ● ● ● ● ● ● ●

Horse People

After leaving the Gentry, I went to the dungeon and had a short meeting with Pierce and Milly to exchange information and coordinate the investigations we were conducting for the killers of the Calders and Darlene Huckaby's mare.

I almost wished for a straightforward, garden-variety murderer. My two victims were just as dead, but these killers would probably be a lot tougher to find. Worse, much worse, even if we did catch the perpetrators, the ludicrous American criminal justice system wasn't likely to do much to "just" another drunk driver and "just" a guy who brutalized an animal. The drunk would be a "victim" of alcohol and "not responsible." After all, alcoholism was "a disease," so how could the poor guy be blamed? The horse mutilator would evade *his* responsibility by coming from a "dysfunctional home" and being an "abused child." Psychobabble liberals and other reality-blind dreamers would hue wise, wring their hands, and get all dewy-eyed about being "compassionate." Meanwhile, Boyce Calder would weep over the graves of his cold, dead wife and baby, and Darlene Huckaby would have nightmares the rest of her life about the horrible, savage evil that crawls free in our society. Not to mention the excruciating suffering of the horse. Even were we to find them and take them down, my two killers probably wouldn't do two years of incarceration collectively before they were released to do it all over again, for—make no mistake about it—true, lasting rehabilitation is a silly myth. That was the biggest crime of all.

Nonetheless, however briefly, I would lock the two maggots up for as long as I could. If I could find them.

I filled Pierce and Milly (she now neatly uniformed) in on the findings of the accident reconstruction experts. Pierce brought me up to speed on last night's investigation of the carnage in Gordy Huckaby's barn.

"Them footprints on the bottom of that feed bucket probably ain't gonna do us much good for identification," Pierce said, looking like a polar bear in reading glasses as he consulted his notes. "The mud and horse shit was too smeared to be of any use in court, I think. We took photographs and casts of what clear imprints there were and sent 'em off to the FBI lab, but I doubt they'll be able to name a boot brand or size or even pinpoint irregularities that we could use to make a connection in court. Just too smeared. Checked for prints of course, but they ain't many viable surfaces in a horse stall—just the few pieces of hardware and that plastic feed bucket. We ain't come up with any prints that ain't one of the Huckaby family. They was some blood smears that was probably from his hands, but no latents. Guess he wore gloves. Nobody saw anybody or any unaccountable vehicles. Went over that stall with Tom Bonner's metal detector, but didn't find nothin' but a small buckle Gordy identified as off one of his halters. Me and the boys searched the whole area around the stall and barn last night with flashlights and again at first light this mornin'. Nothing weird there, either. State lab did call about that suspected semen sample Dr. Chu collected. That's what it was, all right. He cut that poor horse seven ways from hell, and he gets his rocks off doing it. We got us a serious nut, Lewis, a really fucked-up strangeoid."

I considered Pierce's clinical determination. Odd. If somebody was going to engage in a sex act with any other creature, wouldn't they prefer to do so barehanded? Was the butcher both psychotic enough to have sex with an animal before slaughtering it yet realistic enough to appreciate the hazards of leaving fingerprints, and thus preplan measures to avoid same?

"Pierce," I said, "get Double-Parked to send out an inquiry requesting responses from any jurisdictions experiencing anything like our horse killer. I doubt this guy just began his career last night. Let's find out if anybody else has been blessed with him.

"Milly, make sure everyone gets the lookout for that dark red damaged Ford F-350 truck ASAP. Make sure it's on the net throughout the area. Notify Roanoke County to really watch those back-alley body shops for the truck. I hear Boyce Calder's making noises about tracking down whoever wasted his family. He's a good kid, but he's very aggressive and he's under a huge strain right now. I don't want him out bounty hunting on his own, and the best way to stop that is for us to get to the perp first.

"On the horse case, we got a lot of the farmers grumbling about going after Roadkill, and somebody's going to get killed if they try that. So let's tighten up. Emotions are high in both these cases and people are going to run out of patience quick if we don't make arrests soon. Merlin Sowers roped me into some kind of riding affair this afternoon which I can't get out of, but I'll dispose of it as soon as I can and get back in here to help."

"Lewis," Pierce said, looking at me, "are you sure you don't want us to pull Roadkill in for questioning? I agree that this don't seem like his kind of thing, but then, he's a real strange dude. And like Gordy said, who else coulda done it?"

"Who else could've done it isn't good enough for me to arrest a citizen absent anything else to connect him with the crime, Pierce. I don't put anything past anybody; hell, if Milly had the plumbing I'd think she did it, but—"

Milly sniffed. "Shit. Maybe *you* done it. Naw, come to think of it, *you* ain't got the plumbing, neither."

I grinned wryly. You never put one over on Milly. "But the biggest problem I have with thinking Roadkill did the horse is why would he suddenly start now, after all the years he's been skulking about these mountains? No. I'm not dragneting every Looney Tune in the county because a bunch of superstitious farmers are nervous about them. We need more to go on. Besides, finding Roadkill, let alone catching him, is a damned sight easier said than done. He'll panic if we try to pull him in, and he'll fight, and somebody is likely to get hurt. I'm not going that route until I see some firm probable cause."

Like Sergeant Joe Friday and his partner, Milly and Pierce nodded soberly, and they split to carry out their tasks. Thank God for good people.

At Mountain Harbor, Arnold had curried the mud from Moose's thick winter coat and had brushed her and combed out her blond mane, tail, and fetlocks. She looked downright presentable for a giant horse straight out of the Conan legends. Arthur led her onto the trailer, which creaked under her weight and settled on its dual-axle springs. I hung her saddle, bridle, and blanket in the tack closet on the trailer and put my portable radio on the seat of the truck.

"Try not to git shot this time," Arthur suggested.

The big diesel Ford hummed through its automatic gears as I pulled the trailer through the stone gateposts at the mouth of the Mountain Harbor drive and accelerated down the highway.

Retired Professor Mitchell Whitley and his wife Helen probably paid more each year just to tend the miles of high, wooden equine fencing on Laurel Ridge Farm than I spent in mortgage payments on the best house I ever owned. Mitch Whitley had a Ph.D. in ceramic engineering and had patented a process that successfully adhered insulation tiles to the space shuttles and that proved neatly adaptable to several profitable manufacturing applications. This and a few technical books he had written accounted for the incongruity of an impressive estate like Laurel Ridge Farm on a professor's salary.

The driveway to Laurel Ridge Farm began where a heavy pair of wrought-iron gates swung back from between two high, curved stone sections of ornamental wall at the highway. It traversed a gently upsloping pasture bordered in gray stone fencing. When I topped the hill, Laurel Ridge Farm presented an awesome sight. The house was huge, but instead of being of the white-columned, carry-me-back-to-old-Virginny style of architecture, it was a cedar-sided and shake-roofed structure with a lot of smoked glass that looked like a giant, broad-roofed Swiss chalet with an American twist. It was three stories high and recessed against the far slope of a small, shallow valley dotted with majestic old spruces and pines. The stables and barn and a small indoor riding ring were of the same general design. Not a bad return on the invention of a little cosmic glue.

Several people were either sitting their mounts talking to each other or they were riding about one of two fenced show rings, jumping artificial barriers set up therein. All were duded up in that English riding gear, including knee-high boots, riding coats, and black helmets. As I let the rig ride the second automatic gear down the drive, I studied them. Mitch Whitley wasn't hard to spot, looking spiffy on a big Hanoverian, his pipe jutting from his jaw. Plump Helen Whitley waved at me. I flicked the headlights back at her. With the Whitleys, also mounted, was a distinguished, rigid-looking man in his fifties on an incredibly muscled hunter-jumper. Merlin and Arlette Sowers were present, not surprisingly, though Merlin and horse were suitably attired in English duds and saddlery instead of the fourth-of-July gaudy gaucho outfit. A very serious-looking stout man sat on a horse slightly to the rear of the other mounted riders. Watching from her horse just outside the ring was a distinguished-appearing woman whom I suspected was the horse queen I'd been commissioned to impress.

In one of the riding rings, still another impeccably attired woman was cantering a sleek black horse, occasionally soaring effortlessly over the jumps set up in the ring. Even from two hundred yards away, I didn't need to be told she was Karin Steiger.

Eight horse people riding and wearing the best money could buy. They were going to just love Cody the Barbarian.

As I parked the rig and got out, those mounted trotted their horses my way, sitting erect and posting precisely in the manner of lifelong European-correct riders—everyone except Karin Steiger. She spurred her horse and jumped the animal over the ring fence. While everyone else dismounted for introductions, she galloped up and ground her mount to a roping-horse stop without so much as blinking. The other horses stirred at the violent arrival of the younger woman's animal. Such hotrodding is regarded as gauche among the

English equestrian set, but this woman didn't seem overly impressed with convention.

In police work, you learn fast to see what you're looking at. As I surveyed the gathering group, three things registered with me quickly. One was that Karin Steiger was even more lovely in daylight, another was that the horse queen was a woman of immense poise and grace, and the other was that the serious guy in the back who looked like a professional soldier was wearing a concealed handgun. Certain lumps beneath even stylish riding gear can have only one meaning.

Curious.

The gun-toter stood to the rear, almost at attention, clearly an employee of someone in the group. Karin Steiger remained upon her horse and studied me. I had to tear my eyes from her. The rigid man was in his fifties and had the commanding look of an aristocrat accustomed to moving a lot of people to a lot of activity with softly spoken words. The horse queen was a striking woman who bore the carriage of a lady of breeding, a woman born to silver and leather.

The rigid guy and the soldier looked at me with undisguised disdain, but I'm used to it. People are typically uncomfortable around cops, and the rich tend to regard us as necessary but regrettable fixtures, like septic tanks. It is common to offset one's discomfort with a certain superior contempt. Strangers look at me and they see a Rodney King whacker with a big gun and a tiny sense of humor. Never mind that when a criminal like Rodney King threatens *them* or *their* property they scream for his heart on a silver tray.

Bearded Mitch Whitley, pipe in teeth, thrust his hand forward to welcome me. "Sheriff Cody!" Mitch said with genuine warmth. "Welcome to Laurel Ridge Farm. Glad you could find time in your busy schedule to join us."

"Professor," I said, shaking his hand.

"Sheriff Lewis Cody," Mitch continued, "allow me to introduce you. You know my wife Helen, and of course Merlin and Arlette."

Merlin nodded nervously, thinking no doubt of how much money he had riding on me.

"Sheriff Cody," Helen Whitley said, warmly. "So nice to see you. Elizabeth is one of my most accomplished little riders!" Helen probably said this to the parents of all her riding students, including those whose kids couldn't ride a seesaw, but it still felt nice to hear.

"Thank you, Helen. Elizabeth is fond of you, and she's made great progress with your expert help. I'm grateful."

Helen beamed. Always stroke the hostesses. They control the food.

"Sheriff," Mitch said, turning us toward the horse queen, who walked up, smiling broadly, "may I present Meriah Reinholdt? Meriah, Lewis Cody, Sheriff of Hunter County."

Meriah Reinholdt was a slender, stylish woman who stepped forward aggressively, yet with the grace of one who probably grew up in expensive private schools, studying dance. Her hair was black, liberally streaked with gray, but she was clearly a woman to whom nature had been kind and who had in turn taken good care of herself. She lent nice lines to her coat and tight riding pants. She seized my hand in both of hers and cocked her head to one side, looking me squarely in the eyes, and firing a gleaming smile she probably knew entranced men.

"Sheriff Cody," Meriah Reinholdt said, "I've been looking forward to meeting you!" Her accent was the enchanting Portsmouth dialect of Southern. Aristocratic but warm and sexy.

"My pleasure," I replied. "Is it Mrs. Reinholdt?" I despised the trendy bullshit title *Ms.* and refused to use it.

"I'm divorced many years, sir," she said, flooring me with yet another incredible smile, "but please, if I promise to remember that the first name your mother gave you wasn't Sheriff, will you promise to call me Meriah?"

There're girls, there're women, and there're ladies, the country song goes. I was clearly beholding the latter. I knew when I was being charmed by a pro. "Deal," I answered.

Meriah took my arm as though I were her escort for a cotillion, and she steered me masterfully toward the other strangers in the crowd. She began with Rigid.

"Lewis, I'd like you to know Dr. Eicher Dietrich, a retired surgeon in New York, possibly the leading eventing rider in the world——"

"Possibly?" Dr. Dietrich said primly, raising an eyebrow.

Meriah laughed. "—and a good friend for many years."

Dietrich was as tall as me, was ramrod erect, and had the hard, lean face of a hungry eagle. He removed his black velvet-covered helmet slowly while studying me. I met his gaze and held it. He had steel-blue eyes and short-cut silver hair, as one might have expected of a senior riding master. Without smiling or speaking, he offered his hand, and his grip was like a hydraulic vise. This guy made me wonder if there really were such a thing as an Aryan supreme race.

"And Lewis," Meriah said, turning me toward the younger woman still who sat her horse, gazing down at us with what appeared to me to be an air of amused contempt, "this is Karin Steiger, with the German Equestrian Team. Karin is in the U.S. to train under me for the Olympic games next summer at Atlanta." Meriah averted her gaze from me briefly, sadly, I thought. "Eicher and Karin are engaged. They will be married after they compete for the gold in eventing at the games."

Sometimes, into the life of a man there comes a woman whom he knows will become important to him. He may not know what impact she will have on him or whether he will regret it, but he knows she will do things to him he will never forget.

11
....

Love at First Sight

Karin Steiger's look was foremost of confidence and ease; then it was of amusement—not ridicule or contempt now, just a subtle amusement.

Karin's splendid if nervous horse danced, but she controlled him casually with almost imperceptible twitches of the reins and pressures with from knees and heels, all the while never taking her eyes from mine. She removed her riding helmet and ran her gloved fingers through her strawberry-blond hair, still looking at me with a peculiar smile a little higher at one side of her mouth than at the other. She extended her right hand slightly as though she expected me to walk over to her and shake it as she remained mounted.

She wore tight English-style riding breeches that emphasized the sort of muscular thighs common to figure skaters, serious dancers, and competitive horsewomen. I sensed assumed authority in her and did not wish to succumb to it. I stood where I was and nodded at her, holding her gaze. Her amused smile remained but her eyes narrowed slightly and she let her hand descend slowly to her saddle.

"The good sheriff and I have met," Karin said.

Instantly, Dr. Dietrich snapped an alarmed look at Karin, followed by a suspicious one for me. "Really," he said, archly.

Karin ignored Dietrich and eased her mount nearer to me, still gazing steadily at me. "Indeed. Sheriff Cody was so kind as to direct me to Laurel Ridge Farm last night."

Meriah Reinholdt discreetly eyed Karin, then Dietrich. I wondered what was afoot among these people.

"What's his name?" I asked, stroking her gleaming black horse on its pedigreed nose.

"Bitter Stone," Karin answered. "I trained him from a colt. This summer, he will become the most famous horse at the games." She glanced with challenge at Dietrich.

"That will take more than sheer overconfidence, be assured," Dietrich hissed with a brittle smile.

"Lewis," Meriah said quickly as though trying to head off a scene between Karin and Dietrich, "we are expecting one additional guest for this afternoon's ride who hasn't arrived yet. While we're waiting, perhaps you'll show me your horse. Merlin tells me she's quite unusual."

"If you liked *Jurassic Park,* you'll love my horse," I said, thinking how swell a horse named Moose was going to be regarded by people who owned hot-blooded mounts with names like Bitter Stone and Grand Teuton. "But there's a point of curiosity I'd like to settle first," I continued. I disengaged from Meriah and walked through the little group to the hard-looking man now dismounted and standing to the rear. He glanced toward Dr. Eicher Dietrich. I stopped before him, pulled my leather jacket up, and tucked it between my waist and the grip of my pistol. He eyed me warily. I balanced myself and watched his hands. "I haven't been introduced to this gentleman," I said. "Are you a police officer, sir?"

From behind me, Dietrich spoke instantly, with authority. "Klaus is in my employ, Sheriff Cody. You need have no regard for him. Klaus!" Dietrich commanded, causing Klaus to jerk. "Leave us." Klaus moved without hesitation.

"Wait a minute." I said. Klaus stopped and eyed me as if I were a cow patty before glancing again at Dietrich. I rested my right hand on my pistol and extended my left. "I'll ask you to hand me your weapon."

Klaus froze and Dietrich strode casually near. "That will not be necessary, Sheriff," Dietrich said in his smooth but commanding tone, as though the matter were quite concluded. "Klaus is my associate. He is none of your concern."

"Dr. Dietrich," I said, still watching the beefy, cold Klaus, "I don't care if he's the disciple Peter. He's carrying a concealed gun in my jurisdiction, and that makes him my concern. I'll have that handgun, sir," I concluded, staring Klaus in the eye.

"Lewis!" Merlin said with obvious distress, no doubt seeing his big land deal flashing before his eyes.

"Gun!" Helen and Mitch Whitley exclaimed simultaneously, aghast. Mitch had written letters castigating the NRA and guns, which I had read in the *Roanoke Times* in years past.

"Out of the question." Dietrich said flatly. "Klaus is my bodyguard, Sheriff Cody. He is my responsibility. I forbid you to disarm him."

"Lewis!" Merlin whined. "Dr. Dietrich is a world figure in the competitive equestrian community. You know how those nuts attacked Monica Seles and that skater girl . . . Kerrigan! Dr. Dietrich has received threats in past years! You can't expect—"

"And we thank you fer yer support, Merlin," I said wearily, cutting him off. I turned to Dietrich. "Doctor, let's clear the air on a little point of confusion you seem to be suffering. In Hunter County, Virginia, you don't do the forbidding, I do. Now, Klaus here can surrender his weapon, right now, and I'll hold it for you while you're in Hunter County. And we'll all live happily ever after. Or I'll take the gun and lock him up for carrying a concealed weapon." I focused on Dietrich. "And anybody else who breaks a law in the meantime." He glowered at me, his nostrils flaring slightly, like a grizzly bear stuck in the ass with a sharp stick.

"Gentlemen," Meriah Reinholdt said, stepping between us, smiling graciously. "It's much too lovely a day for any unpleasantness. Eicher, I doubt you will be assailed by hordes of terrorists in these beautiful mountains. Surely Klaus would be . . . more comfortable unarmed?"

Helen Whitley piped up. "I will have no . . . *guns* . . . in my home!" she said indignantly, like she had just been told a Serbian mortar squad was coming to dinner.

"Out of the question," Dietrich repeated with force.

"This is unacceptable, Sheriff Cody. I demand to speak to your superiors at once."

I sighed. "Dr. Dietrich, I'm a constitutionally elected official. My superiors are several thousand Hunter County voters. And I promise you, they're not going to be outraged when you tell them I won't let strangers carry concealed guns around their community."

I glanced around. The laser-eyed Karin Steiger was observing everything from astride her horse. Merlin Sowers looked like a kid whose kitten has just been run over. I looked back at Dietrich.

Dietrich glanced at Meriah Reinholdt, then he stared at me again with the sort of ice-eyed assessment a Mafia don displays when making a mental note to arrange for some adversary to sleep with the fishes. "Meriah, darling," he said, smiling meanly without taking his eyes from me, "I have maintained steadfastly, from the moment you broached the notion of locating your new stable in this . . . peculiar locale, that it was a poor choice. Surely this . . . sheriff . . . confirms my misgivings." I had to hand it to Dietrich; he didn't go down easy.

Nobody said anything for several seconds, during which I could practically hear Merlin Sowers going into terminal arrhythmia. Then Meriah laughed lightly, watching me. "I'm not so convinced, Eicher my dear. All I've seen so far is the only man in twenty-two years I've ever known to say no to you and stand by it. Besides, the issue is that he be able to work with me, not you. Now let's dispense with this foolishness, Eicher. Please have Klaus comply with the law, and let's be on with our day."

Dietrich pulled his eyes from mine and looked at Meriah. He was controlled but obviously steaming. He flashed his gaze at Klaus and snapped his head toward me. Klaus eased an expensive Beretta automatic from beneath his coat and handed it to me, eyeing me with menace. Dietrich's expression was that of a man already plotting to get even. I knew I'd made myself a pair of enemies to bear watching.

"Right, then!" Mitch Whitley announced, "If everyone will mount and gather by the house, it's a great day for a ride!"

"Thank you, Mitch," Meriah Reinholdt replied. "Sheriff Cody and I will unload his horse and then we'll join you."

Helen and Mitch mounted, reined about, and cantered away, small dirt clods arcing from the horses' hooves. Arlette Sowers followed stiffly. Dr. Dietrich mounted, near Karin Steiger, and waited with obvious irritation for her attention. When she continued to watch me, he prompted her. "Karin!" he said sharply. "Our hosts are waiting. We should—"

Karin whipped her gaze to Dietrich like Leonard Bernstein slamming the Boston Philharmonic to a sudden stop. Her look would have pitted titanium. Dietrich looked coolly at me, then he yanked Grand Teuton about and fired short, chromed spurs into his sides. The big gelding dug and cantered away, followed crisply by Herr Klaus and mount. When Karin looked back at me, her expression was all sweetness and light. She bore an expression that said "I know what you're thinking; I was thinking it before you." She pressed her calf subtly into her horse and rode after the others.

"Unusual woman," I said, lamely.

Meriah Reinholdt took the reins of her horse from Merlin and advised him we would see him in the dining room. Reluctantly, he mounted and rode after the others. I unloaded the confiscated Beretta, and Meriah and I led her horse toward my rig. "Isn't Karin beautiful?" she replied with apparent sincerity. "She's the daughter of Ambassador Goss Steiger, the German ambassador to the United States, you know."

"So she told me last night. And yes, she is painfully beautiful."

Meriah looked at me. "What an interesting way to phrase it, Lewis. Painfully beautiful. Very appropriate. I suspect poor Eicher will come to appreciate that in time."

I let that one pass for the moment, as we walked to my trailer. I took a deep breath. "Mrs. . . . Meriah, you seem like a lovely woman also, and I'm led to believe it would be a real boon to Hunter County if you located here. Those are two good reasons why I wouldn't want to say anything to discourage you, but I have to be straight with you. I don't have the staffing to devote special attention to any one stable in the county. I'd certainly do everything I could for you, but if you expect some serious security problems with your operation, then you're going to need a lot more than a little mountain posse like mine."

Meriah Reinholdt laughed gracefully. "How refreshing to talk to someone at last who doesn't sound like they're glad-handing me! I appreciate your candor, Lewis." Meriah stopped suddenly when I opened the side-door of the trailer. "My word, what a magnificent Belgian! She must be over seventeen hands!"

"Eighteen and some change," I said. I locked Klaus's blasting iron in the truck, then I dropped the ramp, un-chained Moose, and led her off the trailer. She shook her head and snorted, and Meriah's lithe mare stirred nervously. Meriah cooed softly to calm it.

"Look, Meriah, as long as I'm being so straight-arrow, there's one more thing I need to make you aware of before you hear it from someone else."

Her smile faded to sadness. She walked to Moose and stroked her silken nose. "Bless your heart. You're going to tell me that some human monster killed a local farm girl's mare last night."

I looked at her. "My compliments to your intelligence network," I said, dryly. "Is that all you know about it?"

"You mean there's worse than that?"

"I'm afraid so. Whoever did it is a sexual deviate of some kind." I paused, hoping she could deduce what I was saying without my having to supply the sordid details.

Meriah sighed and looked away up the long drive toward the highway, which was out of sight. "Here comes our other guest, I believe."

I followed her gaze and saw a late-model maroon Chevy pickup truck towing a color-matched, tag-along horse trailer slowly down the drive.

Meriah turned to face me. "Lewis, people kill horses sometimes. And usually it's for money. Frankly, I'd be more worried if what happened last night was an insurance scam or a contract hit on a competition horse. There are a lot of people who'll do that. But if your horse killer is having sex with the animal, it means he's mercifully a rare mental abnormality, so when you catch him, the odds are we'll not see another like him. The same can't be said of the financially motivated variety of horse killer, I regret."

"I don't want to mislead you," I told her. "I don't have the proverbial first clue on this freak yet."

"Lewis, I have had land experts here quietly for two weeks, and they've rendered their reports. I'm going to buy Merlin Sowers's property. I'm going to locate one of the finest stables in the world here. I have left it up in the air because I wanted to sweat the best price out of Merlin, of course, but also because I wanted to meet you. I'll be as candid with you now. I had you checked out by the private investigators of my law firm, and I know you have a wonderful reputation. You'll catch this . . . person; I'm confident. And you and I are going to get along splendidly." Meriah winked at me. "Don't tell Merlin just yet, but so you can relax and enjoy the ride, I'll tell you I was ninety percent sold before I came today. Now I'm certain." She was looking right into me.

I eyed the horse queen. "Welcome to Hunter County," I said, heaving the heavy Australian stock saddle and pad onto Moose's back. I drew the cinch and looked at Meriah Reinholdt again. "I hope you haven't put too much faith in me."

"My God, that horse is huge," Meriah whispered. She continued, "I've been successful in a very demanding sport-business, Lewis," Meriah said, watching the maroon truck and trailer pulling up. "Some of it has been good fortune, but a lot of it has been that I am an excellent judge of people. I know there aren't many I can trust, but I believe you are one."

"Thanks for the kind words. I'll try to live up to them," I answered.

"Lewis," Meriah hesitated, looking at me with a subtle sadness, slight crow's feet at the outer corners of her eyes. "Eicher Dietrich has been a good friend for many years. And he's indisputably a master at the equestrian arts, but he is not without his . . . shortfalls. One is that he is very proud and he cannot abide being embarrassed. He won't be here long, but while he is, be careful. He has a mean streak and he holds a grudge forever."

I was still looking at Meriah Reinholdt when I heard the door to the maroon truck thump shut, and I smelled a familiar perfume. I turned to see Julianne Chu smiling up at me. Her casual clothes were gone, replaced by polished black riding boots, tan riding pants snug over shapely hips, and a black, narrow-waisted hunt coat with a white silk ascot at the throat. Her short black hair curved inward just beneath her ears and framed her wide, cute face.

"Sheriff Lewis Cody," Meriah said. "I'd like to introduce Dr. Julianne Chu, a marvelous veterinarian and a friend of several years."

"Thank you, Meriah," Julianne said, "but Lewis and I are acquainted." She smiled gracefully at us. "Sheriff Cody doesn't know it yet, but someday he's going to marry me."

Meriah Reinholdt laughed again, gracefully, melodically. "Congratulations, Sheriff Cody! Dr. Chu is a very determined young lady, in my experience. I've never known her not to achieve a goal. You'll advise me of the wedding date, of course."

I still looked with amusement at Julianne. She looked at me pleasantly as though there were nothing remotely outrageous about what she had just said.

"In due time, Mrs. Reinholdt," Julianne said, a twinkle in her big brown eyes.

Meriah laughed anew. "If you will excuse me, I will leave you two to your mutual embarrassment. Mitch is right; what a beautiful day for a ride!" I gave Meriah a leg up as she mounted; she blessed me with one more lovely lady's smile and rode toward the big home midway up the shallow mountainside.

I helped Julianne back her sleek little gray Arabian gelding off the trailer.

"What's his name?" I asked her.

"Yang! I delivered him myself five years ago. I knew at once I had to have him and made the owners an offer on the spot. Isn't he beautiful?"

"Quite."

"And your incredible Belgian, Lewis! You didn't tell me about her."

"You didn't ask." I saddled Yang, who seemed more the size of a large dog, next to Moose. "Incidentally," I said to

Julianne, "I didn't thank you for your assistance last night at the Huckaby farm. I'm sorry that had to be your introduction to Hunter County."

"Not at all. I was glad to help. My word! I thought you were going to have an insurrection on your hands! All those men so angry. And with guns!" Julianne set the cinch tension on her saddle.

"It was an ugly situation. They were pretty amped up, but I can't blame them."

"Dad's going to love you, but Mom will be a problem," Julianne said, grinning with charm.

"Pardon me?"

"My dad's a retired State Farm Insurance agent who always wanted to do something more exciting like police work. But Mom will have a rhino when she finds out I'm marrying a cop."

I gave Julianne a wry look along with a leg up onto her mount, my nose about five inches from her tight little fanny. "Yeah, well, tell ole Mom not to freak just yet. Marriage and me have a way of not working out." I stared at distant Buffalo Mountain as I had a brief flash of Lucia. I turned to Moose and ascended to the comfortable Australian stock saddle. Moose snorted and wagged her huge head up and down.

"Karma," Julianne Chu said, still smiling. She clapped a black-velvet riding helmet on her head and secured it. She looked doll-like on the horse.

"Excuse me?"

"Karma, Lewis Cody," she answered with a shrug. "Nothing we can do about it." She gigged the handsome Arabian gently and it trotted away toward the Whitley mansion.

I heeled Moose, and the big, muscular horse clopped briskly in pursuit of the little Arabian gelding and its puzzling rider.

12
•••••••••
Riding

Mitch Whitley on his chocolate-colored Hanoverian led eight other riders, absent the delightful Klaus, slowly away from Laurel Ridge, graduating from a walk to a slow trot, everyone briskly posting. Mitch was giving the horses plenty of time to warm up.

Moose had a jarring trot, possessed as she was of fence-post legs set far apart, and her spine gave not a whit under my weight, so posting her trot was like riding a motorcycle down a staircase. She had a canter as smooth as a schooner on a gentle sea, so I wished Mitch would pick up the pace soon.

Mitch, Eicher Dietrich, Meriah, and Karin Steiger rode abreast in the lead. Arlette and Merlin Sowers, Helen Whitley, and Julianne Chu rode loosely in the center. Moose was eager to run, but I held her back, bringing up the rear. Soon, the pace did pick up. I was relieved when Mitch went to a canter and I could let Moose into her oceanic rolling lope.

The group passed the gap and flowed over brown winter grass, down an easy slope, and toward a flat patchwork of cultivated fields and pastures. The horses seemed game, even Merlin Sowers's poor overworked mare. Under the November sun, the crisp air was cool enough to keep the horses from lathering, yet warm enough to be comfortable.

We crossed into a manicured pasture bordered by stone fence. It was dotted here and there with various jumps, ranging from large logs to short wooden dams to hedgerows. Karin galloped away to jump some of the obstacles. The Whitleys, Julianne, Meriah, Merlin, and Eicher Dietrich cantered slowly at other jumps, arching gracefully over them.

Julianne lifted her little bottom in her saddle and her Arabian soared nimbly over the barriers. Karin Steiger assaulted the jumps like a charging Cossack, her heavily muscled mount barely breaking stride to clear the jumps. Clearly, Bitter Stone was born to run and Karin was born to ride. Her performance seemed effortless, but I knew enough about what she was doing to know how good a rider has to be to so smoothly marry with the horse and the laws of physics, how critical it is that the animal be kept in stride and take off from precisely the correct spot. Incorrectly done—rarely, even if correctly done—it could get a horse destroyed and a rider hospitalized or killed.

I had to hand it to ole Merlin; he was good; but he was a long way from Karin's class. Even I could see an almost indiscernible hesitancy present. Merlin was dead weight his animal had to bear. Karin had moved in and occupied the soul of her horse, rendering it an extension of her own body. Even Meriah Reinholdt and Eicher Dietrich, both obviously in leagues of their own, were not riders of the caliber of Karin Steiger. They were pros, but they had neither the natural oneness nor the total abandon Karin knew.

Eventually, we emerged from the pines onto a ridge overlooking another shallow, broad valley similar to the one that held Laurel Ridge Farm except that at the bottom was a small, clean lake. Mitch reined in and Meriah pulled alongside him, but I knew without being told that we were beholding the site upon which Meriah would build her stable. It was easy to see what drew her. It was gorgeous land.

Eicher Dietrich was unimpressed. He drew alongside Meriah, sitting his mount with erect, show-perfect posture. Sweating in spite of the cold, Merlin Sowers edged his horse near enough to listen.

Eicher expounded loudly in the tone of a university

lecturer. "It's all very pretty, Meriah, but you're not running a dude ranch, you're establishing a serious stable. This quaint outback is still too remote to attract the genre of equestrian society you appeal to. It is a mistake, I tell you!"

Merlin looked distressed, but Meriah never removed her gaze from the pretty valley. "Thank you, Eicher, but for once I think you're wrong. They'll come. They'll come once because they know me, then they'll come back again and again for the beauty of this land. Word of mouth will make this one of the best-known stables in the country in less than two years."

Merlin rolled his eyes heavenward.

Karin Steiger's face was flushed and it shone with her smile. She was a woman clearly in her element. She easily commanded her high-strung horse, whose beautifully defined muscles rippled with its barely contained frenzy to run. "You're wrong, Eicher!" Karin called. "Meriah has made a splendid choice! It will be famous, and everyone will say the great German equestrienne, Karin Steiger, was the first Olympic champion to ride here!"

With that not-so-demure announcement, Karin reined her horse about and gigged it, and together they soared smoothly down the rolling slope toward the lake. The remainder of the group struggled to keep their anxious, excited horses from following, with the exception of Moose and me. Moose stood calmly, breathing easily, observing the goings-on with alert curiosity.

Julianne. Chu rode next to me on Yang, who danced nervously. Julianne watched Karin rocket toward the lake. "Modesty is not what Helga, She-Wolf of the SS, does best," she observed.

"Ooooh," I said, wincing. "A little bitter, are we?"

Julianne sighed. "Well, there is no denying some envy on my part. She is criminally beautiful, and she is indeed the favorite, followed closely by Dr. Dietrich, to take the gold in eventing in Atlanta next year. If she doesn't kill her prize competition Thoroughbred in the meantime. Bitter Stone is a phenomenal jumper and very strong in the dressage. Karin will very likely become the first rider in three Olympic games to defeat the famous Eicher Dietrich."

Julianne's tone became subdued. "First, she took his heart, and next year, she will take his eminence as well."

I looked at Dietrich on Grand Teuton. He was watching Karin and Bitter Stone fly, as were we all. I thought I detected a trace of wistfulness in his eagle's gaze for an instant.

When I looked back at Julianne, I found her watching me with her big, brown eyes, her round mouth so perfectly plump. "She will steal you, too, Lewis Cody," Julianne said softly. She heeled Yang gently and he walked away with her, leaving me thoroughly baffled.

For a moment, we all watched Karin circle the small lake, twice jumping its feeding creek, and start back toward us. Then Meriah Reinholdt walked her horse alongside Merlin Sowers and she extended her hand. "Merlin, we have a deal. I'll buy on the terms we discussed."

I could see Merlin lose fifteen pounds on the spot.

13

•••••••

Sparring

The entire outer wall of the Whitley dining room was a smoked-glass window providing a panoramic view down the meticulously graveled drive to the riding ring and stable, where all the visiting fancy horse trailers and pickup trucks were parked. A small, picturesque creek, bordered by pines, flowed along the low ground, passing beneath an arching stone bridge in the drive.

The dining-hall ceiling rose twelve feet, supported by thick, polished, laminated wooden beams. A fire crackled in a broad brick hearth opposite the huge table that was by the window. Women in neat gray uniform dresses scurried about with silver tureens of steaming food and crystal pitchers of beverages. A gentle aria permeated the room from several hidden speakers. As soon as we stepped inside, a maid materialized and took our coats. Julianne wore a fine suede vest over her white high-collared blouse.

Julianne excused herself momentarily. "Save me a seat!" she said, walking down the thickly carpeted hall.

I gazed about at the impressive Whitley home. It was a warm but very elegant place with lots of exposed walnut, original art, and fine old early American furniture.

Most of the guests were already eating as I entered the room. Mitch Whitley sat at the head of the table in an ornate antique chair. "Sheriff Cody!" he called over the hubbub. "Take a seat anywhere and dig in! A little postride snack!" He waved generally at the immaculately set table. I took one of a pair of empty side chairs, thinking that if this was Mitch Whitley's notion of a snack, I couldn't wait to see his formal dinner.

I don't know where she came from, because I had not seen her when I came in, but Karin Steiger was suddenly in the chair next to me. She had freshened her slight make-up, I suspected, and her perfume was barely detectable, but delectable. Her fragrance wasn't sweet and wholesome like Julianne's; it went quickly past a man's brain to the root of his penis. Down the table by Professor Whitley and Meriah Reinholdt, the imperious Dr. Eicher Dietrich glared at me. Horse people are strange folks.

"Waitress," Karin commanded quietly but firmly, freezing one of the passing women in gray. Her English was perfectly enunciated with only a taste of German accent. "I'll have hot tea with a quarter lemon."

She rotated her head on a long, slender neck exposed by her side-draped hair, faced me, and smiled. The effect was every bit as stunning as she must have known it would be. Her brows rose and fell away over long eyelashes and the sort of sleepy bedroom eyes most women would kill for, and some men have killed for. She, too, had disposed of her riding coat and wore a long-sleeved, ruffled white silk blouse that was cut to expose a tender, fetching cleavage, a typically Karin flaunting of the traditional hunt club high-collared blouse. A cameo hung from a black velvet choker and lay tilted in the soft, pale cleft.

Women. What magic they can be.

She sipped casually from a crystal glass of water, eyeing me all the while. I think she was waiting to see if I would break into nervous chatter. I bided my time, enjoying her beautiful face. She was clearly on a mission of some kind and would get on with it in her own time. Soon she did. "I don't think I have ever seen such an enormous horse as yours, Sheriff Cody; certainly not under saddle." Karin sipped again from her water glass. "For what dreadful personal inadequacy are you attempting to compensate?" She assumed that amused look again, her eyes narrowed, her smile—as before—higher at one side than the other.

Some women like to spar. I've known a couple. My turn to be amused.

"Money," I answered after a brief pause. "That diamond on your hand would probably fund me a badly needed additional deputy for a year."

"Wasn't it the American composer with the German name, Irving Berlin, who wrote that diamonds are a girl's best friend?"

"I pity the woman who believes that," I said. "Anyway, it was a guy named Jule Stein. That's . . . an engagement ring, is it not?"

Karin Steiger paused just a hair on that one, and her look of amusement faded minutely. "Sometimes," she answered. "Sometimes it is a barbed hook tearing at my throat. German country policemen are pitifully paid as well. Why did you not pursue something more . . . remunerative, instead of becoming an ambition-void civil lackey?"

My own smile broadened. "I'm a dedicated servant of the people," I told her. "I do it for truth and justice and honor and for, well, does the word *pussy* mean anything to you?"

Karin laughed richly, a sexy, happy laugh. "Of course, Sheriff Cody. We have small felines in Germany."

"Well, that's why I turned down the chief executiveship of worldwide Mitsubishi and became sheriff of an obscure tribe of Republican pygmies."

"Of what?"

"Nothing." Good. I had upset the rhythm of her attack.

I looked up the table to see Dietrich still staring. The servants began to place dishes of food before the guests. Conversing diners and the bustle of the wait staff afforded privacy of conversation.

Karin Steiger didn't stay off balance for long. "You're not married," she said, glancing at my ringless left hand. "At your advanced age, that can only mean you're a dismal failure at relationships."

I looked at her, trying hard to look grim, with a tiny trace of sorrow. "It could mean I'm a widower," I said.

It almost worked. A barely discernable glimmer of doubt flashed across her eyes, but she recovered.

"It could also mean you are gay," she answered as a waitress set her tea before her. "But I doubt that as well."

Julianne Chu strode into the room, her straight black hair and her breasts bouncing slightly with her stride. She paused only briefly upon sighting Karin and me, and it dawned on me that she had asked me to save her a seat. I had intended to, but Karin Steiger had captured it, along with my attention. Julianne glided by us toward an empty chair near Meriah Reinholdt. In passing, she didn't speak or look at us, but she let her left hand trail lightly over my shoulder and neck, a subtle gesture not missed by Karin, who glanced up.

China dishes of steaming asparagus spears and thinly sliced roast appeared from behind us.

"Dr. Chu is lovely," Karin said, turning to her food.

"I've noticed." I addressed my own meal.

"She just sent me a signal that you're hers."

"Not likely; I just met her. Besides, I'm not anybody's."

"You just met me." Karin sipped her tea, gazing at me from the corners of her eyes. She set the cup down. "But I can make you mine, if I desire to."

I considered her. "You're a rare beauty, I admit," I said. "But I don't do ownership very well. Anyway, you're bought and paid for by the ole führer over there. If you weren't, you wouldn't be engaged to marry a man you clearly despise."

Karin released an amused sniff, a smile pulling lightly at one side of her incredibly pretty mouth. Believe it not, a woman's mouth is what I notice first about her.

"Eicher comes from very old and established German money, probably at the expense of thousands of European Jews. He is useful, aside from being devoted to me, but no man will ever own me."

"I believe that," I said emphatically. The roast was delicious, and the asparagus was tender all the way down the stalks.

"Eicher tries. He fails."

I looked up from my food. "You and the delightful Dr. Mengele must be a marriage made in heaven. I can't wait to see your children."

"Eicher is not without a certain charm, Mr. Cody—"

"That's pitifully paid Sheriff Cody, thank you."

"Lewis, I prefer. My career permits no time for children.

My 'tubes were tied,' as you Americans say, years ago. Eicher is quite in love with me, actually."

"He's old enough to be your father," I said, chewing asparagus and thinking my mother would have scolded me for talking while eating. "He should know better."

Karin looked down the table at Dietrich. When I followed her line of vision, I saw him now engaged in conversation with Meriah Reinholdt and Helen Whitley.

"He's nineteen years older," Karin answered. "He is one of the smartest and strongest men I've ever known, easily the best rider I ever met . . . next to me, of course. But he loves me, and that will subdue the most able man. I like older men, Lewis. The only regret I have about my father is that I could never make love with him."

"How do you know? Did you try?"

The smallest hesitation. "Yes, as a matter of fact. Papa remains the only man I ever wanted to seduce whom I could not."

"Well, hell, nobody's perfect," I replied. I lifted the glass of red wine that had been placed before me. I sniffed its fabulous aroma and set it down with great regret.

"You don't drink," Karin observed with a trace of disgust. "How stalwart."

"I drink," I said. "I'm an ambition-void civil lackey, remember? I'd kill Mother Teresa for a sip of a fine French burgundy like this stuff. But I don't let my people drink alcohol when they're on duty, so . . . lead by example and all that. For a spoiled Kraut princess, you don't have much accent."

Karin fought the urge to smile. "My father was named ambassador to the United States when the Wall fell and we reunified. For almost his entire career prior, he was a diplomat with the West German embassy in Washington. I attended private school in Virginia from when I was ten to when I returned to Hamburg to attend university."

I put my fork down and turned to face Karin. She faintly smelled at once of flowers and horses. Karin Steiger was a freak of nature: she was possessed of an extraordinary, earthy woman beauty I was uncomfortably drawn to, a beauty that acts upon all the senses, not merely vision.

"You are a remarkably lovely woman," I remarked, as though talking to myself.

Almost sadly, Karin looked at her food and replied, "I know. I learned early on that I was beautiful, and I learned the power of that beauty." She returned her gaze to me. "The curse of it is that it makes men want to worship me, and it makes women want to hate me. I don't want to be either worshipped or hated." She rotated on her chair to face me. "That's what intrigues me about you, Lewis Cody. I sense a man who could love me but not worship me, if you just had the . . . stamina. Unlikely for someone who never aspired to more than a mere policeman's lot."

I grinned, chewing my roast beef. "Shoot, even if you did have more charm than a constipated warthog, I haven't worshipped anything since Vietnam." I squinted, gazing through the high, smoked-glass window at the carefully landscaped grounds around Laurel Ridge, then I looked back at Karin's incredible face. "But I don't love you, either."

Karin dabbed at her succulent mouth with a dark-green linen napkin, then she rose and hit me with another of those tilted smiles. "I can fix that," she said, and she walked slowly from the room without looking back. I could still smell her in the air as she walked away, her hips rolling gracefully beneath the tight riding pants.

I once saw a stallion tear down a five-foot-high creosoted wooden paddock fence to get at a mare in season. I know exactly what drove him.

As I led Moose toward the truck and trailer, Mitch Whitley trotted briskly after me.

"Sheriff Cody!" he said. "I wonder, do you mind if I call you Lewis?"

"No. Of course not, professor," I answered.

"Mitch, please!" he said grandly. "Lewis, Helen and I are having a few friends over for drinks tonight. Everyone you've met today and a few others. About eight. We hoped you would join us."

I thought for a moment. I hated to commit to something else that might command my time when I needed it elsewhere, but then I had two thoughts. Mine was an elected office, and I was being invited to hobnob with some of the county's more influential people for a first time. Under the circumstances, it would not be entirely wise to turn down this invitation. Then I looked past Mitch and his horse to the stable, where my decision solidified. Karin Steiger stood by her horse, allowing it to drink. She had unbuttoned her tunic, which swung away from one breast, and she stood with her weight on one leg, her hip cocked. She threw back her head, tossing a strand of hair from her eye, and she sighted down her nose at me with that look of amused challenge.

"Thank you," I told Mitch Whitley. "I'd be pleased to attend, assuming I don't get waylaid by the job."

"Wonderful!" Mitch boomed. "Helen and Meriah will be delighted to hear that!" He turned smartly about toward the stable before I thought to ask him what the attire would be. It wasn't hard to guess, though, that Mitch would probably not be wearing cutoffs and flip-flops.

I untacked Moose and led her easily into the forward stall of the big, clean, gooseneck trailer, which smelled like fresh straw. I gave her an apple and was scratching her ears when the left front trailer door flew back with a bang, flooding the interior of the trailer with the rays of the low afternoon sun. Moose jerked her huge head. "Hooo," I said softly.

Karin Steiger stepped into the trailer and closed the door behind her. Her riding coat still lay open and the little cameo bobbed in the soft cleavage, framed by the ruffled collar of her blouse. Without preamble, she walked to me, looking me full in the eyes. Her expression was void of coquetry and bore only the slightest smile; it was the calm, merciless, predatory look of a lioness on the hunt. She lunged at me from a step away and shoved me with both her palms on my chest. As she must have known would happen, it took me by surprise, and I lurched back against the breast bar of the empty stall. Moose looked on curiously.

I had barely recovered my balance, but my composure was still lagging when she threw both her arms around my neck and pulled herself to me. I was suddenly and vividly aware of her heat and her perfume and the splash of her hair against my face.

At once she was kissing me feverishly about my left ear, a barely audible, hungry little moan in time with her breathing. She chewed frantically at my ear, biting it almost to pain, sucking at the lobe with her wet lips. The whole side of my head and neck warmed and tingled. My breathing, like hers, quickened fast. Her moist, warm breath flowing against my ear was electrifying.

I had almost caught up with her when she suddenly seized me by the hair with both her hands and kissed me hard on the mouth, a probing, gouging, carnivorous kiss full of soft lips, brutal teeth, and wet tongue. She made me hard as Virginia fieldstone. She made every cell in me scream for her. Then she released me and punched me stoutly in the chest with her palms again. By now, I had gained my footing and didn't give, so her shove propelled her backward slightly.

I tasted salty blood and gooey lipstick. Absently, I thought I heard a car pulling up outside; a car door thumped. Karin Steiger's drilling eyes bore a defiant look of triumph, for the moment at least, not without cause.

"I can own you if I want to, Lewis," Karin whispered hotly, breathing hard. "And I want to."

She threw open the door, jumped to the ground, and slammed the door behind her, leaving me with a spinning head and an erection of extremely high atomic gravity.

You will appreciate that this sort of thing doesn't happen to me every day, so I required a moment to compose myself. I wiped a slight lipstick trace on the back of my hand and let my breathing calm.

When I stepped from the trailer I found I had heard a car pull up. It was the black Nissan Pathfinder of one ragged-looking Corporal Boyce Calder.

I had never known Boyce not to be meticulously neat in appearance, a trait he no doubt garnered from his father, a very correct retired army sergeant major. So it was the more shocking to see him now, leaning against the fender on the opposite side of his car, looking at me with the haunted eyes of a Holocaust survivor. He wore a day's dark beard, and his short hair stuck out in places like he'd just gotten out of bed, though I doubted seriously that he'd even been to bed since the previous night, the last night his wife and baby were alive. And he had the thousand-yard-stare I'd seen on so many battle-wasted fellow Vietnam vets. Boyce was dressed in faded jeans, cowboy boots, and a denim shirt. His service automatic was stuck beneath his belt in the front of his jeans. His hollow eyes shifted from me to something behind me. I twisted to see Karin Steiger walking slowly away, glancing seductively over her shoulder at us, those Marilyn Monroe hips rolling ever so slightly. Boyce was eyeing me with disgust when I turned back to him.

"Boyce," I began, feeling as weak as I must have looked and sounded, "I was going to give you a call later this evening. We're—"

I halted because of the hoarse, choking tone of Boyce Calder's voice.

"You . . . your office told me you were out here . . . Sheriff Cody. I . . . wanted to see what you were doing about . . . about . . ." Boyce paused, took a deep breath while gazing wildly about, then let it hiss out through pursed lips, his jaw trembling. "About . . . my baby . . . and Cathy. I wanted to see if you'd . . . But . . . I guess I can see you got more important things to—"

"Boyce," I said, "listen to me a minute, please. I—"

"You go to hell!" Boyce croaked, with sudden vehemence.

"Boyce, I—"

"You go to hell!" Boyce tried to yell, but his voice was shot. He shoved off from his car and yanked open the driver's door. "My wife! *My* Cathy! *My* little Stevie!" Boyce lurched off his car.

"Boyce—"

"Our baby, goddamn you! Some drunk son of bitch *killed* them. And *you* . . . and all you can do is . . . play horsy with the rich fat cats!"

"Listen to me, damn it!"

"No!" Boyce choked out, pointing a finger at me. *"You* listen! *You* listen! Maybe all this awful thing is worth to you . . . is playing touchy-feely with some woman in your goddamn horse trailer! But by God, I *will* find the bastard that killed Cathy . . . Cathy and . . . my . . . my baby. I *will* find the drunk fuck *without* your goddamned help! And when I do! And when I do, I will *kill* the miserable son of a whore thirteen times!"

Boyce pounced into his vehicle, the car rocking with his weight. I ran around the nose of the car.

"Boyce, will you wait a damned minute? I'm trying—"

The young trooper pointed at me again. I could see a tear streak glistening on his cheek. "You go to hell, Sheriff Cody! I thought better of you than this!" Boyce rasped pitifully, gesturing toward Karin, who stood distant, watching us. He jammed the car in reverse, and he looked at me once more with eyes both sad and bitter. "I thought better of you than this, Sheriff Cody," he whispered once more.

Boyce Calder gunned his car rearward, whipping it about when it cleared my horse trailer. He slammed it into a forward gear and roared away up the Laurel Ridge drive toward the highway. I watched him go, feeling small enough to swing my legs off the edge of a three-dollar bill.

I heard a horse's feet clopping on the drive behind me. I turned to see Julianne Chu leading Yang past me to her rig. She stopped, petting the little Arabian on its silky nose. I glanced at where Karin was last seen, but she was now gone.

"Always, she brings suffering," Julianne said absently, as though to herself. Then she looked at me. "And she has you already."

"Nobody 'has' me," I said, sighing, still feeling rotten about Boyce's confusion.

Julianne dropped Yang's halter rope and she walked to me. Capping off a day of surprises, she stood on her tiptoes and kissed my cheek. "She has you," Julianne said softly. "She has you, but her curse is that she cannot keep you."

"Where do you *get* all this hocus-pocus?" I said, my exasperation beginning to show.

Julianne stopped once again and looked back at me. "I just hope she does not destroy you, too."

I was about to ask her what the hell that was supposed to mean when my radio sounded off.

"Sheriff One," Milly's voice broadcast.

"Sheriff One," I said into my little portable radio.

"Lewis, you ten-seven yet?"

"More or less. What do you have?" I slid into the truck.

"Ain't sure, Lewis, but it sound like another one of those . . . um . . . uh . . . animal complaints, you know?"

Oh, Christ. "Where, Milly?"

"Up ole Mr. Henry Tucker's place. Up other side of Bram's Ridge, you know?"

I knew. "Okay, Milly. I'm en route."

"Ten-four, Sheriff. Be advised, Rescue en route. Caller said Mr. Tucker was havin' another stroke."

"Damn!" I hissed without transmitting. I cranked the big diesel and buzzed the window down. "Hey!" I called to Julianne Chu. "Want to go to another delightful little Hunter County vignette?"

It took Julianne about a second of staring at me to grasp what I meant. She hurriedly pulled Yang to a nearby empty paddock, released him, and closed the gate. She ran to her truck and retrieved the thick, aluminum briefcase; then she hurried to my truck and climbed in.

14

• • • • • • • •

Collateral Casualty

As I drove the heavy horse rig over mountain roads toward the Tucker place from Laurel Ridge Farm, I felt it jerk from Moose's shifting her bulk about to keep her balance. Julianne Chu looked at me with those impossibly huge eyes, her smooth, shining black hair jouncing with the movement of the truck. I told her of a day in the early sixties when I was sweeping the sidewalk outside Daddy's old country hardware store on the square in Hunter.

It was a Saturday morning and the square teemed with farm families in town. The men filed in and out of Dad's store, buying ammunition and chain and fence, and the women shopped other merchants on the square for food, bolts of cloth, and canning jars. Eight older farm boys were gathered by the statue of Captain Jedidiah Hunter on the courthouse lawn across from E. H. Cody Hardware, eyeing passing groups of girls, who giggled and peeked back at them from the corners of their eyes. The boys either smoked or spat tobacco juice, and they whispered remarks to each other over which they guffawed loudly. A weathered old pickup truck chugged out of the parking space by the boys, and into that spot Mr. Henry Tucker promptly maneuvered his polished black four-wheeled light carriage, drawn by a splendidly groomed black Tennessee Walking Horse in gleaming harness.

Mr. Henry Tucker had the delicate, poised, but not swishy bearing of a retired ballet dancer in his late forties, which he was. He had recently bought the old Cobb Woolwine farm on the Buffalo Run River and had moved there from New York, which in Hunter County was pronounced Nyu Yark City. He had created a stir because of, among other reasons, his propensity to go about attired in a white linen suit, in his elegant horse-drawn carriage. He had especially been noted arriving in the carriage at the First Presbyterian Church on Sunday mornings in the company of a Giles Putnam, a younger man from Nyu Yark City who was also meticulously dressed. It was said that Mr. Henry Tucker and Giles were afforded a pew of their own in the back of the sanctuary, which I found odd at the time, but then, I found a lot of things odd. Still do.

Even on this summer day, as he tied the beautifully groomed horse to the parking meter and charged the meter with a nickel, Mr. Henry Tucker wore his trademark white suit with white silk vest and tie and white shoes. He completed his uniform with a dapper white straw hat with, needless to say, a white silk band.

I studied him that Saturday morning, not for the reason everyone else stared at him, not because he was visually unique, but because I had an urgent problem that it occurred to me Mr. Henry Tucker might be able to fix.

A week earlier, I had heard a woman in Lady Maude's Café remark that Mr. Henry Tucker lived with a man fifteen years his junior named Giles Putnam. This somehow evoked sly looks and knowing smirks from the women discussing him, an observation I, as an eighth grader, thought was curious but otherwise unremarkable. I also didn't care that he was said to "have money," and to "not need to work." What caught my interest that day was another comment whispered by the women. Mr. Henry Tucker was a . . . . dance . . . teacher, they tee-heed, clearly implying that should mean something, too. Whatever it was supposed to mean went right by me. What it did mean to me was that perhaps this man could save me from a fate worse than death.

In the seventh grade, I had fallen slam crash in love with the most beautiful creature in the entire universe, my classmate Patsy Nolan. My hormones were coming ashore and the mere smell of Patsy Nolan brushing by me in the cloakroom made me dizzy. In her innocent way, she occasionally sat in a dress with her legs slightly apart, which galvanized me with erections that in turn caused me to pray I would not be called upon to stand up. I worshipped Patsy Nolan's tender thighs and devastating smile, and I dreamed away many a classroom hour about our getting married, how many kids we'd have, and how she'd greet me lovingly upon my return from the office. The latter was a little cloudy because I had no idea what I was going to do as an adult, but there was nothing cloudy about my crush on Patsy Nolan. I was love-wrecked.

For an agonizing year, I suffered miserably because Patsy didn't even seem to acknowledge that I existed, and I was way too shy to bring it to her attention. But by the eighth grade, I was taller than most boys in my class and had filled out enough that one day Patsy Nolan looked at me and smiled instead of ignoring me.

Patsy reduced me to jelly with those flickering eyes and changed the meaning of life for me. "I . . ." she stammered, as painfully shy as I was, "I . . . was hoping you might ask me to the American Legion dance. . . ." I later learned that this was the most terrifying moment of Patsy's life because she was convinced she was plain and I would have no interest in her. Ignorance is not bliss.

My exceeding joy at learning of our mutual infatuation had a dark side, though. I didn't know how to dance. Worse, I had tried, and I knew I could no more dance than I could fly. I was fumble-footed, dance was mysterious and confusing to me, and my every exposure to it had been a humiliating debacle. My poor mother had tried her heart out to teach me, but gently gave up. I was trapped. I would die before I would pass on taking Patsy to the dance, but I was scared witless that I would look like a fool before her and my whole class when I did. Big problem. The dance was two weeks away and I was beginning to lose sleep worrying about it. So, by the morning Mr. Henry Tucker got out of his quaint carriage on the square, I was desperate.

I was hurriedly trying to decide how to approach Mr. Henry Tucker about my dilemma when I was distracted by a howl of plainly mean-spirited laughter from the tobacco-sucking older farm boys on the courthouse lawn. I looked up to see them all looking at Mr. Henry, who smiled pleasantly at them. As he walked past them, one of the bigger boys muttered something I couldn't hear from my vantage across the street. The boys cackled at the remark, whatever it was. Mr. Henry Tucker stopped suddenly. I could see him stare straight ahead, then resume walking. The boy then spoke loud enough for me to hear him. "I said, *hey,* queer!" he yelled at Mr. Henry Tucker's back.

It should be noted here that in the Hunter County school system, in the time of President Kennedy, sex education wasn't even defined as such. Once a year in senior high school, the girls would be called to the auditorium and the boys would be herded to the gym, and nervous teachers of the same sex would bravely wax on about "certain urges." The speeches were short and never seemed to specify much except that one could get nasty diseases doing "it," and it was important to wait until after one was married. As an eighth grader, all I knew about sex was what I gleaned from the lurid and uninformed swagger stories of older boys.

"I said, hey, queer!" the boy repeated, and his cohorts snickered again. Mr. Henry Tucker didn't stop walking this time, but I could see a distinct sadness narrow his eyes. Nonetheless, he raised his head, carried a pleasant smile, and tipped his hat to a passing woman who was beholding the spectacle in embarrassment.

To this day I envy the dignity displayed by Mr. Henry Tucker that morning.

It was all very puzzling to me. I ducked back into the store, which was crowded with farmers browsing in the bins and barrels of hardware or socializing with each other about crop prices and some weird place nobody had ever heard of called Vietnam. "Daddyyyyy!" I hollered over the hubbub.

"Yes, son?" Daddy called from over in the salt blocks. He was busy, but my daddy was never too busy for me.

"Hey, Daddy! What's a *queer?*" I shrieked, and the store got real quiet, real fast.

In his cluttered back office over our lunch sandwiches,

Daddy explained that a queer was a man who "liked" men instead of women.

"Well, shoot, Daddy," I said. "You like men, don't you? You go fishing with Mr. Harmon all the time."

At this point, Daddy took the parent's fifth amendment and told me I was too young to understand, but then he looked me hard in the eye. "Listen to me, Lewis," Daddy said very seriously, "you stay away from Mr. Henry Tucker, and stay away from that Giles fella, too!"

"But . . . why, Daddy?" I said, feeling my dance problem beginning to compound.

"Because I told you to, son," Daddy said, which I knew was the end of the discussion.

I debated furiously for two days. I trusted my daddy, who had never misled me, and disobeying him had been, up to that point, beyond consideration. Further, if he was leery of Mr. Henry Tucker, I knew I probably ought to be also. But . . . I was taking Patsy Nolan to the American Legion Youth Dance in twelve days and I couldn't outdance a stoned giraffe. And no less than my own true love was at stake here.

The following Tuesday after school, I fired up Daddy's ancient Massey tractor, which he rarely used anymore, since his hardware business left him no time to farm, and I drove it six miles over the firebreak road and through the creek to Mr. Henry Tucker's fastidiously kept house on the Buffalo Run. Flowers poured from black-painted planters hung on the polished railing of the white wrap-around front porch with the swing. I took a deep breath and rang the doorbell.

Mr. Henry Tucker opened the door in his classic white attire, except that he did not wear the coat or hat. "Good afternoon, sir," he said, and my tongue stuck to the roof of my mouth.

He waited patiently as I stammered and tried to speak.

"I can't dance!" I finally blurted, breathing hard.

Mr. Henry Tucker frowned thoughtfully. "Excuse me? What did you say?"

I ripped off, "I can't dance and I'm taking Patsy Nolan to the American Legion Youth Dance twelve days from now and I can't dance and if I look like a fool in front of Patsy Nolan and everybody I'll have to kill myself 'cause I can't dance!"

Giles Putnam appeared in the foyer behind Mr. Henry Tucker. "Henry!" he said, pleasantly, "who have we here?"

Mr. Henry Tucker thought for a moment. "A young man with a thorny dilemma, I fear," he answered. "Giles, perhaps you would be so kind as to prepare some lemonade for our guest. And a brownie, I believe."

"Why, of course," Giles Putnam said, and he hurried off.

"I can't dance! And I'm taking—"

"What is your name, my young friend?"

"Cody! I'm Lewis Cody, sir. My daddy runs the hardware store!"

"Of course. I thought I'd seen you before. Let me see if I understand you . . . Lewis. You wish for me to teach you to dance?"

"Yes sir! I'll pay you! I got twenty-two dollars and forty-one cents; you can have it all except I need to keep twenty cents for the drink machine to buy Patsy and me a Nehi! I got to learn to—"

"I . . . ah . . . I charge a dollar to teach a young man to dance, actually. First, I must ask you something, to determine if you can learn to dance."

Oh Lord, I thought, *I'm doomed already.* "Yes sir?"

"Did you . . . ah . . . did you walk from that . . . implement . . . to where you now stand?"

I looked over my shoulder at the old Massey tractor, wondering if this was some kind of trick question. I looked back at Mr. Henry Tucker. "Uh. Yes sir."

Mr. Henry Tucker smiled warmly and opened the screen door wide. "Then you most certainly can learn to dance! Do come in."

And learn to dance I did, for two hours each day, which I alibied off to playing ball with friends. "First," Mr. Henry Tucker told me, "you must dance like no one can see you. Then, you must dance like everyone can see you." I thought I was hopeless, but Mr. Henry Tucker would never entertain that notion. He patiently instructed me, and occasionally he and Giles would demonstrate, gliding flawlessly about the huge living room to 78- and 45-rpm records. He taught me how to hear what I listened to, and he broke me of looking at my feet. He taught me the twist, which was the trendy rage of the time, and he taught me to waltz, and he taught me to "simply hold your young lady, and move together in love." He destroyed my fear and made me feel like I was Elvis Presley and Fred Astair combined. All this he accomplished in eleven days. For a dollar.

At the end of the first day's lesson, Mr. Henry Tucker asked me, "Lewis, do your parents know you're here?"

Uh oh, I thought. "No sir."

Mr. Henry Tucker sat back in his chair and studied me with his hand on his chin. "I think it best that you not tell them, Lewis. Ordinarily, I would never counsel you to keep secrets from your parents, who are wonderful people, I'm sure, but I believe that if you tell them you are seeing me, they will prohibit you from doing so any further."

I certainly had planned not to tell Daddy I disobeyed him, but the mysterious, vaguely threatening implications that the women in Lady Maude's Café, the courthouse lawn punks, Daddy, and now even Mr. Henry Tucker himself seemed to be suggesting were piquing my curiosity. He seemed a wholly delightful if slightly peculiar man to me, and further, he was saving me from a fate worse than death. "Why, sir?" I asked Mr. Henry Tucker.

I saw that same look of sadness come across his patrician face that I had seen on the square the previous Saturday. He seemed to be searching for the right words. "I . . . look at human relationships a bit differently, Lewis," he answered, "in ways that are hard for many people to understand. And people tend to fear and hate what they do not understand. It would be best if you kept our association between us, at least for now."

This explanation was still perplexing, but I elected not to pursue it, as I had my own reasons for keeping my dance lessons a secret.

The night of the American Legion Youth Dance was a hallmark in my life. I hit that dance floor like a kid possessed, and Patsy Nolan was thrilled, as were, I noted, a few of the other girls present. I twisted in a way that would have made Chubby Checker hang his head; never mind why. And when the music slowed to the "Tennessee Waltz" and most of the boys stared nervously at the girls clustered on the opposite side of the American Legion Hall, I swept Patsy Nolan about the dance floor like Rhett Butler drew Scarlett O'Hara in her mourning dress.

Late in the evening, Patsy suggested we go out on the back deck of the Legion Hall, because of the heat, I thought. I was right, in a way.

At a dark edge of the deck, under the stars that glitter in rural mountain skies, Patsy Nolan gave me The Kiss You Never Forget. "Don't go away!" she said. "I've got to go to the powder room, but . . ."—she looked at me with what I now know was dawning womanhood—"I'll be right back. You won't go away? Promise?"

I wanted to tell her a four-wheel-drive three-hundred-horsepower diesel gangplow tractor couldn't move me from that spot on its best day, but all I could do was nod. She smiled hugely, kissed me again, and ran inside.

I was trying to get my breath when I heard clapping coming from the area between the Legion Hall deck and the nearby river. I shaded my eyes from the floodlights and looked and could make out two men sitting in a horse-drawn carriage, applauding, Giles frantically, with a tear in his eye, and Mr. Henry Tucker gracefully, with a smile of pride. There was no sadness in his eyes.

Patsy Nolan hurried back out through the sliding glass doors. "Who are you waving at?" she said, throwing her arms about my neck. The hoofbeats of a Tennessee Walker were fading away.

I thought about explaining to Patsy, but I didn't know how. "Friends," was all I could say.

Julianne Chu and I turned off the highway onto the drive to Mr. Henry Tucker's just as the med unit came screaming in from the volunteer firehouse in Perry Hollow.

Wearing jeans and a green wool shirt, Giles Putnam met us in the drive of the showcase home on the Buffalo Run River. Julianne slid to the ground and yanked her case from the rear of the truck. Giles was a slight man, well into his sixties now, but other than a slight limp, he was still quite fit. He was crying.

"Oh, Lewis! Thank God you're here! It's Henry! He's had another stroke!" Giles Putnam paused and wept again.

Andy Harmon, the paramedic who pronounced Cathy Calder dead the previous night, hurried from the big boxy ambulance. Two other medics followed, carrying their gear.

"This is Doctor Julianne Chu, Giles," I said gently. "Doctor Chu is a vet. Where's Mr. Henry?"

"He's up there," Giles said, sniffing. He pointed to a wooded hill about a quarter mile away. "Come with me; I'll show you!" Giles indicated an old green Land Rover standing nearby. "He's with Orlando. Orlando is . . . dead. She's . . . oh my God, Lewis, you cannot believe what someone has done to that poor horse. It's . . . it's . . ." Giles Putnam looked up at me. He was lost for words, but his expression told the story. He was terrified.

We bailed into Giles Putnam's Land Rover and he drove up a dirt trail toward the wooded hill. The rescue paramedics rocked along behind in the ambulance.

"Lewis," Giles wailed, "you know how Henry has always loved his horses. Everybody knows. He's eighty-one years old and he's had Orlando for eighteen years, since she was born. He's . . . he's heartbroken, Lewis! He can't even talk! He won't come down from there! I'm sure it's another stroke! The doctors said last time . . . they said—" Giles began to weep again.

"When did you find the horse dead?" I asked Giles.

Giles brought himself under control as the old Land Rover ground up the rutted road. "Henry went to harness Orlando about . . . oh, noon or so, I guess. He's so stiff now with his arthritis, you know. But he insists on having his horses and he won't let me harness them for him. He'd have to admit he's getting old. Through the kitchen window, I saw Henry hobbling out to the upper pasture with a halter and a carrot, looking for Orlando. He wanted to drive down to Slayer's General Store. He likes to talk politics with old Mr. Slayer, you know? I didn't think any more about it until almost an hour later, when it occurred to me I hadn't seen Henry come back or heard him go out the drive. I looked out and saw the carriage still in the stableyard and I thought, oh my god, Henry's had another stroke! I was frantic! I drove all around the upper pasture and down on the river stretch. Finally, I found him in the woods by the vineyard. He . . . he was just sitting there by Orlando, just staring! And that horse, Lewis! Somebody has . . . has . . . *destroyed* that poor animal! I've never seen . . ." Giles broke into tears again.

"Easy, Giles," I said, "we're going to have to think of Mr. Henry now. He's going to need you to be under control when we get up there."

"You're right, of course, Lewis," Giles said. He drew a deep breath and let it out slowly. "It's just . . . I have never seen anything like what has been done to Orlando, Lewis," he said, looking over at me. "Who . . . what could *do* such a thing? I mean, we've had vandals bash our mailbox and paint . . . epithets on the barn once, but—"

"This has nothing to do with your . . . life style, Giles," I said. "He didn't single you out. I'm afraid he's already done it at least once that we know of, at Gordy Huckaby's place."

"Oh no! That little mare the Huckaby girl competes with? Oh Lewis, no. Who . . . what . . ."

"I don't know," I answered, feeling as lame as when Boyce Calder left me less than an hour earlier. "But I'm goddamn sure gonna find out." I noticed Julianne staring at me.

Mr. Henry Tucker lay on his side in the leaves just inside the woods, about twenty feet from the carnage. Bloodstains smeared his suede driving coat, and he stared blankly without blinking. His hat lay upside down in the leaves, and he was balder than I remembered his being the last time I had seen him, months before.

"Henry!" Giles cried, and he hurried toward the old man. The young paramedics rushed past him and descended on Mr. Henry. Giles dropped to the ground, cradled Mr. Henry's head in his lap, and caressed his forehead. At first, they worked feverishly, cutting clothing back from Mr. Henry's pale white chest, Andy listening with a stethoscope, and but then their pace slowed markedly. Andy sighed and stood. "He's dead, Sheriff Cody," Andy said without turning. He closed his eyes and rubbed the bridge of his nose. "At this point, CPR is not a viable option."

Giles gently closed Mr. Henry Tucker's eyes. We stood quietly, listening to the soft sobs of Giles Putnam intersperse with gusts of the cold November wind. In time, one of Andy's men helped Giles to the Land Rover to drive him back to the house where he would now live alone. Andy Harmon, Julianne, and I examined Mr. Henry's body enough to be certain his death had not occurred from any assault, then I released the body for removal by the paramedics.

It wasn't hard to tell that the butcher had visited. All the signs were there: vicious slashes about the rear and throat of the once-beautiful black mare, and multiple stabs along the right side. Massive quantities of blood ran in rivulets through the low places in the forest floor, turning the brown, dry leaves wet and dark. There were marked dissimilarities in the method of restraint: the horse lay on its left side, the head elevated, bound by the neck to two trees, and the hind feet had been roped to separate trees. As the animal now lay, her head was suspended by a rope and her rear legs were crossed. The eyes were a cloudy bluish white. Still another rope was tied to the root of the animal's tail.

Julianne moved quickly about the sleek, still, black mare, examining it. Blood smeared her riding boots and her pants, but she didn't seem to notice. She opened her aluminum case and withdrew a needle device about eighteen inches long with the thickness of a large nail. She knelt on one knee against the sleek body, probed with her free hand about the dead horse's side, located a spot, and without hesitation, she sank the long needle into the body. She seemed to be feeling for the depth and path of its penetration. When it was inserted nearly to its chromed grip, she withdrew a clear plastic tube from the thick needle and discarded it. She then inserted a long wire, tipped with what looked like the mouth end of an oral thermometer, deep into the hollow steel needle. She connected the wire to a hand-held electric digital display.

I studied the rope. My father had run a hardware store and I was blessed with a pretty broad knowledge of work done with the hands, and the tools and equipment used to augment that work. The rope was half-inch manila hemp and appeared to be new; it was stiff and had no kinks or dirt or any of the worn look of used rope. Whoever had bound the poor horse knew knots well. He had used a simple and very effective tension-maintaining method with the rope that local farmers called a "winch knot." Unfortunately, I reflected, the rope was as common as Coca-Cola, and tracing it was unlikely. I began to circle about, looking for a discarded wrapper or anything else that could tell a tale.

"Seventeen Celsius," Julianne said, and I turned to see her extract the blood-smeared needle apparatus from the horse's corpse. "About sixty degrees Fahrenheit." She glanced at the Lady Rolex on her arm. "I'd say the time of death was about noon or one o'clock. I can pin it to the quarter-hour when I can determine the ambient temperature and consult my tables." Julianne turned her back to me. "Take my coat off, please," she said. I peeled her coat from her and laid it over a low tree limb. Julianne began to draw sleeve-length clear plastic gloves up her arms. She looked at me. "I'm going to try to obtain a vaginal swab. That's what the people docs do when . . . when they're trying to verify rape." She turned back to the horse.

I continued to find nothing. The leaf-blanketed ground sloped down in the direction of the horse's head, and the leaves were churned up, predictably, but there was nothing that might yield a footprint or a fingerprint. I looked for hairs or fibers caught in the bark of the trees, for anything but leaves on the ground. About ten feet away, I found a stick two inches thick and nearly two feet long. It was broken on one end and was bloody almost its entire length. I didn't pick it up; I didn't have to to know what it meant.

I heard Julianne behind me. "Oooh," she said, pained. I turned to see her stand, one of her gloved arms bloody. She held her booted feet apart and her head down and displayed an expression of fury. "There's a *stick* in her!" Julianne Chu shouted, which surprised me, given her usual poise. "A *stick!*" she repeated, her voice cracking, her breathing rapid. She stripped the long gloves from her arms and flung them wildly away, staggering in her rage, tears showing in the corners of her eyes. "The bastard stuck a . . . a . . . a *goddamned stick* in her! I hate this bastard! I *hate* him!" Now she was shouting, heaving. I walked to her. She jabbed a finger at me. "You . . . you've got to get him! Get him! Get him! Get him!" She began to cry, and I took her in my arms reflexively. She lay her head against my chest and cried. "You . . ." She raised her head and pushed back and locked eyes with me. "We! *We* have to *get* this creature!"

I heard a car engine and pulled my gaze from Julianne to look toward the dirt trail bordering the nearby pasture. Pierce's tan cruiser was rocking to a stop. He heaved his bulk from the car. "Lewis?" he yelled.

"Here." I called. Julianne was wiping her eyes.

Pierce lumbered into the scene and paused briefly, his lips pursed, eyeing the atrocity in the leaves. "Same guy?" he asked.

"Looks like it," I said. "Christ, I *hope* there's not more than one."

Pierce looked at Julianne Chu, who was shrugging into her black riding coat, her back to us. "We . . . uh . . . we got another problem, Lewis," Pierce said in his Hoss Cartwright baritone.

I looked at him.

Pierce sighed. "It's Boyce Calder, Lewis. He's out of control."

15

•••••••••

The Other Hand

I had Pierce radio the dungeon to call Mountain Harbor and have Arthur bring my unmarked cruiser to Mr. Henry Tucker's place. He could return with the horse rig. By the time Pierce and I had completed interviewing Giles, Arthur rolled into the drive looking a bit incongruous, driving an antenna-laden silver police car in his old fedora, bib overalls, and denim coat.

Predictably, Giles hadn't been able to tell us anything useful. He was grief-stricken, and could only lie and weep.

Julianne had regained her composure. I asked Arthur to drive her back to Laurel Ridge Farm to pick up her own rig. Before we left, Julianne reached as though to touch me, but withdrew her hand. "Are you coming to the party at the Whitleys' this evening?" she asked me.

I nodded.

"Then I'll see you tonight." She squeezed my arm. "Get this monster, Lewis!" she whispered. "He hurts for fun. Let me know how I can help, but get him!"

There was a sleazy pool hall on 619 called the Dixie Rider, frequented by the long-haired and bearded Harley set. I knew some of the patrons were PCP and coke traffickers, and almost all of them were pot users, but on the whole, they policed their own and kept a low profile, so I left them alone unless I caught them dirty somewhere else. They never called the police, for obvious reasons, but they had called this afternoon. A "crazy-assed" off-duty state trooper had hit the Dixie Rider like Clinton aides hit Vince Foster's office after the body was found.

Pierce and I parked our cruisers among the dirty pickup trucks and chromed-up motorcycles in the gravel parking lot at the ugly black-painted concrete-block saloon. It had been as dark as a cave inside the windowless Dixie Rider on past occasions when I had come to pay social calls, but now the fire lights were on. The owner, a tattooed silverback mountain gorilla delicately named Richard "Big Dick" Boneventure, was pushing a broom about a nasty room in which there had clearly been a spirited dispute. Broken glass, wood splinters, and overturned furniture completed the decor.

The place stank of cigarette smoke, booze, and sweat. Most of the remaining six patrons slouching about drinking beer had on greasy jeans, boots, and black T-shirts cutely accented with chains, black leather vests, sunglasses, and bandanas or black leather Harley caps. Several wore big folding knives in leather belt pouches. Most had bruises, torn clothing, and/or bleeding places on them, and they weren't exactly overcome with emotion to see us.

"You held a party and didn't invite me, Dick?" I said, looking around.

"This ain't funny, Sheriff!" Dick roared with a voice made ragged by fifty years of carcinogenic smoke. He harpooned a fat finger at me. "You motherfuckin' cops is in trouble now! I'm suin' y'all's asses off! You pigs ain't got no right to come in here and trash my place and harass my customers! I'm gonna sue your mother—"

"Yeah, yeah, Dick. I get the message." I said. Pierce leaned against the wall by the door, his shotgun dangling toward the floor from a hamhock hand. "Why don't you just tell me what happened."

"That goddamned Trooper Calder, that's what happened!" Dick ranted, waving his hairy arms. "Come in here all wild in the face, want to know who drivin' that banged-up pickup truck out front. We tole him go fuck himself! He grab up a cue stick and liked to killed all of us! Busted my whole place up! Ole Jimbo tole him, 'Awright, by God, motherfucker, it's my goddamn truck! What's it to you?' That crazy-assed kid flung Jimbo on the floor, stuck a goddamn gun in his face, and tole him he had two seconds to say how that truck got bent. Hell, ole Jimbo liked to shit! I went for my ole double-barrel, and Calder turn that gun on me. I dropped the shotgun and picked up the phone to call y'all, and that crazy-assed motherfucker *shot* my goddamn telephone right off the *bar!* Phone's in fifty pieces on the floor! Had to go 'cross the street to call! Look at that bullet hole! He's fuckin' crazy! I heard his bitch and his tax deduction got snuffed, but that don't give him no right to do this! I'm gonna—"

"*Hey!*" I shouted, silencing Dick Boneventure, veins standing out on his bald forehead. In a quieter tone, I continued. "Calm your big ass down, Dick, and just tell me what I need to know. How *did* that truck get damaged? And better none of you tell me to go fuck myself."

The room was quiet, except for Dick's labored breathing. He must have had a nuclear-powered heart to keep that phenomenally fat body alive, given the smoke and chemicals he had ingested in half a century. Finally, Jimbo spoke. "Like we tole Trooper Calder, Sheriff, Petey backed into me about two nights ago. Ain't that right, Petey? You dumb fuck."

"Jimbo ain't shittin' you, Sheriff," Petey said, looking disgusted. "I was fucked out of my head last week. Got me some bad shit outta Roanoke. I backed my ole Firebird into Jimbo's truck. Swear to God."

God had never heard of Jimbo and Petey, and vice versa, but they didn't sound like they were lying, and in police work, you get a sense for liars. More to the point, I knew Jimbo Wheeler's ratty old truck, and it was a Chevy half-ton, not a Ford F-350 ton truck. Jimbo's truck didn't have extruded hub lugs.

"See there?" Dick bellowed. "I'm gonna call State Police Internal Affairs, have that crazy fucker brought up on charges! I'm gonna sue—"

"How much for the damage, Dick?" I interrupted, taking out my billfold. Dick cleaved his sentence in midsyllable and eyed my wallet.

"Aw . . . 'bout a thousand ought to cover it, I reckon."

"Sure, Dick," Pierce growled. I turned to see him with his own billfold in hand, the shotgun crooked in his arm. "And my sainted grandmother's whippin' Hulk Hogan's ass on 'Wide World Of Wrestling' tonight. Get serious."

"Jeez, Dick," I added. "We're just trying to help you out, and here you're trying to sell us a ski lodge in Death Valley."

Pierce continued coldly, "A grand *will* cover it with a good nine bills to spare." Pierce tossed two twenties and a ten on the floor. "Me and the sheriff will keep the spare, thank you."

I handed Dick another fifty. He took it and scooped up Pierce's money with a sneer. "And Dick," I said, catching his eye. "If you or anybody or the goddamn fairy godmother so much as mentions Boyce Calder's name to VSP Internal Affairs, two of my deputies will become faithful customers of yours. They'll buy a beer a day and they'll listen to the lovely music, every hour of every day you're open. They'll be nice, but of course, if they should suspect anything illegal, why, they'll have to take steps to protect you and your customers."

"Well, hell," Dick mumbled, fingering the cash. "On the other hand, I reckon this'll take care of it."

"It'd better take care of everything, Dick," I reiterated.

"What the fuck," Dick said, meeting my gaze. "I guess if my ole lady an' one o' my rug rats got smeared by some drunk asshole, I'd be a little riled myself. I reckon we're singin' the same tune, Sheriff."

I slammed open the door that gains entry to the booking room and secretaries' cubicles that comprise what used to be the main courtroom of the original stone courthouse, now the Hunter County dungeon. Sergeant Milly Stanford had her overcoat on and was about to leave.

"Milly, I need to see you and Pierce in my office," I said, irritated with the state of affairs and my inability to do anything effective so far. Further, I was very worried about Boyce Calder. Pierce was right; Boyce was out of control, and an out-of-control man with a gun was a problem.

"Sure, Sheriff," Milly answered. She dropped her voluminous leather purse on the spot with a crash.

"Christ." I grinned at her in spite of myself. "What's in that thing, your bowling ball collection?"

"Hell, somebody got to have some balls around here," Milly retorted without a pause, walking toward my office.

"Cindy!"

"Yes sir, Sheriff!"

"Get me Trooper Boyce Calder on the phone, ASAP. Tell him I want to talk to him, and I don't mean later."

In my office, Milly briefed me that despite all the intense efforts of my people, including several deputies working on their own time, no one had turned a whit of information on a damaged maroon Ford F-350 pickup truck. She assured me that, as I had suggested, she'd spent the afternoon going through the yellow pages calling every body shop in a fifty-mile radius to have them look out for the truck. The deputies had stopped six similar trucks since last night, but none of them had fresh damage or any indications of recent repairs.

"Okay," I told her, "but tell 'em don't let up. He's gone to ground with that damned truck, or somebody would've seen it. It's tough to keep secrets like that in these hills. Sooner or later, he's going to have to move it to get it repaired and erase the evidence. Let's everybody stay awake. I assume nobody's heard anything?"

"No, Lewis," Milly said. "I've had the boys pumping all they snitches and Dick Tracy wannabees and ain't nobody heard nobody talking about bein' in no wreck."

"Pierce." I sighed. "Nothing new on this butcher nut?"

Pierce looked embarrassed, like he thought he should have closed the case by now. "Naw, Lewis. Ain't nobody heard nothin' there, neither. I got Double-Parked querying the NLETS net for anybody who mighta had this creep before, but so far he ain't got shit. I got a man doin' a scene survey out at the Tucker place, but tell you the truth, I don't look for him to find nothing. This weirdo don't leave no tracks in the snow, Lewis; he's a phantom."

Double-Parked was our endearment for a local twelve-year-old named Park Soon Park, the delightful only son of a Korean immigrant widow who cooked for Lady Maude.

146

Double-Parked was the sort of computerphile every modern business had better know at least one of. He was a cop wannabee and a computer game freak who used to hang out around the dungeon. Two years ago, we discovered he could program, trouble-shoot, and fix our relatively primitive computer systems better, faster, and cheaper than the professional firms out of Roanoke. We kept him supplied with police shoulder patches for his collection, a scanner radio for his room, and gave him ride-alongs several times a month; in exchange, he was the resident computer wizard for the Hunter County Sheriff's Department. Without Double-Parked, we'd close down in a day.

I sighed again and threw a wadded telephone note into the crackling fire in the old stone fireplace in my office. "Damn," I mumbled. "Well. Y'all know what to do; just bear down and make sure everybody keeps doing it. If we keep the wires strung tight, then time is with us. Sooner or later, one of these creeps will slip up and leave us a sign. Let's don't miss it."

My intercom buzzed and I answered it.

"Line one, Sheriff," Cindy said.

"Boyce Calder?" I asked.

"No sir. I'm trying him, but State doesn't know where he is and his family doesn't, either. His car phone isn't answering. This guy on the phone says he's got some information, but he'll only give it to you."

"Thanks, Cindy. Keep trying Trooper Calder 'til you get him. Have the night clerk do the same, and if you find him, tell him to call me ASAP; give him my home phone if you need to."

I switched to the speakerphone and leaned back in the creaky old judge's chair. "Y'all listen to this," I told Milly and Pierce. "We might finally be getting a break." I punched the blinking button. "Sheriff Cody," I said.

"Uh, yeah, hey Sheriff Cody, it's me, Buster Walney? I was . . . well, I was out at Gordy Huckaby's last night, you know, when the . . . well, when Darlene Huckaby's little horse got . . . well, you know."

"Sure, Buster," I said amiably, "What can I do for you?"

"Well, Sheriff, you told us to tell you if we seen something, you know?"

"What did you see, Buster?"

"Well, Sheriff, I seen ole Roadkill today. This afternoon about two."

My eyes and Pierce's connected. "Yes. Are you sure that's who it was?"

"I'm goddamn positive, Sheriff. Folks see him—what, once a year? And he ain't somebody you forget. It was Roadkill, all right. Great big-assed nigger wearin' all buckskins, had that big ole compound bow and deer arrows slung on his back, and he was carryin' him somethin'—I don't know what. Gone in a flash like a damn cat. Look like that damn Bigfoot thing out in Alaska, you know?"

"California, I think," I said.

"Whatever. One o' them countries. Scary goddamn son of a bitch, just the same. I like to shit."

"Where'd you sight him, Buster?"

"Well, up there a-creepin' acrost that ole firebreak road up by old man Henry Tucker's place, you know?"

I sat forward, Pierce locked his eyes on the speaker phone, and Milly stopped chewing her gum in midchew.

"Good eyes, Buster. I appreciate your help," I answered. "What else did you see?" I suddenly realized I was holding my breath.

"Just one thang, Sheriff," Buster Walney twanged. "He had somethin' ain't no tellin' in that one hand, you know?"

"Yeah."

"Well, Sheriff, I damn well seen what he was a-carryin' in his other hand."

"Yes."

"He was carryin' a big ole knife!"

16

....

Party Time

"Hold *still*, Uncle Lewis!" Elizabeth scolded, standing on a chair before me and yanking the knot of my necktie. "I'll never get this straight if you don't hold still!"

"Has the concept of oxygen in mammals been run by you yet?"

"Oh hush, big baby, and be still!"

"Listen, you little hussy," I replied, "has it occurred to you that I've been dressing myself about five times longer than you?"

"Well, I would think you would have it right by now!" Elizabeth said, pulling at the collar of my shirt. "You can't go to Professor and Mrs. Whitley's looking like nobody cares how you dress!"

"How about self-esteem?" I asked. "Has that been broached yet?"

"Pooh. Who ironed your shirt? Me. Who was going to wear it looking like an elephant slept on it? You. Mrs. Whitley knows I'm . . . I'm *responsible* for you, Uncle Lewis!" Elizabeth smoothed the sides of my leather sport coat. "Now. That's better! Now you look like Keanu Reeves. Well, almost."

"Who the hell is—"

"He's like Harrison Ford, only not so fossilized. But you

look great! Thanks to me." She jumped down from the chair and admired her handiwork.

"Thank you," I said dryly.

She smiled. "You are bosh, Uncle Lewis. Righteously bosh, if I say so myself. Bosh is like 'cool,' only not so—"

"Fossilized. Yeah, yeah."

"Are you going to see Dr. Chu tonight?"

Hmmm. Arthur and Elizabeth had been talking. "Ah, well I don't know. I mean, yeah, I think she'll be there. Why?"

"Oooooh, just wondering. You think she's cute, Uncle Lewis?"

"Um. Yeah, she's very pretty. There's another woman who will be there, too, and she is Boone and Crockett Trophy beautiful, trust me."

Elizabeth's eyes brightened. "Really? Who is she?"

"A German woman, daughter of the German ambassador, in fact. She's some kind of famous equestri—"

"Karin Steiger?!" Elizabeth fairly screamed. "You're going to a party with *the* Karin Steiger?"

"Let me guess: you've heard of her."

"Heard of her! Uncle Lewis, Karin Steiger is the heiress apparent, the queen of darkness, the bosh rider of the century! She's in all the journals. She was even in *Sports Illustrated* last summer! She's the favorite to defeat the famous Dr. Eicher Dietrich in eventing at the olympics in Atlanta next year. Incredible! Wait here!" She sprang from the room and I could hear her little socked feet pounding down the hall to her room. Shortly, they pounded back. "Here's the *Sports Illustrated* with the article about her, Uncle Lewis. You've got to ask her to autograph it for me!"

"I'll see what I can do," I said, taking the magazine. Karin and her charger were on the cover, arching over a jump at some riding event. It was a closeup, and her concentration and staggering beauty were unmistakable.

"Come on!" Elizabeth squealed, dragging me by the arm. "Let's go show Polly how bosh you look!"

At the door to the veranda, Elizabeth told me I should be in by midnight because, "You're like, you know, not too young? And you gotta—uh—you work in the morning."

"You're a real ray of sunshine," I muttered, kissing her on

the top of her head. "Now carry your own little butt to bed. Tomorrow's Friday."

Elizabeth hugged me. "Last school day of the week!" she cried. "I'm gonna ride Dublin all weekend! G'night, Uncle Lewis!"

The Whitleys' daughter, Christine, opened the carved oak door to the enormous shake-roofed house at Laurel Ridge Farm. Pleasant music floated out on the warm air, and voices chattered within. "Sheriff Cody!" Christine said warmly, although we'd never been introduced. "My, you look—ooh! I've never seen you without your uniform."

I take as a definite compliment a genuine-sounding *ooh* from a pretty, sweet-smelling young woman dressed to kill, even if she is seventeen.

"Bosh, my . . . niece says," I mumbled, thinking I'd have Elizabeth sign off on what I wear more often. I looked through the broad cathedral foyer into a capacious, softly lit, and sunken living room beyond. About two dozen people in cocktail dress stood about or sat on beige leather sofas, socializing. In a corner, a formally dressed pianist and violinist sat by a polished black grand, playing their instruments. A woman in a gray maid's outfit snatched my overcoat out of my hand and disappeared.

"You look pretty damn fine yourself," I said, looking at tall, lithe Christine, who smiled. "Decided where you're going to school yet?"

"Are you kidding, Sheriff? Mom and Dad went to Princeton, my grandfather went to Princeton, and both my brothers are in Princeton."

"I get the picture. Good luck."

Christine laughed. "Thank you, Sheriff Cody. Esperanza will bring you a beer; you prefer it cold and Norwegian, I understand."

"How in the—"

Christine laughed again. "Dad always has one of us call around to find out what potential guests drink," she said. "He learned that in his fraternity at—"

"Princeton. Right. Amazing."

The doorbell rang again. I excused Christine and, discreetly, I hoped, I appreciated her retreat. Thank you, Mother Nature. Blessed indeed is the fruit of thy womb.

Karin Steiger had a disturbing way of materializing out of nowhere. I stepped toward the living room, still eyeing Christine Whitley, and bumped gently into the soft breasts of Karin, who must have seen me coming but chose not to move or put out a hand. I stepped back and apologized before I realized whom I'd run into.

It takes breeding and a certain female cunning to be able to dress with grace and good taste and yet remain thunderously sexy. Karin Steiger wore a sleeved tangerine dress of a rich knit fabric that is cruelly unforgiving of flaws in the figure yet which showcases a taut body such as Karin's like no other miracle of textile engineering. It was a proper look for the occasion, completely sophisticated and in taste, but one that ruled male eyes and which utterly commanded a man to consider what it would be like to touch the wearer.

Karin wore that plutonium-based perfume, which, together with the rest of her, was erotically incapacitating.

"She is a tasty peach now," Karin said, slipping her arm through mine and looking at Christine Whitley. "She is as pink and sweet as a fresh-water clam, but in ten years, she will be a cow like her mother. I believe *frumpy* is the American word."

"Bam, slam," I said, proceeding with Karin to the edge of the big, crowded room, breathing her in as deeply as I could without hyperventilating. The steady drone of conversation was softened by the subtle, expert talents of the pianist and violinist. "Youth, woman's eternal enemy!" I told Karin while I surveyed the room. "Thy jealousy scalds my cloistered ears." I glanced down to see Karin field that one with a wry smile. We stopped before descending the two steps to the sunken portion of the exquisitely appointed living room.

Karin absently scanned the room from our elevated position, her smile fading. "Women like that child fear women like me, Lewis, not vice versa, I assure you. I am never jealous, merely realistic." Karin's light German accent rolled the *r* in *realistic*. More softly, she added, "I know what it is like to be hated for possessing youth and beauty. I begrudge no woman hers."

I followed Karin's visual sweep of the room. She dropped her head on my shoulder affectionately, partly for my benefit, and partly, I suspected, to tweak the jealousies of the other men in the room, most of whom either stared or discreetly side-eyed us over their crystal wine goblets while talking. Karin Steiger was very difficult for a man not to look at. Some of the women, notably the elegantly dressed Arlette Sowers, glanced apprehensively at Karin, then looked to see who the man they were with was watching. Karin's fiancé, Dr. Dietrich, stared like an eagle at a rabbit that didn't have long to live.

A servant floated by and offered me an ice-coated stein. She prepared to pour me an equally icy bottle of Norwegian brew, but I told her I preferred it from the bottle.

"Regardless," Karin continued, her voice barely audible over the sound level in the broad room, "what would a wet little country filly like Miss Whitley want with an aged, impotent, dirt-poor, beer-swilling municipal servant like you?"

"Here, now! I don't swill, I gulp." I drew a delicious, frigid swallow of the Norwegian.

"Nonetheless, you are about as attractive to a baby like Christine as that repulsive Klaus, skulking in the corner over there."

"Moooooo," I said. Standing by a big elephant-ear plant, Klaus spotted me, gave me a tiger-eyed appraisal, and shifted his gaze. He had been a professional soldier in somebody's army, I was sure. He was in excellent physical shape and he had the hard eyes of a man who'd seen— perhaps caused—a lot of death.

"Speaking of cows . . ." Karin whispered. She stepped back and smiled sweetly at Helen Whitley, who was closing at twelve o'clock low.

"Sheriff Cody!" Helen said graciously, climbing the two steps from the living-room floor and extending her hand. "We're so pleased you could join us!"

"The pleasure is all mine, Mrs. Whitley. Thank you for the kind invitation. You look lovely. It's easy to see where your beautiful daughter gets her grace."

Helen's eyebrows rose. "Why, Sheriff Cody! Aren't you sweet? Flattery will get you everywhere. Please enjoy yourself, Sheriff." Helen glanced at Karin, adding in a minutely different tone, "I doubt that will be difficult. Later, I'll introduce you to anyone you haven't met." She smiled broadly at me and hurried away.

I turned back to Karin. She paused to take a glass of white wine from a tray offered by a servant, then stepped toward me, only to be deftly headed off at the pass by a stunning Julianne Chu, who came suddenly and deliberately between us. Karin pulled up short, firing a brittle look at Julianne's back.

Forget everything I ever said about Julianne Chu looking cute and wholesome. She had on an ankle-length silk Chinese gown with a high collar and a slit at one side that gave a glimpse of her thigh. Her dress was black but was embroidered in gold thread with pagodas and gracefully arching bridges over quiet, tree-draped ponds. It clung to curves on her that annihilated the innocent image forever. I wouldn't know diamond from glass, but I doubted her elaborate earrings were the latter. She seemed a foot taller than usual until my eyes finally got to her tiny but tall black patent-leather heels. Clark Kent never effected a change like that in any phone booth.

Julianne Chu turned her head slightly, as though wary of Karin Steiger behind her. Then she fixed me with her lovely eyes and smiled. "Good evening, Lewis," she said, cocking her head to one side. "I thought you'd appreciate some intelligent company . . . as a little diversion."

Karin collected herself, walked around Julianne, and sipped her wine. "A very little diversion at that," she said, giving Julianne another look that would have set off the smoke detector if we'd been standing any closer to it. Karin looked at me and her fury vanished, replaced instantly by that expression she must have known no man could ignore. I know what you're thinking; I was thinking it before you. "Lewis," Karin said pleasantly, "I will leave you . . . temporarily . . . to the dragon lady." Karin turned, giving me a calculated view of the fine curve that swooped down from her shoulder, into the slim recess at the small of her back, and then sweetly out over plump bottom. She eyed me over her shoulder with half-closed eyes. "Perhaps she can do your laundry." Karin flowed down the steps into the crowd. Eicher Dietrich hurried to her, and she handed him her empty glass before leaving him standing alone. He looked at me with an expression somewhere between hurt and rage.

"Karin the destroyer," Julianne said bitterly. "Even the man with the heart of ice succumbed to her charms. She bent Eicher like she bends everybody, and now that he loves her, she is using that love against him. She's breaking him down one thread of resolve at a time, so that by the time they get to Atlanta he won't have the will—let alone the skill—to defeat her. Karin stops at nothing to win. It's almost enough to make you feel sorry for Eicher, except for two reasons. He'd be just as ruthless if he didn't love her."

"The second reason?"

Julianne continued to eye Karin hotly. "And the second thing is, Eicher richly deserves his demise for the rotten way he did Meriah."

I saw Julianne look briefly at the rug, then up at me. She forced a smile, cementing my sudden realization that there was more than one unusually beautiful woman in the room.

I waited, but Julianne didn't seem inclined to elaborate on what Dietrich did to Meriah Reinholdt. There was one point of curiosity I could no longer pass on. "Julianne," I asked, "what the hell *is* it with you and Karin?"

"Nothing," she replied, lightly. "Shall we sample the hors d'oeuvres?" She moved away, but I placed a hand on her arm and she stopped. "Wait a minute," I said. "I asked you a question we both know 'nothing' doesn't answer."

Julianne Chu studied my eyes for a moment. "I . . . I had a husband two years ago, Lewis." She bit her upper lip and glanced at Karin, who was charming Professor Whitley on the other side of the room. "Then Karin had him, but only until she tired of him." Julianne looked back to me. "And one night not long thereafter, I found him with his brains all over the ceiling of our bedroom," she whispered, tightly. "Does that answer your question?"

17

•••••••

Tête-à-Tête

"Never ask a question," my grandmother used to say, "unless you're sure you want to hear the answer." Julianne's brutal reply answered some questions pretty succinctly, but it opened a worm can of new ones at the same time. Before I could recover, I heard Professor Whitley calling to me over the music and talk. I glanced at where he stood next to Karin; he was beckoning me to join him, ostensibly to meet a number of people near him I didn't know. I could bet, however, that his attention was directed to me by Karin, as a counterthrust at Julianne. I was getting a little nervous at becoming the football of the moment in what was apparently much more serious a game between Karin and Julianne than I had thought.

When I looked back to Julianne, she was gone.

I carried my beer to Mitch Whitley's little assemblage near Karin. Mitch introduced me around, mostly to fellow academicians and their spouses. I drank slowly, but the instant I drew off the final sip, another gray-suited ghost swished by and the bottle in my hand was suddenly cold and full again.

Soon, and inevitably, the conversation turned to traffic tickets. Noncop people don't seem to feel a policeman at a party is capable of discussing anything other than law enforcement, and the only exposure most nice folks have ever had to the cop world is the dreaded speeding citation. As always occured at such mixed gatherings, half the accounts by those present of their travails with The Man were humorous admissions that they had been wrong, and half were thinly veiled declarations of the officer's ignorance and incompetence. I'm used to it.

"Sheriff Cody!" Mitch Whitley said, taking me aside by the huge fireplace. "You're aware of the hunt I'm hosting this Sunday?"

"Yes, Professor," I answered. "You and Helen put on a remarkably generous charity event, I understand. Commendable."

"Thank you, Sheriff, but I was wondering if you'd like to join us?"

"I'll have a deputy here for the traffic, Professor. I doubt I'll have—"

"No, no," Mitch interrupted. "I don't mean officially! Helen and I were hoping you might attend the dinner on Saturday night, and ride with us on Sunday."

I suppressed a smile. I could see me now, gallomping about on Moose in that crowd of equestrian purists, even if I possessed a red coat and one of those little black-velvet helmets. "Thank you, Professor. I'm grateful for the invitation. I'd be pleased to have dinner with you Saturday, but as for the ride—"

"Lewis," Mitch said, "You do know what is meant by *hilltopping?*"

All I knew about fox hunting was what I'd learned listening to excited accounts by Elizabeth, who was being groomed for the fox-hunting crowd by Helen Whitley. I knew *hilltopping* meant those riders who did not ride with the main hunt but who would ride less formally in a separate group that observed, usually from hilltops—hence the term. "Sure," I told Mitch, seeing that I wasn't going to be able to get out of this charity hunt as neatly as I had hoped.

"Good! Then we'll expect to see you at the ride as well. You and your magnificent Belgian will be a high point of the weekend!"

"I'll bet." Now I did smile as I thought. Politically, attending the hunt was appropriate. Strategically, someone from my department needed to be present anyway. My being here would free a man for the road. "All right, thank you, Professor. We'll be there."

"Splendid!" Mitch crowed. "Excuse me, please." He hurried to meet a couple who had just arrived.

I craned around, searching for Julianne, but never saw her. Regrettably, I didn't see Karin, either.

I did see ole Klaus again, though, hulking by the large plant on the raised approach to the sunken living room. He stared at me without any posturing malice, only with a cold, fearless, carnivorous gaze. Presumably, he was still steamed because I took his gun away. I returned the stare calmly until he pursed his mouth ever so slightly and flicked his eyes away. Never let 'em stare you down in your own sandbox.

I also spotted Meriah Reinholdt, resplendent in her dignified dress, every hair in place. She was in a group, by the twelve-foot windows that looked out on the dark grounds of Laurel Ridge Farm, with Merlin and Arlette Sowers and Eicher Dietrich. Meriah saw me, her attack-smile flashed, and she hooked her head in a coy way, summoning me.

"Meriah," I said on arrival. To my surprise, she lifted her face to kiss me lightly on the cheek, casually, while acknowledging remarks vociferously being offered by Merlin Sowers. The gesture was at once subtle and endearing. She, too, bore a charming fragrance. Women. What wonders.

Merlin seemed nonplused by the sight, and promptly lost his train of thought. Arlette Sowers looked on through narrowed eyes. Both Merlin and Arlette appeared to be well into their cocktails, which was little wonder, since both had become substantially richer by the land deal Merlin closed with Meriah. I nodded at them.

Silver-haired Eicher Dietrich looked like the ranking executives from Mercedes-Benz I had seen in a TV news clip recently, visiting some new plant they'd opened in North Carolina: humorless, aloof, expensively suited and hard as trilonite. "Doctor," I said, engaging his eagle's gaze.

"Cody," he said without moving anything but his lips, as though begrudgingly acknowledging one of his lawn-care workers.

"Lewis!" Merlin said brightly. "I was just telling everyone what happened to you last year; that little girl killed by her father! It was a shootout like the OK Corral!"

Oh, thanks a lot, Merlin, I thought. I really needed to be reminded of poor Peggy Sloan at a party. "Merlin exaggerates my exploits," I said, trying to think of a quick way to change the subject.

"Doubtless," Eicher Dietrich observed, still eyeing me like I was a large hog.

"Nonsense," Meriah replied pleasantly, as though quite used to Dietrich's surly rudeness. "It must have been horrid. Why, Merlin says a state police officer was shot during the engagement, as well."

Boyce Calder. Fabulous. Why didn't we dredge up Vietnam, my divorce, and my daughter's death while we were on this lovely nostalgia bent? Then I'd have all the major distressing memories in my life condensed into one charming party topic. Maybe Julianne could deliver a treatise on the heart temperatures of psychopathically abused horses. Merlin, I ought to choke your bleary red eyes out.

"Hmmm," Eicher Dietrich said, coldly amused. "I suppose you—how is it you cow boys do? Did you shoot the gun out of his hand, and then ride your oversaddled cow horse into the sunset?" He stared at me over his wine, pleased with himself.

I'd had enough of Dietrich. It was time to take up the gauntlet. I leaned close to him and caught his eye. "Actually, since you ask," I said to him, "I shot the man seven times with a riot gun at close range. Then I beat his body with the shotgun until the stock broke. And then I beat him with the steel section until they pulled me away." I paused. Dietrich's left eye twitched minutely. "What else? Oh yeah. I didn't ride off into the sunset, Doctor, I collapsed weeping on the bloody corpse of a child I had promised to protect. It was an inglorious occasion, you can believe me."

That pretty much quelled the subject for all concerned. Even Dietrich had nothing to say, though he continued to hold my gaze.

"Cheers," I said to everyone, and I drew on my beer.

We were rescued from a pregnant silence by Karin Steiger, who strode toward us on long legs, her breasts

159

trembling minutely beneath the soft sweater dress, in time with the strike of her heels on the floor. At once, Merlin sucked in his ample gut and stood straighter, Arlette studied her drink with a slight sneer, Eicher Dietrich's hard glare suddenly softened, Meriah Reinholdt looked at the rug, and I felt a stir in my dick from mental flashes of hot kisses in a horse trailer. A pretty impressive effect for one woman, I thought. I was glad to see her, not only for that stunning female presence, but because she offered a diversion from the pall that had descended on the group.

Karin gave Eicher a cool glance. "Lewis," she said, "you remember my . . . fiancé, Eicher Dietrich?"

Dietrich hooked an arm about Karin's waist, probably to remind me whose woman he considered Karin to be.

"Some of us," Karin said, a trifle sweetly, subtly shifting to escape Dietrich's clutch, "used to be able to ride the wind, but are shortly to become has-beens."

"Big talk; little woman," Dietrich replied, smiling with his mouth but not his eyes. He averted his gaze and sipped his wine.

"And some, of course, weren't really that good in their exaggerated, fading prime," Karin purred, watching me.

Dr. Dietrich sucked a sharp breath through his nose. "Still others are so self-obsessed as to confuse dubious bedroom talents with equestrian greatness."

"Oh, please," Meriah said, moving deftly to separate me from Karin, "can't you two wait until Atlanta to tear each other's souls out? Lewis, walk with me to the deck. I need some fresh air." With that, we were headed for the sliding doors to the huge deck outside.

"I love them both," Meriah said as we stepped out into the biting November air. "But they are like most world-level competitors in any sport: they are ruthless and unable to separate their sport from the rest of their lives. That becomes tiring occasionally."

"Are they always as vicious with each other?" I asked.

Meriah released my arm and examined the stars in the clear sky. "Only since Karin ascended to fame in the eventing world. Eicher has been the undisputed master of eventing for twelve years now, dominating all the major competitions, including four Olympic games. He's still extraordinary, but he's lost his edge, if I must say. And Karin is brilliant. If I can keep her from riding her prize jumper to death, she will upstage Eicher at Atlanta, and I'm not sure he can handle that."

"They seem to hate each other," I observed.

Meriah smiled weakly at me. "Karin and Eicher are two of a kind: brilliant, driven, and passionate. Each is the only person in the world the other considers remotely their equal. It's colder than I thought out here. Shall we go inside?"

We stepped into the warm if noisy room near the two excellent musicians. "You seem to know a lot about them," I told Meriah.

Meriah stopped, looked at me briefly, then she looked across the room at Karin and Eicher, who seemed to be in heated discussion.

"Yes," Meriah whispered. "You could say that, Lewis." She looked up at me sadly. "Perhaps it's because Karin is my daughter, and before Eicher was Karin's lover . . . he was mine. Excuse me."

Meriah walked slowly away through the clusters of drinking and conversing partiers without looking back.

Damn, I thought, *horse people are strange folks.* I didn't know the half of it. Yet.

18

•••••••

Strange

I was going to have to reconsider my aftershave lotion. Two lovely women had dropped bombshells on me in Mitch Whitley's living room at Laurel Ridge Farm and then disappeared. I still couldn't see Julianne Chu among the guests, but then, there were many rooms in this big house.

Having dropped two beers on an empty stomach, I was now moved to find a bathroom. I picked my way through the throng to a hallway and followed it to what logically might have been a bath, but it was occupied. A home this opulent would of course have several, so I continued into the house farther from the noisy crowd in the big living room. The hall soon led to a dark library lined with bookshelves and what apparently was Mitch Whitley's collection of M. C. Escher's strange art. Mobius Curves of giant ants, staircases that led up until they were seen to lead down, fish that evolved into birds then back to fish in the same tableau. Escher, the engineer's artist.

Against one wall of the library was a massive antique roll-top desk that I noted only because it had four tiny television monitors built into it where the upper drawers might otherwise have been. I assumed they were security camera screens, although they were now dark.

I groped my way across the library and into still another hall. Halfway down on the left, I found the room, which,

given that I had to whiz like a racehorse, was now tanta-
mount to the Holy Grail. I felt for the light switch inside the
doorway. The lights illuminated a narrow room tastefully
wallpapered and carpeted, about twenty feet long with
ceiling-height shelving full of house-cleaning supplies on the
left. An avocado-colored washer-dryer set was recessed into
room-length walnut storage cabinetry on the right. On the
wall over the washer-dryer was another walnut storage
cabinet that extended the length of the room. Off the end of
the corridor on the right was a small half-bath, but it was
the correct half for my problem. As I made my way past the
appliances, I noticed both were operating, the dryer in a soft
whisper and the washer throbbing, rum-rum, rum-rum.
Both machines were very warm to the touch. A blue plastic
basket of laundry sat on the adjoining counter, containing,
among other items, I was moved to notice, pantyhose, bras,
and lacy bikini panties belonging, I presumed, to the
delectable Miss Whitley. I shrugged out of my suede coat
and dropped it on the oscillating washer.

I took care of stand-up business in the cramped little
bathroom and stepped into the corridor with the washer-
dryer. I was zipping up my pants when I caught a sweet
scent on the air; it dawned on me that I was no longer alone.

Surprise, surprise.

Karin Steiger was leaning against the wall by the door to
the hall, her arms crossed, that same look of amused disdain
on her face that I had seen earlier in the day. I searched for
the genes of Meriah Reinholdt but I saw none; Karin must
have taken her looks from her father, Ambassador Steiger.

What does a man say to a beautiful woman who follows
him to a remote cubby in a huge house during a party? I
wasn't sure, either, so I said nothing.

I rubbed my forehead and enjoyed the sight of that long,
slender body seductively painted in the soft tangerine
sweater dress, sleekly hosed legs rising from tall heels,
strawberry-blond hair waving onto her shoulders, and a
delicate neck descending into the loose turtle-neck of the
dress. Her lips were shiny, slippery red and formed a smile
unique to Karin that rose higher at one side of her mouth
than the other, revealing a flash of white teeth. Thank ya,
Jeeee-sus!

Sexy seems too trite a word when applied to such a sensually overpowering woman as Karin was that night, but sexy she was. She was more than a blessed body beautifully prepared, she was a woman who was clearly glad she was a woman and exulted in it. There is such a power in that bearing. Karin had mastered that power, and she knew it. I felt my mouth pull with my own sense of amused admiration.

Between the visual impact of her and the implications that were settling in, my heart rate began to increase. There remained no sound in the room but the rhythmic rum-rum, rum-rum of the hot washing machine.

The best defense is a good offense, I decided, so I moved toward her. At the same moment, she stepped toward me, and we met by the thrumming washer. I put my hands at her waist on the swell of her hips, and I bent to kiss her gently on the fine fur at the side of her neck beneath her ear. She placed her hands on my shoulders, tilted her head, and drew a deep breath. Her lifting breasts forced from the soft collar of the dress a current of warm air bearing the fragrances of a woman that sear the brain and heart en route to the cock.

I held her firmly but not entrappingly so, pulling the heat and smell of her into me, and I drew my lips lightly through the down on her neck. I could feel her breathing become deeper and faster, and she let go only the tiniest moan, but it was brutally erotic. I lifted my face to look at hers. Her mouth was parted slightly to facilitate her rapid breathing. Her tongue was wet and pink, and her breath was warm and clean on my face. Karin's eyes gave me caution, though, for there was something . . . strange . . . in them, and their message placed me on guard.

But, as if to dismiss my alarm, Karin slid her arms around my neck and began to kiss me, softly at first, in multiple places upon my mouth, tugging at my lower lip. Then her kisses grew more urgent, and she slipped her tongue into me, wriggling, alive. I grew hard against her belly and she hunched against me there. She fed upon me, consuming as much as kissing, and she raised a fever in me that begged for her.

Then, without warning, she pushed back and she slapped me so hard my left eye twitched and watered, and the left side of my face felt napalmed. It took me totally by surprise, but it shocked more than it hurt. And it hurt a lot. I gritted my teeth and throttled the reflex to strike back, lowering my fist. When I could focus again, I saw Karin standing before me, still breathing hard, her head back and a look of excited triumph on her face like a figure skater after a championship performance.

I stared at her, trying to make sense of the situation, a wasted effort. I picked up my coat from the washer, never taking my eyes from Karin's lest she move on me again. She did. She swatted the jacket from my hand and took another vicious cut at my face, but I saw this one coming and seized her wrist before impact. Karin cried out in frustration and yanked her arm, but I held it, squeezing hard until her fingers trembled. She squealed in anger again, kicked me in the leg, and bit my hand at her wrist, drawing blood and securing her prompt release. I had flash of a time when I let my hand get too close to a table saw.

Karin stepped back, still with that amused contempt in her expression. She raised the hem of her dress to her muscular rider's thighs, showing the tops of those stockings with lacy elastic bands to hold them up, then she came up with a knee and fired a lightning kick at my crotch. She was as fast as a snake, as might be expected of someone in superb condition, but then, I made a living locking up the fast and strong. I raised a knee and deflected the kick. The dress stayed bunched at her thighs.

Before she could regain her balance, I seized her by the shoulders and wrenched her about me; she flailed at my face with both hands, about half the shots connecting. I shoved her back from me, and she caught herself on the hot washing machine, which was still obliviously drumming away, rum-rum, rum-rum. I slowly backed away toward the open door to the hall, never taking my eyes from Karin. She looked about furiously, grabbed a plastic container of detergent from the shelves, and hurled it at me. I jerked my head to one side and the soap sailed into the hall, bouncing off the far wall.

Karin stood heaving. Her dress had descended to its correct position, but her expression now changed. The smile of amusement was gone and only the contempt remained. She snatched up my jacket from the floor and flung it at me with an angry cry, but I had begun to understand. I let the jacket hit me and slide to the floor.

Still watching Karin, I pulled the necktie from my collar before she might choke me to death with it. Then I kicked the door shut and I thumbed the lock button.

Now it was Karin's turn for surprise. Her eyes widened from their angry squint and her mouth opened. Instantly, she recovered, and the amusement was back. She charged.

I met her halfway. She swung at my face again, but I ducked inside and seized her by the waist. She slapped at the back of my head while I hoisted her into air and slammed her down onto the groaning washer-dryer, her head to my left. She thrashed and pulled at my hair, but I jerked loose from her. I turned to my right, pinned her with my hip, and yanked her dress and slip to her waist, exposing white panty briefs, curly strawberry-blond hairs fluffing from the sides of the crotch. I spread her legs and buried my face between her thighs for a little feeding of my own. I rooted at her through the damp, silky nylon and cotton. She was hot and wet and musky. And good.

In all men dwells the wolf, the Cherokee say.

She bucked and struck at my back, but shortly she grabbed my belt with her right hand and the overhead walnut cabinet with her left, and she lifted herself against my digging face, uttering a subdued sound that was half fury and half desperation, struggling to breathe.

I raised just long enough to rip her panties at one thigh and slide them partway down the other, then I sucked at her again. She was as pink and open as a mare in season.

Karin rolled her head from side to side, moaning while I tried hard to give her something to moan about. When I was so amped I thought I'd explode, I straightened, pulled her from the machines and sat her hard on the washer, her head thumping against the cabinet. She fought, but I pinned her to the cabinets with my shoulder, staying clear of those teeth, and I fumbled in the basket of laundry to my left, withdrawing a brown strand of pantyhose. Karin still struggled, but she was losing her strength. I caught one wrist, forced it upward against the brass pull-handle on the front of the cabinet above her. There I lashed it with one leg of the pantyhose. I drew the rest of the stout nylon beneath Karin's chin and through the brass handle on another cabinet. Finally, and with no small combat, I bound her other wrist to the second handle.

There is a time in any endeavor of import when it is too late to turn back.

Karin thrashed, but I had heaved hay bales and arrested men; I knew how to tie something so it stayed tied. I stood between her knees and wrenched the knit dress and slip above her breasts, finding she had done me the favor of a front-hook bra. I unhooked it and did myself the favor of savoring its contents. Her nipples were small and rigid, the latter of which I'm given to believe meant she was either excited or cold. Cold didn't seem an option.

Enough with the delicate foreplay. I kicked off my pants and underwear, seized Karin by the outsides of her thighs, and lunged long and deep into her. God, the sweetness of that slippery wet heat. I hammered at her, my knees thumping the door of the washer, her shoulders rocking the cabinet behind her, my balls and her bottom warmed by the hot, throbbing appliance. Rum-rum, rum-rum. She gripped me with her heels, and twisted her head to free it from the pantyhose, but she was held. I kissed her consumptively, daring her to bite me, but she only sucked at my tongue as though trying to swallow it.

I was close and I was not alone. I stroked into her feverishly, chasing the wave. She pulled one cabinet door open, which released her head and allowed her to put one arm about my neck. She was crying and reaching hard with her counterthrusts, reaching for me, for herself, clutching me to her with her freed arm and her heels.

I plunged my face against her neck and streamed within her, pounding the washer with my knees and driving her against the cabinetry. She cried out in gasps and threw her middle against me in a desperation of her own.

We held each other, fighting to breathe, our faces slippery against each other, semen running from her, down my balls, and over the front of the thrumming washer. Rum-rum, rum-rum.

When my knees were spent, I untied her wrists, and we slid to the floor, I on my back and she face down atop me, crying, kissing me softly, her tears dripping upon my face. I looked into her eyes and stroked the side of her beautiful face with my hand.

The machine drummed on. Rum-rum, rum-rum.

In a time, maybe five minutes, Karin rose, backed away, and looked at me as though she could not believe what she saw. There was a faint redness on her chin where her bonds had marked her.

She tugged the dress over her hips and straightened it. Her panties hung about one ankle; she removed them and balled the torn garment in her fist.

I stood, wary, watching her, not sure what she might do.

Karin backed to the door; there her eyes half closed, her lips parted slightly, and her slight, one-sided smile slowly consumed her face. She felt behind her for the doorknob, never taking her eyes from me, and she unlocked it. Karin threw her torn panties at me, and I caught them. She pulled the door open, slipped through it, and was gone.

I washed and dressed and examined myself in the mirror. My face still stung, I had a small abrasion on my lower lip, there was a slight scratch beneath my left ear, and the knuckle of my right hand was swollen and seeped blood from a tiny toothmark. My back was sore, I had strained a right arm muscle, I still breathed harder than normal, and I could barely stand.

The words of a jogging chant from my Army days came back to me: If a woman don't kill you, she'll drive you insane; my woman's got me down, but I sure do love the pain.

Jesus Jericho, I thought.

I was crossing the dark library en route back to the party when I could tell something was wrong. The music had stopped and a woman was wailing.

I trotted quickly down the hall to find Eicher Dietrich in the corner near the piano, kneeling over a prone and sobbing Arlette Sowers. All the guests were standing around, looking shocked and bewildered, except Merlin Sowers, who was pacing about, his head in his hands, moaning, "Oh my God, oh my God, oh my God . . ."

Meriah Reinholdt caught sight of me. Karin was nowhere to be seen.

"There you are, Sheriff!" Mitch Whitley called urgently, hurrying to me. "We've been looking everywhere for you! A . . . a terrible thing has happened!"

I was still trying to soak it all in when I saw Julianne Chu striding briskly toward me, carrying my overcoat and shrugging into her own. She stopped, eyed me briefly as though hurt, and she pitched me my coat.

"Let's go," she said softly, "Merlin Sowers's son just called, hysterical, evidently. He . . . just found Arlette's mare. Looks like our creature has hit again." Julianne turned for the door, continuing in a choked tone. "He's cut the head off this time."

19

• • • • • • • •

He'll Do It Again

The big silver Chevy slid through the cold winter night, flashes from the grill and dash strobes pulsing blue in the trees zipping past on either side. Julianne Chu had thrown her aluminum vet's case in the back seat, and she now rode grimly beside me.

I called the department on the radio to advise them where I was going. Cindy answered. "Ah, ten-four, Sheriff. We were about to call you at the number you left. Sheriff Four's already on the way—we got the call from the Sowers boy. Uh, Sheriff, Tim—Timmy Sowers—he sounds like he's real shook, screamin' on the phone and all."

"Okay, Cindy. Call Pierce. Tell him we're going to need to do the whole nine yards. Again."

"Ten-four, Sheriff Cody. Sergeant Stanford already called Captain Arroe. And Sheriff Cody? I asked Timmy Sowers if he saw anything. Said he saw a large black male subject armed with a knife run from the barn just before he found the . . . the ah . . . animal . . . situation. Sounds like Road-kill, Sheriff."

"Cindy, call the state prison camp and tell them we need a tracking dog fast. Add all available units to this call and give them the description. Tell the deputies nobody goes in those woods after Road—after the suspect without backup."

"Ten-four, sir."

I glanced at Julianne, who was looking at me. "You have the smell of her all over you," she said simply.

I couldn't think of any charming reply to that observation, so I concentrated on swiftly driving the unmarked cruiser toward the Sowers estate. We drew up fast behind a car on the road; I gave the electronic siren button a short push and shot by the car, noting it was a Dodge Caravan occupied by a young family.

"I'm not surprised," Julianne continued, as though tired. "When I couldn't find you or Karin, it wasn't hard to guess she had . . . gone after you already."

I swerved to miss a possum crossing the road. "Julianne," I said tersely, "what's the story with you and Karin? How long have you known her?" A string of cars appeared ahead in my lane. I switched the siren to yelp. Brake lights flashed and cars moved quickly to the shoulder. I flipped the siren off.

"About thirteen years," Julianne answered, staring out the passenger window at the trees and occasional houses sweeping by. "During veterinary school, I worked summers for Meriah at her stable near Washington. Karin came over from Germany in the summers to study under Meriah. She and I were only passing acquaintances until about three years ago, when Karin met Jonathan, my husband. I didn't know it then, but Karin consumes men for sport. She is deadly beautiful, and she knows the power she has over men. She delights in seizing men by their hearts . . . usually beginning with another part of their anatomy. She uses them until she uses them up, and then she discards them, broken . . . or worse. If she can take a man from the woman he is attached to, so much better the fun. She is utterly shameless."

"What happened to Jonathan?" I asked her, watching the road. "It's none of my business, but tell me anyway."

She said nothing for a moment, as the car rushed swiftly through the night. Then she sighed. "Karin came over in August that year. I was staying at Meriah's for a month, tending the horses that her students had brought in for training." Julianne drew a deep breath and expelled it slowly. "Jon was tall, a lean, beautiful man. He was a mountain climber, a tour-level tennis player, a leader in his medical school class . . . and a sweet lover. I never loved a man like I loved Jon Chu. She . . . Karin had no *need* for Jon, or even any *desire* for him, past a physical one! She certainly didn't love him. She just took him. For sport. For fun. Just to show she could do it. That's how she sustains her self-image. That's how she gets her kicks."

"So—" I began.

"She took him!" Julianne continued, raising her voice. "She seduced his body, and then she seduced his heart, and finally, his soul. Jon fell in love with her, and when Karin was convinced she possessed him at her leisure, she put him down cruelly. He wrote me a note saying he loved Karin and he was ashamed of what he had done to me . . . and then he put a shotgun barrel in his mouth and pulled the trigger with his toe. I found him and the note in my bedroom at Meriah's guest house."

I winced. I had worked a couple of shotgun suicides in my years as a D.C. cop. They were vividly messy, even for veteran cops. God knows what it must have been for Julianne Chu, so much in love, to have found her husband so disposed. I glanced quickly at her again, and saw her wipe a tear from her eye.

"When . . ." Julianne composed herself. "When I confronted Karin, she just said, 'He was weak.' She didn't even send flowers to his funeral. She just went home to Germany after the summer, like Jon never existed."

I mulled all this over for a time. "What keeps you . . . what connects you to Karin still?"

"Meriah Reinholdt's prominence in the horse world, I suppose. Karin is Meriah's star student, of course. And I have become something of an expert at equine lameness problems. I have worked on many of Meriah's most valuable horses over the years. Karin and I don't come into contact often. We're here now only because Meriah is buying the new land. She asked me to consider relocating here as well."

"I'm amazed you can stand to be around Karin, considering."

Julianne Chu pursed her round lips, staring. "I was crippled with bitterness for a long time, it's true. But my father saw what it was doing to me and he straightened me out; at least he taught me to live with it. He told me that to hate Karin like I did then was to hate a wolf for taking a lamb. Certainly one is prudent to protect one's lamb, Dad said, but to hate the wolf is pointless. It only does what it must, by its nature. To hate it only harms the soul of the hater. I wish I could say it was easy to embrace that philosophy, but eventually I did. Then, too, with maturity and experience, I have come to know that, in time, Karin will destroy herself. The truth is, now that I understand her, I pity her. Especially now." I could see from the corner of my eye that Julianne was looking at me. "She's trying to break Dr. Dietrich, and she has a hold on him because he loves her. He is strong and she hasn't broken him yet, but next summer at Atlanta she will break him. She will steal his thunder, she and Bitter Stone will win the gold in eventing, and Karin will reduce Eicher to the one thing he cannot stand to be, second best."

"You don't seem all broken up over that notion," I observed.

Julianne continued to stare out her side window. "It is impossible for me to feel any pity for Eicher. Just as Karin was viciously heartless to Jon, and to me, so was Eicher cruel to Meriah. Meriah loves Eicher, still. They were an item until two years ago, when Karin set her sights on Eicher, after she . . . disposed of Jon Chu. Then Eicher dropped Meriah as though she'd never existed. Meriah is a wonderful, generous, giving lady. She's been like a second mother to me, closer in some ways than my own. Eicher Dietrich crushed her. I'll despise him until his dying day for that. Karin will slay Eicher in Atlanta. Then she'll discard him like he discarded Meriah. And no, I'll shed no tears on that day."

"There's the drive to the Sowers estate," I said, cleverly. I slowed the cruiser, looking around as though I might see Roadkill Rudesill creeping about. I didn't.

One of my black deputies, Tom Bonner, was first on the scene. His marked cruiser sat in the circular drive before the Sowers home, its blue lights probing the darkness. The house was one of those see-how-rich-I-am Southern-ostentatious white-columned mansions. Sowers money went back a long way in Hunter County. With his hand on his holstered gun, Tom hurried through the front doors and down the steps to meet us as I slid to a stop.

"Hey, Sheriff," Tom said, peering around, "man, am I glad to see you. Way the Sowers boy be talkin', he seen *Roadkill,* man!"

"Where's Timmy?"

"Inside. He run down here to use the phone. He pretty fucked up, Sheriff. Excuse me, ma'am." Tom tipped his hat to Julianne Chu.

"Where's the horse, Tom?"

"Timmy say up at the barn. I ain't been up there yet. Cindy say you tole us wait for backup, since it's Roadkill an' all."

"You did the right thing, Tom. Wait here. The rest of the shift is responding, and State's supposed to send us a K-9. Keep everybody here until the dog shows up so we don't confuse the scent."

"Yes, sir."

Julianne and I hurried inside. Sixteen-year-old Timmy Sowers, all knees, elbows, and feet, sat on the sofa in one of those showcase living rooms that never gets lived in unless somebody dies or gets married. He held his head in his hands, sniffling, his shoulders shaking. When he looked up, he had terror written all over him.

"Hi, Tim," I said. "How're you doing, son?"

Timmy looked only briefly at the unexpected sight of a splendidly dressed woman carrying a metal case. "I . . . I . . . I—" He wept again.

"Take it slow, Timmy." I put my hand on his shoulder. "Tell me what happened."

The boy looked at me through red, swollen eyes. He trembled visibly and was clearly very frightened. "I heard the horses raisin' hell, Sheriff Cody! I was watching TV and there was a quiet spot in the sound, you know?" I nodded. "And I heard the horses raisin' hell, whinnying and kicking the stalls. I ran up to the barn 'cause Mom's old mare, Windsong, is in foal, you know? Mom told me to let her know right away if Windsong showed any trouble. And . . . and . . . oh God, Sheriff Cody! I turned on the lights and . . . and . . ." The boy fell back on the sofa, covered his face with his hands, and wept, out of control. Soon, he stomped his feet and began to scream. He had gone over the edge into hysteria. I would learn that, considering what he'd seen, it was a miracle he took so long to do so.

I knelt, avoiding the boy's huge flailing feet. I grasped him by the back of his neck and pulled his head to my shoulder, speaking into his ear. "Timmy, *listen* to me. Hush. Listen to me. I need your help here. I understand you saw somebody. Ssssh. Hush. Tell me what you saw, son."

Timmy Sowers sucked deep, fast breaths trying to calm himself. "I ran down to the barn, Sheriff Cody. I ran in the door on this end, and flipped on the main light switch. At the other end of the barn, running out, I saw him! I was so scared! I was *so* scared, Sheriff Cody! He was so big and he had a big knife in his hand and he was running fast, sort of crouched over, like a . . . like a *leopard* on National Geographic! He was carrying something under one arm. It was that . . . that crazy guy, you know? That Roadkill guy!"

"Have you ever seen Roadkill, Timmy? Before tonight?"

"Well, no, Sheriff, but I know who he is. Everybody's heard of him, the crazy, giant black dude that lives like a hermit and eats dead animals off the road like buzzards! This was him! Big, strong guy with long hair, carrying something . . . dark, under his arm! And a huge knife in his other hand!"

"Did you see his face?"

"Uh, no, he was running away into the dark."

"You're doing great, Timmy, you're a big help. What was he wearing?"

"I . . . I don't remember! It was brown . . . sort of brown. I don't remember! I was so sc-scared!"

"What was he carrying, Timmy? What was the dark thing under his arm?"

"I don't know! I don't know! I couldn't see! I was so scared!"

"I know, son," I said, patting the boy on the shoulder. "That's okay. You've done good."

Car headlights shone through the windows, along with arcing blue flashes. I left Julianne to comfort Timmy Sowers while I went outside. Pierce and another of my deputies, Hollis Beach, had arrived, but behind them were the

Cadillac Fleetwood of Merlin and Arlette Sowers and the silver Mercedes sedan of Mitch Whitley. Besides Mitch, the big Mercedes contained Eicher Dietrich, Karin, and Meriah Reinholdt. I wasn't happy to see the civilians, because they could only gum up the works.

In half an hour, the rest of my duty deputies and the corrections department K-9 unit arrived. It took some doing to keep Merlin and Arlette Sowers from going to the barn in the interim, but I convinced them that Timmy had left Julianne no doubt that the horse was dead. There was nothing to be gained by hurrying to the barn, and if we all went up there and started milling around, we could destroy the dog's ability to distinguish a scent. Arlette quickly busied herself with Timmy.

I caught Eicher Dietrich eyeing me with distinct malice. This guy just didn't tire.

The corrections dog handler climbing out of a dark-green Suburban was Mr. Cale Willis, a grizzled old ex-trapper who'd been tracking men in the Blue Ridge Mountains since the fifties. He wore denim coveralls, a Massey-Ferguson ball cap, and serious boots. On the end of a leash he restrained a goofy-looking bloodhound he called Old Bob.

I led a group composed of my people, Merlin Sowers, Julianne, Mr. Willis, and Old Bob to the stable fifty yards behind the Sowers home. Julianne Chu looked more than a little incongruous in her oriental gown and dress coat. I insisted everyone else remain at the house until the scene was secured. My deputies' flashlight beams swept erratically about the bordering woodline. I suspected they were thinking what I was thinking, that Roadkill Rudesill with his compound bow could put a broadhead arrow into the heart zone of a running deer at forty yards. He'd been seen doing it. On the way, I briefed Mr. Willis, who briefed Old Bob. "Here, Bob! Easy, Bob! Now *easy*, Bob!" Old Bob didn't feel very easy. Neither did I.

At the barn, Mr. Willis went ahead, with Old Bob tugging his leash, down the brightly lighted aisle to the only open stall door, while I held everyone back at the entrance, watching.

When Old Bob drew even with the open stall, he recoiled

visibly and growled. "Ho, Bob," Mr. Willis said soothingly, but then he, too, came to the door.

"Oh," Mr. Willis said, yanking on Old Bob's leash. "Oh." Then he sniffed sharply, exposed gritted teeth, and exclaimed, "Oh, good gawdamighty. Good gawdamighty." He staggered back against the opposite wall of the aisle. I thought for a moment he was having an attack; so did Julianne, and we both rushed to him. He was transfixed on what he saw in the stall. "Good gawdamighty, Sheriff Cody. I ain't never seen nothing like that. Never."

Julianne sucked a sudden breath and covered her mouth.

"Jeee-sus . . ." Pierce whispered.

Merlin Sowers was right behind me. He began to shriek like the woman in a cheap horror movie who has just confronted the monster. Tom Bonner grabbed Merlin's arm just before he went down.

I was rendered stone mute for a long moment. I wouldn't have thought the creature's savagery could gotten worse than the scene at Gordy Huckaby's barn, but I was wrong. Arlette Sowers's pregnant mare had been restrained with ropes, per the earlier incidents, but this time a bloody ax was imbedded hard into a six-by-six corner post. The horse's belly was gaped open, blue strings of its contents trailing from within. It got worse. The animal's head lay grotesquely propped, inverted, against the oak-planked wall of the stall, six feet from the other remains, the tongue extended, eyes white.

I recovered. "Tom!" I shouted over Merlin's howls. "You and Hollis get Merlin to the house and then get back up here. Move! Pierce, secure this scene; make sure nobody touches that ax until we can process it. Mr. Willis, take the dog that way to the end of the barn. The suspect was seen exiting there. See if you can get a track. Go! Get going! If you get a scent, yell at me. Don't track into those woods alone."

"You can goddamn well count on that, Sheriff," Mr. Willis mumbled, tugging Old Bob down the barn aisle.

Pierce and I stepped gingerly into the stall. The butcher had hobbled the rear feet of the poor horse again, this time with several strands of baling twine, which is usually laying around any horse barn. The head was what gave me the coldest chill. It lay several feet from the corpse, in a position that suggested it had been flung there.

It had to have weighed at least eighty pounds.

I heard the latches on Julianne's veterinary case snap. Shortly, she appeared in the doorway, carrying the tools of her profession. She wore those arm-length clear-plastic gloves again, and her dress was pulled up to her thighs and knotted. Pierce glanced at her shapely legs. I had a flash of Karin Steiger about to kick me where it hurts. Julianne stepped near the horse's hacked body and knelt in the pooled blood by the open belly.

I studied the ax without touching it. The steel single-bit head was clotted with body matter and the handle was smeared with blood. I could see nothing that looked like a fingerprint, and I wondered again if the butcher wore gloves. What worried me most about the ax was that it was sunk two full inches into a solid oak post, across the grain. Oak is an extremely dense wood and I have used an ax all my life. I knew the power it took to drive an ax that deep into oak.

Then I heard Old Bob yelping in shrill squawls of pain.

Pierce and I scrambled from the stall, Pierce drawing his pistol, both of us envisioning Old Bob with a broadhead shaft through him. We ran out into the dark stable grounds to see Mr. Willis shining his flashlight at the ground and Old Bob rolling in the dirt, pawing at his nose.

Mr. Willis hooked the flashlight under his arm and knelt by the writhing bloodhound. He wet his finger with his tongue and dabbed it into the dirt; then he sniffed what stuck to his finger. He flinched, squinted, and snorted.

"Shit!" Mr. Willis spat. "I knew it! Goddamn cayenne!"

"What?" I said, running up with Pierce.

"Pepper! Goddamn cayenne pepper! Same stuff they use in that new chemical mace that'll take out even a man on PCP. Son of a bitch has done throwed down cayenne pepper! Old Bob's got a snoot full of it; he ain't gonna smell nothin' fer hours!"

"Damn," Pierce said, holstering his gun. "So much for tracking Roadkill tonight."

"Oooooh! No! *Nooooo!*" Julianne Chu cried, from inside the stable, startling me and causing Pierce to spin about. We rushed back to the stall to find her still on her knees by the devastated horse. In her gloved hand, she held what appeared to me to be a strand of entrail trailing into the mare.

Julianne looked up at me through wide, scared eyes. Eyes that knew. "I know what he was carrying, Lewis! I *know* what he was carrying!" she all but screamed.

I looked again, and then I knew, too. What Julianne held wasn't gut, it was umbilical cord.

"It was the *fetus*, Lewisssss!" Julianne cried, on the edge of her control. "The crazy bastard took the foal fetus with him!"

A new voice sounded from the doorway. "Whaaat!?"

I looked up to see Pete Floyd, the newspaper editor, standing aghast, holding both sides of the stall door for support.

"He cut the—?" Pete gasped and swallowed like a bass flopping in the bottom of a boat. "He . . . took the fe . . . fetus? Roadkill took the horse *fetus? To eat* it? He took—"

"Pete," I said.

"Oh my God," Pete mumbled, and then he fled.

Fabulous, I thought, my hands on my hips. *Just fucking fabulous.*

179

20
....

Amazing Grace

The stately old stone Christianburg Methodist Church was surrounded for blocks by scores of marked and unmarked cruisers of the county and town police forces of southwest Virginia. Many VSP cruisers were also present. I parked the silver Chevrolet unmarked in a spot reserved for me by a young, dress-uniformed Virginia state trooper. As we got out of the car, I noted a television relay van parked nearby with its antenna telescoped forty feet above it. Sergeant Milly Stanford and I, both in our own dress uniforms of tan, were directed to the church by still other troopers choreographing the funeral of Cathy and Stevie Calder.

Inside there were a hundred cops in formal uniform seated in the pews to one side of the church, and as many civilians seated on the other. The state police commander, Colonel Able Clair, with his wife and a delegation of his officers, sat near the front, behind Boyce Calder's weeping mother and stoic father. At the other side of the chapel were people I took to be Cathy's parents, and other relatives.

Only one pertinent individual was missing. Corporal Boyce Calder hadn't been heard from.

A powder-gray casket rested on a stand before the altar, closed. Next to it was a pearl-white coffin about three feet long. There is nothing on earth so obscene as a three-foot-long casket. Flowers flooded the choir bay.

I hate funerals. I hate the goddamned organ music, the cloying smell of the flowers, and the black mood. I especially hate police and police-family funerals, though I know it is wise to make a parade of such occasions, to remind the public of the danger its police officers face in its behalf, and in this case, to highlight the tragic scourge of drunk driving.

The black-robed preacher did his thing. A girl about Cathy's age stood in the loft and sang "Forever Young" while mothers wept and fathers hung heads and police officers bitterly vowed to get even any way they could with every drunk driver they could find.

Two splendidly uniformed honor guards of Virginia State Police troopers marched slowly down the aisle and bore the caskets to the cemetery in a glade beneath tall pines behind the church. There, under a small tent, they were lowered. On a rise several yards away, a kilted piper began "Amazing Grace" in the slow, mournful, exquisite strains possible only with a bagpipe.

And still there was no trace of Boyce Calder.

Before leaving Christiansburg, Milly and I went by a formal wear place and I rented a tuxedo to wear to the Whitleys' charity hunt dinner dance. We arrived at the dungeon an hour later to learn that all hell had broken loose.

"Jesus, Lewis, am I glad to see you!" Pierce said as we walked in to the old courtroom that was now our administrative area. "Newspaper people—even TV people—from Roanoke and Richmond been calling here all morning. Looks like Pete Floyd put the horse-killer story out statewide. Look at this!" He shoved a copy of the *Roanoke Times* at me. A mercifully small blurb at a lower corner of the front page was headed: HORSE BUTCHER STALKS HUNTER COUNTY.

Pierce continued frantically. "Merlin Sowers has been screamin' for you, Lewis. Newspaper people been calling for you, wanting a statement, and the Roanoke TV people asked for directions on how to get up here. Damn, Lewis, they talk like they want to make a feature for the evening news out of this."

"Lovely," I said. Milly hurried to her desk.

"That ain't the half of it, Lewis. Another horse turned up slaughtered this morning."

"Damn! This guy is tearing us *up!* Where this time?"

"Hollis and Tom are out there now doing the work on it. It's one of Merle Pflegar's prize Plantation Walking Horses, and Lewis, he is hot. Says that horse was worth thirty thousand bucks. Talking about suing the county. Says he hears it's Roadkill and he demands we catch him before he kills any more animals."

"A mare, I assume?"

"You bet."

"Any hard evidence?"

"Hollis and Tom ain't found shit, but one of Merle's stablehands was comin' to work and he seen something. Says he seen a big man in dark clothing at the far range of his headlights, crossin' the road near the Pflegar place. Just seen him for a second."

"Roadkill?"

"It was a short sighting a long way off, and he ain't never seen Roadkill before, so he ain't sure, but the description fits. Who the hell else *could* it 'a' been?"

I took a deep breath, strolling toward my office with Pierce on my heels. "Well, that's all just fucking peachy keen, Pierce. You got any other rosy little tidbits for me?"

"Well, yeah, Lewis, since you ask. Boyce Calder surfaced."

"At least he's alive. That's good news."

"Not exactly. You know Phillip Yarmouth?"

"Railroad engineer? Lives out on Trace Creek somewhere?"

"That's him. Well, his boy Clark wrecked Phillip's old pickup truck the same night the Calders were killed. The kid was drunk and was drag racing with some of his little maggot buddies. Lost it and hit a tree. He knew old man Yarmouth would beat the bejesus out of him, so he took it to Bealor's Garage to get it fixed. Bealor had the word on damaged pickup trucks, and he notified us. Double-Parked put it out on the computer, and somehow Boyce got wind of it. He went out to the Yarmouth place this morning and abducted Clark Yarmouth at gunpoint."

"Oh shit."

"Phillip says the kid's okay now. Boyce apparently dragged him out, tied one of his legs to a fencepost, the other to his car, and told him if he didn't make words about how the truck got damaged, he was gonna drive off and forget him."

"Oh shit."

"Yeah! Thank Christ Clark Yarmouth somehow convinced Boyce to call his little drag racing buddy, Cootie Hopkins, and confirm the story. He untied Clark and left him lying there."

"Do we know where Boyce is now?" I asked.

"Hell no. But of course Phillip Yarmouth cain't decide who he wants to kill first, Clark, Boyce, or us."

"Unbelievable. I don't suppose a B-1 bomber loaded with live nuclear devices crashed into the courthouse, did it?"

Pierce sighed. "Not yet."

"Swell. So we still don't know where Boyce Calder is, and we still don't have any idea who scrubbed his wife and baby, right?"

"Well, at least we know Roadkill has been doing the horses."

I sighed now. "Yeah. It sure sounds like it. At the least, I've got to pull him in for questioning, maybe a lineup."

"You? What do you mean you, Lewis? Let's get dogs and men and let's go take him."

"No. I'll get him."

"Lewis, the guy is as big as I am! And he's a lot crazier. He cuts baby horses out of their mothers and carries them off to eat 'em, for Christ's sake! This is nobody to fuck around with."

"If we track him with dogs and people, Pierce, he'll panic."

"Gee, that's sad, Lewis. I'll give him a 30.06 sedative. He'll calm down."

"No, that's not the smart move. Not yet, anyway. By the time we run him to ground, he'll have killed somebody—maybe several somebodies—and we'll probably have to kill him to take him."

"Shit happens."

"Not yet. I have an idea I want to try first."

"It'd better be good, Lewis, or you'll be the next body that gets cut high, wide, and deep."

I went into my office and changed into my duty uniform. I shrugged into a brown military sweater and pinned my badge to the holder sewn to its left front.

On my desk was a note that said, Merlin Sowers—07:10, Merlin Sowers—08:30, Merlin Sowers—10:05, Merlin Sowers—11:22. I dialed Merlin's office but was told he was not in for the day. I dialed his home and Timmy Sowers answered.

"Hey, Tim," I said, "how're you feeling?"

"Hey, Sheriff. It's been a rough night, sir. Dad and me tried to keep Mom from finding out about the . . . you know, what he did to the . . . foal and all, but that doctor with the German name, you know?"

"Dietrich."

"Yeah, him! He told Mom what happened and she's been nuts, Sheriff Cody. She was up crying all night. Mom's scared as hell; Dad's been yelling all night. I . . . I'm scared too, Sheriff Cody. Will he come back?"

"I doubt it, Tim. So far he hasn't hit the same place twice that I know of."

"Sheriff, that guy Dietrich, he's been trying to get Dad to make trouble for you. He says you knew it was Roadkill two days ago and if you'd got him then . . . then this wouldn'ta happened. Dad's pretty upset."

"We're all upset, Tim. You hang in there. Look after your mother. Better times are coming."

"Thanks, Sheriff. Listen, you better be careful be—"

I heard Merlin's voice in the background. "Who the hell is that, Timmy? Is that the sheriff? It goddamn well better be! Gimme that phone. Hello!"

"Hello, Merlin." Merlin was microdelighted.

"Well! It's about time, Lewis! I'm glad you could find some time in your busy schedule to—"

"I had to attend the Calder funerals, Merlin. You know that."

"I'll tell you what I know, goddamnit! I know that if you'd arrested Roadkill two days ago when you first knew he did these awful horse killings, I wouldn't be out a twenty-thousand-dollar hunter-jumper and a valuable foal, and my wife wouldn't be keeping me up all night squawling! *That's* what I know!"

"We're working on it, Merlin. Merle Pflegar also lost a horse sometime this morning."

"Jesus Christ, Lewis! What's that make it now? Five?"

"Four."

"Well, that's four too many! You got to stop this guy, Lewis, and I mean right now! That Dr. Dietrich is on the phone with the press people in Roanoke, making this out to be a major disaster, and you out to be an incompetent boob insensitive to animal rights and the equestrian community. He's a big name in the horse world, Lewis, and he's laying it on thick, and let me tell you something else! I have only a verbal commitment from Meriah Reinholdt on the land deal. She hasn't signed anything yet, and Dietrich knows it! He's trying his damnedest to talk her out of it. If this horse killing goes on, the whole damn thing could fall through! You got to get Roadkill *now*, Lewis! Now! I know he's a Vietnam vet and you are, too, and all that bullshit. But you shoulda locked him up years ago! Then none a this would've happened!"

"Being strange isn't illegal, Merlin. No evidence has ever linked Roadkill to any crime. I couldn't just lock up——"

Merlin's voice got shrill. "I don't want to hear that bullshit, Lewis! He's a nut! He skulks about these mountains like the creature from the Black Lagoon, and he eats dead animals run over in the goddamn road! Now he's cutting expensive foals out of the goddamn mares to carry 'em off and eat *them!* The man is obviously a dangerous freak! Any sheriff with any goddamn sense would've found something to arrest him for years ago! Now you get him, Lewis! You get the crazy son of a bitch *now!* You hear me? You get him now, before he kills another horse and *fucks* my whole land deal!"

I held the phone back from my ear, after a painful bang. When I listened again, there was only a dial tone.

"Oooookay," I mumbled to myself, setting the phone down. "That just about covers that."

* * *

"Milly," I growled, stalking through the booking room on my way to the door, donning my Stetson and carrying my brown bomber jacket.

Milly looked at me. Her brows knitted and her lips pursed. "Where you goin'?" she asked suspiciously.

"If you haven't heard from me by ten in the morning, tell Pierce my idea didn't work out. He'll know what to do."

Milly frowned and waddled quickly across the room to block my exit. "Hold it, white boy. I ast you where you was goin'!"

I smiled at her in spite of my mood. "I'm going after Roadkill."

"Whaaat?!" Milly howled, following me out to my car, waving her plump arms, blowing puffs of vapor in the air. "By you*self?* Is you sick in the head? Lemme git you some backup right—"

"Milly," I sighed. "I've been all through this with Pierce. Trust me, okay?"

"Sheeeit. Las' time you tole me that, you like to near got youself beat to death!"

"Thanks for the worry, Milly. I'll see you in the morning."

"Worry!" I heard her yelling as I drove out of the dungeon parking lot. "Hell, I ain't worried! Why I'm gonna worry about you gettin' you damn fool white ass whupped? Go *on* after that crazy niggah! What I care? You better be back by ten in the mornin'! You hear me, Lewis Cody?"

"I love you too, Sweetums!" I called as I buzzed the window up.

One thing nagged at me. Milly was right. The last time I told her I didn't need backup, I almost got killed.

21
• • • • • • • •
Roadkill

At Mountain Harbor, I had Polly pack me some food, and I changed into my hunting boots. I dragged out my old aluminum-frame backpack and stuffed it with matches, a huge police flashlight with fresh batteries, a down vest, and a serious sleeping bag.

Elizabeth had come in from school and I sent her to Arthur's tool shed for a small plumb ax. When she brought it back, she said, "Well, I don't care what you say, Uncle Lewis, I still think it's a funny time of year to go camping." Elizabeth looked at me with that same gimlet-eyed frown I'd just seen on Milly Stanford. What is it about women that they always know when you're woofing them?

I heaved the gear and an excited Gruesome into the cruiser and drove east for that part of Hunter County that climbs the west face of the Blue Ridge to border national park territory about halfway up. The sun lay orange just above the distant Appalachians behind me.

As far as I knew, Roadkill's real name was Garvin Rudesill. He was born in a little shack in east Hunter, what used to be called Niggertown, back when the courthouse had three restrooms: men, women, and "colored." When he was fifteen, he lied about his age and joined the Army. Birth records were frequently vague in those years, especially in mountain Virginia.

Garvin Rudesill was huge but lean and fast. Shortly after arriving in the Republic of South Vietnam, he became what was respectfully called a *lurp,* an expression derived from LRP, meaning long-range patrol team. Seven-man lurp teams were transported by helicopter to the boonies, sometimes even into Cambodia and Laos, usually at night. They attached themselves like deadly leeches to large North Vietnamese Army units and followed them, reporting their movements in radio transmissions that were almost always whispered, so close were the lurps to the enemy. Sometimes they directed air and artillery strikes against their hosts. They remained so engaged until they ran short of food and radio batteries, which was commonly a week or more, or until they were discovered, when they had to fight their way to a landing zone for emergency extraction.

Lurp patrols were excruciatingly tough, dangerous expeditions that demanded only the very best professional jungle soldiers. Among other skills, a lurp was occasionally required to kill an NVA sentry with a knife or wire garrote without making a sound. Garvin Rudesill excelled as a lurp for two tours in Vietnam, earning the Silver Star and four—count 'em—four Purple Hearts.

He spent his postwar Army years in clandestine endeavors not fully explained in the records the Army released to me after I was elected sheriff. It was clear he was in the desert when the Iranian hostage rescue went sour, and he was in Beirut for a time.

Garvin surfaced in Hunter County in the late eighties to become a spooky mountain legend in his own time. He was one of many military veterans who had spent years in a deadly craft with brave compatriots of loyalty and courage, who was unable to reconcile his life with the seemingly petty values of domestic America. A man who had been forged in the brotherhood of combat found ridiculously trivial the racial obsessions of both sides of the interminable black-white squabble. He who had lived by a code of honor found himself unable to tolerate a society that was increasingly forgetting the concept. Like many of his brothers of the experience and time, Garvin Rudesill took to the woods, where he could as nearly as possible live the life he needed to live.

One night, a local schoolteacher named Bess Warren, then about fifty, was driving home in the rain on County 12. She was squinting through flapping washer blades when a nicely antlered buck leaped in front of her pickup truck. She slammed on her brakes, but the truck crashed into the deer anyway. The buck broke a truck headlight and shattered the windshield before flying over the roof onto the dark road behind. Bess Warren slid her truck to a stop just shy of the ditch, with a white-knuckled death grip on the steering wheel, eyes bugged, mouth open, gasping, on the verge of tears. It was maybe three solid minutes before she could collect herself. Bess considered deer to be among God's gentler and thus more precious creatures, and she abhorred the idea of leaving one maimed in the road on a dark, stormy night.

She decided she would walk back up the road and locate the deer. If it was dead, she would call County Roads to collect it. If it was still alive, she would go for her husband, Dave, who would return and put it out of its misery.

On foot, Bess Warren trudged back up the watery road, while lightning flashed, thunder bashed, rain poured. When she reached the spot where she thought the deer might be, she stopped, looking around at empty, rain-slick pavement. Then, out of the ditch, not ten feet from her, an enormous dark creature stood upright with a throat-cut, bleeding, hundred-ten-pound deer flopped over its shoulder. Lightning bleached the scene brilliantly and she saw the creature turn toward her. All she would be able to tell authorities later was that he was "eight feet tall and black as Othello, with hair like Medusa and eyes like Thor!" Bess Warren taught drama, as well as algebra, at Hunter County High School.

When Garvin Rudesill, carrying an adult deer, crossed a twelve-foot road in three strides and vaulted a split-rail fence to disappear into the woods, Bess Warren's reaction had not been so eloquent. She stood in the dark rain in the middle of County 12, trembling, screaming against the thunder, and urinating down her legs.

The legend was born. By the time Bess Warren's horror

story passed its five hundredth retelling, Garvin Rudesill had become a monster ghoul who fed on squashed animal corpses rotting on the roads of Hunter County. It didn't take much creativity to assign him the nom de guerre he would forever be known by.

Not long after the Bess Warren episode, a girl of sixteen named Cleta Hawkins was riding her bicycle home from school when she struck a patch of loose gravel and crashed. Bike helmets were not exactly the rage in Hunter County then. Cleta Hawkins struck her head on the pavement when she went down and was temporarily knocked cold as a divorce lawyer. The real problem was that Cleta had come to rest in the middle of a country road, just over a sharp rise. Anyone topping the rise in a vehicle could not avoid running over her, and anyone viewing the scene would have found this hazard obvious. Garvin Rudesill heard the crash from his vantage in the woods bordering the road, and he did see the hazard.

Garvin had worked on many a shot-up soldier and, after checking Cleta's pulse and breathing, he determined she was relatively unharmed, save for a few abrasions. But clearly she could not safely lie in the road until she regained her senses. So Garvin set down his powerful compound bow with its attached rack of deer arrows, and he picked up Cleta Hawkins in his arms. He was about to deposit her next to her bike, on soft moss beneath a tree, when Cleta came to. She took one look at the bearded and scarred black face and voluminous dreadlocks of the buckskin-clad giant carrying her, and she put Bess Warren's screams to shame. Cleta had been taught all her young life that "niggers," among their other undesirable traits, lived to "do ugly things" to sweet young country white girls. Beauty and the beast was not a theme that occurred to Cleta Hawkins.

Meanwhile, back at the mobile home, Cleta had been missed by her mother, who, like most mothers, closely monitored the expected arrival times of her tender daughter. Mrs. Hawkins was driving down the road she expected to find Cleta on when she crested that very rise just in time to see "Roadkill" gently place the hysterical Cleta Hawkins on her feet. Cleta squawled and ran, sobbing, Mrs. Hawkins screeched to the top of her lungs, and the hapless Garvin Rudesill melted into the woods.

Predictably, accounts of this event quickly decayed into a brutal assault and rape attempt upon a lily of mountain maidenhood by a carrion-eating monster nigger. There hadn't been such a call to arms in Hunter County since carpetbaggers had made the mistake of thinking there were defeated yokels in these mountains to be exploited out of their money and daughters.

At the time, I was still a deputy, one of several responding on the "rape" call. From my car on a nearby dirt road, I watched a formidable platoon of farmers, all armed to the teeth, trailing behind a dozen yelping hounds. They were crossing Emmitt Cutter's farm, hot on the trail of something as yet unseen. My boss of the time, the corrupt former sheriff, Oscar Wheeler, rolled up in his cruiser, mouthing a soggy cigar with wet lips, and he observed the men and dogs in the distance. He chuckled and exhaled a cloud of blue smoke, his elbow out the window.

"Hear 'em hounds?" Wheeler said. "They on that nigger! They on his track!" I listened to the dogs baying. Wheeler was right.

I was disturbed. I had confronted plenty of mobs as a D.C. cop in the early seventies and, regardless of the merit of their cause, they were all ugly. People, like dogs, get excited when in packs, and they behave with a mindless viciousness no one of them would consider independently. I had never seen this Roadkill guy, but at least until he had a trial, he deserved better than being shot to hell by enraged mountain men and torn to ribbons by slavering hounds. Or vice versa.

I wiped sweat from my lip. "If that bunch gets him before we do, they'll kill him, Oscar," I said.

Wheeler cackled, watching the hounds and rifle-toting men run. "Yeah," he said. "Ain't that a fuckin' shame?" He was still cackling as he drove away toward town.

I could see that the tracking party was now climbing Emmitt Cutter's high pasture toward the wooded mountain above it. I knew the gravel road from which I observed the chase wound around the hollow and cut through the woods above the pack. I stood on the big-block Plymouth and blew down the road.

High up the mountainside, I caught sight of a dark figure limping across the road ahead, leaning on some sort of bent stick. I skidded to a halt in a cloud of gravel dust, and bailed out with my shotgun. I found blood trails in the dust and a rip of tanned deerhide caught on the rusty barbed wire bordering the narrow road. I climbed the fence and went only about thirty feet into the woods before I almost fell over Garvin Rudesill. I grunted and jumped as though I were about to step on a snake, and I drew down on him with the shotgun. Over my sights I saw a huge, sweat-glistened, bearded black man wearing hand-stitched deerhide pants, shirt, and one moccasin. His hair was woven into shoulder-length dreadlocks. He had a large knife that he held out at me defensively, but his bow was broken from being pressed into duty as a crutch. The long Fiberglas arrows had been abandoned. Garvin was heaving desperately for breath, and his face was distorted with pain because his left ankle was swollen like a ripe eggplant. He'd lost the moccasin from the injured foot and the foot was sliced, bleeding, and caked with dust.

An awkward pause ensued while I collected myself and Garvin realized I wasn't going to kill him out of hand.

"I wasn't trying to hurt the child!" Garvin groaned through gritted teeth.

"Drop the knife," I said, sighting down the shotgun, "or you're one dead son of a bitch." I could hear baying hounds grow nearer.

"I never tried to hurt the girl, man, I swear!"

"Last call on the knife, mister. Drop it or you're fertilizer."

Garvin let the knife fall from his hand. "Ooooh, Lord!" he groaned. "Ankle's broke bad. God, it hurts!"

I stepped near, still holding the shotgun on him, and I kicked the knife away. I was confused. I had the "rapist," but my instincts told me something wasn't kosher. Further, if all those dogs and men found us, I knew I probably couldn't keep them from taking Garvin from me, given what they believed about him. They were an armed mob of Southern men avenging a perceived threat and, worse, an insult, to their daughters by a "deranged nigger." They'd take him, and they'd kill him, and if I obstructed their "justice," they might well kill me, too.

The baying of the dogs grew louder: aaaroooo! aaaroooo! Garvin's eyes widened and turned toward the sound.

"Listen, man!" Garvin hissed, his jaw trembling from the pain of his purple ankle. "That child wrecked her bike and I found her in the road! I was only tryin' to set her off the road before she got run over, I swear to God. Arrest me . . . or shoot me, man. But do somethin' 'fore them 'necks and their hounds get me. That ain't no way for a man to die!"

I glanced toward the hounds, still out of sight down the mountain, and I made a fast decision. "Damn!" I spat, angrily, hoping I wasn't making a big mistake. "Get on your feet, quick!"

"What? Ankle's broke, man! I cain't walk."

I lowered the shotgun and extended my free hand to Garvin. "You better do the best you can, King Kong. You're too damn big for me to carry, and if we stay here, we're both in a lot of shit."

Garvin's Rudesill's big hand closed around my wrist.

I thought we'd never get Garvin back over the fence and stuffed into the back floor of my car, but finally we did, and the old Plymouth rocketed down the mountain road as the first of the hounds were coming out of the woods in the dust behind us.

It was after dark by the time I helped Garvin stagger into the woodsmoke-scented old farm home on Bram's Ridge, which my grandfather left me, years prior. In the living room, I sat exhausted in Grampa's overstuffed chair with the shotgun placed on the armrests in front of me. Across the room on the equally worn sofa, Garvin Rudesill lay passed out from his agony, breathing in short gasps, while I tried to figure out what to do with him. Beside me, Gruesome growled suspiciously at Garvin.

Jesus, I thought, *now what the hell am I going to do? If Wheeler finds out I spoiled the vigilante party, he'll fire me, and he'll probably arrange for Rudesill to die "resisting arrest."* Exhausted, I was still mulling all this over when I fell smack asleep.

About one A.M., I jerked awake and seized the shotgun.

The couch was bloodstained, but it was empty like the rest of the house. In the kitchen, I could see Garvin had poured Gruesome a pile of enough dog food to feed a kennel for a week. "Some goddamn guard dog you are!" I groused. He looked up, blissfully crunching away, not terribly concerned about the escape of his new buddy, Garvin Rudesill. In the front hall, I noted that my grandfather's stout hickory cane, with the deer-antler handle bearing his initials, was missing from the umbrella stand by the door. Outside, there was nothing but darkness and crickets.

Two weeks, in which I declined to mention apprehending and then losing the infamous Roadkill, went by. During that time, the county attorney investigated the incident and determined that no evidence existed to suggest, let alone prove, that Garvin Rudesill had possessed any intent to do harm to Cleta Hawkins. The hillfolk were unconvinced and continued to peer warily at the woods at night like Irishmen watching the foggy moors for a werewolf, but officially the matter was dismissed.

One dark night three months later, in my grandfather's bedroom, I came awake to Gruesome's low growl, and I heard the weathered old gray planks of the back porch creaking. I crept downstairs in my underwear with my shotgun, but could see nothing behind the house through the wavy glass of the kitchen window. When I turned on the back-porch light, I looked down to find my grandfather's hickory cane, clean and undamaged. Beneath the cane, neatly folded, lay a pair of deerskin riding chaps of the most exquisite workmanship I had ever seen. They were new, but they had never seen a factory. The tanned leather was finely stitched with leather thong, and the legs were secured at the sides with flap-covered buttons hand-carved from deer antler. The chaps fit me perfectly.

Now, many years later, I was on my way to apprehend Garvin Rudesill again. If I was lucky.

I drove as far up an old jeep trail as the Chevy could reasonably climb, and stashed the car in the trees. I humped into the backpack, and Gruesome and I started up the west face of the Blue Ridge.

We hiked up the rocky trail for almost two hours,

stopping only once to drink from a spring. The second hour was slow climbing in the deepening darkness before we entered a natural cathedral of towering hemlocks hundreds of years old, bisected by the headwater stream of the Buffalo Run River. I deposited the pack, which by now seemed to weigh six hundred pounds, and built a crackling, roaring blaze much bigger than I needed just to warm beef stew. I put the stew pot on a rock near the fire to warm and took out my pistol.

"Easy, Gruesome," I said softly, patting his head. "Easy, boy." I pointed the weapon at the mountainside and let rip nine rounds, three close together, three far apart, and three more close together. The muzzle flashes lit the massive hemlock trunks and the mossy ground around them. Gruesome flinched and ran near my feet. I slapped a full clip into the pistol, decocked and holstered it, and picked up the brass hulls ejected by the gun.

Nobody knew where Garvin Rudesill lived, but I had always suspected it was near. I knew of this splendid part of the western slope from boyhood days of hiking. I knew also that deep beneath the forest floor ran caves with Shawnee drawings smoked upon the ceilings. My instincts told me Garvin would choose this isolated, majestic part of the county to make his bed. The shots had echoed in the cold, hemlock-scented mountain air, and soon the smell of wood-smoke would carry as well. I was betting I wouldn't have to find Garvin Rudesill. He would find me.

I ate slowly, savoring Polly's rich, spicy stew, and I sipped a tasty Virginia chardonnay chilled in the creek. After I washed cooking gear in the stream, I restoked the fire to a raging pyre and settled down to read some favorite Shel Silverstein poetry. Over an hour later, I was halfway through "Rosalee's Good Eat's Cafe" when a deep, calm voice sounded from downwind, beyond the limits of the firelight. "What you want, man?" I sincerely hoped the next sound I heard was not a broadhead deer arrow slicing into my chest.

Gruesome recoiled, barked, and scrambled about. "Hush," I whispered to him.

I stood without looking around, and stepped to the fire. I slowly set my pistol on a rock in plain view. "Got some good wine from Linden Vineyards here," I said. I drew off the bottle again before setting it on the moss a few feet in front of me. I backed away and sat down on my pack.

"What you come here for, Sheriff Cody?" the bass voice repeated from a different place in the darkness.

"I came to arrest you for killing four horses in the last two days, Garvin." I patted Gruesome and pushed him down by me.

Soundlessly, Garvin Rudesill emerged from the darkness, walking slowly, loose, like a panther in no hurry. Strapped to one of his calves was a large knife in a scabbard. At the end of a long arm he was carrying a high-powered Fiberglas compound bow, to which was affixed a clip of four long razorhead arrows. I had seen good mountain archers work out; I knew Garvin could nock one of those arrows and put it clear through me faster than I could stand up off my pack.

I remembered Garvin vividly, of course, and thus was not surprised at his size, but I noted he now wore treebark-camouflaged insulated winter pants and coat, as well as expensive store-bought boots. More strikingly, though, Garvin looked younger than I remembered, and then I realized why. He was no longer bearded, but clean shaven, and his hair was cut to a short conventional length. Truth was, despite the scars on his face, he looked downright human.

Garvin "Roadkill" Rudesill approached the wine bottle and lifted it without taking his eyes from me. He backed away near the edge of the firelight and sank to his heels still holding the bow. He sniffed the good wine, drank from the bottle, and eyed me.

"I don't kill horses," he said simply. "I kill a lot of deer. Some turkey. Found a rabid black bear last year and I killed her. But I don't kill horses."

I sighed and studied Garvin Rudesill. "I know. They're all mares, and this guy also has sex with the poor animals before he butchers them. I figure it gets pretty lonely up here for you, but not *that* goddamn lonely. Further, if it was you, I figure you'd have started long ago. Problem is, one of the horses belonged to old Mr. Henry Tucker; was cut up like a mortar casualty yesterday about one P.M. I got a witness who says he saw you cross a fire road by the Tucker place about the same time."

The fire popped and a cascade of sparks rose while Garvin stared. "I might have been there, might not. But I didn't kill anybody's horse." Garvin's eyes were incredibly intense.

"Then I got another witness says he saw you carry off a foal fetus from the Sowers stable last night."

"A goddamn unborn baby horse? Your . . . witness . . . been watchin' too much TV. I was somewhere el— I was nowhere near the Sowers place last night."

I considered that Timmy Sowers admitted he had never seen Garvin Rudesill before he saw whatever he saw fleeing the stable last night.

"Can you prove it?" I asked.

Garvin watched me for a very long pause. "No."

I tossed another branch on the fire. "You got to come in with me, Garvin," I said, raising my head to look at him. "Now."

Instantly, Garvin rose to his feet and I resisted the urge to go for my pistol on the rock. He strode gracefully to me and set the wine just out of my reach before returning to his spot and squatting again.

"Never happen" was all he said.

I leaned forward and retrieved the bottle. "It's got to happen, Garvin. The whole county is gunning for you. It's like fucking Transylvania. You have to let me make a show of taking you in and questioning you. I'll let the witness see it wasn't you he thinks he saw, and then the heat will be off you. I won't have the evidence to hold you and I'll have to turn you loose. But I've got to go through the motions." I drank. "So do you."

"Like hell I do. You try to take me, I'll kill you."

"I know that, Garvin, but then what? Then my people and the state will come after you with dogs and horses and jeeps and helicopters. And men like you. Oh, you'll lead them on a merry chase. You may even kill a few of them, but in the end, they'll get you, because you'll have to sleep, and they won't, because they can work in shifts. You've tracked people, Garvin. You know what I'm saying is true."

Garvin stared hotly, tense. But he said nothing.

"Bottom line is you've got no choice, Garvin. You're going to have to trust me whether you feel like it or not."

Garvin regarded me intently for an excruciatingly long minute. Then he rose and picked my 9-mm Sig-Sauer up off the rock. He moved slowly toward me with the loaded pistol in his hand.

Oh, you're so smart, Lewis Cody, I thought, watching Garvin cast quivering shadows on the hemlocks. *You're sooooo fucking smart. You better pray you haven't outsmarted yourself this time.*

Five feet away, Garvin stopped. I could see his jaw muscles clench. Suddenly, he pitched the pistol to me, which I barely caught in time.

Then he placed his bow and knife on the moss at my feet.

22

Barbarians at the Gate . . . and Within

An hour into the trek down from the hemlock stand, in spite of our slow pace, due to the darkness and rocky surface, Gruesome began to give out. He never let on, of course, but he limped painfully. I dropped the pack and Garvin's weapons, scooped up the huffing Gruesome, and continued. Gruesome lapped wearily at my face.

Garvin "Roadkill" Rudesill observed all this in silence, then he snatched up his bow and knife and my pack, like it was an empty milk carton, and trudged along behind me. At the car, I locked the bow and knife in the trunk along with my pack. I let Garvin ride in front, contrary to standing policy, which required prisoners to ride handcuffed in the back seat behind a steel-mesh screen. Garvin's wrists were too damn big to get handcuffs on, anyway.

At three A.M. in the morning, I had fond hopes of getting Garvin to the dungeon without being observed, but it wasn't to be, for one simple reason—and another not so clear.

It was, after all, a Saturday morning, and farmers stir early, some earlier than others. As I slowed to make the turn onto Main, under Hunter's only street light, of course, that same redneck goon I had to tighten up out at Gordy Huckaby's barn, Roscoe Lee Byner, drove by in his dolled-up pickup truck. I hoped he wouldn't notice, but from the

199

way he braked suddenly and gawked, I knew that was blowing in the wind, too.

Then, when I got to the dungeon, I saw a strange car parked under the spreading pine in front of the Western Auto. I could barely make out someone in it. I turned into the jail parking lot and steered into my reserved space. When I got out, the unfamiliar Mercedes coupe rolled by in the street with its lights off. I could see what I needed to see, though. Klaus.

Inside, my night-duty deputy, Newby Biddle, nearly suffered a myocardial infarction. He was asleep at the radio console, and he wasn't expecting me, let alone the fearsome Roadkill. He sprang up in shock, staring at Garvin.

Garvin paused at the open door to an isolated cell at the end of the empty holding block. He drew in a deep breath and let it out slowly, eyeing the cell. I let him take his time. It wasn't hard to imagine the trepidation a man with his definition of freedom would have about being locked in a cage. Finally, ducking his head, he walked in and lay on the bunk, hands behind his head, and stared at the ceiling.

In my office, I flopped on the couch, real tired, covered myself with an army blanket, and tried for a couple hours' sleep. Gruesome curled up at my feet.

It was still dark out, at 06:20 A.M., when Newby shook my shoulder. "Sheriff? Sheriff, I hate to wake you, but you'd better look outside. We got trouble."

I parted the blinds and peered down at the street before the jail complex to see Newby was dead right. From the elevated window, I looked down on a television news van that was parked at the curb, beyond the high fence composed of wrought-iron spears linked together. The truck's microwave antenna telescoped high in the air. Spotlights were being set up on tripods and some guy in an NEWS NOW! sweatshirt was panning the dungeon with a shoulder-mounted video camera. Worse, a crowd of locals, including my boy Roscoe Lee, stood across the street. Oh, hot damn. Ain't we got fun.

"Get Pierce and Milly on the phone, Newby," I said. "Tell 'em to get in here. Send somebody after Buster Walney. Hold the night shift over on station, and brief the day guys to stand by here for instructions. Put somebody at the gate now. I don't want anybody inside the fence that I don't authorize. Move."

"Yes, sir!" Newby hurried out.

I called Pete Floyd of the *Hunter Press* at his home, and told him he might want to join the crowd at the jail. I told him that I had Garvin Rudesill but that I had not charged him, pending his being ID'd by Timmy Sowers and Buster Walney.

In an hour, the crowd outside had tripled with farm people in town for Saturday logistics who had gotten the word; Roadkill was captured. Under Pierce's command, my people had secured the gate to the compound and Milly was fielding phone calls. The news personality, a well-dressed black woman, had requested an interview, but I sent word out to her that I was busy and would brief them within an hour. My deputy showed up with a sleepy-looking Buster Walney in tow. I had Buster wait in a side room.

Just as I was about to tell Milly to call Merlin Sowers and have him bring Timmy in, she called to me from the outer office. "Pierce say Merlin Sowers here, Lewis! Demand to come in!"

"Let him in," I grumbled.

"They's a Dr. Eichman Dietmun or somebody with him."

"He stays outside. He's not a player in this."

"Okay, Lewis!"

Merlin stormed in with an embarrassed Timmy in tow. "Let me tell you something, Lewis!" Merlin bellowed. "I am chairman of the Hunter County Council, and don't you forget it! I do not expect to be stopped at the gate to this facility and have to request permission to enter! Do you understand me?"

"Tim," I said, "would you wait outside a second? Close the door." When the door clicked shut, I turned on Merlin. "Now you listen, Merlin. I am Sheriff of Hunter County, and I'm elected, just like you. I don't answer to you and you know it, so don't tell me how to run my department. Now carry your ass out of here until you calm down."

Merlin simmered down. "I want to see Roadkill," he demanded, "right now. I want to see the man who butchered my mare, and tell him what a despicable bastard he—"

"No. Road— This is not a zoo, and *Garvin* Rudesill is not on display. If you keep your mouth completely shut, I'll let you stay for the lineup; otherwise, you're obstructing justice, and there's a cell for you out there."

"You—! You dare—!" Merlin spluttered indignantly. Gruesome growled menacingly from the hearth. Merlin eyed him with concern. He turned in a circle and got a grip on himself. "All right, Lewis, we'll do it your way! But you'd better not fuck this up! You'd better not make a mistake!" He stuck a finger at me. "You hear?"

Merlin stomped through the booking room and out the front door. I watched through the window as he angrily pushed past the gate detail to be met by Eicher Dietrich, who was resplendently horsy in a tweed coat, turtle-neck sweater, riding pants, and tall polished black riding boots. He was clearly dressed for his role as the preeminent world horseman.

I had Timmy Sowers wait in my office, and I sent Pierce outside to gather five of the biggest, meanest looking black men from the curious crowd across the street, offer them an opportunity to see the infamous Roadkill up close, and take the five around back. I took Garvin out back to the lot behind the jail, out of view of the crowd out front. There, I told the five men Pierce collected to get their gawking over with and stand in a line, with Garvin fourth from the left, facing the jail. I went inside, got Buster Walney, and led him to a high window opening out onto the rear lot where the five scruffy farmers and Garvin Rudesill stood puffing steam in the chill morning air, unaware they were being observed.

"That's him!" Buster hissed. "That's the crazy nigger I saw crossing the firebreak up by old man Henry Tucker's!"

I squinted at Buster. "Which crazy nigger, Buster?"

"The tall one! That's Roadkill in the flesh, the dude with the camoflush suit and all the scars on his face! Fourth from the left!"

Garvin Rudesill.

"What?" Timmy Sowers said, five minutes later. "You mean one of these guys is supposed to be the one I saw at the barn night before last?"

"Take your time, Tim," I said. "Tell me if you recognize anyone."

"I'm not sure, Sheriff Cody," Timmy mumbled, peering at the men in parking lot.

"Tim, a couple of those guys have beards, but a few of them don't. Remember, a beard could have been shaved off. I need you to be certain."

"I—I don't know. It was dark, and I didn't see him too well, and I was scared as hell . . . but, you know, Sheriff Cody, I didn't think about it 'til just now, but the man I saw had sort of a humped back, like real bad posture, you know? I can't be certain, Sheriff; I'm sorry. I can't say for sure if he was one of these guys or not, but I don't think he is."

I had the five citizens thanked and dismissed, and I had Pierce move Garvin back to his cell. Through my office window, I could see everyone in the street gather excitedly about the five men who'd shared the lineup with Garvin. The TV woman pushed through the crowd with a microphone.

I thanked Timmy Sowers and asked him to wait in Milly's office. I didn't want the kid mobbed with questions and challenges by the crowd out front, most of which was ready to pull the switch on Garvin, and I wanted to avoid the possibility of Merlin's embarrassing the boy in front of all those people.

Buster Walney's ID'ing Garvin wasn't enough to hold Garvin, since all Buster saw was Garvin near the scene of Mr. Henry Tucker's place near the time Mr. Henry's horse was slaughtered. Timmy Sowers's testimony was critical, as he was the only person so far who'd seen a smoking-gun suspect. I was disappointed that he couldn't categorically dismiss Garvin as a suspect, because it muddied up being able to release him, which I had implied I would do when I talked Garvin into coming in. If Garvin got the idea I'd misled him, he'd become very dangerous to my people handling him, and to himself. Not to mention me. I was considering my options when Milly leaned in the door. "Lewis, that Cynthia Haas, lady runs that little jewelry store up on the square, you know?"

"Yeah. I just talked to her the other day about that little piece of silver I found at the Calder wreck. What about her?"

"She on the phone. Say she got to talk to you."

"This is a lousy time, Milly; can't I call her back?"

"She say now, Lewis. Won't say why. Say she got to talk to you right now."

"Milly, anybody turn anything on the Calders yet?"

"Ain't nobody seen nothin', Lewis. Billy and Otis been snoopin' around on they own time, but whoever hit 'em has done gone deep. Ain't nothing showin' so far."

Damn, I thought. That made this horse affair even more sour. I would have to spend precious manpower handling Merlin, Dietrich, Garvin, and the press, to say nothing of whoever really was killing horses all over my county—manpower I should be pouring into finding the Calders's killer.

"Hello, Cynthia," I said into my phone, "how are you?"

Cynthia Haas's voice sounded strained, worried. "Sheriff Cody, I . . . I need to see you, immediately."

"Well, come on in, Cynthia."

"No. No. I can't do that, Sheriff Cody. I need you to come here, to my home. And please don't tell anyone about me."

"Cynthia, if I remember, you live way out on Perry Hollow Road—"

"Near the school, yes, a brick two-story; second house past the—"

"I know the house, Cynthia, but I'm up to my ears here in—"

"Please, Sheriff!" Cynthia suddenly pleaded, as though about to break into tears. "Please! It's so important! It's about Gar—Mr. Rudesill, and I can't possibly do this over the phone. Please. You've got to come."

"Twenty minutes," I said and hung up.

I walked as unobtrusively as possible out to my cruiser, overhearing the TV woman doing a clip for her camera. All attention was on her for the moment, which I hoped would allow me to get to my wheels unnoticed.

"—with News Now, live before the Hunter County Jail in the little mountain town of Hunter, Virginia. Sources have revealed that an arrest has been made in the slayings—the horrible mutilations—of several Hunter County horses, including a prize fox-hunting horse, called a hunter-jumper, belonging to prominent Hunter County banker Merlin Sowers. With me now is Mr. Sowers. Mr. Sowers, I understand you've just had a briefing with Hunter County Sheriff Lewis Cody. Can you confirm that an arrest has indeed been made?"

I leaned on my car. I should have gotten in it and driven it, but I was morbidly fascinated.

"Uh, yes, uh," Merlin began eloquently. "I uh . . . we are pleased to announce that through . . . uh . . . intense cooperation by all facets of the Hunter County government . . . uh . . . we have brought to the bar of justice the . . . uh . . . hideous person responsible for . . . uh . . . these terrible horse mutilations. Yes." Merlin tried to look important, but looked instead more like he had acute stomach trouble.

"Mr. Sowers, we understand the alleged mutilator is a man known locally as Roadkill. Is that correct?"

"Uh, yes. He . . . uh . . . well, he is . . . thought to . . . eat dead animals off the . . . uh . . . the road." A murmur hummed through the crowd.

I'd heard enough. I cranked the car and was turning past my deputies onto the street before I was spotted. I ignored the tumult of cries and questions and accelerated. On the radio, I advised Milly to tell the media people their briefing would be delayed for an hour.

It was beginning to turn light when I turned off Perry Hollow Road into the drive to Cynthia Haas's pleasant home. I noted one of the garage doors go up. To my surprise, Cynthia stood in the garage waving me into it. She wore jeans and a sweater, and although fourteen hard years of caring for a dying invalid husband had aged her, she looked like she had in her little jewelry shop, better than I could remember seeing her in recent years.

Thoroughly baffled, I pulled into the garage and Cynthia buzzed the big door shut. Gracefully, she led me through her immaculate kitchen and into another of those perfect living rooms nobody uses for anything, this one less ostentatious than the Sowers parlor, but no less formal. I considered it lucky for both of us that she hadn't led me past the marijuana crop alleged to be in her greenhouse. She motioned me to a couch, and she sat on the edge of a beautiful old Windsor chair, her knees together. She tried to smile, but it faded. Cynthia Haas swept a nonexistent strand of hair from her face.

"Would . . . ah . . . would you care for some coffee, Sheriff?"

"No thanks, Cynthia. I want you to try to relax. I can see you're tense. Is there any way I can make it easier for you to tell me what's bothering you?" I tried to appear relaxed, but I wished she would get on with it so I could get back to matters at the dungeon.

About eight years ticked by. Finally, Cynthia drew a wavering breath and spoke. "Sheriff Cody, I . . . ah . . . I hear you have Gar—Garvin Rudesill in custody for . . . for killing horses."

I never failed to be impressed with the speed and scope of the Hunter County gossip system. "He's being questioned, yes."

"Sheriff Cody, Garvin Rudesill is innocent. He didn't kill anyone's horses. He couldn't have." Cynthia Haas looked pained.

"Cynthia . . . I myself doubt that Garvin did the killings. But someone saw Garvin near one killing and another witness saw someone who looks very much like him running from the Sowers stable Thursday night."

"Nonetheless, he is innocent."

"Cynthia—"

"He was here, Sheriff Cody."

I listened to the grandfather clock tocking in the hallway for a good ten seconds. "Road—Garvin Rudesill was here?"

Cynthia looked at the floor and nodded her head.

"When?"

"Thursday night, when they say Mrs. Sowers's horse was . . . mutilated, and all of the previous afternoon when Gordon Huckaby's . . . animal was killed."

I was still out to lunch. "Cynthia, Garvin Rudesill was *here,* with . . . *you?*"

She looked up sadly. "Is that so hard to believe, Sheriff?"

"Well, no. I mean, not that a man wouldn't want to be with you, but . . . Garvin—" *What the hell was Garvin Rudesill doing here?* I wondered. *Chopping firewood for food?* I studied Cynthia, trying to absorb the shock. "Cynthia, I'm lost here. I—"

"He was here! Consequently, he could not have committed at least two of the horse killings. And if he didn't do those two, I'm sure you'll agree it's very unlikely he did the other two."

I began to recover from the shock. "Can you prove Garvin was here?" I asked her. "Any other witnesses, I mean?"

Cynthia raised her head. "Are you saying my word is not sufficient for you, Sheriff Cody?"

I rubbed my forehead. "Cynthia, I'd like to free Garvin, because I don't think he did the crimes, but there is a lot of heat on me to arrest him. The whole damn county, except you and me, thinks he's guilty, and not without some reason. I need proof. Evidence."

She rose suddenly, distressed. Again, she swept away the hair that wasn't there. "If I could provide you with incontrovertible proof that he was here during at least one of the horse killings, Sheriff Cody, would you release him?"

"Probably. What proof?"

Cynthia fretted and paced and then seemed to calm, as though she'd made up her mind. "Please wait here," she said and she disappeared down the hall toward the bedrooms. In a moment, she returned carrying a VCR cassette. She took it to the living-room TV and slipped it into the VCR player in the cabinet beneath the TV. She turned to me. "I . . . I think we'll both be more comfortable if you watch this tape alone, Sheriff. I'll be in the kitchen. Please . . . please note the television in the background, if you . . . if you . . . can." She pressed the buttons and walked primly out, her head high.

I leaned back on the couch, totally buffaloed, and watched this mysterious videotape flicker then clarify on the screen. The volume was low but audible. It was a picture of a living room and a couch. Actually, I saw upon examination, it was the same perfect, no-use living room that I was now in and the couch on which I sat. I rubbed my chin and frowned in confusion. The very television I was now watching was running in the background of the picture, displaying a CBS on-scene report on an air crash in Oregon, its volume barely audible, a report I remembered seeing aired on my bedroom TV the day of the Huckaby horse killing. I remembered seeing it while I was dressing to ride shortly before the idiot from Richmond shot at Moose and me. Actually, I considered later, the live news report had been at about one P.M., the same time Darlene Huckaby's little mare was cut up. I remembered the news coverage vividly because an airliner crash took my little girl from me, years ago. My Tess.

Suddenly, the screen darkened, blotted out by something crossing very close to the camera. As the figure in the video moved away from the camera position to the couch on which I now sat, I jerked bolt upright and stopped rubbing my chin. I looked twice, and then again, but it was real. The person on the tape was none other than Garvin Rudesill, and he carried in his arms one obviously delighted Cynthia Haas.

Both were nude.

23

• • • • • • • •

News Now

It was stunningly unreal, but there it was, quite without doubt. As the tape ran, the heavily muscled Garvin Rudesill made love to the heretofore homely Cynthia Haas on the very same couch on which I sat. I tore my eyes from the television to look down uncomfortably at the couch. I looked back at the screen in time to see beyond doubt that Cynthia and Garvin had indeed obtained full value for whatever had been paid for this couch. I took back everything I said about Cynthia Haas's living room. She'd sure learned how to live in it.

I felt compelled by a sense of respect for Cynthia's privacy to run over and turn off the tape, but I watched it for another half minute, long enough to examine the TV still shown in the background of the picture. I was sure. I wasn't seeing a rerun. It was live at the time of this lovers' encounter. The tape had been made at almost precisely the time Darlene Huckaby's horse was destroyed at least ten miles away. I hit the stop button and removed the tape from the player.

I turned around to see Cynthia Haas standing before her living-room bay window, her arms crossed, gazing at the pink hues of the rising winter sun. "Eight months and seventeen days ago," she said softly, still staring out the window, "I was . . . gardening in my greenhouse out back. I looked up to see him crossing the edge of my yard near the woods. We sort of saw each other at the same time. I had heard about him, of course, but he didn't look particularly menacing. He was huge, certainly, and he was hairy as an ape with all that beard and hair, but to me he looked . . . sad. Lonely. He would later tell me I was the first woman who had laid eyes on him in Hunter County who had not run away screaming. We just looked at each other for a moment, and he disappeared, but a week later I saw him again, this time just squatting in the wildflowers, watching me work in the greenhouse." Cynthia sniffled. The sun burned into the room. "I started leaving food out there by the woodline and occasionally I'd find it consumed. One day, I left a book, Pat Conroy's *The Prince of Tides*. One of the characters is a Vietnam veteran who is driven to a life of isolation on an island off South Carolina. I was trying to tell him I understood him. God. All those years of hauling Gene to VA hospitals, those unnerving caverns of war-wrecked, lost souls. All those devastated veterans. Oh God, yes, I understood."

Cynthia sniffed abruptly, and dabbed at her eye. She continued. "One evening, he came while I was gardening, and I was shocked. He had shaved and cut his hair, and he had brought me the most lovely doeskin dress he'd made with his own hands. It fits me perfectly! It's so beautiful!" She dabbed more tears. "It was a slow process, Sheriff Cody, but he trusts me. I've won his heart. I know he loves me, even if he still won't come in from the woods." She turned to face me, tears wetting her eyes. "And finally, for *once* in my life, I have a whole man!" Cynthia looked at me with the eyes of a woman in love.

"Cynthia . . . " I said slowly, looking at the tape cassette I held, trying to collect my head.

She too glanced at the tape, and she blushed and turned away. "We—we just decided to film ourselves one day. For . . . fun. Then we sort of made it a habit. We . . . like to watch them together . . . and, when he's away, the tapes, they help me—"

"I understand, Cynthia," I said. "It's perfectly reasonable. Lots of folks do it."

Cynthia resumed watching the rising sun. "Sheriff Cody

. . . my . . . my little business depends on the good and proper socialites of Hunter County buying their jewelry and china and silverware from me. It depends vitally on them registering their daughters' weddings with me. If . . . they— if they knew about . . ." She glanced nervously at the tape. "If they thought I even entertained the . . . the 'monster who eats dead road animals,' a . . . black man . . . they'd . . . my little business would be ruined."

I looked at the sun. "Did you tell me Garvin was with you all day Wednesday?"

"Yes. I closed the shop that day and left a sign saying I was out of town. Did you see the news program on the TV? I had forgotten it was on. The volume was down, and we . . . weren't watching."

"I saw it. I know what the tape proves. He couldn't have done the Huckaby slaughter."

"Or poor Arlette Sowers's horse, Sheriff Cody! He was with me all Thursday evening. We just had dinner and slow-danced until late, but he was here, I swear!" Cynthia was crying.

"I believe you," I said, handing her the tape.

Cynthia took the tape and lay her head on my chest, weeping. "Please let him go, Sheriff Cody! Please release him. You can't know what it must be like for him . . . confined . . . locked up! He can't take that for long! Please let him go!" The woman sobbed wretchedly.

I held her by her shoulders, patting her gently.

My "unmarked" car sure didn't fool anybody. I was spotted fifty yards away by the now-huge crowd before the dungeon.

People were sitting on car hoods and in the backs of pickup trucks. They leaned against the wrought-iron fence and smoked or chewed, shuffling to ward off the cold. It was Saturday morning in the mountains, and the word was out: Roadkill, the eater of the decomposed, the butcher of horses, the stealer of the unborn, was captured. Everybody had come for a glimpse of the monster.

The news van was still present, and when I was seen approaching the dungeon grounds, there was a flurry of activity around it. Slowing for the turn into the compound,

I saw Merlin Sowers and Eicher Dietrich stop their conversation to eye me.

I pulled through the gate and my deputies held the crowd outside. I got out, slammed the door, and stalked through the gate to pay some dues. The black newswoman and her camera buffalo hustled my way, as did Merlin, Dietrich, and Pete Floyd.

"Sheriff!" the attractive newswoman called, scurrying as fast as her skirt and heels would permit. "Sheriff Cody! Amanda Daniels, Sheriff Cody, News Now. Sheriff, we understand you have captured the man responsible for the brutal torture-slayings of several horses here in Hunter County!" The camera guy angled for his picture. People were crowding near. "Sheriff Cody, how do you answer the charge, leveled by famed horseman Dr. Eicher Dietrich, that you dragged your heels in making this arrest, needlessly allowing the torture-slaughters of still more prize horses?"

I glanced at Dietrich, who eyed me down his nose, plainly closing in for the kill.

"In spite of the popular fervor, Miss Daniels," I said tersely, "there has not been adequate evidence to—"

"Adequate *evidence?*" Eicher Dietrich exclaimed incredulously, stepping close. The newswoman knew when she had a live one by the tail. She snapped a visual command to her cameraman, and both maneuvered to include Dietrich in the picture. Daniels held her microphone toward Dietrich. "Adequate *evidence?*" Dietrich intoned still again, his eyebrows arching. "Absurd! Even the most uninformed resident of this . . . community . . . has known for years that this Roadkill person was a dangerous man, yet he has been negligently allowed to run free! I must tell you, your . . . sheriff . . . here"—Dietrich cast a disdain-ripe sneer at me—"is a disgrace to your community! Not only has he failed to make a timely arrest, causing the needless suffering and loss of fine, valuable animals, he has been wholly uncooperative with the effort by my long-time friend, Meriah Reinholdt, to bring a thriving new equestrian industry to Hunter County, one that would provide jobs and a vitally needed boost to the county tax base!"

"Dietrich," I began, but I choked it off. I didn't suppose it would improve my fast-eroding image to knock the "famed horseman" flat on his Aryan ass, live before a major statewide news crew.

"In fact," Dietrich said, raising his voice over the crowd's mumbling, "in fact, your very own Mr. Merlin Sowers, who has suffered the painful loss of an expensive and beloved mare as result of Sheriff Cody's incompetence, has informed me that Sheriff Cody was reluctant to even meet with Mrs. Reinholdt to discuss her proposal!"

The crowd buzzed. I looked at Merlin, who looked back, distressed and confused. He shrugged his shoulders at me.

Amanda Daniels whirled on Merlin. "Mr. Sowers! What can you tell—"

"W-well," Merlin stammered, "I d-didn't exactly—"

"Mr. Sowers!" Eicher Dietrich demanded, hotly skewering Merlin with his eagle eyes. "Did you or did you not tell me this very morning that Sheriff Cody had to be coaxed and offered a political tradeoff before he would agree to even discuss this wonderful new venture for Hunter County?"

"Well, yeah, but—"

"Exactly!" Dietrich ripped. The crowd stirred once more.

"Sheriff Cody," newswoman Daniels said, stabbing the microphone at me, "is it true you accepted a 'political tradeoff' in order to—"

"I asked Mr. Sowers to extend the mortgage of a cancer-stricken local farmer, wholly unrelated to me, yes. I doubt that'll eclipse Watergate."

"Sheriff Cody," Daniels said, slightly confused, "what will the suspect be charged with?"

"Not a goddamned thing," I said, instantly regretting the bleep that would punctuate my remark on tonight's news. "I'm releasing him immediately."

You'd have thought I had just asked Daniels to suck my dick. The entire assembly gawked at me for a brief, silent moment, and then all hell broke loose.

"Release!" several people bellowed at once. It was hard to tell if Dietrich, Merlin, Daniels, or others in the crowd were the loudest.

"You're cutting that bastard *loose?!*" Merlin howled.

"This is outrageous!" Eicher Dietrich shouted. "This is an outrage to the equestrian community worldwide! This is a gross display of insensitivity to animal rights! This—"

The crowd of citizens yelled, "Hell no!" and other less-subtle expressions of protest.

Daniels couldn't decide whom to say what to. She poked the microphone in every direction.

"There is no . . ." I shouted, pausing to let the crowd quiet. "There is no evidence linking the individual in question, Garvin Rudesill, with any crime whatsoever. Specifically—" I was drowned out by roars of complaint. In a moment, they subsided. "Specifically, I have just been made privy to irrefutable evidence establishing that Mr. Rudesill has an alibi eliminating—" More yowls of protest covered me.

"Sheriff Cody!" Amanda Daniels cried over the noise. "What evidence do you have that the man known as Roadkill was not involved with these brutal horse killings?"

Now the crowd quieted quickly, but this was the question I had been dreading. I took a slow breath as the suddenly hushed crowd struggled to hear. "Elements bear . . . on this case . . . that do not permit me to detail that evidence at this time."

"What?!" Merlin Sowers screamed.

"This is an incredible miscarriage of justice!" Eicher Dietrich repronounced.

It was probably a good thing for me that the grateful, adoring citizens of Hunter County had no handy source of tar and feathers.

"Sheriff Cody!" Daniels shouted over the din. "Surely you can do better than—"

"I will not detail the information that bears on this matter at this time," I repeated, "but I remain convinced that insufficient evidence exists to charge Garvin Rudesill with the crime of—"

I was soundly roared down in a crescendo of protest. "No!" the crowd howled. "You cain't let that crazy nigger loose!" a voice suspiciously like Roscoe Lee Byner's called, and the crowd sang out its support.

I could barely hear Merlin Sowers over the ruckus.

"Goddamn it, Lewis! Are you *nuts?* Is this some stupid Vietnam buddy thing? 'Cause if it is, you're in trouble! You hear me?"

"Outrageous!" Eicher Dietrich shouted, also drowned in the din. "A travesty of unparalleled—"

"Sheriff Cody!" Amanda Daniels shouted, struggling to keep her footing among the jostling, highly agitated surge of citizens. "Sheriff Cody!"

At this moment, the shrill, injured-dog yelp of a police siren deafened everyone within fifty feet, and all heads turned to see a marked sheriff's cruiser roll out of the gate from the jail complex smack into the crowd, its blue lights flashing. People stepped lively in every direction to make a path for the car, which was clearly being driven like the driver didn't give a fat damn if a path was opened or not.

The cruiser lurched to a stop near me, and a really pissed off Sergeant Milly Stanford got out, slamming the door behind her with a vengeance. "Y'all shut the fuck *up!*" Milly roared, never one to stand on grammar.

The crowd, including an astonished Merlin Sowers and a perplexed Eicher Dietrich, gawked.

"I said *shut up,* goddamnit!" Milly repeated, and the entire crowd did. Milly waddled toward me, pushing the newswoman back with a meaty hand in her chest. "*Git* outta my way, sister; git dat goddamn micaphone outta my face 'less you wanna eat it! I got a important message fo the sheriff!"

Milly sauntered up to me, slapped a piece of paper in my hand, and turned to the crowd, her pudgy arms crossed, a belligerent wrinkle to her big nose. God, I love that woman.

I read the message, sighed, and walked over to Amanda Daniels. To her startled surprise, I snatched the cordless microphone out of her hand. "All right, pay attention!" I said. "I hate to spoil this little kangaroo court you people are having here, but about five minutes ago, Reverend Edmund Hodges just saw a man who looks like Garvin Rudesill—who has been in my cellblock since four A.M. this morning, I remind you!—attack a horse belonging to Reverend Hodges with an axe! Now if this little inquisition is over, and you folks will excuse me, I've got work to do!" I pitched the microphone to the dumbfounded Amanda Daniels, and stalked toward the gate to the dungeon. Behind me, a stunned crowd stood in silence.

The flashing cruisers of Pierce Arroe and Tom Bonner screeched out of the gate, headed for Reverend Hodges's place. "Get a perimeter out! Use everybody!" I shouted at Pierce as his car bounced onto the street. He gave me a thumbs-up and his cruiser engine roared, Tom hot on his heels. Other deputies were rushing to their cars.

"Milly! Call State and tell 'em we need the dog again!"

"Got it, Lewis!"

"Hey!"

"Yes, Lewis?"

"Thank you, darlin'!"

Milly beamed.

Inside the holding block, I trotted quickly to the last cell. "Got a message for you, Garvin," I said, hurriedly unlocking the cell. I looked at him and smiled. "Cynthia says tell you she loves you."

On the way to Reverend Hodges's home, Gruesome whined and sniffed at a blanket covering something in the rear seat of my cruiser. I bounced into Cynthia Haas's driveway. The garage door was up, so I blazed into the garage, sliding the cruiser to a halt. Cynthia Haas came running from her kitchen in time to see me open the trunk. Out of the back car door climbed the immense Garvin Rudesill. She cried out and rushed into his arms. Gruesome was confused.

I set Garvin's bow and knife on the concrete, took a last look at Cynthia crying in Garvin's embrace, and Gruesome and I blew hard for the Hodges farm.

24

•••••••

The Holy and the Hellish

Horse victim number five was still alive, but that only made the occasion more horrible. The animal was bound by several strands of barbed wire from a roll in the storage shed of the Reverend Edmund Hodges's small stable, near the woodline well behind his neat, modest frame home. The wire had cut deep, and what the wire hadn't severed, a lunatic with an ax had. Predictably, it was a bloody, pitiful scene. Worse, the creature had taken the ax to Ed Hodges and his dog.

Mercifully away in town, Mrs. Hodges was shopping with little Tara Hodges. Ed had been walking his Irish setter in the brittle winter leaves when he heard thumps of hard impact against the walls of the tiny two-stall stable where Tara's little quarter horse mare was sheltered. Then he heard the shrill cries of a horse in terror.

Ed and Murphy the Irish setter scurried to the stable, Ed thinking maybe a snake had gotten into the stall. Ed was considering that you don't see many snakes in November when he ran into the little barn and saw a sight he was in every respect unprepared for.

Edmund Hodges was one of those academicians raised by academicians, a well-meaning but hopelessly naive theologian who eternally wore a tepid, bless-you-my-son smile. He was forever going on about the intrinsic goodness of the human soul, the power of love, and my favorite, "God's holy mandate to forgive." Ed was the kind of guy the Nazis, the Khmer Rouge, and the Bosnian Serbs just adored. Ed Hodges struck me as someone raised to think that if you pretend something sweet long enough, it'll come to pass. Consequently, he was a little more than mildly disturbed to find a six-and-a-half-foot semihuman creature fucking his daughter's barbed-wire-strung pony. The ax the creature kept swinging into the thrashing animal's back probably didn't help cement Rev. Hodges's concept of the basic good in all men, either.

To his credit, Murphy the Irish setter didn't put much credence in the reverend's benevolent theories. He immediately charged, took a chompful of the creature's hairy right thigh, and did a little thrashing of his own.

The creature yowled through ragged teeth and came disconnected from the horse, his long matted strands of hair flying. He swiped at Murphy with the ax while Rev. Hodges shook, arc-welded in horror.

Murph took a bad slash in the right shoulder, but not bad enough to make him unclamp the creature's bleeding, tearing thigh. The next blow struck him in the head, however. Luckily, the creature's quality control had slipped a little in the melee and it was the flat side of the blade that struck the gutsy dog. Murphy was only sent reeling instead of being decapitated.

Ed Hodges tried hard to scream as the creature hobbled about, covered in blood, roaring in pain, and clutching up his pants with the hand not occupied with a wet plumb axe. Ed had plenty to scream about under the circumstances, which included the writhing, squealing horse expelling blood like a lawn sprinkler, but all he could do was croak and gasp.

Ed recovered when the creature staggered toward him and raised the ax. The Lord spoke to Ed at the last second and told him to haul balls for the house, pronto. The ax tacked a portion of the tail of Ed's cardigan to the stable wall, but that didn't slow him down any. He looked over his shoulder just long enough to see the butcher loping into the woods behind the stable.

A different dog and handler responded from Corrections this time, Old Bob having been temporarily put out of service at Merlin Sowers's place two nights ago. Remembering the cayenne pepper trick, I had the dog handler sweep fifty meters beyond where Ed Hodges had seen the creature disappear, to locate a track. In seconds, the dog locked on and took off. I sent two men ahead of the general direction in cars, and the rest of us ran after the dog and handler, all of us packing enough guns to make the NRA stand up and cheer. We didn't run far. The dog tracked about a quarter of a mile to a dirt road and then lost the scent. It was obvious the creature had made it to a vehicle and split. Curses, foiled again.

Back at Rev. Hodges's, I saw a familiar maroon pickup truck parked in the paddock. Inside the tiny stable, the bloody ax still protruded from the wall, a rip of sweater yarn hanging from it. In the stall, Julianne Chu was readying a large syringe full of a drug that would mercifully put what was left of Tara Hodges's little mare to sleep. Julianne looked at me with a drained expression, knelt in the blood-saturated straw, and inserted the syringe. In a moment, she checked that the pulse had stopped, then she stood and threw the syringe toward her equipment case in disgust. She stripped off rubber gloves, wadded them and hurled them after the syringe, and she stalked out to her truck. I had the feeling something in her was condemning all men for the male perversity of the butcher. Or maybe she was just blaming me for thus far failing so miserably to stop the abuses and slaughters.

I went to the house. By paramedics, on the couch in still another pristine, ceremonial living room, Ed Hodges was pale as the Shroud of Turin, but basically unhurt. The paramedics left. In gasping fragments, Ed, wide-eyed, described to me a huge man with Howard Stern hair, several days' beard growth, and extremely muscular build. The creature was said to have thick black eyebrows, a broken Arabic nose, and yellow, pitted teeth. Well, at least I could eliminate Keanu Reeves as a suspect.

"What race would you call him?" I asked.

"I . . . I don't know, Sheriff. He was almost . . . Middle

Eastern, dark-skinned but not negroid in feature. His eyes, Sheriff Cody!" Rev Hodges croaked. "His *eyes!* I have never *seen* such . . . such . . . malice! Such *evil!"*

I asked Ed to keep the sexual aspect of his observations under wraps and explained why. He understood. He said he was going to move his family into the church in town, until we caught the creature. I didn't tell him that, at the rate we were going, he'd better pack a lot of clothes.

At the dungeon, everyone kept a low profile, hearing me swear and throw things in my office. Milly stood by patiently; she'd seen me lose it before and she knew I'd blow it all off and get over it. She knew it was a disgraceful way for a grown man to behave, but she forgave me.

"God*damn* it!" I roared. "Milly what the *hell* is the matter with us? We haven't got the first clue on this *fucking* horse nut, and I can't look Boyce Calder in the eye without hanging my head! What the *hell* are we overlooking?" I slammed the center drawer to my desk. Behind me, the Rotary Club plaque on the wall crashed to the floor. "Double-Parked! Get in here!" I yelled.

"Yes, sir, Sheriff, sir!" The great little Korean kid yiped and set the world land speed record, carrying his notepad and pencil, the laces of his Reeboks trailing in the breeze. He wore oversized Bermuda shorts and a VPI sweatshirt that would have swallowed Pierce Arroe.

"Double-Parked, Rev. Hodges said this creep is built like a studio wrestler. That kind of muscle only comes from hellacious physical labor, or exceptional devotion to conditioning, or . . . or it comes from being in prison and having nothing to do but lift weights. You get on that glass-faced devil in there and ask it for information on recently released convicts over six feet four inches tall! Any race but Oriental, as long as they're dark-skinned. I'm especially interested in anybody who did time for bestiality or animal sodomy. Get into the NLETS net, start with Virginia, and work your way out in a circle to the other states. Keep punching buttons 'til you get something I want to hear. Get going!"

"Yes, sir!" Double-Parked spouted, and he fairly blazed from the room.

I stared out the same window from which I had observed the crowd of righteous earlier in the morning. Calmed, I asked Milly, "What's the kid enjoy, Milly? What's he get off on? Comic books? Music? Candy? What?"

"Well," Milly said, smiling slyly, "other day, I heard him say he done busted a wheel off that raggedy old skateboard of his."

"Excellent. Detail somebody in the office to go find him the best skateboard made. Send 'em to Roanoke if you have to. Take it—"

"Outta you check. I know."

"Milly, what else can we do about Boyce's wife and child? What are we failing to do?"

"Lewis, the boys is searching every cave, every vacant barn, every log road, every garage it don't take a warrant to see into, and a few that might. They askin' around, they listenin' in the bars, and they surprise-visitin' every body shop in the county. Billy and a couple others been circulatin' out-of-county body shops on they own time. The description, what little we got, is out all over the eastern U.S. This is real po-leese work, Lewis. This ain't the movies. We can dig and we can keep our eyes and ears open, but we ain't magic. Truth is, ain't much we gonna be able to do 'til the son of a bitch makes a move. Long as he hides that truck and keeps quiet, we ain't gonna find him. And you know it."

"Any word on Boyce?"

"Nobody seen him since he threatened to drive off with one of the Yarmouth kid's legs tied to his bumper. Left messages on his machine, but he ain't been heard from. State say they done had a man at his house in Christiansburg, but they ain't found him, neither."

"How the hell could he just drop out of sight? Christ, I'm beginning to think we couldn't find our own ass with both hands and a five-cell flashlight."

"Boyce is a cop, too. He'll be hell to find if he don't wanna be found. Listen, Lewis, don' forget you gotta attend Mr. Henry's funeral at fourteen hundred. You dress uniform's still in the closet." Milly waddled out.

I was exhausted. I had been up most of the night, had been on a long hike over rocks in the dark, carrying a pack or a dog, and had enjoyed one hell of a morning. And I had to attend Mitch Whitley's charity dinner at 7 P.M.

I had a warm, arousing mental flash of Karin Steiger's violent, fabulous body. My back was still sore, and I would never look at any washing machine the same way again. I needed some rest, big time, but I would not fail to pay my respects to Mr. Henry Tucker.

I was gratified to find the First Presbyterian Church packed with Hunter Countians of all races and social stations, come to pay their respects to Mr. Henry as well. He was laid to rest in the old cemetery behind the church. It was somehow reassuring to believe that the enduring dignity of Mr. Henry Tucker had overcome the ignorance of prejudice. Rest in peace, Mr. Henry.

I told Milly where I would be, and I drove home to Mountain Harbor. I inhaled a large bowl of Polly's beef stew, soaked my aching bones in the hot tub, and I smashed to sleep.

I hate tuxedos almost as much as I hate funerals. If Mother Nature had meant for man to look like a penguin, she'd have given him fins and webbed feet. Elizabeth was impressed, though.

"Wow, Uncle Lewis! You look righteously—"

"Bosh. Yeah, yeah."

Elizabeth studied me and frowned. "You look tired, Uncle Lewis. You gotta—"

"Have to. Should. Need to. Anything but 'gotta.'"

"Okay! You need to stop camping out on work nights!"

"Can't argue with that. Have you fed Dublin and Moose tonight?"

Elizabeth rolled her eyes and propped her hands on her hips. "Of course!"

"Good. Listen, Sugar. You know about the . . . ah . . . horse killings, right?"

"Are you kidding, Uncle Lewis? While you were asleep, you were on the five-o'clock news in Roanoke! All about Tara Hodges's daddy and the crazy man trying to hurt him! And he killed Tara's pony! I called Tara on the phone after school when I found out, and Tara cried and cried!"

"I know, darlin' girl; it was a terrible thing. Now listen to me, Sweetheart. Don't . . . ah . . . don't be riding by yourself, and don't go to the stable when Arthur isn't out there, until I tell you different. Understand?"

Elizabeth's cute little mouth pursed and she frowned. "Sure, Uncle Lewis. Why?"

"Just until . . . this horse guy is taken care of. Okay?"

Her eyes widened and she gasped. "Uncle Lewis, you mean he might try to . . . to *hurt Dublin!* You don't think he'd come *here?"*

I held her to me and she clutched me about my waist. "No, no. Don't get all worked up, now. He hasn't even been seen in our half of the county. I doubt he'd ever come here, and if he did, Arthur would . . . handle him. Let's just be cautious for a little—"

"Don't let him kill Dublin, Uncle Lewis!"

"Shhh. You're getting all upset for no reason, now. We have an alarm system on in the stable, and Arthur's been told to stick close. Moose and Dublin will be all right."

Elizabeth sniffed but seemed convinced. "The news lady showed film of you talking to the people at the dungeon. Boy! You and Sergeant Milly must've said some baaad things. They bleeped and bleeped and—"

I winced. "Yeah, well, public speaking isn't what Milly and I do best, I'm afraid."

Downstairs, I sat Elizabeth down for the dinner Polly was serving her and Arthur.

"Sheriff," Polly said, sliding a plate in front of Elizabeth, "Miz Hodges called today. They stayin' down at the church a few days until . . . well, you know, until y'all catch that crazy man. She ast if 'Lizbeth kin spend the night with little Tara tonight. Kinda give her some company, you know? Told her I'd ast you."

Polly knew very well I wouldn't object or she would've broached the subject away from Elizabeth.

"Can I, Uncle Lewis? My homework for Monday is done!"

"Well, in that case, I don't see how I could object. Sure, Sweetheart. Have fun."

"Thanks, Uncle Lewis!"

I kissed her on the head and went to my car.

Just as my cruiser rolled to the stone gates by the road, nearly a mile from the house, a black Nissan Pathfinder pulled out of the tall pines to the left of the drive and stopped before me. The driver exited, and I understood why nobody had seen Corporal Boyce Calder.

I stuffed the Chevy in park and got out. Boyce looked ghastly in the bright headlights. His hair was disheveled, he wore three days of dark whiskers, and he looked like he hadn't eaten or slept in weeks. He wore the same jeans, shirt, and boots he'd had on the day I saw him last at Laurel Ridge Farm. They looked slept in, as I was sure they were. Boyce also still had a gun stuck in the belt of his jeans. He walked very slowly, putting each foot directly in front of the other, in the weaving gait of a very tired man.

"How . . . was . . . the funeral?" Boyce croaked, spacing his words, pausing often to breathe. He was near collapse, and his voice was still shot.

"As nice as funerals get, Boyce," I replied gently.

"How . . . how did Ca—Cathy . . . look?" Boyce's jaw hung open and he stared at me from the tops of his eyes. "And my baby boy?"

"The . . . caskets were closed, Boyce. But the music and the words were pretty. They were buried with dignity and grace, son. Everyone missed you."

"Shit. I couldn't come. I couldn't stand to see them . . . to see them . . . put my Cathy in a hole in the ground. Bury her! *Bury* Stevie! Oh! Oh . . . he was so beautiful!" Boyce's voice seized. He lay his head back and sobbed at the bright November moon.

"Boyce—"

"I loved her! Oh God, I loved them so much!" Boyce wept.

"I know, son. I—"

"I can't *find* him!" Boyce shouted, more to the towering pines than to me. "I can't *find* the son of a bitch! I wanna kill him, but I can't *find* him!"

"I know, Boyce. He's gone deep. We haven't turned anything, either, and I swear to you, we are looking hard."

Boyce pulled his gaze from the moon and looked at me in my tux with disgust. I knew what was coming.

"Yeah. I can see how hard you're . . . looking, Sheriff Cody." Boyce sniffed loudly and wiped his face on his sleeve. "I . . . listened to the radio this afternoon. I see how looking for some asshole killing horses—*animals!*—is more important than—"

"We're doing both. This is no lousy hired hitter electrocuting horses so the owners can collect insurance, Boyce. This guy is hacking them up with knives and axes. He's a dangerous nut. If you heard the radio, then you know he went after Rev Hodges this morning. He's dangerous, Boyce; the timing is rotten, but I have to get this freak, too. I swear my guys are doing everything possible—"

"I don't give a *shit* about your goddamn *horses!*" Boyce swung his arm and staggered to get his balance. I stepped to help him, but he held up his hand in warning. "And I don't need your fucking help!" Boyce stabbed a finger at me. "You kiss the goddamn rich guys' asses all you want! I *will* get this motherfucker! I *will* get him, and I *will* kill him! So help me *God,* I will!"

"Boyce, listen to me," I said. "You can't keep this up. You're about to drop and you're getting wild. Somebody's going to get hurt, and you're going to draw more grief you don't need. Come on up to the house with me and—"

"Fuck you!" Boyce slurred. "I don't need you! I don't need anybody! I'll get him!"

I moved toward Boyce again, but he suddenly tensed and slapped his hand onto the pistol at his belt.

"Boyce—"

"Back off, man! You back off, Sheriff Cody! I'm not going anywhere with you! Back off!"

I stopped, and spread my hands to my sides. He was a big, grief-stricken kid with a gun, who knew how to fight. If I tried to take him by force, one of us would get hurt bad.

Boyce staggered to the door of the idling four-wheel-drive vehicle. He glared again at me. "I'll get him! I swear to God! He didn't *bury* that truck in these rocky mountains! That fucking truck is here somewhere, and that murdering bastard is, too! I'll get him, and I will *kill* him dead, I swear to God!"

Boyce Calder slammed the truck door viciously, crunched the machine into gear, and fishtailed out onto the highway in a squawl of hot rubber and howling engine. I ran to the stone gate posts in time to see his lights disappear around the turn toward Hunter.

I knew how awful he felt. When my little girl—when my little Tess—was killed, I thought I would come apart from the agony, and I spent many a long night sitting in my dark bed with a pistol in my lap. I knew how utterly destroyed Boyce Calder felt. And I knew how dangerous he, too, was becoming.

25

•••••••••

Turkey in the Straw

After my troubling encounter with Boyce Calder, I continued to Laurel Ridge Farm. When I topped the wooded rise between the estate and the road and was able to see down upon the shallow valley in the bright moonlight, I began to appreciate the magnitude of the charity event Mitch and Helen Whitley had planned. Near the covered riding arena where tonight's dinner dance was to be held, there were five acres of parked horse transporters. Most were elegant goose-necked trailers with cabins built in the front, towed by expensive big Ford, Chevy, or Dodge dualies. A few were tag-along trailers hitched to Suburbans or pickup trucks, and there were no few dedicated horse vans and long gooses pulled by large road tractors. The cream of the eastern horse establishment, nearly a hundred of them, anyway, had arrived at Laurel Ridge Farm.

I noted that Mitch's main stable and a smaller one near it were ablaze with light, and several grooms were bustling about, tending the collection of prize hunting horses within. I doubted the butcher would be attracted to such an event, but evidently Mitch Whitley was taking no chances.

As I eased down the drive in the silver cruiser, it wasn't hard to imagine the most popular topic of conversation among those equestrians, newly arrived in Hunter County, late the horse-murder capital of the world. Nor was it hard to envision how warmly I'd be received.

I suppose I have to admit that there is one redeeming value to tuxedos, which is that one normally wears them to affairs resplendent with women dressed to the nines. Walking into the warm, brightly lit arena, I was pleased to see Mitch's thousand-dollar-a-plate charity dinner would not be a disappointment.

The arena had been temporarily floored in linked parquet wood panels, on which sat dozens of tables covered in dark-green tablecloths with red napkins and place mats. The chairs were wooden and plushly padded; no steel folding chairs for the horsy aristocracy, especially not at a grand a head.

Mitch had gone all out; you had to give him credit. The place was extensively decorated and Mitch had even arranged for three huge crystal chandeliers to be hung from the roof beams of the arena. The place must have been as expensive to heat as the Hunter County dungeon.

Fifty well-heeled riders for the next day's hunt had brought spouses, older children, or other acquaintances with them, most of whom would not ride with the actual fox hunt, but who would observe from vehicles or horses not involved in the hunt. There were some media people, and, consequently, the guests numbered well over two hundred.

Someone waved a hand at me. It was Pete Floyd, the newspaperman. I waved back, hoping he would let me get through a decent meal without asking about the Calders or the lost legion of horses.

At the left end of the arena, a spacious dance area remained clear, and a small, elegant band played at one side. The end of the arena was occupied by a raised dais, on which, at dining tables, sat Mitch and Helen Whitley, Merlin and Arlette Sowers, Eicher Dietrich and Karin Steiger, and Meriah Reinholdt. There was an empty chair by Meriah. A few of the guests, splendidly attired in tuxes or colorful gowns, danced to the fashionable music, but most sat or milled about, drinking and conversing.

Two photographers circulated about, snapping smiling groups of horse dandies. I recognized at least one woman I knew to be a writer for *The Chronicle of the Horse*.

When I strode into view, through the tunnel beneath the bleachers that surrounded the arena, more than a few heads turned my way. Everybody loves an entrance, but I could have passed on this one.

On the dais, I could see Karin lock onto me instantly. That supremely confident expression of amused contempt was alive and well on her entrancing face. Dr. Dietrich glanced at Karin, wondered what she watched, and followed her gaze to me. He turned to stone before my eyes.

Out of nowhere, everybody's favorite storm trooper, Klaus, appeared, blotting out the light like a solar eclipse.

"You have an invitation?" he growled, standing squarely before me.

I looked at Klaus's wide granite face. I was convinced he was a former German soldier. From his bearing and his devotion to Dietrich, he had probably been a senior sergeant. He had the look of a Mafia mechanic who killed for a living and found the profession remarkably satisfying.

"No one enters without an invitation," Klaus rumbled with a sharp German edge to his speech. He gave me a cruel smirk. "I have instructions to keep out the rabble."

I looked at him, more amused than offended. "I didn't rent this getup to muck stalls in, precious. Professor Whitley will confirm that I'm invited, if you want to check with him. Excuse me." I moved to step around him.

Klaus again stepped in my way and poked me in the chest with a finger. I froze and locked eyes with him. Klaus patted me about the waist while I restrained the urge to kick him where he'd remember being kicked. "No invitation, no admittance. Those are my instructions."

Wonderful. I was going to have to fight my way past the Fourth Reich to get my dinner.

I examined Klaus, who was stoically unemotional except for a glimmer in his eyes that signaled a readiness to do battle. "Listen, Adolph," I said casually, "I'm tired and I'm hungry. I don't have the energy for some macho confrontation with you or your boss. Just carry your ass over to Mitch Whitley and tell him I'm here."

"You will leave." Klaus commanded, edging nearer and poking me again. "Now."

I tried to count to ten, but I only got to three. "You touch me again, you rewarmed Goebbels, and I'll lock you up for assault if I have to deputize all of hell's angels to do it."

"Klaus!" Karin Steiger snarled, suddenly near. She followed with a blistering diatribe in German that I could not understand but which probably meant "carry your ass." Klaus eyed Karin, then me again. He smiled that arrogant smirk at me once more and faded away, to my joy, I admit. Taking him alone would be like arresting a yellow-eyed rodeo bull coming out of the chute.

Karin was supremely elegant in a black gown that dived into her soft cleavage in front, highlighted by the little cameo, now on a gold chain. In the rear, the dress displayed her fine, pronounced back muscles almost to her waist.

"I thought y'all did away with Nazis," I said.

"Eicher's robot often exceeds his authority," Karin hissed, still hotly eyeing the retreating Klaus. "Soon I will have to deal with him." She whipped her gaze to me, and just as instantly, it converted to soft grace and charm, accented by that Karin smile, higher at one corner than the other. She took me by the arm. "Come! There is a seat for you at the dais. You've been a busy man since we last . . . met, I hear."

We strode past dancers, across the floor to the dais, watched rather widely by everyone from the guests to the arctic Eicher Dietrich.

"Yeah," I said, "'tis the season of joy. Almost, anyway." I was acutely aware of Karin's warm, bare shoulder against me. It splashed me with memories of Thursday evening in the Whitley laundry room, and that, in turn, set off a hormonal firestorm in me. I glanced at the softly undulating upper surfaces of Karin's breasts as we walked, trying not to appear too much like a drunken sailor in a topless bar. I was deafened by the thrum of the washer, seared by the smell of her perfume and her heat, flooded by images of her panting, clinging to me, thrusting against me. Again, I felt that narcotic power she exuded, magnetic yet frightening in its strength.

Mitch Whitley descended the dais steps and walked our way. "I'll leave you in the capable hands of our grand host!" Karin said, nodding at Mitch. She squeezed my arm hard before releasing it.

"Good evening, Lewis!" Mitch said warmly, shaking hands. "I'm delighted you could be with us. It's been a trying day, I understand."

"I've had better, Professor. Glad to be here. You've really done the place up."

"Thank you. It costs a fortune, but it's good for the charity, everyone has fun, and it's an opportunity to see old friends. Listen . . . Lewis. I was hoping you'd be able to tell us you've made some progress in these horse killings. Terrible timing, this thing, what with Meriah about to announce her new stable and all."

"I can imagine. We have eliminated one popular suspect and we have a better description, Professor. We are doing everything we can. I can't stay long tonight, as I'm sure you can appreciate."

"Of course. Lewis, if I may suggest, perhaps it would be in the interest of a pleasant evening if you and Dr. Dietrich avoided each other. I—"

"An excellent suggestion, Professor," I replied, "one I was already planning."

"Thank you, Lewis. I must attend to the opening remarks. We have saved a seat on high for you there by Meriah!"

I walked past the rear of the podium. Helen Whitley smiled, but I was studiously ignored by Merlin and Arlette Sowers and, needless to say, Mr. Personality, Eicher Dietrich.

Meriah was engagingly gracious. The charm of a true lady has no equal. I sat beside her and gazed out on the crowd, now moving to their seats at the request of the bandleader.

The floral arrangements on the table were fragrant, but they reminded me of the Calders' funeral. I felt Meriah's hand pat mine beneath the table. "He tried to kill a man, today, I hear. A minister?"

"Yes. Close call. This guy is a psycho right out of Bram Stoker. I . . . Meriah, I'm sorry that all this has to spoil your announcement about the new stable. It's the worst possible development from a publicity standpoint, not to mention the tragedy, and I apologize for not having been able to dispose of it yet."

Mitch Whitley dinged a wineglass with a spoon and

adjusted the microphone on the podium. Those guests still unseated moved for their places.

"I know you're doing what you can, Lewis," Meriah answered as the crowd hushed for Mitch's remarks. "I do not underestimate the ghastly difficulty of your task. You'll get him, I know. And when you do, there will likely not be another. It will be a year before I open in Hunter County. By then he will barely be a memory."

Mitch Whitley welcomed his guests warmly, and introduced everyone on the dais. There was a restrained smattering of applause when Eicher was recognized, and another for Meriah Reinholdt. When Karin was introduced, an extended hearty applause filled the small arena. Dietrich contributed a token clap or two while staring straight ahead. There was no smattering when I was introduced.

"And now," Mitch boomed over the speaker system, which made his voice echo throughout the decorated riding arena, "once again, Helen and I are gratified to see so many of our fine friends in attendance. It is a joy to have you all with us, and on behalf of the Greater Virginia Children's Christmas Fund, we welcome you once again! Now, please enjoy a delicious dinner, a donation at cost, I might mention, by Roanoke Valley Catering . . ." Mitch invited a round of applause. "And afterward, my dear friend, Meriah Reinholdt, has a special announcement for you! Following Meriah's happy news, we will be honored to hear the remarks of another figure who is no stranger to the horse world, four-time Olympic gold medalist Dr. Eicher Dietrich. Then, we dance the night away! Tomorrow, we ride to the hounds!"

Mitch sat to a broad roar of applause, and the caterers invaded.

As all I had eaten in the last twenty-four hours had been a bowl of stew, I welcomed the good roast turkey and dressing set before us.

"I don't see Dr. Chu," I mentioned to Meriah.

"No," Meriah said, smiling, "bless her heart. She insisted on spending the evening in the barns with all the horses, tending to them after the long hours on the road that most of them have endured."

"Once a vet, always a vet, I suppose," I said.

"To tell you the truth, Lewis," Meriah said, looking at me, "I think she is quite taken with you. I think she feels Karin has you in her spell, and that disturbs Julianne. Does Karin have you in her spell, Lewis?"

I thought for a moment. "I don't love her, Meriah, if that's what you're asking. But I won't pretend that I'm not affected by her phenomenal magnetism as a woman."

"I do love her," Meriah said. "She is the 'love child,' we used to say in those days, of German Ambassador Goss Steiger and me. We had a tempestuous affair in the late fifties, and when I found I had been careless, I also found I wanted a child very much at that point in my life. Goss took her from me. He had—still has—powerful connections. He took Karin to Germany, and I was unable to fight his strength in the German courts or his political clout here in America."

We ate in silence for several minutes.

Toward the end of the splendid dinner, I looked down the table at Karin and Eicher. Karin seemed to be surveying the crowd, and Eicher was withdrawing an elegant pair of eyeglasses from his inside coat pocket. Karin sensed my gaze and shot me that look of challenge I had seen in Mitch Whitley's laundry room two nights earlier. Dietrich donned his glasses, and I was surprised to see how much older the glasses made him look. There was something odd about him, I thought, but I could not put my finger on it. He withdrew a folded paper containing, I assumed, notes for the remarks he would deliver shortly. Eicher, too, became aware of me, and his steel-blue eyes engaged me, piercing, even through his glasses. He glanced quickly at Karin, and then resumed glowering at me. I still found something indefinably odd about the picture he presented.

"Meriah," I asked, sipping my wine. "What are those two doing together?"

Meriah paused from her eating and looked at me. She knew whom I meant. "I believe they are two consummate competitors, Lewis, who have found in each other the one personality they cannot dominate, either personally or on the riding field. Eicher . . . poor Eicher . . . loves Karin. Karin has found Eicher to be the ultimate prey to be conquered, I suspect. She respects him and she envies his renown in the riding world, but it evokes only a passion to defeat him."

"Not much of a basis for a tranquil marriage," I observed.

"They'll *never* be married," Meriah said with surprising vehemence. I looked at her, trying to fathom what she was implying, but she studied her food.

Again, I looked down the dais at Dr. Dietrich. Again, he looked at me with white heat. Suddenly, I dropped my fork. I knew what was odd now. It was his glasses.

Meriah looked at me. "Lewis, are you all right?"

I struggled to collect my thoughts; when I did, I rose from my chair. "Excuse me, please," I mumbled to Meriah Reinholdt. To the surprise of everyone at the dais, I bolted down the steps and trotted across the floor to the exit tunnel.

I ran through the cold night air to the larger of the barns where all the horses were stalled for the night. In the lighted stable, several people moved among the horses, providing them with water and hay, covering some with colorful horse blankets. There was nothing here but stalls for horses and a few small tack rooms. Not what I sought. I exited the opposite end of the large stable and dived into the smaller, but it, too, was only quartering for horses. I was trotting down the aisle when I heard a familiar voice. "Lewis?" I stopped and turned to see Julianne Chu standing beside Yang, her pretty little Arabian gelding. "Lewis," Julianne repeated, looking at me with concern, "is something wrong?"

Seeing Julianne in the dim barn lighting, I was struck by how very beautiful a woman she, too, was. She wasn't the sort of stupifyingly gorgeous that Karin was, yet the simple, perfect symmetry of her face, the delicate, round lines to her lips, and the big brown eyes constituted a quieter but equally absorbing beauty.

Julianne wore a stylish light-green ski jacket over a dark-blue turtle-neck sweater, along with jeans and the sort of high rubber boots you wear when you're walking around fifty horses in stalls.

"Julianne! You look . . . very nice." I never sounded so lame.

Julianne blushed charmingly and studied her feet. She raised her head and melted me with a smile. "Why, thank you, Lewis. Is that why you came out to the barns in your tuxedo?"

"Not exactly, Julianne. But it sure did make the trip worthwhile. I . . . ah . . . I'm looking for something."

"What?"

"I'm not sure, but I'll know when I find it. Excuse me." I trotted toward the far end of the smaller barn.

"Lewis!" Julianne protested. "What are you—?"

I was outside trying to see what I could of the other outbuildings under the winter moon. A hundred yards up the gentle mountain slope, backed against the woods that rose to the summit over a mile distant, stood still another barn, unlit, this one a huge agricultural barn, distinct from a stable.

Julianne Chu ran into the darkness beside me. "Lewis! What's wrong? Why are you so—? Lewis!" I was already running for the barn.

I had horse manure on the soles of my patent-leather tux shoes by the time I reached the big barn, fumbled around the entrance, and found a light switch. When light illuminated the interior, it revealed a broad, roof-high center aisle with no exit at the other end, as the barn was sunken against the rising mountainside. Several wide enclosures ran off the sides of the aisle, most of which contained Mitch's antique collector automobiles, beneath dust covers. In one was a large John Deere tractor with the long steel bars of a hydraulic hay-roll lift mounted to its front. In another was a hay baler. The loft was stacked with standard bales of hay, but three of the enclosures off the ground-floor aisle were stuffed with those huge rolls of hay five feet high, rolled into the high stalls two rolls wide and stacked three rolls high like cans of beer in a dispenser. I ran all the way to the end, looking in each stall, but I didn't see it.

"Damn!" I spat.

"Lewis!" Julianne cried, running into the big aisle behind me, more than a little exasperated. "Will you *please* tell me what you—"

"Ah!" I yelled, cutting her off. I scrambled back to the last stall.

"Lewis!"

I seized the cords of the first roll and pulled, and the heavy hay roll revolved toward me. I dived into the rolls behind.

No.

I moved to the second stall stacked three high with hay rolls. The lower layer of rolls was pinned by the upper two, so I jumped onto the lower row and heaved on the front left roll of the second layer, but it wouldn't budge. With a little examination, I learned why, and I knew I'd finally found it.

The rolls were tied into the stall with lengths of baling twine, which had sunken into the surface of the rolls. I opened the tiny Swiss army knife on my key ring and sawed at the tough twine. Julianne looked on as if I were losing my mind.

The twine parted with a snap. I folded the little knife and heaved again on the roll in front. I had hay all over my black tux, and my hands were chafed by the tight vinyl bindings securing the big hay rolls. Slowly the first left roll began to turn forward. I heaved it back and scrambled back out of its way as it rolled forward and dropped to the floor. And there it was, surrendering all secrets like King Tut's tomb.

I was looking with immense satisfaction at the hay-littered right side windshield and hood of a crimson Ford F-350 pickup truck with a damaged right front fender. And extruded hub lugs.

"I knew it!" I exulted, and I climbed onto the stall wall to shove the second roll off the hood of the truck. I dropped between the wall and the truck, and examined the damaged fender. Blue paint transfers. Fresh.

"I *got* you, you son of a *bitch!*" I cried.

"That's . . ." Julianne stepped apprehensively around the hay rolls, which were taller than she, into the stall. "My God, Lewis . . . that's Dr. Dietrich's truck!"

"You bet your sweet ass it is!" I said.

"He . . . Dr. Dietrich is notorious for insisting upon driving his own horses. He doesn't trust anyone else. He had this truck specially ordered to pull his—"

"It was his eyeglasses!" I crowed, hugging Julianne, lifting her off the ground, to her astonishment.

"What?" she said, totally confused. "Eyeglasses?"

"His eyeglasses are missing a tiny piece of trim! A small, tooled piece of silver trim is present over one lens, but it's missing from the other lens! I *got* the bastard!"

"Lewis, I—"

"It's that piece of silver I found at the scene of that double fatal hit-and-run accident Wednesday night! Dietrich was *there!*"

"Lewis, no! Are you trying to say Dr. Dietrich—"

"Killed Cathy and Stevie Calder! You're damn right. Now I'm going to go lock that arrogant prick in a cell!"

"Lewis, wait. How do—"

I scrambled around the hay rolls to run down the barn aisle. I was about to give Mitch Whitley's horsy guests a surprise they'd never forget.

Then, into the only exit from the barn walked a cold ex–German army sergeant in a tuxedo.

"Klaus." Julianne whispered.

He walked casually toward us, carrying a pitchfork.

26

• • • • • • • •

Gotcha

Julianne Chu and I stopped, but Klaus didn't. He slowly
advanced down the aisle of the barn, turning the pitchfork
over in his hands, the six long steel tines like the claws of a
Kodiak brown bear, a not altogether inappropriate analogy,
given the bulk and strength of the man wielding it.

Gun? What gun? Who takes a gun to a dinner party in
peaceful, remote Hunter County? Only rookies with black-
glove complexes carry their guns with them to a private
party. Not me. Oh no, I was no dummy. I wasn't going to
lug some heavy, bulky gun to a lousy horse-people party. I
had one in the car, of course, but the goddamn car was a
quarter-mile away!

Klaus stopped, watching us, and, like a hydraulic machine, he calmly bent double the outer four tines with his
bare hands, leaving only the middle two extended. I knew
why. Two tines would be harder to block and would
penetrate much deeper when they hit.

Klaus smiled and chuckled. "You were so . . . efficient,
Sheriff Cody," he said tersely, now advancing, still turning
the ugly old pitchfork. "You relieved me of my weapon as if
I were one of your common Negro criminals. No one ever
relieves me of my weapon. Were it not for Dr. Dietrich's
orders, I would have taught you whom you were talking to
in a way you would not have forgotten."

I studied Klaus as he grew nearer. "You're buying into a lot of grief here, Adolph," I said slowly. "I know you weren't driving, so that means you're not involved. Yet."

Still advancing one measured step at a time, Klaus drew the back of one hand across his mouth, never removing his gaze from me. When the hand cleared his face, it revealed gray teeth and a mean smile.

"I am, of course, involved; and it is you who has . . . bought grief. We all suffer our vices. The doctor is perhaps a bit too fond of your fine Tennessee whiskey. I have warned him often about drinking so much when he drives, but . . . the doctor cannot stand to be driven by anyone. After we unloaded the horses that night and dropped the trailer, he insisted on driving to the ABC store in Christiansburg." Klaus shrugged and chuckled again. He was a real party boy. "The doctor . . . he is a commander, not a listener."

"Beat it, Julianne," I said. "Get out of here."

"No!" Klaus ordered. You will remain where you—"

"You listen to me, mister," I said sternly. "You—"

"Silence! I have listened to you more than I care to already. It is regrettable that Dr. Dietrich killed some insignificant policeman's woman and child, but he is far too important a man to become embroiled in your petty legalities! He must compete in Atlanta. I am afraid he cannot risk a jail sentence. You should have minded your own business, Mr. . . . Cody."

"I'm the law, you dimwit; homicide *is* my business."

Wrinkles appeared where Klaus's nose met his brow, and his teeth bared. "Nonetheless, you have made a big mistake."

"Bullshit. What the hell do you think you're going to do, murder both of us? That's going to cure your boss's little hit-and-run problem? You're real bright, Adolph; maybe I could sell you an Amish Learjet."

"You underestimate your enemy, Mr. Cody, a regrettable error in combat. You followed the delicate Fraulein Chu to a remote barn, where you attempted to rape her, and, as she defended her honor, of course, you choked her to death. I heard screams. I fought you off bravely. I even had to kill you to protect myself—alas, too late for poor Fraulein Chu. In the meantime, of course, the truck simply disappears."

This wasn't going well. I ripped out of my tuxedo jacket, holding it by the collar and twisting it.

From twelve feet away he made his move, much sooner than I expected. He was right; I'd underestimated my enemy. Big mistake.

The heavy man was in excellent shape, I was dismayed to note. He covered the distance in about four bounds and went for me with the pitchfork. I whipped the jacket at the pitchfork tines, which was just enough to deflect it from hitting me about stomach level, causing it to barely clear my side. When he jerked the pitchfork back, the jacket was jerked with it. While he shook the garment off the points, I frantically searched about for some kind of weapon. The best I could find was a four-foot length of rusty chain draped over a stall wall.

The chain clattered as I drew it off the wall, which gave Klaus a brief moment of pause, but only a brief one. He knew what I knew, that a chain was an unwieldy weapon, very difficult to control and almost as likely to injure the user as the usee.

Klaus chuckled still again. This guy was really getting on my nerves. "Oh! You veesh to make a sport of it! Goood! Goood!"

We looked like a couple of dumb gladiators in an old Roman slave epic; him chuckling that *fucking* little laugh and me hoping I didn't brain myself with my own chain. I swung the chain in slow, vertical arcs at a varied rhythm I hoped Klaus could not successfully time. Skillfully, he was inching closer without appearing to.

His eyes widened just slightly, telegraphing his move by a half-second. When he lunged again, I swung the chain, again narrowly deflecting his stab. Immediately, he withdrew and stabbed again and I was slow with the chain. The tines hit me in the chest painfully, but the effort to swing the chain had caused me to lurch rearward, which lessened the impact and limited the damage to two shallow, searing stabs.

Damn! I remember thinking. *I guess this means I lose my deposit on the tux.*

The chain, in the meantime, had swung several loops around the handle of the pitchfork and snagged in the bent tines. Klaus yanked and I held. He stabbed from close range, but I blocked it by stretching the two feet of chain I still held between my hands. Invention is the mother of necessity.

Klaus became enraged, which I did not interpret as a good sign. He planted his feet and heaved rearward, staggering me forward and pulling the rusty chain several links through my grip, which hurt like hell. I knew I couldn't hold on for the mighty jerk he was gathering himself to make. He'd yank me right into the pitchfork tines. Klaus grunted and jerked the pitchfork back, but his luck was used up. The old tool had sat out in years of sun and rain. The metal tine section of the fork pulled right off the end of the handle, leaving Klaus having brought a stick to a chain fight. He backed up a step, staring with no idle concern at the rotted end of the pitchfork handle.

"Thank ya, *Jeeee*sus," I said, weak with relief at being spared the undignified death of a pond frog. *"Yeah!"* I yelled, feeling much better now, untangling the pitchfork tines from my lovely chain, as Klaus backed still farther. "Oh *yeah!* They don't make pitchforks like they used to, huh, Spartacus?"

I whipped the chain in a high overhead arc. To his credit, Klaus kept his cool and gripped the pitchfork handle at both ends to ward off the chain. However, for all their awkwardness, chains do have redeeming traits as weapons. One is you can develop one hell of a lot of speed at the tip. I heaved on the chain hard and it cut through the pitchfork handle like a bush hog, impacting the ground in a cloud of dust. The next swing with the chain caught Klaus over his upraised forearms and head, slashing his scalp and breaking one arm with a soothing crack—soothing to me, it goes without saying.

I whaled the living shit out of Klaus with the chain until I became aware of Julianne Chu yelling, "Stop it, Lewis! *Stop* it! You're going to *kill* him!" I stopped, about to pass out from my thundering heart, thinking I was *way* too old for this Hollywood shit. Klaus was hunched on all fours on the dusty, straw-littered ground, bleeding and moaning. Julianne moved to help him.

"Leave him!" I shouted. Julianne froze.

"Lewis, he's hurt bad!"

"Tough shit. Don't get where he can reach you."

I circled around behind Klaus, looped the chain around his neck, and dragged him, choking, to a ten-by-ten-inch barn support post. There, I sat him back against the post and chained his neck to it, knotting the chain behind the post out of his reach. With one broken arm, Klaus wasn't going anywhere.

"And now," I said, leaning on the barn post to catch my breath, "a word from our sponsor!"

I heard Dr. Eicher Dietrich's bold voice over the public-address system as I strode through the entry tunnel beneath the bleachers into Mitch Whitley's lavishly decorated riding arena, a gun tucked in the small of my back and a pair of handcuffs in my hand. Julianne Chu struggled to keep up on her short, if shapely, legs.

"—of us who have spent our lives appreciating and enjoying the equestrian arts might challenge the old American phrase that a dog is man's best friend," Dietrich spoke eloquently. "Indeed, many of us might declare that at least man's most noble friend is the horse." A chuckle bubbled from the attentive guests at the many tables lighted by candles. Waitresses moved about, collecting dishes. Only a few people seated near the tunnel entrance noticed me, coatless and speckled with hay, my white shirt stained with two spots of blood. They eyed me with alarm and nudged or glanced at the person nearest them. Maybe my little bow tie was crooked.

Dietrich waxed on, not noticing the small stir developing in the relatively dark table area beyond the dais lights. "It was my intent to speak to you this evening about our splendid U.S. Equestrian Team, and the challenges before us at Atlanta this summer. But events of the past few days move me to address a more urgent issue, that of the appalling failure of law enforcement in America to appreciate the needs and rights of the equestrian community and, indeed, even of the noble horse itself."

I bided my time, gathering my breath, anticipating a certain sound for which I knew I had only a few minutes to wait. Dietrich forged on with a vengeance.

"Unfortunately, right here in Hunter County, we find one

of the worst examples of this dismal failure," Dietrich went on, peering at the crowd through his evidentiary eyeglasses, the glasses with only one of two original tiny pieces of silver trim remaining on them, "in the form of Sheriff Lewis Cody."

Keep yapping, you arrogant fuck, I seethed, thinking of a chopped-up young mother and her unrecognizable baby. *Your ship's about to dock, sweetpea.*

Another stir rumbled through the crowd while, gradually, more people began to notice me standing in the darkened entryway. I looked at Mitch Whitley, who was looking with distress at Meriah Reinholdt, who in turn was staring icily at Eicher Dietrich. I noted that Karin had seen me and was looking alternately from Dietrich to me with just a touch of excitement showing in her eyes. She could sense something was in the works.

"As you can see," Dietrich indicated my empty chair on the dais, "Sheriff Cody has not had the decency to honor the invitation to join us tonight, extended him by our good friends Mitchell and Helen Whitley. Indeed, he has abruptly walked out without so much as a word of thanks to his hosts. I think this is a graphic of example of the contempt Sheriff Cody has demonstrated at every quarter in his dealings with the equestrian community. He has resisted the establishment of the marvelous stable my dear friend Meriah has just announced she will build here, and he has callously disregarded the esteem in which we all hold the noble horse by failing to adequately pursue the perverse killer now savagely preying upon defenseless horses in Hunter County. This despicable—"

I heard it. The lawman's lullaby. Sirens in the distance moving rapidly closer. I stepped into the arena and casually walked toward the dais, tucking handcuffs in the front of my belt as I walked.

"—clearly indicates an attitude of ignorance and insensitivity toward horses and horse owners all too prevalent in American police management circles." Even more people began to take note of me as I walked along the edge of the dining area, began to whisper among themselves and point discreetly, began to glance from Dietrich to me. Absorbed in his diatribe, Dietrich was still under the impression that he was damning an absent man. The faint, distant sirens grew nearer and the audience murmured again, glancing nervously at me. I paused at the end of the dais, and the crowd grew suddenly silent.

Dietrich moved on with his harangue. "My friends, I submit to you that we must confront this ignorance and insensitivity on every front! We must demand consideration of—" Dietrich spotted me climbing the steps to the dais.

"My, my," Dietrich said, recovering from his surprise with aplomb. "It seems Sheriff Cody has elected to grace us with his presence after all. I'm most pleased."

"This one's for you, Boyce," I mumbled, passing behind Merlin and Arlette Sowers and Professor and Mrs. Whitley. Sirens outside became quite audible.

"Perhaps Sheriff Cody would care to enlighten us on his—" Dietrich cleaved his remarks. He now heard the whooping sirens of two of my deputies arriving, and it began to dawn on him that it might not be a wonderful day in the neighborhood.

Merlin Sowers gawked at me, bits of hay clinging to my black tux pants, two bloody spots staining the front of my white shirt. He whispered heatedly, "Lewis! What—?"

Mitch and Helen Whitley craned about in their chairs as I passed behind them. On the other side of the podium, Meriah watched intently, and Karin seemed slyly amused.

I stopped behind the podium as Haskel Beale and Otis Clark, my deputies, ran into the arena through the entry tunnel. They jerked to a stop, then spotted me on the dais. I waved them forward.

Dietrich turned to face me, struggling to grasp what was happening. Rather deftly, I thought, I reached with both hands and removed Dietrich's glasses. I folded them and slid them into my pocket. Dietrich jerked slightly as the glasses slid from his head, and a theatric gasp emitted from the crowd. He looked as though I'd just slapped him. "This—! What? This is outrageous! I demand to—"

Haskel hurried onto the dais and handed me a folded document. I slapped it down hard on the podium. "Dr. Dietrich," I said, my voice carrying on the speaker system, echoing through the hushed arena, "that is a warrant for your arrest for the manslaughter of Catherine and Steven

Calder, and for felony accident hit-and-run. Put your hands on the podium, Doctor."

To say that all hell broke loose would be like saying Desert Storm was a little loud. Many in the crowd stood in shock. All joined in a loud collective stir. Merlin Sowers shot up like a Saturn booster yelling, "Whaaat?!" Meriah Reinholdt lowered her face to her hand. Photographers raced to flash shots of the scene. The writer from *The Chronicle of the Horse* hurried forward as fast as her tight gown would permit. Even the shock-proof Karin Steiger looked solidly surprised.

Eicher Dietrich was not amused. "You're insane!" he said. "You'll never—! Don't you *dare* touch me!"

I seized the good doctor by his right wrist, pulled it to me enough to extend his arm, and struck him upward with my left palm behind his right elbow, causing him to rotate left into the podium. I shoved his head down against the podium, where it hit with a thunk that resounded over the PA system throughout the building.

"You have the right to remain silent!" I said, ratcheting a handcuff onto Dietrich's wrist. "Anything you say may be used against *you* in a court of law!" He struggled strongly. It took effort, because Dietrich had panicked in surprise, and professional competition riders are necessarily in excellent physical shape, but I held him against the heavy dais by raising the cuffed wrist high behind him. *"You* have the right to consult an attorney before answering questions!" I grappled to gain a grip on his remaining wrist. We rocked the podium, jarring the microphone from its holder. It fell to the floor below the dais, emitting several painfully loud bangs over the speakers, startling the crowd, evoking a few squeals and shouts. As I leaned over Dietrich, he frantically whispered music to my ears, "You'll never prove it! You'll never prove it! I was *drinking!* It was an accident, damn you! It was a simple *accident!"* His words were uttered with his head jammed against the podium, but a couple of glances told me he'd been clearly heard by the Whitleys, by Karin, and by Meriah Reinholdt.

Dietrich thrashed in rage, but I held him. "Thanks for the confession, Doc," I replied, bending his left wrist near his right to handcuff it, too. "Now we add DWI to the charges."

When the cuffs secured both his powerful arms, I pulled him from the dais.

"You'll *never* prove it!" Dietrich hissed again, to the profound shock of Mitch Whitley, who now stood near. My deputies pushed past Mitch to take control of Dietrich.

"Dream on, doc," I said looking him in the eyes, "I got the truck, and I got a witness!" He blanched visibly.

Pandemonium reigned in the arena. The crowd noise had risen sharply. The *Chronicle* writer was yelling at me. Pete Floyd was knocking over chairs trying to reach a spot where he could photograph Dietrich. Karin stood, her incredible body lithe in that black gown, craning to see Dietrich, who wrestled futilely with my deputies as they moved him toward the dais steps. Meriah watched from her chair, her hand to her lips, a tear gleaming in one eye.

Merlin Sowers was apoplectic. "Lewis!" he squawled, crowding past Mitch Whitley to me. He grabbed me by the arm. "Lewis! Have you lost your goddamn *mind?* That's *Eicher Dietrich,* for Christ's sake!"

"Support your local police, Merlin," I sighed, moving to the podium.

I retrieved the microphone wire and fished it up from the floor in front of the dais. "Ladies and gentlemen," I said loudly but calmly, my voice ringing in the arena. The crowd noise began to subside. Merlin took his hands from the sides of his head and gawked at me. "Ladies and gentlemen," I repeated forcefully into the mike, "if you will take your seats for a moment . . . I'd like to offer a word of explanation."

People moved to their seats and the murmur declined.

"Folks . . ." I began, searching for some appropriate commentary on the spectacle of the year for the horse world. "Ladies and gentlemen, I apologize sincerely to you and to your hosts for this unpleasant interruption of your evening." I paused. You could have heard a mouse fart in that arena. "I . . . cannot give you a lot of detail tonight, as doing so could prejudice a criminal case . . . but I will tell you that, regrettably, evidence has surfaced which lends probable cause to believe that Dr. Eicher Dietrich killed a local young woman and her baby Wednesday night in a hit-and-run traffic accident." A renewed murmur ran through the guests on the floor of the arena. "Ladies and gentlemen, while I have your attention . . . I would like to tell you that I ride a horse of my own, which I am extremely fond of. I do appreciate the beauty and joy of the horse, and I have from the beginning welcomed Mrs. Reinholdt's splendid new stable to Hunter County, as she can attest. As most of you probably know, there is . . . someone . . . who has attacked five local horses recently. I assure you that I have the greatest concern for these crimes, and I and my entire staff will continue to devote maximum effort toward arresting the responsible individual as soon as possible. Once again, I apologize for the interruption of your evening; I hope you will enjoy the remainder. And now I will ask you to excuse me, as I must see to my duties. Good evening."

No one made a sound, which didn't surprise me. I had just dethroned the king and radically altered the entire eventing scene for the Atlanta Olympics.

27

•••••••

No Rest for the Weary

Eicher Dietrich screamed for his lawyers all the way to the dungeon. When we brought him into the booking room, he screamed that he was a personal friend of the governor, that he would have us all fired, that he would sue each of us and the county. It was remarkably satisfying to see genuine fear replace the arrogance in his eyes when the cell door rolled shut. Clearly, it occurred to Dr. Eicher Dietrich that perhaps that clang was a sound he should get used to.

Klaus's last name turned out to be Breithopf. Under guard, he was taken to a Roanoke hospital to be treated for a . . . chain of problems.

Pierce had Dietrich's fancy truck dragged out from the round bales and impounded for evidence. We attempted to question Dietrich about the accident, and to try to learn whether Klaus had assaulted me independently or through any collusion with Dietrich. By then, however, he'd collected himself and refused to answer questions until conferring with his attorneys.

It was nearly midnight when I finally pulled into the garage behind Mountain Harbor, casting a paranoid eye toward the stable. I crossed the creek to the stable and disabled the alarm system. After checking on Dublin and Moose, I dragged my ass to the house, after resetting the alarm. I had a start when I found Elizabeth's bed empty, before remembering she was spending the night with Rev Hodges's family down at the church. Gruesome was missing, too, and I knew he was also at the church, sleeping blissfully between Tara Hodges and Elizabeth, no doubt snoring like a walrus with a gunshot wound to the lungs.

I showered and collapsed into the prairie-sized bed. The pace of the last few days was catching up with me. With Arthur asleep over the stable and Polly in her apartment over the garage, I was all alone in a twelve-thousand-square-foot mansion, and I felt like it.

I slept the deep dreamless sleep of the exhausted until some dark hour when I imagined I felt something sharp upon my neck. Then I had fitful visions of the mad butcher standing in the room with a knife at my neck. As it too frequently does, my hand crept beneath the quilt to a familiar place near the edge of the bed, like a worried child's hand for a teddy bear. My fingers slid around the hard-rubber textured grip of my pistol. I squeezed it and felt the ridges in the trigger, and it gave me a much warmer feeling of security than my teddy bear ever had.

Again, I thought I felt a mildly painful prick at my neck, and again I suffered mindflashes of the butcher standing over me, that terrible knife that had wreaked so much savage evil held to my neck.

I was half right.

My eyes opened and my whole body flinched. I suddenly became aware that I was not as alone as I had lamented earlier. I could plainly see the gleam of a grooved knife blade placed at my cheek just beneath my right eye. In the pale light of a November moon shining through the bedroom window, I could only make out a silhouette behind the knife but, together with the scent of a woman on the air, it was enough.

"If you move," said Karin Steiger in the darkness, "I'll cut your eye out." My right eye twitched at the pain of the blade against the cheek beneath my eye. Never relenting the touch of the knife, she knelt on the bed and straddled my waist with strong legs draped in a long denim skirt. Her weight settled solidly onto my belly. My brain raced to order the extraordinary events into some meaningful, understandable pattern, not with much success.

All the panic-driven fears that would affect most anyone under the circumstances coursed through me, and I jerked again, but the knife anchored my head down. Any knife in such a situation would have seemed like a sword, but this one was big. My eyes focused on a round steel ring at the root of the blade. A bayonet.

"How the hell did you get in here?" I croaked, remembering even as I said it that in my weariness I had not locked the French doors to the den when I came in. You didn't lock houses in Hunter County. My hand slithered slowly beneath the quilt for my steel teddy bear, only to stop inches short of reaching it. It was a big bed.

"You have *ruined* the life of the man I am engaged to marry," Karin whispered. The knife dug in a little deeper. I could feel the skin tear as the tip penetrated.

"Ow! Christ! Not half as much as he ruined the lives of a sweet young woman and a baby," I growled. "Now you listen to me good. If you aren't going to use that goddamn thing, get it the fuck out of my face, or I'm going to ruin another life right here and now!"

For a disconcertingly long moment, the woman sitting astride me with the bayonet digging into my face said nothing, though I could hear her labored breathing hissing in the dark. I contemplated going for her, but if she was determined and quick, she'd stab me through the eye. At a minimum, if I grabbed her wrist, I risked raking the point of the knife through my eye.

Then the fragrant, moonlight-silhouetted figure raised her head and laughed that sexy, earthy woman laugh I had so enjoyed at Mitch Whitley's dining room table three days before. She removed the knife from my flesh, tossed it to the side on the bed, and laughed still more richly. I wasn't laughing.

In midlaugh, I seized her by her hair with my left hand and wrenched her off me. She gasped and tumbled onto her back. I scrambled to get astride her, forgetting for a moment in my rage that I was nude. I pinned her to the pillow with a handful of her hair, and felt my cheek with my other hand. It slid about in oily blood.

"You *fucking* lunatic!" I hissed. "You could've blinded me!"

Karin found the whole thing just immensely amusing. With a hand over her eyes, she laughed again, not with scorn or meanness, but with genuine amusement. I was having difficulty grasping the humor.

I groped about the quilt in the dark 'til my hand hit the bayonet. I seized it and placed its edge to Karin's tender throat, which took some of the giggle out of it for her. She inhaled sharply and breathed rapidly. "That instrument is very sharp!" she said.

"You're goddamn right it is!" I answered, wiping the blood on my hand across her cheek. I pushed back, inserted the blade, edge up, through the thin, fuzzy fabric of the sweater she wore, at her navel, and slit the fabric all the way to her chin. The sound of parting fibers was distinct, even above our heavy breathing. She was right. The knife had the honed edge of a razor. Karin drew a sharp breath through clenched teeth as the blade tip slid past the side of her neck. Her white nylon bra reflected the moonlight. I slipped the knife beneath where the cups were joined and sliced it. The two halves, elastic and suddenly freed of their ample load, sprang to the sides, and her breasts jiggled with her struggle.

With the edge down, I drew the blade sideways across her nipples, slowly, carefully, not enough to cut her but quite enough for the little nipples to swell and quiver with the passing of the blade. Karin breathed in short, quick spurts.

"I noticed it was sharp about the moment you stuck it through my face!" I said.

"I . . . borrowed it from Klaus's room," Karin said, her clipped German accent rolling the *r*'s in *borrowed* and *room*. Even with the bayonet against her neck, Karin began to giggle again. "It . . . ah . . . I don't think he'll be needing it for a while!" She cracked up laughing yet again.

I had to admit that was pretty funny. I smiled in spite of myself. I took the damn bayonet off her chest, suddenly becoming very aware that her breasts stood straight up splendidly though she lay on her back, and I knew from the washing machine encounter that there was no silicone enhancement.

"I ought to lock you up," I said, not sounding very convincing even to myself.

"Ooooh," Karin cooed. "Is he angry?" she asked sweetly.

At the same time, she gripped my waist and slid beneath me, placing her face beneath my dangling penis. She took me in her hand and kissed me on the tip and the sides, slowly, lovingly. "Oooooh," she said softly again, "Did we make him angry? Ooooh. So sorry." She continued to kiss my rapidly hardening dick. "So sorry," she repeated, closing her eyes and rubbing my cock along the sides of her face and across her lips. Then she began to lap the bottom surface like a lollipop, holding the penis in one hand and caressing my balls with the other. She evidently thought a man of my caliber could be pacified by a little oral gratification. That crazy Columbus thought the world was round, too.

For a woman to be really good at fellatio, she has to enjoy it for her own sake, gaining real oral satisfaction for herself in the process, for it is better shared than served and best drawn out over time. Some women know, and some don't. Some care, and some don't.

Karin did and did.

When the thousand-year orgasm consumed me, she swallowed and lapped and swallowed and lapped as though voraciously hungry. Then she smiled in triumph as though she had achieved something, which indeed she had. The wetness on her face gleamed in the moonlight and the metallic smell of semen hung in the air.

I stripped Karin Steiger of her underpants and indulged myself in oral gratification, which I had no trouble enjoying for my own sake. There is nothing so deliciously slippery as an aroused woman. In time, it became her occasion to cry out and release and embrace my skull between her thighs.

While we floated in blissful satiation, Karin said, "I suppose I should thank you for eliminating my biggest competitor in the games this summer. I regret that I will not be able to defeat him directly. It is a shame. I admire much of Eicher, of course, but it was a terrible thing he did. It is so like him to place himself above the law."

"Yeah," I said, holding Karin. "Well, I wouldn't spend the endorsement money just yet, if I were you. My case against him ought to be bulletproof, but there is no integrity left in the American court system. Dietrich could get himself a cobalt lawyer who might plead him off or block evidence in some way. Even if he goes down for two whole manslaughter charges, he may only do a few months, the way sentencing is done these days. It's sick. And then we wonder why our crime rate is so high and getting higher."

When I slept again, Karin atop me, even the butcher did not intrude. Even the intense Karin breathed deep in slumber.

Sometime before dawn the phone rang. I rolled a sleepy Karin off me, propped on my pillows, and groped for the phone. I searched for the digital clock: 6:08 A.M.

"Cody."

"Lewis?"

"Yeah, Pierce. Good morning."

"Maybe not. He's done another horse."

"Shit! This son of a bitch is relentless!"

"Sometime last night. Plowhorse for one of those Mennonite families other side of Saddle Mountain. Went out to feed about half an hour ago and found it."

"Mare?"

"Of course. Strung up and cut up in the bank barn. Same song, sixth verse. Just talked to Billy and Neil on the radio. Nobody saw shit. No weapon on the scene. Nothing different about the scene that they see so far."

I drew a deep breath and let it out. Karin stirred. She lay her head on my chest, the back of her fine, slender neck toward my face. "All right, Pierce. I'm coming in. How's Dietrich?"

"Sulking, mostly. Newby says he didn't sleep at all. He's done called his lawyers, of course. But they ain't here yet."

I hung up the phone. Yawning, Karin asked, "Your maniac. He . . . has killed another horse?"

Another ring of the phone cut off my answer.

"Cody."

"Lewis? It's me. Lucia."

"Lucia!" I said, stunned. "It . . . it's good to hear your voice."

Karin Steiger instantly began to play with my dick, stroking it slowly, adding to my confusion. But I didn't tell her to stop.

"I'm . . . fine, Lewis. I'm . . . I'm afraid this isn't a social call."

Karin began to lick me again. My head, the one with ears on it, felt like a careening bobsled crashing from one wall of the run to the other, from one surprising train of thought to another erotic one and back. Again and again.

"Lucia, what's up?" I asked, trying to concentrate despite the wet ministrations of Karin's tongue.

"Lewis, I have been retained by Dr. Eicher Dietrich. His law firm in New York just contacted me."

"At six A.M. on Sunday morning?"

"Exactly. I want Dr. Dietrich released on bail immediately."

"What is this, Lucia? You know how the game is played. He sits in jail until court convenes tomorrow morning, when he's arraigned, charged, and bail is set."

"Not this time, Lewis. A copy of a court order from the seventh circuit in Roanoke just rolled off my fax machine. It sets bail at twenty-five thousand dollars and orders the immediate release of the accused. This guy plays hardball with some heavy hitters, Lewis. You've got to release him, now."

"All right, Lucia," I said with resignation. "I'll be at my office in forty-five minutes." Karin continued to play with me.

"Lewis?" Lucia said, her tone switching from counsel for one of my prisoners to a woman I had shared love with.

"Yes?"

"What about you, Lewis? Are you okay?"

At that moment, Karin slipped me into her mouth. Her head bobbed up and down slowly. Her fine back muscles shone sleek in the moonlight. I stopped breathing momentarily.

"Lewis?"

"Uh! I'm . . . fine, Lucia. Ah, how are things with . . . uh . . ."

"John. John Blake. It's good, Lewis. He's a fine man."

"I'm glad," I replied, sincere but having difficulty keeping the strain from showing in my voice. Karin was competing, as she always did, this time against another woman, for my attention. And as she always did, she was winning. "I'll see you in forty-five minutes. No. Better make it an hour. 'Bye, love." I banged the phone down.

Karin laughed again, gently but genuinely, and she rose, straddled me, and took me in. She began to rock to and fro, her head back, her eyes closed. I closed mine.

With no warning whatever, Karin seized me about the throat with both hands and jammed with her thumbs until I thought my Adam's apple would collapse. I cursed my stupidity even as I choked to breathe and get her off me. But Karin Steiger, like virtually all top competitive women athletes, especially those accustomed to commanding thirteen-hundred-pound horses, was strong, fast, and balanced. About the moment I felt my brains were going to squirt out my ears, I drew both fists up hard, hitting her wrists and breaking her grip. She grappled to regain it, and even in the struggle, in the pale moonlight from the window, I could see the look of fevered excitement on her face.

I was still inside her, even as she thrashed, and if the truth be known, I was close to coming in spite of it all. Still she clawed to get at my throat. I succeeded in hooking a leg across her face and throwing her to the floor. She had barely hit when she rolled, cried something German in anger, and came back like a leopard for an antelope fawn. I caught her coming in, and with her momentum, I rolled her over me. She fell off the far side of the bed and dragged me with her.

I hit the floor and Karin hit me with her open hand across the side of my head, succeeding at last in pissing me off mightily. "God*damn* it!" I gasped.

We wrestled about the floor until I was able to pin an arm behind her with one hand and seize the back of her hair with the other. I gained my balance, whirled her about me, and stuffed her, face down, on the mattress, her knees extending to the floor. I dropped to my own knees between hers, forcing her thighs apart. She bucked and jerked and I released her arm to use my hand to guide myself into her. As she was quite wet and open and I was still slippery with her, it didn't prove difficult. Karin groaned tightly, and pushed back with her arms. I bent over her, seized both her wrists, and pulled them behind her, causing her to collapse forward on the mattress with a grunt. I bound her thumbs in one fist and reached beneath her wrists with my other arm, taking again a fistful of the hair at the back of her head. Now, secured beyond escape, she arched her back, head high, and repeatedly pushed herself back into me, counterthrusting my strokes, crying high, nasal, primal noises of copulation. Oh, those sounds.

I was sweating profusely, my chest was heaving, my whole body was rigid. I had symbolically defeated her, taken her, conquered her. I had raped her in the fantasy of us both, even if a certain consent had been present from the beginning. I can hear the feminists screaming now, but the effect was still incredible. When I felt the warm wave cresting, I released Karin's thumbs and hair, slid my arms beneath hers, and gripped the fronts of her shoulders. I sucked her earlobe and pulled her hard against me until I poured and poured and poured.

By the blue winter moon, I could see Karin grinning over her shoulder like the Cheshire cat. "You witch," I whispered, so very tired. "You'll kill us both."

We slept.

I opened my eyes to find her standing near me in the darkness, her clothes bundled in one arm. She bent and kissed me. I was startled to see that tears ran from her face onto mine. "Lewis," she whispered, "I just want to live! I want to *feel* my life!" She turned, and as she walked toward the bathroom, I saw her stagger to the side and drop to one knee.

I threw back the guilt and rose. "Karin, are you all ri—?"

She stood shakily, her feet apart, and she waved me off. "No! There's . . . it's nothing. Just the darkness."

When Karin was gone, I stood naked at the window and watched her little Porsche slide across the blue-and-white landscape. My face was swollen where the bayonet had pierced it; my throat was sore. Several muscles ached, and my knees had carpet burns. "Christ almighty," I whispered to myself, stumbling to the shower, "we have *got* to stop meeting this way."

At the dungeon, there were two news vans in the street and the marked and unmarked cars of several print media people. One reporter waved at me to stop, but I just waved back and drove into the compound.

Eicher Dietrich looked like cellblock life didn't agree with him, but Lucia Dodd looked lovely despite the fact she'd been up for two hours. Seeing her for the first time in weeks set asunder the carefully constructed little cage in which I'd placed my feelings for her. She was all business, but I was not surprised.

We processed Dietrich's release in stiff silence but for the required remarks. When Lucia paid the bail, Dietrich was handed his effects. He snatched his tux coat from my deputy, and stabbed a finger at me. "You will regret this, Sheriff Cody! You do not know who you're—"

"Dr. Dietrich!" Lucia interrupted firmly, "It is not in your interest to threaten officers of the law. My advice to you is to remain silent and follow me. Now!" Lucia immediately headed for the door without looking back. Dietrich followed after one more glare at me.

A pitiful twenty-five grand bond—Dietrich only needed to post ten percent—for a drunk who killed two people was typical of the disregard for human life that the courts had assumed. It was galling, but I'd had to get good at accepting injustices I could do nothing about.

I yawned and looked around the booking room. As it was Sunday, no office personnel were supposed to be present, yet there at his computer console was Double-Parked. He was characteristically so absorbed in The Binary Demon that he was oblivious of anything going on around him. He had not so much as noticed Dietrich's histrionics, as he tapped away at his keyboard and eyed the result through his glasses. By his feet sat a brilliantly striped new skateboard.

I walked over and patted him on the shoulder. He jumped as though he'd thought he was alone in the room. "Oh hi, Sheriff! Hey, thanks for the skate! Man, it is bosh to the rim!"

"You've earned it many times over, Double-Parked. I'll be lucky if the feds don't get me for violating child-labor laws with you. How's it going?"

"Oh, nah so good, Sheriff Cody. I put out queries for recently released prison inmates over six feet four of a dark-skinned race. 'Specially anyone serving sentence for animal-related crimes. Come up with a big fat goose egg. Paht of the problem is there is no common database. All states have their own database for their own facilities. Common data-base for federal institutions, of course, but no one released in the last thirty days matches that profile. I'm having to query the state prison systems independently. Very slow."

I patted the kid's shoulder again. "Thanks, Double-Parked. This case is a cast-iron bitch, and I need all the help I can get. Just do the best you——"

I was suddenly distracted by shouts, thumps, and other sounds of tumult from outside the dungeon. I hurried to the door and looked out at the parking lot to find Eicher Dietrich being thrown over the hood of Lucia's Lexus by a ragged but enraged Boyce Calder. Lucia Dodd attempted to intervene and Boyce shoved her flat on her ass.

"I'll kill you!" Boyce grunted at Dietrich, his voice hoarse. "I'll *kill* you, you murdering drunk!"

I went out the door at a dead run. I reached Boyce just as he had pinned Dietrich to the hood of Lucia's car and his free hand closed on his gun. Grappling with Boyce Calder was like tackling a D-8 Caterpillar. "Boyce! Stop it!" I yelled, but Boyce had just found someone he'd been looking very hard for. He released Dietrich and flailed at me. It was pretty clear he was over the edge. Fatigue, grief, and rage had taken their toll. Newby Biddle joined the fray, but Boyce was too much for the both of us. Had Boyce been anyone but a friend whose crushing grief I understood, I would have employed more force without concern for injuring him, but I wanted to subdue him without hurting him in some way that would only compound his woes. Newby no doubt had the same thought, but we were losing. The fact that Boyce was hysterical and exhausted was all that kept him from maiming one of us.

The news people were videotaping everything from their vantage outside the compound, shoving and jockeying for position, shouting and pointing.

From somewhere, the cavalry arrived. Pierce Arroe hooked a huge arm around Boyce's neck and lifted him from the ground. I jumped in and removed Boyce's gun from his belt. Boyce thrashed, but Pierce held him comfortably.

I stood, winded. Dietrich was pale, was bleeding from his lip and nose, and was being examined by Lucia Dodd.

Lucia turned on me. "You get him under control, Lewis!" she demanded, stabbing a finger at the struggling Boyce. "If he gets within shouting distance of my client just one more time, I'll get a warrant for his arrest!"

"We'll handle him, Lucia. Are you hurt?"

Lucia took a moment to collect herself. "No. No, I'm all right, Lewis. I just fell when he pushed me."

"Good. I'll talk to you later. Get Dietrich out of here."

Lucia seemed confused for a brief moment. She reached to touch my hand, our eyes met, then she shepherded Dietrich toward her car.

"Pierce, you and Newby get Boyce inside. Move! Let's get the hell off everybody's TV."

I ignored the calls from news people and followed my men inside the dungeon. In my office, Pierce and Newby heaped Boyce onto the old leather couch and I waved them out. I patted Pierce on his huge shoulder as he went by.

I gave Boyce time to weep it out and collect himself as much as he could. "It's wrong, it's wrong, it's goddamn *wrong!* My Cathy and Stevie are *dead* and that son of a bitch walks free! It's *wrong!"*

I let him continue in a similar vein until he ultimately collapsed in a low, wracking sob.

"Boyce," I told him, "for your sake, as well as Dr. Dietrich's, you've got to let us handle this. I swear I'll hurt him as bad as the law will let me, Boyce, but if you get near him again I'll lock you up for your own good. Do you understand me, son?"

Boyce sighed and wiped his eyes. He nodded his head. "Yes, sir. I understand."

I walked Boyce to his car after he refused my offer to have a deputy drive him home. He assured me he was under control and he felt able to drive safely.

"Go home, Boyce. Go home and let your family help you through this. You're only making it harder on yourself and your family. Let me handle Dietrich. Go *home,* Boyce."

He closed the door to his black Pathfinder before looking at me with those Holocaust eyes. "I don't have a home anymore, Sheriff Cody," Boyce Calder croaked. "I just have a house. And I can't face living in it alone."

To my relief, Boyce drove away in a normal manner toward Christiansburg.

I took a moment to give the media people an update, then I left them shouting more questions through the fence.

I almost made it through the door to the dungeon when I was virtually run over by a hysterical twelve-year-old Korean computer genius.

"I did it! I did it! I did it!" Double-Parked screamed, waving a strip of edgeholed computer paper. "I did it, Sheriff Cody! I found him! I found the horse killer!"

28

●●●●●●●●

The Fairer Sex

I shushed Double-Parked and hurried him inside the dungeon. He was about to bust.

"I got him! I got him! I got—"

"Easy, Doubled-Parked," I said, amused. I led him by the hand into my office. "Calm down a little for me. What do you have?"

Double-Parked slapped the computer sheet down on my desk, beaming. He paced about my office, bouncing on his tiptoes as he walked. "I got him," he whispered over and over to himself.

I scanned the readout before me.

```
TO:   HUNTER COUNTY VA SHERIFFS DEPARTMENT
      4566277VA1237
      OLD COURTHOUSE BLDG
      HUNTER VA
FROM: ILLINOIS DEPT OF CORRECTIONS 3654811IL4471
      RECORDS DIVISION
      12811-A WEST BILLINGS AVE
      MARION IL
SUBJ: NLETS QUERY 94345-0198 HUNTER CO SHERIFFS
      DEPT
REQUESTING AGENCY:  PER YOUR QUERY 94345-0198/
      S:M/ R:N-H/ H:76+/ W:UNK/ A;UNK/ E:UNK/
```

HA:UNK/ OTHER IDENT CHAR: UNK/ OFF:BESTIALITY-
ANIMAL SODOMY OR OTHER ANIMAL/ RELEASE
DATE: 050194+///
**** NO MATCH **** ILL DEPT OF CORR INMATE FILE///
<<<<< HOWEVER/ BE ADVISED >>>>>> ANIMAL SEX
OFFENDERS ABSENT COINCIDENT HUMAN VICTIMS
ROUTINELY ASSIGNED ILLINOIS PSYCHIATRIC CRIMINAL
DETENTION CENTER 3654812IL7666 318 PARIS BLVD
BLOMBERG IL/ END/////////////

A second page documented a query to the psych center,
and a third printout bore the reply that had Double-Parked
so excited.

TO: HUNTER COUNTY VA SHERIFFS DEPARTMENT
      4566277VA1237
      OLD COURTHOUSE BLDG
      HUNTER VA
FROM: ILLINOIS PSYCHIATRIC CRIMINAL DETENTION
        CENTER 3654812IL7666
        318 PARIS BLVD
        BLOMBERG IL
SUBJ: NLETS QUERY 94345-0198 HUNTER CO VA
        SHERIFFS DEPT
******* FED PRIV ACT NOTICE: THIS INFORMATION SUBJ
TO FED PRIV ACT/ CONFIDENTIAL/ FOR LAW ENFORCEMENT
DISSEMINATION ONLY/ PENALTY FOR PRIVATE OR OTHER
UNAUTHORIZED USE/// *******
REQUESTING AGENCY: PER YOUR QUERY 94345-0199/
**** NO MATCH **** IL CRIM PSYCH DET CTR PATIENT
FILE/// >>>>>> HOWEVER/ BE ADVISED <<<<<< IF
R: BROADENED TO INCLUDE C:/ ONE (1) >>>>>> MATCH
<<<<< AS FOLLOWS:
      S:M/ R:C/ H:77/ W:243/ A:31/ E:GRN/ HA:BLK/
      OTHER IDENT CHAR: TATTOO "MOM" HEART ARROW
      UP RT ARM - SCAR UP LE ARM - TOP RT EAR
      MISSING/ OFF: DESTR OF PROP (DROPPED PER PLEA
      BARG) - *** ASLT ON POLICE OFF *** (DROPPED
      PER PLEA BARG) - SPEED TO FLEE CAPTURE
      (DROPPED PER PLEA BARG) - RECKLESS
      DRIVING (DROPPED PER PLEA BARG) - EIGHT (8)

COUNTS UNLAWFUL SEX ACT IE ANIMAL/ SENT: 18
MOS OBS + TRTMNT IL CRIM PSYCH DET CTR/
RELEASE DATE 102894 (PAROLE)///
MATCH ID: LN: HORROW/ FN: CALEB/ MN:{NONE}/
DESC AS ABOVE/ PAROLE ADD: NEW BEGINNINGS
RESIDENCY APT 234/ 8484 GROVER CLEVELAND
PKWY CHICAGO IL/ PAROLE PH:3125558922/ PAROLE
EMP: CARDUCI WHOLESALE MEATS 3491 LACY ST.
CHICAGO IL/ PAROLE PH:3125552400/ END/////////

Double-Parked handed me a second sheet that listed an
extensive arrest and incarceration record for this Horrow
person, beginning at age fourteen and ranging from burgla-
ry to drugs to animal cruelty. I read the whole thing once
more, carefully, while Double-Parked watched, breathless.

"I don't know, Double-Parked," I finally said, dubiously.
"This guy is six-five and two-forty-three, which makes him
the right size, but he's white, and all our witnesses say our
horse killer is black or some other dark-skinned race. And
this guy's from more than five hundred miles from here."

Double-Parked looked crestfallen. "But that match, Sheriff Cody! Size, offense, date of release!" he said, distressed.

I studied the intense boy, hoping it wouldn't be necessary
to disappoint him. Without speaking, I reached for my copy
of the Hunter County phone book. "Forget it!" Double-
Parked said. "No Horrows in there; I checked! Come on!"
He bolted out of my office into the booking room. I followed
him to the big table in the corner, which held the huge
property-tax map book. Double-Parked had turned all the
giant pages except the tax-base index in the back. "Look!"
Double-Parked exclaimed, pointing at the page.

In tiny letters, several hundred names down in the third
column, under *H,* was Horrow, Adeline Christine, Mrs.,
plat 445-819, map 38-G-14, RR 3, Box 249, Hunter, VA
22909. I sucked at my teeth and studied the page. I turned
to map thirty-eight and looked up block G-14. The page was
flat, but I knew the general area it referred to, which was
very steep and remote. As near as I could tell from the
property plat, this Horrow woman lived way up in an
isolated hollow on the far side of Saddle Mountain. I had an
idea. "Come on," I said to Double-Parked, and we went

back to my office. I switched to my speakerphone and called Amos Cotter, the Hunter postmaster, at his home. I asked him for the name and number of his Route Three carrier, then I dialed.

"Hello?"

"Beedie Weinczek?"

"Maybe. Who's askin'?"

"Beedie, this is Sheriff Lewis Cody. I—"

"Oh my God! Has Malcolm been in a wreck? Is he all right?"

"Nobody's hurt, Mrs. Weinczek; this isn't about a wreck. I need to ask you about someone on your route."

"Oh, praise the Lord. Sure, Sheriff. What can I do for you?"

"Horrow. Adeline Horrow. What can you tell me about her?"

"Mmmm. Box . . . two-forty-nine, I think."

"That's her."

"Well, cain't tell you much, Sheriff. She moved in way up that holler maybe a year ago, I reckon. Don't rightly remember. Woman about fifty. Quiet gal, kinda heavy-set. Ain't seen her but twicest or so. Lives in a ole cabin way up the holler over the creek. Rough road. She don't git much mail, just her electric an' junk mail an all, which I leave in her box down by the main road."

"Anybody else live there?"

"Not I ever seen, Sheriff, but I only been up to the house twicest. Fer sher, ain't nobody but her git mail there."

I thanked Beedie Weinczek and hung up.

"Double-Parked, you've done a hell of a job here, but it looks a little thin. The suspect's semiblack and your guy is white. This Horrow guy lives in Chicago and our nut is here. Big-time here. The Horrow person here, evidently, is a quiet woman in her fifties who lives alone. I'm afraid all we've got here is a coincidental last name matchup. Nice try, though."

Double-Parked looked as though he was about to cry. His shoulders slumped, and he looked at the old hook rug, his lip trembling. He turned to walk out, clearly dejected. I felt rotten as John Wayne Gacy.

"Wait, Double-Parked. Hold on. Don't get all down.

264

You've done a great job here, son. But sometimes—hell, nearly *all* the time—things don't work out."

Double-Parked was obviously not redeemed in his own eyes. "I was so sure, Sheriff Cody. I've spent hours and hours—"

I got up and went to place my arm on the crushed kid's shoulder. "I know. I know you've worked like a galley slave on this, Double-Parked, and I couldn't be more proud of you, son." I thought for a moment. "Tell you what. I've got a few hours to kill before I have to go to the big charity foxhunt out at Professor Whitley's place. After I get some breakfast and do some paperwork, I'll drive up to this Horrow lady's place and make certain there's no connection."

"Thanks, Sheriff Cody," Double-Parked mumbled sadly, "but you're right. It's unlikely. I just wanted to find him so bad I guess I put two and two together and got five. Sorry."

"Never apologize when you didn't do anything wrong, my young friend. Beat it up to Lady Maude's and get yourself some food. You get sick and not only will your momma kill me, my whole damn department will bind up and colic." Double-Parked walked slowly out, his head still down.

I was sad for Double-Parked and for me and Hunter County's hapless horses. I had the Calders's killer, but I was still no closer to finding the butcher. And there was little doubt he'd do his savage thing again, soon.

I walked out to my cruiser, glad to see the news people had bagged up their toys and shagged it back to wherever they came from. Now that Dietrich was released and nothing was pending in the horse case, they'd evidently lost interest, which I could live with.

As I was about to get into my car, a Porsche yowled into the spot next to mine. Karin Steiger got out, already dressed for the afternoon ride in her hunting coat, tight tan riding pants, and long black boots. She looked amazingly fresh and lovely to have spent most of the night wrestling with me at Mountain Harbor. She bore a smug, knowing look.

"You look twice your advanced age this morning," Karin cooed. "I fear you are no longer up to the challenges of the night."

"You're lucky I didn't blast you into the next world," I said wryly. "I probably ought to search you for weapons."

Karin slid closely by me. "I seem to remember you did 'blast' me, more than once. And you are right; perhaps you should search me." With that, she placed her hands on the roof of my cruiser, spread her booted feet widely, and arched her back, which had the intended effect of extending her rather tasty pear-shaped ass. She looked over her shoulder at me.

I glanced around, praying no one was watching.

"Well?" Karin said.

Satisfied that no one was around, I spanked Karin hard on her sweet round bottom, with a resounding pop. She yiked and stood up abruptly, holding her fanny, her face flushed but still smiling.

"That outfit is so tight you couldn't be hiding a paper clip under it," I said. "Shouldn't you be faithfully supporting your beloved fiancé or something?"

"Eicher is in one of his venomously righteous moods, damning everything and everyone, including me. I can't stand him when he's like that."

"We'll be lucky if he doesn't shoot us both," I said, not coincidentally looking around.

"Nonsense. Klaus is in Roanoke Hospital under guard. Eicher was your staff's guest for the night. No one knows anything about our . . . tryst. Isn't that what you Americans call it?"

"Combat sex is what I would call it."

Karin smiled again, always with her mouth slightly higher at one corner than the other and that sinister twinkle in her eye. "Nonetheless, Eicher doesn't sully himself with violence. He assigns it to Klaus instead."

"Who sullies pretty damn good."

I heard a vehicle behind me, turning into the compound. Before I could turn to see who it was, Karin, who was already looking in that direction and could see, seized me about the neck and kissed me hard on the mouth. Instantly, I figured out that the vehicle approaching us had to be a maroon pickup truck with Julianne Chu in it. I disengaged from Karin, who clung to my neck until I pushed her back.

She still radiated with her victory expression. I wiped lipstick from my mouth.

I was right. Julianne parked and slid down from the truck. She, too, was already dolled up in her fox-hunting duds and she, too, looked damned fine, her pretty, Orientally lidded eyes examining Karin and me.

"Good morning, Lewis!" Julianne said with what I took to be a forced brightness. She flooded me with that huge, happy smile of bright, straight teeth and wide eyes, as though I'd just given her flowers for no reason. "I'd give you a good-morning kiss," she said pleasantly, the smile still glowing, "except my mother raised me better than to throw myself on a man in public like a starving street whore."

Ding. Round two.

"What was that about your mother and street whores?" Karin replied sweetly.

Julianne glanced at Karin. "Perhaps your hearing is going the way of your morals."

"Excuse me, but—" I tried to say before Karin counterattacked.

Karin's banter tightened a foot-pound or so. "I would prefer deaf promiscuity to setting myself up as a self-pitying neovirgin, living monument to a dead husband. A weak, spineless, dead husband, in fact."

That one stung Julianne. She paused, her jaw trembling, her eyes locked on Karin. I felt sorry for her. Karin understood what all ultimate competitors know, that there is no such thing as a fair fight, only the ones you win and the ones you lose. In Karin's school of competition, the only thing ruled out was losing. Period.

Julianne looked at me, her head high, though there were tiny, shiny puddles at the corners of her eyes. "Lewis, I had hoped we could have breakfast together." She glanced again at Karin. "But . . . I suspect your appetites have been seen to," she said softly. Julianne turned and walked to her truck. She closed the door, started the truck, and buzzed the electric side window down. "Don't be fooled, Lewis," she said, plunking the truck into reverse, "she can't love you. It isn't in her. You're only a trophy for her wall." Julianne backed the truck, turned it around, and drove out.

I opened my car door.

"I'm going with you," Karin said, marching around to the other door and pulling it open.

"I'm just going to the boonies to check out a thin lead on the horse killer. You won't find it very interesting."

"Nonetheless, I'm going." Karin dropped into the seat and clipped the belt.

"Not if I say you're not, you aren't."

"You won't," Karin said with quiet confidence, looking calmly out at the distant peak of Buffalo Mountain. "You may not love me yet, Lewis. But you crave how I taste and smell and sound, and you admire how I give no quarter and seize what I want. You feel challenged by me, and that excites you and piques your male nature. You'll take me with you because I'm pure female, and you like having me around." Karin turned her head to gaze at me. "If I'm wrong, tell me. And you'll never see me again. If I'm right, drive."

Passing the town square, I said to Karin. "You were a little hard on Julianne."

"You know better," Karin said, watching the old buildings slide by. "You know there are only the vicious and the dead. There is no nice way to kill someone."

29

•••••••••

Mommy Dearest

Way up on the Blue Ridge, including parts of Hunter County, there are places you can reach overland only with great difficulty in modern, low-slung cars. The roads regress from pavement to gravel to rutted rock, from graded cuts to mere gouges in the mountainsides where the trees have been beaten back. Even high-performance police cruisers are reduced to the speed of the horse-drawn wagons for which the roads were originally and barely cut. If one listens on quiet summer evenings, sometimes lone, mournful violins or plaintive banjos can be heard on the pine-scented breeze.

Karin Steiger braced herself against the dash as I eased the big silver Chevy down a steep, bumpy grade in low gear, into a shallow creek, and up the equally steep far side. I winced as the bottom scraped on rock.

"Better we should be mounted," Karin said. She peered at the graying winter sky. "Mmmm. I hope the weather remains dry for the hunt this afternoon. Bitter Stone is sure-footed, but any riding is treacherous in mud."

I examined the sky myself. Rain, soon.

A small, worn farm home perched on a steep slope came into view beyond a zigzag split-rail fence. I let the Chevy rock to a stop for a precautionary survey.

"What is it?" Karin asked, sitting up.

269

"Nothing. It's just a good idea to see what you're looking at."

The Adeline Horrow place needed a lot of work. I saw an abused old GMC pickup truck sitting in the front yard. Not the sort of vehicle you expected a woman in her fifties to be driving, but again, in this setting it wasn't beyond reason. Besides, the truck bore no rifle rack. Smoke was wisping from the chimney of the small two-story gabled clapboard home of weathered planking and sloping front porch. In the rear were a chicken house, a tool shed, and a small barn through which daylight shone from the missing boards. A satellite TV dish stood in tall weeds at one side of the yard, tenuously connecting the place with the twentieth century. Still, it bore no signs of a shiftless man in residence. No junk cars or car parts lay about, no hunting dogs jerked at chains and bayed, no chain winches hung from tree limbs. No beer cans in the yard. There was no evidence of farming beyond a small fallow vegetable patch to one side of the house. Nothing besides possibly the truck indicated anyone other than a middle-aged woman in residence. I eased the car forward. When I glanced from the trail to the house I could have sworn I saw a front window curtain move like someone had held it aside to peek and then released it.

We parked by the truck and got out. I looked into the truck, glancing warily at the house occasionally. The truck was dusty, as were all vehicles that traversed dirt roads, but was otherwise unremarkable. The Virginia tags and inspection sticker were current. I noted the seat was set about four inches forward from the rear of the cab. A man six and a half feet high would have it all the way back. On the seat were a pack of those supposedly feminine, thin death weeds in a flowery package, and an empty Big Gulp cup.

I considered having Karin wait in the car, but there was nothing to indicate an unusual risk, and I knew she wanted to see what life in mountain America was like. She followed me onto the porch.

I lifted my little portable radio to my mouth. "Sheriff One."

"Sheriff One," Cindy answered.

"Hold me out at the Adeline Horrow residence, off 621

west from Cherokee Gap, across the creek, second right to the end."

There was a pause while Cindy scribbled the directions. "Ten-four, Sheriff One. Eleven twenty-two hours."

Colorful, cheap curtains shrouded the windows and the door glass, obscuring any view within. I rested my hand on my gun unobtrusively and knocked.

The door opened slowly to a tall, overweight, imposing woman who was probably in her early fifties but looked about ten years older. Her graying hair was the sort of Frankenstein's-bride frizzy that somebody should have shot hairdressers for years ago. She was dressed in turquoise Spandex stirrup pants way too tight for her flabby thighs, with a maroon sweatshirt that had a portrait of a plump, sneering, unpleasant woman on its front. ROSEANNE FOR PRESIDENT! exclaimed words superimposed over the image. A warm, cloying odor flowed from the house, equal parts tobacco smoke, dirty laundry, and coffee.

The woman sucked deep on her stinkweed, looking first at me and then with incredulity at Karin in her riding finery. She expelled a rancid blue cloud, squinting through it at me. She nervously shifted her weight from one foot to the other. When she snatched the cigarette from her lips, she straightened the fingers of both her hands. Her eyes had the hostile fear of someone who has hated cops for a long time. I've seen it often.

"Yeah?" she said, belligerently. Her voice had a hard, whore's edge to it.

"Adeline Horrow?"

"Shit. You already know that or you wouldn't be standing here. What do you want?"

Oh, joy. Several thousand delightful Hunter County hill folk I could have taken Karin to see, and we get Miss Manners.

"I'm Sheriff Lewis Cody. This—"

"Hell, I can see you're the law. What do you want?"

"I need to ask you some questions, Mrs. Horrow. If we stepped inside, we could save your heat."

"Suit yerself," Adeline snapped, and walked away.

We entered a stuffy living room that was definitely not

one reserved for funerals and weddings. I had a mindflash of an astonishing videotape of Cynthia Haas and Garvin Rudesill. I still hadn't gotten over that.

The Spartan poverty of the place was offset by hand-woven doilies, a thick hooked rug, cracked vinyl furniture draped with quilts, and, by the fireplace, the requisite TV. The sort of plastic figurines one wins at the county fair for popping enough balloons with darts sat on the small tables at each end of the couch beneath the window. There was a gray corona of grimy handprints around the wall light switch near the edge of the doorway that led past the bottom of a stairway and into the kitchen. No photographs were on display. None. On a stained coffee table were several copies of women's magazines and a newspaper that headlined TEN-YEAR-OLD BOY HAS BABY BY ALIEN! Let's hear it for literacy.

On the end of the table was a large steaming electric pot of rich-smelling coffee, a sugar bowl, and a cream pitcher. There was only one mug. Karin stood gracefully, subtly surveying the room.

Adeline drew on her cigarette again. I struggled to breathe. "Well, you're here," she said with resignation. "So ask."

"I don't think I've ever seen you before, Mrs. Horrow," I said. "Have you lived in Hunter County long?"

Adeline Horrow paused, thinking that one over but trying hard not to look like it. "About a year or so, I reckon. My husband passed away; he was with the railroad. Lord, wadn't for the retirement, I'd be on the welfare with the niggers." Adeline inspected Karin from head to toe. "I ain't rich, but I ain't no welfare nigger."

"Where did you live before you came to Hunter County, Mrs. Horrow?"

"Ah . . . well, Indiana. Valparaiso. Buford—that's my husband—Buford was with the railroad. When he had the stroke, I moved out chere. I ain't in no trouble, am I Sheriff?"

"No, ma'am. I just—"

"Hell, that's a relief. I ain't done nothin', but o' course, you laws don't need no good reason to lock somebody up, do you?" At this, Adeline Horrow let rip a burst of startling laughter while pinching the dancing cigarette in the corner of her lips.

I laughed lightly to be polite and in an attempt to put her at ease, while I looked past the foot of the staircase into the kitchen. In midyuck, I choked. I heard the ceiling over our heads creak. It was barely audible over the laughter. Neither Adeline nor Karin appeared to notice, but I was listening.

"You live here alone, Mrs. Horrow?"

"Alone? Why sure! It's hard on—"

Battle stations.

"—an old widow woman, but I get by with my little garden and the retirement. Why . . . ah . . . why do you ask, Sheriff?"

The ceiling creaked again, this time like a falling tree. Adeline Horrow's grin faded just a hair. "Uh . . . 'cept for my boy, o' course! But he's just a-visitin'. He don't stay here. Here, I'll git him." Adeline walked to the foot of the stairway. "Uh, Juh—ah . . . John? John? Git down here right now! Meet the *sheriff!* The *sheriff's* here!"

"Karin," I said casually, "go wait in the car. Now." She glanced at me with alert interest, but she didn't move.

Out of view, I could hear the stairs creaking sequentially as someone descended. Someone heavy. Adeline walked stiffly back near us. Her mouth smiled, but her eyes weren't with the program.

When "John" reached the foot of the stairs and turned to enter the room, I knew instantly that Double-Parked was truly a genius. My little Korean buddy was a silicone-chip detective par excellence; he was magic. He was right. Dead right. I reached for my radio as casually as I could manage.

The man was six-five and slim, and his hair was shoulder length, woolly black. He was Caucasian, but his skin was very dark, hairy at the arms and neck, and his face carried several days' black beard stubble. His cheekbones were pointy, yet his cheeks were hollow and his nose was hooked. He hunched forward at the neck like many tall people do, giving him the appearance of looking at you from the tops of his eyes. Together with the rigid muscles in his arms and shoulders, the impression was that he was . . . hunchbacked. He walked with a slight limp at the right leg;

Murphy the Irish setter had nailed the creature in Rev Hodges's little barn in its right thigh. If I had any doubt whatsoever now, it was vanquished by his eyes, predatory, pitiless eyes that studied calmly from deep within hollow pits. I knew beyond any doubt: I beheld the butcher.

He stuck a cigarette into his mouth and lit it slowly with one of those plastic lighters, moving his eyes about the room, soaking every detail in, especially Karin. I saw his eyes pass over my holstered pistol and the portable radio in my hand. He exhaled and squinted briefly at the burn of the smoke.

"John!" Adeline, said pointedly. "John," she repeated, telling him he had a new name. "This here's Sheriff Cody."

Without altering the piercing, merciless gaze of those eyes, the man stepped forward and smirked without parting his lips, which held the cigarette. He offered his hand, and I pretended not to notice. I wasn't about to let him get a grip on me anywhere, let alone my right hand. I scanned him for weapons, but he wore jeans, socks, and a heavy, plaid flannel overshirt, untucked, that could have hidden a bazooka.

And he smelled faintly. Like decaying meat.

"Caleb Horrow?" I asked. He froze and his smirk vanished. Adeline Horrow's happy-face was history also.

Caleb Horrow let his hand drop. "So you know." His voice was hollow, like a strained whisper. "So what?" He eyed Karin coldly, then looked back at me.

"Caleb, I need you to come into town with me, for a little while."

Horrow straightened, looking about eight feet tall from where I stood. "What the fu—what for, Sheriff? You ain't got no right to harass me just 'cause I done time." He spoke slowly, dragging the last syllables of each sentence, sounding like a rasp being dragged over metal.

Horrow had long, bony fingers, like vulture talons. The nails were long and I shuddered to think what a forensic lab could make out of the substance that blackened the curled tips. He began to open and close his fists slowly.

Adeline Horrow's voice rose an octave. "Now Sheriff, Cale here, he ain't done nothin' since he got out. He's a good boy!"

I ignored Adeline and never took my eyes off Caleb. "No harassment, Horrow. I'm sure you're as pure as Shirley Temple's teddy bear. All I need you to do is appear in a lineup. You've been in lineups before. If my witnesses don't make you, I'll drive you right back here to your doorstep."

"Now this ain't right!" Adeline began. "You cain't—" I cut her off with a wave of my hand.

"Karin," I said, calmly, "go out to the car." She stood cautiously, but didn't leave. I glanced quickly at her, then back at the giant before me. The glance was enough to tell me Karin had that crazy excitement in her eyes. She wasn't going to miss this despite anything I told her.

I could feel Caleb Horrow tensing. He rasped, "What if I tell you I ain't going *no*-goddamn-where with you?" He shifted his weight from foot to foot. It must have been genetic. He was opening and closing his hands rapidly now. "Huh? Suppose I tell you to go fuck yourself?"

I really wish tough guys had a broader vocabulary.

"Karin, get outside," I said. "Look, Horrow, I—"

"You ain't takin' my boy again!" Adeline shrilled, breathing harder, sweat beading on the uppermost of her chins.

Caleb flicked his eyes from my face to the radio and back, his breathing quickening.

Adeline leaned forward right in my face. She waved her hands and almost screamed. "You ain't got no right to mess with my boy! You ain't takin him—"

"Hey! *Easy* here, people," I said in what I hoped was a soothing tone of voice. I needed time and calm to get some backup on the scene. Without lifting the radio, I keyed the transmit button and held it, knowing that my people would hear what was being said, would quickly deduce that I could use some company, and would send it forthwith to the location I had marked out to. That was provided, of course, that the steep mountainsides of the hollow allowed the relatively weak hand transmitter to get out a good signal from inside a structure, and provided Caleb Horrow wasn't clever enough to see that I was calling for the cavalry. "Everybody calm down. Listen . . . Caleb, I know you've got a record, but we're just talking about some routine questioning. Nothing to get excited about. Let's just—"

"Fuck you, Cody!" Adeline screeched, red in the face,

breathing hard. "You laws ain't takin my boy again!" That ought to have waked up my people, if they were hearing my little radio. But then I saw Caleb Horrow's eyes snap to my radio again, and then widen. The jig was up.

"Shit!" Horrow croaked, "he's got that fucking radio on! He's calling help, Momma!"

"He ain't takin' you this time, baby! Momma's right here, honey! He ain't takin' you!"

"Outside, Karin!" I yelled over the din. I whipped the radio to my mouth. "Sheriff One, Signal thirteen!"

"Nooooo!" Adeline shrieked.

"You motherfucker!" Horrow roared, and he went for me.

I went for my gun, but my hand never reached the weapon before he was on me. We grappled, furiously.

Adeline screamed, "Nooooo! I'll kill *you!* I'll *kill* you!" and she lit into me as well. At the first opening, I smashed Caleb over the head with the only weapon handy, the radio. Horrow howled, but with fury, not pain, shaking his head. That was the good news, such as it was. The bad news was that the radio wasn't made for bludgeoning and it exploded in fragments, leaving me holding the battery portion. I sure hoped the message had gotten out. I shoved Adeline backward into an overstuffed armchair behind her.

Caleb came back with a vengeance. He hit me like a train and we fell over the TV, crashing to the floor. Both of us were fighting madly to keep the other from reaching my pistol.

"Nooooo! Noooo!" Adeline screeched, waving her fat arms and hobbling on her knees to the couch.

"Motherfucker!" Caleb grunted into my face with breath that would've stunned an ox, his mutated voice ringing like an old air conditioner. He pinned me to the floor and got a yoke on my neck with one hand. I held his other wrist with both of mine to keep him from getting at my pistol. Horrow was big and in the kind of psychological and physical fighting shape that comes from being a survivor in a mental prison. I tried to get a shin into his balls, and I stabbed at his eyes with my left hand, but he was no beginner. "Motherfucker!" he screamed, slugging me, his coarse voice cracking. With his right hand, he fumbled under his shirt and whipped out a huge Bowie-style knife with dark-brown stains on the blade near the hilt. "I'll cut your fucking *heart* out!" Caleb bellowed, spittle flying from his mouth. I was thinking hard about a new line of work when a chocolate-brown cloud of steaming liquid engulfed Horrow's face. Some of the scalding coffee splashed on me. It burned, but it felt just fine.

A quart or so of barely sub-boiling coffee square in the face didn't feel so mmm, mmm, good to Horrow. He dropped the knife, clutched his face with both hands, and screamed. I shoved him off me and scrambled to my feet. Karin stood to one side, the empty coffeepot in her hand, staring with wide, vivid eyes at Adeline Horrow. Who now held a shotgun on me.

"Don't move!" Adeline shrieked, tears in her eyes, saliva dribbling from her lip. "Don't you move, either one a ya! I'll kill ya! I'll kill the both a ya! You laws is always pickin' on my boy! I'll kill ya! Bury ya bodies! Hide yer goddamn car!"

Caleb was writhing on his knees, clutching his face and wailing hoarsely.

"Where the hell did you get that?" I panted, almost absently, gawking at the double-barreled shotgun. The bore looked like the entrance to the Chunnel.

"She withdrew it from beneath the sofa," Karin said, almost in awe, I thought.

I considered the prevailing physics. All that was necessary was for the hysterical brain of Adeline Horrow to develop a neural impulse that would flash down her arm to her finger, causing it to contract minutely. The trigger would move aft less than a millimeter, freeing a steel pin, which a compressed spring would propel forward. The pin would dent the tiny primer imbedded in the rear of a twelve-gauge shotgun shell. The primer would spark, igniting a powder charge within the shell. The powder would burn at an incredible rate, generating phenomenally expanding gases. The gases would have no room to expand rearward for the locked bolt or radially for the heavy breech. They would push forward against a plastic plug. The plug would roar down the barrel, shoving before it twelve lead balls the size of peas that would exit the barrel at about eight hundred feet a second and go through me like a meteor shower. It would blow the window curtains and glass and about three pounds of meat out into the yard. And all this would occur in much less than half a second.

"Yaaaaaah!" Caleb croaked from his burns, the big, ugly knife on the floor beside him. I hoped he was at least temporarily blind, because soon, he'd probably recover from the pain, and then he might display antisocial tendencies.

"I'll kill you!" Adeline slobbered, gasping for breath, shifting from foot to foot, her eyes bugged, blood trickling from the corner of her mouth. The mammoth bore of the shotgun waved just out of my reach. "I'll kill both a ya!"

"Adeline, listen to me good," I said. "You're buying into a world of hurt here. Give me that weapon." I stepped toward Adeline, hoping to get close enough to deflect the barrel before the necessary chemicals in her brain flowed over the neurosensors that would signal her finger to pull.

Adeline stepped back, sucking hard breaths through clenched teeth. She whipped the shotgun to her shoulder.

"I ain't buyin' into *shit,* you son of a bitch!" she said shrilly, her massive breasts heaving like mating walruses. I fought the panic that screamed at me to charge, to duck, to dodge, to run. Any sudden movement by me might be all that it took to set the tiny impulse on its deadly journey.

"Adeline—"

"Shut up! You *shut* up! Look what y'all done to my boy! He ain't done nothing! He's a good boy!"

The good boy still shook his head in agony, wailing hoarsely.

"He's cutting up horses all over the damn county, Adeline; listen to me! He's sick. He needs help. He needs to be where he can get treatment. You know—"

"Shut up!" Adeline screamed, fairly frothing, rocking maniacally from one beefy leg to the other. *"You shut up!* I don't want to hear that! You're a-lyin'! You're a-lyin'! My Cale's a good boy! He ain't never done all those things! You laws has always been against him! Y'all always picked on him and said all them ugly things! Ever since he was a boy, y'all said he done all them weird things. Y'all *lyin'! Lyin'!* You ain't takin' my boy this time! I'm gonna kill you!"

Contrary to Hollywood-engendered popular myth, it is very hard to shoot someone in a way that kills them instantly. Direct hits in both the heart and the brain, if you can hit that good, frequently leave the shot person with at least several seconds, if not minutes, of life. One man lived for more than twelve years after suicidally firing a spike from a nailgun into the center of his brain, where it remained, and he functioned normally except for periodic headaches. All Adeline Horrow needed to subdivide me was enough nanoseconds of fading life to generate the neural pulse that would pull the trigger of her shotgun. The best chance I had under such a circumstance, my friend the late Doctor Coleby Butler once told me over a chess game, was to sever the spinal cord at the base of the skull, cutting the brain off from the muscles and its life-support system. This I determined would, from the front, require an entry point through the mouth. Even then, Coleby had said, there was no guarantee. Enough neurological energy might be excited by sheer pain reflex to cause adequate contracture of the trigger finger. It is possible to consider all this in a fraction of a second when you are looking up the shiny maw of two shotgun bores nearly an inch wide each.

"Listen to me, woman," I said. I could see the nothing-left-to-lose point was rapidly drawing near. "I'll give you just a count of three to put that gun down."

"Lewis!" Karin said, her voice rising.

"Or you'll what?" Adeline squealed, her voice failing her. "Or you'll what? I'm gonna kill you! Look what y'all done to my boy!"

"One!" I said, staring at Adeline Horrow's squinting eyes.

"Lew-isss!" Karin yelled.

"My face!" Horrow wailed, hoarsely.

"I'll *kill* yooouuuu!" Adeline howled, raising the shotgun.

"Two!" I shouted, frantically rehearsing the precise movements my arm, hand, and fingers would have to take.

"My face! My face!" Caleb dropped his hands and glared at me, squinting with pain. *"Shoot* him, Momma! *Kill* him!"

This dialogue was not showing a lot of promise. I kicked Caleb Horrow hard in the head, bowling him onto his back and causing him to squawl again. As I hoped, Adeline's motherly instinct drew her to divert her vision and examine her pained child for the briefest of moments. It would have to be enough.

Adeline Horrow's eyes flicked to Caleb, and the shotgun wavered slightly off line with my chest. But then her eyes glassed as she realized the mistake she'd made. Both the shotgun and her eyes began to traverse back to me as my hand crawled through space toward my holster. Her gaze turreted about, now almost on me, her hair spinning out from her head, her jowls distorting. The shotgun muzzle was arcing back. My hand impacted the grip of my weapon. Adeline's eyes met mine. The shotgun muzzle swung closer. My thumb broke the safety snap on the holster, my fingers closed on the grip, and my hand rose. Adeline's eyes began to widen as the realization struck her that one of us was about to die. She raised the shotgun barrels. Her mouth opened. My pistol cleared the holster and began an agonizingly slow rise to engage. Adeline's eyes stopped expanding and began to narrow. Her teeth bared. She screamed. Caleb screamed. Karin screamed. Maybe I screamed; I don't know, because all I could hear was the crashing *bum-boom!* of my own heart.

I began the pull of the pistol trigger even as the muzzle rose past Adeline Horrow's paunchy middle. By the time the sights passed her voluminous bosom, the hammer was nearly back to drop point. Adeline's porcine eyes now arrived at a scowl. The shotgun was almost on me. My forefinger crawled rearward. Adeline's mouth extended fully; her nostrils flared. The rage possible only in a mother defending her young burst from the eyes of Adeline Horrow.

The shotgun went off with a yellow-white flash and a concussive boom, missing me by inches. Stuffing from the couch exploded into the air. Broken glass rang like the Notre Dame carillon on Easter morning. Her second blast was still only a nerve spark away.

My pistol slammed hard against my hand, a stiff punch sweeter at that moment than the best orgasm I'd ever known. Flame and light distorted my image of Adeline Horrow's face. The pistol muzzle flinched upward. My eyes closed and my ears rang from the cacophonous blasts. When

I opened my eyes, a dark-red hole just off center in Adeline's upper lip oozed blood in a trickle that reddened her teeth. An extensive pattern of spattered red wetness glistened and dribbled on the wallpaper behind her, framing her head like a scarlet crown. Her eyes had opened also, reflecting a mildly surprised, puzzled expression.

Adeline lurched backward, still clutching the shotgun. The muscle tension in my arm was snapping the pistol down from its recoil apogee to the sight line once again. The shotgun barrel sagged, and I twisted violently to clear its trajectory. Adeline was falling. I struggled to re-aim, squeezing steadily. The pistol snarled and kicked my hand again, arcing a small brass hull over my right shoulder. The shotgun leaped from Adeline's grip even before she crashed into the overstuffed chair behind her. She rebounded and rotated face down to hit the floor, bouncing and then settling.

"Three." I whispered, shaking.

When I could hear again, there was only silence. The air was rank with cordite. The glass had settled. The blast echoes had faded. Karin Steiger stood frozen, her hands extended from her sides, fingers stiff and spread. Her eyes were wide and transfixed and her jaw trembled. Adeline was deader than the Whitewater Real Estate Corp.

Caleb Horrow and the knife were gone.

I kicked the shotgun away from Adeline's body, assumed a two-handed grip on my gun, and scampered to the kitchen, looking for Caleb.

"Are you hurt?" I shouted at Karin.

"Noooooo," Karin moaned, quavering.

I hurried to the still-open rear door and peered over my sights. A white sock foot vanished into the pine thicket behind the house, some thirty yards away. The branches whipped back in place. I couldn't see him, but I fired ten more shots as rapidly as I could into the trees as close to where the fleeing Caleb Horrow might be as I could guess. Spent brass hulls pinged down all over the wooden floor of the back porch. Leaving one live round remaining in the breech, I ejected the empty magazine and stuffed a full one in its place. I ran across the backyard and entered the woods at a different place than I had seen Caleb disappear and, slowly, from cover, I searched for him. All I found was a shiny trace of wet blood on a pine bough. I searched another fifty feet into the woods before backing out and returning to the living room of the Horrow house.

Karin Steiger stood staring at Adeline Horrow's prone bulk, beneath which a red puddle was forming. She raised her gaze to me, and she sprinted into my arms. I decocked and holstered the pistol and held her, to help her pass her fear and shock.

And to quell my own.

30
• • • • • • • •

Momentum

Later, I would consider the pathetically dutiful mother who perceived she was protecting her innocent and abused child. I would consider how misplaced her maternal allegiance was and how sad it was she had to die for it. Adeline Horrow would even wake me on future quiet nights, from tense, sweaty, fitful sleep, as did my Tess, Peggy Sloan, Coleby Butler, and a host of other ghosts who visited me in dark bedrooms in wee hours. But at that moment I had not killed Adeline Horrow. I had combated a hostile shotgun with an organic aim-fire system. And I had won. That was all that mattered. It died and I didn't.

So, standing in the little living room of the Horrow home with one woman dead on the floor and another alive and vital in my arms, I cannot deny I felt the rush. I had fought, not Adeline Horrow, but the death force in life that seeks us all, of which Adeline and the circumstances that placed her there were only instruments. And I had survived. I had climbed to the summit, broken the record, won the home-coming game. I felt the rush, the gladness of being alive, the excitement of the contest, the ecstacy of victory, the simple relief of remaining a little while longer.

I gently pushed Karin back at arm's length with one hand, unable to pull my gaze from hers. She stared at me, tears forming in her eyes, her lip trembling. She turned slowly, unsteadily, as she had in the bedroom only hours earlier. She sat on the stuffing-littered couch and rolled onto her side. She pulled her knees up, clutched them and began to weep softly, whether from shock or fatigue, I did not know. "We die so easily," she whispered. "We go so *soon!*"

My people arrived along with a tracking dog Pierce had wisely called for. I sent Tom, Billy, and Otis with the dog handler past the bloody pine bough on the scent of Caleb Horrow. I had his description broadcast to the VSP and adjacent jurisdictions, and ordered Pierce to conduct the requisite investigation on the shooting. Haskel drove a now-composed Karin back to her car at the dungeon after she gave her statement to Pierce.

As Karin left, walking by me, she looked up at me with a pained expression I couldn't read. The softness defined by a woman's lips defies description. She held up a hand, then reached to touch my face with it.

"Thanks for the coffee," I said to her. "It was good to the last drop."

"You should try the dessert," she replied as she walked away, her spirit back, apparently.

In an hour and forty minutes, Pierce had wound up the formalities. He took statements, photographed the scene, and lifted fingerprints from Adeline's shotgun and other objets d'evidence. He pried a distorted 9-mm slug from the blood-spattered wall and placed it with the other bagged evidence. The rescue squad was removing Adeline Horrow's body to an ambulance when my men and the dog handler came back with the results I suspected. They had tracked to a foot trail that led down the mountain a half-mile to a clearing near a dirt road. There the dog circled, but the scent ended. Caleb Horrow was an experienced criminal who had graduated from the best prisons in the country. Like a pro, he had left an escape vehicle hidden away from his nest.

Double-Parked had a scanner radio in his room at home on which he monitored department activity every hour he wasn't asleep or in school. He was back at the dungeon before I was and, unlike me, he was ten feet tall. He soaked up slaps on the back and other congratulations from the deputies. Without my even asking, he was at his console, hammering away after everything the computer might further reveal about Caleb Horrow. He paused involuntarily to receive a smothering hug from Milly when she arrived, before resuming his pecking and staring down the Information Superhighway.

"He got a current Illinois O/L, Sheriff," Double-Parked called to me as I walked to my office, "but don' know what he drivin' or usin' for license tags. His name and SOC number don't turn anything from Illinois DMV."

"Double-Parked, I'm issuing you a gun, badge, and cruiser son," I called back. "It ought to take a crimefighter like you about ten minutes to bag and tag this creep."

"I'm for that!" Haskel Beale yelled from his desk. "Depity Double-Parked!"

"Chubby Chink rides again!" Otis shouted from the coffee machine.

"Chinks are Chinese, butthead!" Double-Parked said, grinning, never taking his eyes from his monitor screen. "I'm a Slope, and don't you forget it!"

"Oh. Right," Otis mumbled, puzzled.

"Besides, I can't drive!"

"Hell, Doub, you ain't got to!" Otis Clark replied. "You gon' be my partner from now on, and I drivin' you anygoddamn-where you wanna go!"

Everyone in the office laughed and Double-Parked glowed.

I was glad for Double-Parked because he'd earned every ounce of applause, but I was not glowing or laughing. The relief that Adeline Horrow hadn't vaporized me was wearing off, and the sadness of having had to kill her was setting in. It would have been easier to live with if she'd been evil like her satanic offspring, but she'd only been a country woman acting as motherhood had driven her. Adeline's face at the moment the screaming ended and the shots began appeared before me, that wild-eyed, beet-red, sweating, plump face with its bared teeth, spraying spittle. *I'll kill you!* I wondered if she might not have, but instantly banished the thought from my mind. It was moot now, and such reservations were deadly impediments in any future survival scenario. I was confident the grand jury would rule the shooting justifiable, but in the end, it didn't matter. It is better to be judged by twelve than carried by six. Karin Steiger had said it coldly and correctly: there are only the vicious and the dead. There is no nice way to kill somebody.

Adeline Horrow evaporated, but I knew from experience she had joined the Legion of Ghosts. She'd be back. Often.

I put in calls to Pete Floyd and Merlin Sowers to advise them of the morning's festivities, but both had departed for Mitch Whitley's charity fox hunt, which was about to get under way at Laurel Ridge Farm. As though she were listening in on my mind, Milly waddled into the office in jeans and a sweatshirt, the front of which read KNOW HOW TO TELL A DEAD LAWYER IN THE ROAD FROM A DEAD DEER IN THE ROAD? Milly went to the fireplace and chucked another log on the blaze and I read the answer on the back of the sweatshirt: THERE'RE SKID STREAKS LEADING UP TO THE DEER. That joke had been a lot funnier in the days before I'd fallen in love with a lovely, loving, passionate attorney. Oh, Lucia.

Milly turned to me. "You okay?" she asked. Big-city police forces employed elaborate stress debriefing teams composed of psychiatrists or psychologists who moved in to look to the mental health of officers involved in high-stress events. The Hunter County Sheriff's Department's equivalent was Sergeant Milly Stanford.

"I guess. Wondering if maybe if I'd waited another minute, said something different, maybe I wouldn't have had to—"

"I don't wanna hear that shit, Lewis. You a cop, you ain't no social worker. They's too many dead po-leese who thunk when they shoulda been a-shootin'."

I sighed.

"Looka here," Milly continued. "Arthur called. Say he done took 'Lizbeth and Dublin to the Whitley Charity Hunt so she kin ride wit all the other kids—bunch that follow the main hunt wit Miz Whitley. Say he thunk you was s'posed go ridin' out at Professor Whitley's this afternoon, too, and since you ain't back, he figure you got tied up. So he done took Moose and you saddle and ridin' clothes over to Laurel Ridge Farm in case you still plannin' to be there."

"Jeez, Milly," I replied. "Without people like you and Arthur taking care of me, I wouldn't last a week."

"Sheeeeit. Ain't like you never took care of us."

I thought for a moment. There were several good reasons for me to go on to the hunt in spite of—perhaps because of—the morning's violence. Merlin Sowers and Pete Floyd needed to be briefed. I thought it wise to use the *Hunter Press* and the hunt itself as a forum from which to issue an advisory to county horse owners. They needed to be warned to look to their animals and they needed to be given a description of Caleb Horrow. Further, though I thought it remote, it had to be considered that such a gathering of horses might even draw a visit from the butcher. Who knew what he'd do now, given the events of the morning? Then there was Karin Steiger. Most of all, I decided, I needed the distraction, the relief. I was very tired, having slept awfully in recent days, and the death and violence—not to mention the sexual and emotional violence of Karin Steiger—had taken a toll.

I held a short meeting with Pierce and Milly. We set an overtime schedule and arranged patrol plans to seek Caleb Horrow. His description had already been disseminated regionally, including to area hospitals. The blood smear on the pine bough behind the Horrow house made it likely that I had hit the son of a bitch at least once. The deputies would actively circulate among the county hangouts, convenience stores, and the farm co-op, to hang flyers and ensure that as many people as possible knew what Horrow looked like. We had thoroughly searched the Horrow house and property, of course, but had turned up absolutely nothing about Caleb Horrow but a few filthy clothes. He had evidently recently arrived at Adeline Horrow's little mountain home. There was nothing to indicate where he might have gone—no letters, no purchase receipts, no vehicle keys, nothing. Caleb Horrow traveled light.

We advised the men to check the Horrow house, periodically, but there were way too many horse sites in Hunter County to stake out. Without knowing what he drove or where he might be expected to go, there was little else we could do but energize the system to be alert for him and to turn over every rock in sight.

Pierce sniffed and sighed. "Lewis, we ain't got no vehicle description, so he could be three states away by now."

I considered Pierce's words, but then shook my head. "Nothing's impossible, Pierce," I said. "But as far as we know, he has no place to go, and probably no money to go with. He's crafty enough to know that the more he moves about, the more likely he is to be seen and arrested. Further, I think he's dominated by his horse-based sexual psychosis; he knows that if he goes inside again, it'll be a very long time, if ever, before he gets out, and there are no horses in mental wards, no victims of the kind he needs. That's why he never leaves any fingerprints at the slaughter scenes. He knows there is a system at work attempting to put him back in prison, and he does not want to go there."

"Besides," Milly added, "when were we ever so lucky that some creep motherfucker like this punk just moved away?"

"There's one more thing," I said, locking eyes with Pierce. "He has a tattoo on his arm of a heart with the word *Mom* in it; when he got out of the clink, he came straight to Mom. And this morning, the sheriff of Hunter County gave ole Mom a one-way ticket to the Promised Land." I shifted my gaze from Pierce to Milly and back. "He's here, guys; he's still here, and he isn't going to run. I can feel it."

You hear a lot of wailing about the cruelty of the sport of fox hunting, but I find it hard to take the criticism seriously when most of those wringing their hands over the alleged abuse of foxes also seem to think the wholesale murder of human fetal infants is somehow a "woman's choice." Amazing. Regardless, a fox hunt is certainly a visual spectacle, and the Whitley charity event was no exception.

I topped the rise between the highway and Laurel Ridge Farm under a threatening gray winter sky, and could see the shallow valley where the estate, the stables, and the indoor and outdoor riding rings were. The sight was impressive. There were actually three large groups of riders. The hunters proper were a loose cluster of roughly fifty riders who were milling about on carefully pampered, seriously athletic horses, the riders all somewhat uniformly attired in helmets, elegant riding coats, and knee-high boots. The horses blew puffs of vapor into the cold air. Nearby, close to the acres of parked horse trailers, a smaller group of similarly dressed youngsters, most mounted on smaller but no less prepared horses, gathered to follow the main hunt at some distance, under the stewardship of Helen Whitley. Partly upslope, another group of riders, wearing varied but dignified riding attire, were grouped. These riders were the "hilltoppers."

The horses knew the drill and loved the hunt. They pranced nervously, anticipating the run to the hounds.

As I glided down the gravel drive in my cruiser, taking in the scene, two workers known as whippers-in, under the supervision of the huntsman, opened multiple gates on a large, flat container truck. Perhaps thirty tall, rangy hounds spilled out and swarmed about in a frenzy, sniffing the ground and each other, also frantic to get underway. Hounds, mind you. Not dogs. I recognized the huntsman and two whippers-in as being those employed to handle the hounds by the local hunt club, of which Mitch Whitley was the fieldmaster, the Grand Poobah of the club, so to speak.

A rider in the hilltopping group mounted on a little gray Arab gelding raised her hand and smiled wanly. Dr. Julianne Chu looked very good, if a little worried for some reason. I waved back at Julianne and then looked for Karin Steiger, who would be with the distant hunters, but there were too many horses moving about for me not to watch where I was driving.

I rolled slowly among the milling horses, eyeing the children's group. It wasn't hard to find Elizabeth, who was standing in her stirrups on Dublin, waving wildly at me, her face red and bejeweled with a huge, excited smile. As I pulled up next to the Mountain Harbor truck and trailer and got out, Elizabeth came rocketing up on Dublin.

"Uncle Lewis, where have you *been?*" she scolded, reining Dublin in. She looked so precious in her oversize black riding helmet, her proper little black coat, tan pants, and paddock boots, her brow furrowed. "Hurry, Uncle Lewis! Everything's about to start!" Elizabeth was fully charged.

"I'll be there, sweetheart. We had a problem this morning; that's why I'm late. I'll join the hilltoppers as soon as I can."

"Hurry, Uncle Lewis!" Elizabeth admonished, and she cantered off to rejoin the younger riders.

Arthur had groomed and saddled Moose, who looked at

me with her ears up, no doubt wondering what my apple potential was. Arthur hobbled up, his thumbs hooked in the shoulder straps of his insulated coveralls. "Lewis, I hung your stuff in the trailer." The grizzled old man squinted at me. "Miss Milly . . . she say you had to shoot a woman this mornin'?"

I gazed at the group of mounted hunters gathering around Mitch Whitley and his big Hanoverian gelding. I still could not see Karin on Bitter Stone. "Yeah, Arthur. The mother of that nut case who's been . . . killing all the horses. She pulled a shotgun on me. I didn't have any . . ." I paused because it occurred to me that the old man's jaw was quivering and his eyes were watering. He reached out a withered hand and patted me gently on my shoulder.

"Lord, Lewis. My Lord, son. Polly. Miss Elizabeth. Me. What we gonna do if you get your young ass killed?"

I smiled and swatted the old man on his shoulder. "My ass ain't so young anymore, Arthur, but I don't aim to get it killed anytime soon, just the same. Thanks for bringing everything out here. I don't know what I'd do without you, either."

"I'm just glad you okay."

"Me, too, believe me. Listen, Arthur. That Horrow guy is still loose and he's goddamned dangerous. Make sure you keep the alarms on at the estate and keep your eyes open."

"Ever since he caused old man Henry Tucker to die, a-killin' that fine ole mare, Orlando, my Winchester model twelve has been a-hankerin' to meet that fella."

"He's a cutter, Arthur. He hurts other creatures because it makes his dick dance. If he shows up at Mountain Harbor, it won't be to sell Amway. If you see him, take him. Don't show him the first ounce of mercy, or he'll use it to kill you."

"Hummph," Arthur snorted, resuming his brushing of Moose's golden, woolly winter coat. "I went ashore at Omaha Beach, boy. Better men than that son of a bitch have tried to kill me."

I entered the forward portion of the big gooseneck horse trailer. In it, Arthur had hung my tan riding trousers, my brown leather field coat, and a white Irish turtle-neck sweater. Beneath them, he had set brown gloves, a suede-covered rider's helmet, and a splendid pair of brown knee-high leather riding boots that had once graced the feet of the late Dr. Coleby Butler. *Oh, Lord, Coleby,* I thought. *I don't know if I'm man enough to fill those boots.*

The boots fit.

I tucked my gun in the right leather saddlebag on Moose. In the other bag, I stuffed a rolled-up yellow cop's raincoat and a portable radio. Moose and I joined the hilltoppers on the high ground in time to see the huntsman and the whippers-in, on horseback, moving the widely dispersed hounds in an arc a hundred yards west of the hunters, casting for scent.

The hunters spread out in a wide line, following the hounds at a brisk trot, remaining well back to avoid spoiling the scent. Mitch Whitley, acting as fieldmaster for the event, held the lead and, by custom, no one passed him. Farther back still, the children's group followed.

Searching the hunters, I sighted Karin, on the splendid shiny-black Bitter Stone. She appeared to be in a heated exchange with Eicher Dietrich, who was also mounted on his tense, gleaming Grand Teuton. It took either a lot of nerve or insufferable arrogance for Dietrich to appear at the hunt, given the previous evening, but then he didn't get where he was in a viciously competitive sport by quitting in the face of adversity.

In the distance, a contingent of the hounds began to bay and pack up. The huntsman galloped near the excited hounds, blowing notes on a brass horn that carried on the cold air across the expanse of low pasture. The horn aroused chilling flashbacks of North Vietnamese Army bugles tooting outside the perimeter of a helicopter airbase at midnight, barely audible over falling mortars, arcing tracer rounds, and the screams of men. The remaining hounds responded by flowing toward the huntsman. The hunters began to canter across the low flat, and the hilltoppers began to flow along the ridge in the general direction of the action.

"Lewis!" Julianne Chu called. I turned to see her riding Yang in a brisk canter, coming alongside. She looked as lovely as she had in Hap Morgan's living room, her short hair barely visible beneath her hunt cap. She seemed distressed. "Lewis!" she repeated, drawing near, breathless.

Yang broke to a trot and Julianne posted rapidly. "Did that lawyer reach you?" she shouted urgently over the rumble of hoofbeats.

"What?" I said.

"That lawyer, that black woman lawyer, have you talked to her?"

"Lucia Dodd? No. Not since we released Dietrich this morning. Why?"

"She was trying to reach you earlier, Lewis. She asked me if I'd seen you!"

The huntsman's horn had drawn all the hounds together. They bayed in loud chorus and surged away in a charging pack.

"What for?" I called over my shoulder, ducking bits of flying turf thrown up by the horses ahead of me.

"It's Dr. Dietrich, Lewis! The Dodd woman says he's crazy with rage; she can't talk any sense into him!"

The hilltoppers picked up speed. "I've been sued before!"

Julianne spurred Yang and pulled alongside Moose, a frown on her pretty face. "You don't *understand,* Lewis!" Julianne said. "Miss Dodd was trying to warn you that Dr. Dietrich is out of control! She's afraid he's going to try to kill you!"

Mitch Whitley led the hunters to the gallop and the mass of riders thundered after the baying pack. They approached an ancient gray stone wall, and as an ocean wave, they poured over it. The children's group swung wide to flow through an open gate. The hilltoppers broke into a canter for a distant hill.

The fox was in the wind. The hunt was on.

31
· · · · · · · · ·
Wired

The sky grew darker as the hilltoppers reached a grassy rise from which we could observe the hunters following the hounds along a distant creek bed below. Moose stood calmly, breathing deeply and snorting vapor clouds. The other hilltoppers clustered near, many struggling to hold their excited mounts. Over my shoulder, I saw a half dozen pickups and Range Rovers and similar vehicles rocking over the terrain as they climbed the rise from a dirt road. When one truck arrived, two camera men scrambled into the back with long-lensed cameras on tripods. Old English letters on the door of the truck read EASTERN HUNTER MAGAZINE. Julianne drew near on Yang.

I watched the hunters loping in the distance, followed by the young riders. Karin and Eicher Dietrich were tight on the heels of Mitch Whitley in the lead. Among the kids in hot pursuit, my little Elizabeth bobbed frantically on a determined Dublin. I shook my head free of the vision of her going down in that crowd of horses.

"Sounds like Dietrich is a little vague on his Hippocratic oath," I told Julianne.

"It's not funny, Lewis!" Julianne scolded. "The lawyer wasn't kidding; she was frightened! And Dr. Dietrich can be dangerous! There are stories about him and that . . . Klaus person."

I considered Dietrich's threat to be vastly exaggerated. It wasn't uncommon for frustrated toughs or arrogant elitists to threaten cops after arrests. Nor was it peculiar for women unaccustomed to ugly men to be unduly frightened by such threats. Still, I knew Lucia Dodd—Lord, did I. She was an experienced trial lawyer, no stranger to threats, and she was not easily spooked.

"I don't suppose the good doctor was kind enough to detail when and how he plans to follow through, was he?" I said to Julianne, watching Karin raise that beautiful bottom into the cold air, bending low over Bitter Stone's neck as the magnificent horse jumped a fallen tree. Mindflashes of a sweaty, erotic struggle in a moonlit bedroom.

Julianne, too, watched the hunters pursue the hounds. "No. Miss Dodd only said that he was quite intent in his threat and it was imperative that you be warned."

"The fox!" Hap Morgan shouted, whipping binoculars to his face. "By the hollow log! See him, Lewis?"

I saw the long, thick, moss-covered log, long down and heavily rotted, laying among the trees beyond the creek that traversed the low ground. Then I saw what Hap pointed to. The orange doglike head of the fox protruded from the hollow log and craned about to peer after the departing hounds and riders. The hounds now lost the scent and busily circled, snouts to the ground, silent, frantic to regain the scent. The hunters reined in and waited, and the younger riders held their distance. The mounted huntsman and whippers-in moved to collect and direct the hounds.

From our stance on the hill, we could see the fox exit the log and run casually back toward a thick forest in the distance. His black-tipped, bushy orange tail, nearly as long as the rest of the fox and called a brush in hunting circles, floated behind him. Somehow the scene reminded me of a pack of farmers and dogs hungry on the trail of an injured and innocent Garvin Rudesill, years before, yet the fox seemed not desperate but almost smug, as though he were enjoying the game.

"Go on, Br'er Fox!" Hap shouted, grinning. *"Run,* you ole rascal!" Bev Morgan smiled at her husband's excitement. She winked at me.

One rangy white hound with black patches ran along the

creek toward the log, his long ears flapping. Suddenly, he jerked to stop and splashed into the shallow creek. When he emerged from the other side, he lifted his muzzle and howled in delight. He repeated the happy yowl and loped toward the fallen log where the fox had hidden. Instantly, the remaining hounds homed on their comrade, baying wildly as they leaped the creek. The huntsman and whippers-in galloped through the creek, spraying water. The hounds clustered and milled frantically about the log briefly before the original lone hound locked on the scent, bayed, and set off in pursuit of the fox, which was now well out of sight. The hounds streamed away, the whippers-in spurred their horses to the flanks, and the huntsman blew long, brassy notes on the horn. Mitch Whitley gigged his horse and, with Karin, Dietrich, Meriah, Merlin Sowers, and the dozens of other hunters, went hard in chase. Many jumped the creek gracefully, some charged through it, splashing water like fish in a feeding frenzy. The kids' group went in trail and we hilltoppers began to descend the hill toward the creek. The people who were hilltopping by vehicle raced for their cars.

The sky darkened as the hunt progressed, and I knew a cold winter rain was imminent. The horses blew vapor and radiated steam as they thundered in pursuit of the baying hounds, over fields and through woods. The riders swayed to avoid being speared by broken tree limbs, leaning in concert with their mounts as they sailed over fences and hedges and fallen trees. Approaching a deeply sunken Civil War–era wagon road at a gallop, the leading hunters ground their horses to a halt, among them Mitch Whitley, Karin, Dietrich, and Meriah Reinholdt. As the remainder of the hunt charged up from behind, Karin spurred Bitter Stone and the big horse dived down the embankment into the road, leaped it in a single bound, then dug furiously to climb the opposite bank. Dietrich followed immediately on Grand Teuton, leaning way back to maintain his seat, and then the entire hunt spilled into the deep depression of the sunken road and scrambled up the other side.

The hunt entered a slope of widely spaced tall spruces, crested a ridge, and descended to the fast-rushing headwaters of the Buffalo Run River. Here, even the fox had run alongside the near edge, since the tumbling waters of the Buffalo Run raced into Clawmark Gorge, a quarter-mile of deep, rock-walled trough about twelve feet wide, flushed by the roiling mountain stream. One spring, decades ago, a Harvard naturalist had come to fish the famed trout of the upper Buffalo Run and, while crossing the spill of a waterfall, he slipped and was washed over, falling forty feet into the deep, frigid pool at the foot of the fall. Searchers with dogs were later following his trail across the fast stream when one noticed eight parallel claw marks gouged in the moss covering the smooth rock at the head of the fall. They grapple-hooked the body from the black pool beneath. The site was thereafter called Clawmark Fall, similar to the gorge below.

An hour after the hunt began, the horses and even the hounds had begun to slow from the pace, and still the fox remained elusive. The hilltoppers would occasionally lose the hunt, but given the baying of the hounds, the huntsman's horn, and the thunder of fifty horses, it was never hard to locate. There were two falls among the careening hunters that drew the gasps and pointed arms of many of the onlookers. Oddly, one rider to suffer a fall was Karin Steiger, who appeared to misjudge the approach to another old rock fence, causing Bitter Stone to jump from too far away. The horse failed to clear the fence, snagged its rear feet, staggered, and fell. It was not an error riders of Karin's level often made. Karin had fallen before; she saw it coming and cleared the horse as it tumbled. She hung onto the reins, calmed her animal, remounted, and charged to regain her place among the galloping hunters. Fox hunting is not a sport for the faint of heart, as I was soon to learn the hard way.

The hounds entered an extensive forest, and the hunters broke into groups to follow the few, widely segregated paths through the woods.

The children's group took an alternate route, as riding in forest is especially dangerous, owing to low and jagged tree limbs. Julianne and I entered the woods together on the heels of the last of the hunters. Well ahead, I saw Eicher Dietrich rein in and turn to look back at me. Mitch, Karin, and the other hunt leaders disappeared in the forest.

Dietrich immediately spun Grand Teuton and spurred him, scrambling back toward us. I pulled Moose up, wondering what would move Dietrich to depart his position among the leaders in the hunt. Surprised, Julianne drew Yang up near me. The other hilltoppers rode around us into the woods. I watched Dietrich and Grand Teuton closing at the charge. I looked at Dietrich's gloved hands, but they held only taught reins.

At the point where he should have steered away or slowed the horse to join us, he did neither. In a second, I knew a collision was now likely in the narrow spaces of the forest. Moose jerked her head up but stood her ground. I freed a hand to ward Dietrich off, but he had another target in mind.

Julianne Chu tried to escape on Yang, but Dietrich's horse was moving too fast and had swerved too suddenly. Dietrich hauled Grand Teuton down hard, reining skillfully to collide breast-to-side with Julianne's little Arabian gelding. Grand Teuton struck the frantic Yang with a shrill whinny, knocking the smaller horse right off its feet. Yang crashed onto his side in a cloud of dry leaves. Julianne hit with an audible *oof!* and rolled. I was relieved to see her scramble angrily to her feet, glaring at Dietrich and clinging to Yang's rein. Quickly, she moved to quiet Yang, who was lurching to his own feet.

I was astonished. A rider of Dietrich's caliber could only have done this with careful deliberation. "You son of a bitch!" I whispered, gathering Moose's reins. My temper was blowing in the winter wind.

Dietrich looked cruelly at Julianne, then he fired me a self-satisfied, amused sneer. He must have known how I would react, and I regret he was correct. I speared Moose and went for him, but he effortlessly reined about, Grand Teuton dug to accelerate, and the chase was on.

We ran away from the hunt, Dietrich leaning low and swaying gracefully in his saddle, his mount responding instantly to his commands. Enraged, I had given Moose her head and was heeling her high and back on her flanks. She seemed to relish the chase and was digging hard to keep up, but she was no match for an Olympic champion. Dietrich soon had a seventy-five-yard lead on us.

Dietrich looked back one last time, then he pulled Grand Teuton hard to his right and disappeared around an embankment. When Moose and I rounded the embankment, we found ourselves on still another sunken section of the old Confederate wagon trail, with steep, wooded embankments on either side. I was startled to see Dietrich paused in the road as though he had waited for us. *The arrogant bastard!* I thought. *He's so confident he can't be caught that he waited for us!* I heeled Moose and called urgently to her. She snorted and went to warp speed.

Dietrich whipped Grand Teuton about and the superhorse raced away down the narrow, tree-lined roadway at an accelerating gallop. Moose and I were full out when it began to soak through my rage that Dietrich appeared to be leaning very low over his horse's neck. But then he straightened as Grand Teuton flew. I grunted guttural yells to Moose and she somehow called up still more steam. We thundered down the old sunken wagon road hot after Dietrich.

I'm not sure even now if it was my years as a helicopter pilot or just fool's luck. Whichever, shrill alarms now rang through my anger and I saw it not a nanosecond too soon.

It was just a thin, horizontal silver gleam that some cluster of my brain cells recognized as out of place against the blur of green and brown embankment. It was enough for me to dive and fling myself from Moose without hesitation. Even so, the taught, heavy wire caught me on my right shoulder and the side of my helmet, spinning me wildly as I fell. I hit in the leaf-carpeted roadbed and tumbled ass-over-tea-kettle before sliding to a stop face down.

I lay still, gasping for breath and taking damage-control reports from my body. Everything seemed to function according to the owner's manual, but oh Christ, how I hurt. I struggled to one knee and looked down the old wagon road to see Moose standing yards away, watching me.

Dietrich and Grand Teuton had vanished, but I could hear fast galloping hoofbeats fading in the quiet forest.

I mounted Moose with some effort, and rode her back to the treacherous wire. It was quarter-inch braided cable strung so tightly between two stout trees that it twanged.

It was exactly at my neck level.

Only an equestrian expert could know the right height for a tall rider like me and a very tall horse like Moose. Such an expert would know that a horse's head is down at the charge but the rider is up and leaning slightly forward. Only a cunning man would have understood that he could enrage another man beyond caution by viciously attacking petite little Julianne Chu.

Dr. Eicher Dietrich was no fool. He had read me like a book and played me like a violin, but I would never be able to prove it in a court of law. And if my head and I had been lying several yards apart right now, neither would anybody else.

The rain was close enough to smell while Mitch was conducting the awards and farewell ceremony in the covered arena in which I had arrested Eicher Dietrich the night before. There was much handshaking and hugging and kissing in farewell, but most in attendance moved quickly to load their horses and leave before the rain caused trucks and trailers to become mired in mud.

Dietrich was nowhere to be seen.

Mitch and Helen had invited a handful of guests for post-hunt cocktails and, as I was included, I turned Moose over to Arthur, who was loading Dublin and Elizabeth aboard the Mountain Harbor rig.

"Wasn't Dublin *great,* Uncle Lewis!" Elizabeth was clearly exhausted but delirious. "He ran like Bitter Stone! Someday, I'm going to be a star like Karin Steiger, Uncle Lewis!"

"Probably," I said, kissing her on the cheek as she sat next to Arthur in the truck. "But right now you need a shower, dinner, and some sleep. Tomorrow's a school day."

"What a hunt!" Elizabeth exclaimed. "Dublin was great! *I* was great!" Elizabeth giggled, immensely pleased with herself.

"Yes, you were," I laughed, glad to see her so happy. "At the rate you're going it'll be at least two weeks before you make the USET."

Elizabeth laughed again, then she jumped and hugged my neck tightly. "I love you, Uncle Lewis!" she said.

I fought tears as I replied, "I love you, too, darlin' girl."

Thank you, Coleby, I thought. You were right. Your precious daughters have put meaning and love back in my life. Thank you for blessing me with this beautiful child. Oh, Coleby, my fine friend, I miss you so.

"'Nuff o' this foolishness!" old Arthur grumbled. "Polly gon' be puttin' our dinner on the table, girl. We got to go!"

"Don't forget the alarms, Arthur," I reminded him, picturing a tall, craggy, evil-smelling man with a big knife. Arthur nodded. I could still hear Elizabeth crowing about the hunt as they pulled the trailer up the drive in a long line of departing horse rigs.

I hiked between the pair of large stable barns en route to the Whitley home for cocktails, still in my natty riding duds, my pistol tucked into my belt beneath the coat. No more Klaus encounters of the third kind for me, thank you; not with Dietrich trying to guillotine me and the butcher still out there somewhere. The barns were all but deserted now, as this year's charity hunt was officially ended, and all but the Whitley houseguests were pulling out. Big, cold raindrops began to pelt down, and I broke into a jog.

Passing between the barns, I heard the commotion of a disturbed horse, which sounded as though it came from the far end of the smaller of the stables. At first, I took it to be the normal stirring of a horse not happy to be penned up in a stall, but then there was the loud hollow boom of a hoof slamming against a stall wall, followed by a shrill whinny. I peered down the long barn aisle, but could see nothing other than the dark interior of the barn with its multiple stall entrances and its overhead loft. Again, there came the violent sounds of a thrashing, agitated horse. I unbuttoned my suede riding coat and drew my pistol, letting it dangle by my leg, and I moved cautiously down the barn aisle, hugging the left bank of stalls. The cold rain arrived and a steady, drumming drone came from the roof above me, resonating throughout the stable and, regrettably, muffling virtually all other sound.

All the stalls I passed were empty. Whatever was happening to the horse I heard was occurring in a stall near the far end. Again, I heard the thump of a hoof against heavy oak, followed by snorting and a nervous whinny.

As I drew near the stall from which the noise emanated, I

crept slowly, listening carefully but in frustration because of the loud rain on the barn roof. All I could hear were the heavier of the sounds of the stirring horse. I paused before an unusually large stall on my left, the open, bulky half-door of which was swung into the aisle. I peered around the doorway and found the roomy stall empty.

I jumped at the abrupt thump and scramble of the horse in the next stall, and something else. Then I knew I was not alone in the roaring barn with only a frightened horse. My eyes tracked hard to my right and my head began to rotate. When it turned far enough that my ear deployed to the rear, all uncertainty vanished. It was then that, over the Niagara Fall of the rain on the roof, I heard quick, hard-digging footsteps closing fast from behind.

32

•••••••

Animals in the Barn

I'd barely turned when Karin Steiger hit me on a dead run, seizing me about the neck, I stumbled backward and fell into a pile of straw, Karin landing atop me. She clamped her mouth on mine and slurped at me ravenously, making hungry little throat noises through her nose. Furious, I grabbed a fistful of her hair and pulled her away from me. She winced from the pain, gritting her teeth, but that slight smile of arrogant contempt never faded. Her eyes, wide and excited, were fixed on mine.

I shoved Karin off me and scrambled to my feet.

"Goddamn it, Karin, you maniac!" I sputtered loudly over the drum of the rain on the stable roof. I tucked my gun in my belt. "I damn near shot you!" I wiped waxy lipstick from my mouth, drew a deep breath, and let it ease out. *"Christ!* Assertiveness has never been much of a problem with you, has it?"

On her knees, Karin smiled broadly, a fabulously beautiful smile of soft, full lips and white teeth, all of it set off by teasing blue eyes. She tossed her head to fling a strand of hair from her eye. "Oooh," Karin cooed, "thou doth protest too much. We both know why you followed me here."

"Oh, bullshit. I didn't even know you were in here. I heard a horse raising hell and I thought that psycho with the knife might be making another animal rights statement. What the hell are *you* doing here?"

Karin cocked her head to one side, still grinning slyly at me. "Bitter Stone is in the next stall, 'raising hell,' as you say. I take very good care of my best horse, Lewis. I stable Stone apart from the rest, feed only special diet, and provide protection from the cold with a sheet. Bitter Stone is the most significant eventing horse in twenty years, insured for a quarter of a million dollars. Without Stone, I could never deliver Eicher the humiliating defeat he will suffer at the games next summer."

"Hoo," I said, walking quickly into the aisle and peering to see the horse in the next stall, "with you for a fiancée, ole Doc Mengele could get by a long time without any enemies." Sure enough, I saw Bitter Stone pacing nervously, draped in a German Equestrian Team blanket. A small cobweb-draped TV camera was mounted high in one corner of the stall, for purposes of monitoring mares about to foal, I assumed. I'd seen the arrangement in other horse barns.

Karin released a short laugh with a bitter edge to it, audible even over the permeating roar of the rain on the roof. "Eicher and I are . . . dedicated competitors, Lewis. Our engagement is just part of the game; it should not be taken too seriously. Make no mistake, he would cut my throat before he would lose in Atlanta. Shed no tears of pity for Eicher Dietrich."

I returned to the more spacious stall. Karin was still on her knees. Her mouth still smiled, but her eyes were looking far away. She broke off her gaze, looked up at me, and extended her right hand. I took it and helped her to her feet. She wobbled a little, as though dizzy, held my hand tightly, and leaned into me, turning her face up.

A truly lovely, intelligent woman up close is bewitching to a man, to this man at least. The draw is much more than sexual, though it is decidedly that. A woman of substance and achievement offers to a man a gift of herself, a prize so exceedingly more rewarding than a collection of orifices, which is not to discount in the least the degree of lust such a woman generates. When I told Karin I didn't love her, at the Whitley luncheon, she said she could fix that, and I was beginning to fear she was right.

Again, Karin wore that maddeningly teasing smile a little higher at one corner than the other. Her eyes were half closed, but the parts that were open drilled into mine; they glowed with the intensity of the emotion behind them. She put her lips near my ear, again causing that flooding, tingling sensation, like warm honey running over the side of my neck.

Karin pressed her pubis solidly against the front of my left leg, and she kissed me, but differently this time, I was struck to note. It was not her heretofore carnivorous, consumptive assault. For the first time, it conveyed feeling in her in addition to desire; for the very first time, it was not a kiss that took, but one that gave, not a kiss that demanded but one that pleaded. The sudden introduction of vulnerability in her, of the touching of souls as well as bodies, put color in our closeness that blinded with its brilliance. She kissed firmly but with finesse, letting me share the flesh, savor her softness and scent and warmth, even hear the sudden inrush of breath through her nose that conveyed her excitement. At such a moment, a man may in truth be to such a woman only a life-support system for a dick, but it never feels that way. You feel special, as though she has singled you out for the gift of herself, and it feels good. There is no substitute for woman.

Karin broke off her kiss. She seemed to buckle at the knees, but I held her. She studied my eyes as though she'd never seen them. In hers, I thought I saw a trace of pain, but that is often difficult to distinguish from passion at times like this. Then the beautiful, crooked smile was back.

I bent and straightened her, feeling her knees tremble. She turned her head up and to the left, and we kissed gently.

The rain subsided some, and Karin Steiger wept softly, tears streaming down her cheeks. "I just want to live, Lewis," she whispered again and again. "I just want to live."

"I know," I answered, rocking her in my arms," and you work harder at it than anyone I can think of."

"Not hard enough," Karin whispered softly. Then she bent to retrieve her hunt cap from the floor. Twice, she dropped it as though her hand were lifeless. Karin glanced up at me, angry, whether at the cap, her hand, or me, I was unsure. I stepped to help her.

"I can do it!" Karin suddenly snapped, slapping at my extended hand. I straightened, surprised.

Karin snatched up the helmet with her other hand and stood. She swayed dizzily.

I caught her before she fell. She looked at me with a mixture of rage and fear. She flailed at my arms. "No!" she shouted, "I do not *need* any help! There is nothing *wrong* with me!" She pushed back from me and wobbled while searching for balance. Just when I thought she was all right, she suddenly looked very frightened and she turned away from me, bending at the waist and leaning on the stall wall. From behind her I could not avoid seeing a stain spreading black on the inner thigh of her tan riding breeches. She sank to her knees and sat upon her feet, facing the wall, her head bowed.

"Karin," I said, alarmed, stepping toward her. She held up a hand without looking back. The rain noise swelled.

"No!" Karin shouted, sounding as though she was again close to crying. "No! Just leave me! Go away!"

"Are you bleeding, Karin? Tell me what's wrong. Are you all ri—"

"Go away! Just leave—"

"I'm not going any-goddamn-where until I know what's wrong, Karin." I knelt behind her and rested my hands on her shoulders.

Karin still hung her head, but she drew a deep breath. When she spoke, it was like she had striven very hard to bring herself under control. "There . . . is *nothing* wrong, Lewis. I . . . I'm not bleeding. I have just had a . . . a little embarrassing accident, if you must know. All right? Now, please, just leave me with a grain of my dignity. I will be all right. Please. Go to the house and join the party. I will be all right."

"Karin, I hate to just leave you—"

Now I could see she was crying. "Please, Lewis! The kindest thing you can do for me—"

"Is leave. All right, I'm leaving." I stroked the silken hair at the side of her head. As I stood, she suddenly clapped her hand over mine, pinning it to her neck. She slowly rocked her head, rubbing it against my hand, then she released me. "Go," she said. "Please. I'll be all right."

I stood and walked to the door. "Lewis!" Karin called, barely audible in the din. When I looked, she was still sitting on her folded legs, her head bowed, facing away from me. "We lived good, did we not, Lewis? For those moments, we lived good, didn't we?"

I trotted through the rain to the Laurel Ridge mansion, confused and troubled.

33
••••••••

A Killer's Promise

The lovely Whitley daughter, Christine, met me at the door, still in her riding finery.

My bizarre encounter with Karin was still dominating my thoughts. "I need a phone, Christine," I said. She took me by the arm and led me down the hall and left me in Mitch's elaborate library. There, I sat at his huge rolltop desk, with its built-in security television monitors, and I called my office.

"Sheriff's office, Sergeant Stanford!" Milly's voice more demanded than answered.

"Hi, darlin'."

"Hey, Sheriff! I was about gwan call you. Got some good news for you!"

"I could stand some, Milly. Tell me Caleb Horrow ran head-on into Eicher Dietrich, and what's left has to be scooped into body bags with a snow shovel."

"Hell, I just said good news, Lewis, not no motherfuckin' *miracle!*"

"Yeah, okay, I lost my head. What's up?"

"Well, ole Double-Parked, he been a-peckin' away on that goddamn computer, you know?"

"Bless his heart."

"Well, that little smartass figger that since the Illinois

DMV didn't have no vehicle info on Horrow, he'd work the DMV files for the states neighboring Illinois."

"And he's come up with a car on Caleb Horrow!"

"Nineteen-eighty-nine Chevrolet Camaro, two-door, black in color, Kentucky registration: robert-mary-david, one-one-three!"

"Ex*cept*ional! Get it on the—"

"I got it out everwhere, Lewis. I even got the girls callin' all the gas stations and convenience stores in all the area counties. Figger the motherfucker got to have gas, beer, and cigarettes. Somebody gonna see him!"

"Want to get married, Milly?" I asked. I held the phone back from my ear while Milly howled.

"Sheeeit, white boy! You ain't seen the day you could satisfy a woman like me!"

"Can I die trying?"

Again Milly shattered all the glass within fifty yards. She suddenly sobered. "Listen here, Lewis! I done thought about what you said about this psycho, and I think you're right. He ain't runnin', he's a-comin' after you white ass for chillin' his momma! You watch yousef 'til we git this motherfucker, you hear me, Lewis Cody?"

"Yes, ma'am. Put Double-Parked on."

"I done run him off home to eat. Tole him turn that scanner off and git some goddamn sleep! Tomorra a school day!"

"Okay, good. I just wanted to thank him, but I'll do that tomorrow."

"He know you love him, Lewis. That little boy crazy about you."

"Christ, I'm thinking we should take out a key-man insurance policy on the little genius. Got any Peter Pan dust we can sprinkle on him to keep him from growing up and going off to college? The whole damn department will cave in."

"Well, we got a few years to sweat that, I reckon."

"Okay, Milly, thanks. Tell Pierce to put the word out that if anybody spots that car, try to wait for backup before taking him down. Tell Pierce that includes him. I don't want him trying to take him alone in the hope that Horrow will force cause to shoot him. Let's everybody be extra careful.

Caleb Horrow is big and he's meaner than a starved grizzly. If the car is spotted unoccupied, pull back, stake it, and notify. Got that?"

"Is a bear fuzzy? Is white folks uptight? Do the American Bar Association pray to a eight-by-ten color photo of O. J. Simpson every day? Do the——"

I sighed. "All right, all right. A simple yes will get it, Milly. I should be free here in a half-hour or so. I'll call you when I hit the road."

"Watch you dumb ass, Lewis!"

I elected not to tell Milly that my dumb ass had very nearly been separated from my dumb head already.

I entered the big sunken living room where the party had been held three nights earlier, when Arlette Sowers's poor mare met with the butcher. A fast-paced Yanni orchestral number emanated from ceiling speakers, covering a bustling hubbub of conversation. People stood about in their stocking feet with their riding coats open, drinks in hand. One woman, near the fireplace with friends, was dancing solo with the wobbly enthusiasm of someone who was well into her celebratory drink, much to the amusement of her group. I hoped somebody was driving her home.

Mitch and Helen Whitley stood by the piano with Merlin and Arlette Sowers, Meriah Reinholdt, and Hap and Bev Morgan. Merlin was beaming, red-faced, and waving his arms. I gathered from a distance that he was relating his spill during the hunt, much to the amusement of everyone. Near Merlin, Meriah turned from a conversation with Hap and Bev to wave at me. I thought I saw a trace of distress in her gaze. I didn't see Julianne Chu or Eicher Dietrich in the room.

"Lewis!" Mitch hailed, spotting me. I strode across the room to join the group. "A splendid hunt, don't you agree, Lewis?" Mitch declared. "Just splendid!"

"It was pretty damned exciting in places, Mitch," I said dryly. "Congratulations on bringing off a successful charity."

"Congratulations indeed!" Merlin Sowers almost shouted, waving his drink. Hap Morgan eyed the libation and leaned back lest it spill on him in passing.

Helen Whitley said, "Oh my, yes! The weather held off!

No one was injured! No horses were hurt! Everyone seemed to have a wonderful time!" Helen's glowing expression faded suddenly. "Except for . . . except for Dr. Dietrich, of course. What a terrible tragedy." The general merriment of the group took a nosedive.

"Where is the good doctor?" I inquired. "I could stand a chat with him; I surely could."

"I don't know," Helen said with concern, looking about. "I haven't seen him since the hunt."

"Mercifully," Mitch muttered. "Perhaps he's in his room, changing. What will become of Dr. Dietrich, Lewis?" Everyone studied me.

"That's up to the courts, Mitch," I said. "Presumably, he'll show for his day in court and a jury will decide."

Merlin frowned. "We're gonna be famous in the horse world, all right, but not like I hoped. Lewis, will Dr. Dietrich be able to compete in the Atlanta games?"

"I don't know, Merlin. A lot can happen in six months. His lawyers may be able to postpone a trial until after the games. Even if he goes to trial before the games, he may be acquitted." I looked around the room grimly. "After all, he's innocent until proven guilty."

"Innocent until proven guilty," Merlin repeated gravely. "Absolutely! A cornerstone of American justice I heartily agree with!" Merlin sighed and proceeded lamely with a question that clearly worried him. "Mrs. Reinholdt— uh, Meriah—I do hope that the . . . uh . . . recent unfortunate developments . . . uh . . . with regard to Dr. Dietrich haven't . . . oh, negatively influenced you about our lovely community. Uh . . . we . . . uh—"

"Merlin," Meriah said calmly, watching him, "two days ago, I gave you my hand and my word. Ask anyone who has done business with me in the last forty years and they will tell you that both are as binding as my signature on a contract. Eicher is my . . . dear friend, but the stable I intend to build here is business. I never let one influence the other."

"Oh!" Merlin said magnanimously, visibly relieved, "did you think I meant our little deal? Oh, why I never doubted for a—"

"Of course." Meriah looked pained, and glanced at me

before sipping her wine. She seemed to contemplate a moment and then she asked, "Lewis, if Eicher is convicted, what will happen to him?"

"Again, Meriah, that's up to—"

"A judge. I know, Lewis, but you must have some idea!" I was startled at Meriah's uncharacteristic vehemence. Looking at her, I decided that in spite of his having thrown Meriah over for her daughter, Meriah still loved Dietrich.

"Up here, he could go down for manslaughter one—times two. Rural juries are much less inclined to sympathize with drunk killers, especially where dead babies are concerned. He could get several years in prison, of which he would have to serve at least a couple before he sees parole."

Meriah looked stricken. "Oh, my God. That's terrible."

He drove drunk and killed two people. That's *terrible,* I wanted to say, but didn't.

As though reading my mind, Meriah held up a hand and waved it rapidly. "Sorry. I'm not attempting to mitigate Eicher's crime. It's unforgivable. It's just that . . . you have to know Eicher like I do. He isn't a bad man, just proud and impulsive and intensely competitive. Prison will kill him. It would be like locking Bitter Stone in a stall twenty-four hours a day. They'd both go crazy. I know Eicher. He would prefer execution."

"Well, by God he's innocent until proven guilty!" Merlin declared sternly. "I have always said that—"

"No." Meriah said coldly, cleaving Merlin's drivel as with an ax. "No. I know Eicher, and I heard what he said last night. He isn't innocent. He killed those poor people, and even he will go to jail for that." Meriah's lip trembled a bit. "And for him, it will be a slow death . . . that even Eicher Dietrich doesn't deserve. Excuse me, please." Abruptly, Meriah set her drink on an end table and hurried away. Shocked, everyone in the group watched her ascend the steps and disappear into the hall toward the stairs to the second floor.

Hap Morgan coughed. "Plenty enough misery in this to go around, I reckon," he said, swishing his drink.

"There's Dr. Chu!" Helen exclaimed, desperate to break the pall.

Julianne had changed from her riding gear to stylish gray pants topped by a blue sweater and blazer. She'd paid some attention to herself and looked very good indeed. She walked to me with a broad smile. She took my arm on joining the group and exchanged pleasantries about the hunt with everyone.

"Hello, Lewis," Julianne then said to me, drawing us both to a private spot by the doors to the huge rain-soaked deck. "I was wondering what happened to you."

"I was about to say the same thing," I answered. "Are you okay?"

"Yes, thank you. I was more shocked by Dr. Dietrich's charge than injured by the fall. I wanted to change. My clothes were . . . muddy."

Julianne took a small goblet of wine from a tray offered by one of the Whitley house staff. She looked at me over the drink. "What happened with you and Dr. Dietrich, Lewis? What on earth came over him?"

"It makes for a good tale; he tried to kill me, and if I'd been a better idiot, he would have."

"Are you serious?"

"Quite. I'll tell you about it later."

"Where's Karin?" Julianne looked around.

I was wondering the same thing. I hoped she was not still in that cold, damp barn, in her peculiar condition. I had considered asking one of the women to walk down and check on her, but couldn't think of a good candidate for the task in such rain. An aggressive beauty like Karin doesn't acquire a lot of girlfriends. Before I could answer Julianne, Merlin piped up again.

"Dr. Chu!" Merlin hailed us, wobbling our way. "Julianne, we here in Hunter County are wonderin' when we'll know if you're going to join our happy little community!"

"Aw," Hap Morgan grumbled from the piano, "I reckon Julianne can make up her mind in her own time, Merlin; don't rush her!"

Julianne pulled her gaze back into the room. She glanced

at me for a moment with her immense, brown eyes, then at Hap. "Thank you, Dr. Morgan—"

"Hap, dammit."

Julianne smiled. Bev Morgan elbowed her husband with a frown.

"Thank you for the chivalry, Hap, but since Mr. Sowers has raised the question, if the offer still stands, I accept. I'd like to buy in with you."

A burst of enthusiasm exploded from the group that caught the attention of everyone in the room.

"Outstanding!" Mitch Whitley roared.

"Well, hot *damn!"* Hap said, beaming.

"Hap!" Bev Morgan scolded. "Julianne, that's wonderful news, dear!" Bev stepped forward to hug Julianne, followed by Helen Whitley. Mitch snapped his fingers for one of the servants and ordered a round of champagne.

For my part, I was amazed to note that I suddenly felt better—relieved, though I couldn't delineate why. When the commotion subsided, while the house staff scurried about with glasses of champagne, Julianne turned to me, and it seemed natural, not to mention desirable, to hug her myself.

"I'm glad to hear your decision," I told her. "Hunter County needs you."

When I released her, she clung to me and turned her face to my ear. "Karin won't last, Lewis. It's her curse. She can steal anyone, but she can keep no one. When she's done with you, you will need me, too." She kissed me lightly on the cheek, then turned away to accept a congratulatory hug from Mitch Whitley.

"Here, here!" Mitch called loudly. "Everyone have their champagne?" A cheer went up. "Excellent! Hap, would you like to do the honors?"

"Damn straight," Hap said, stepping forward and placing his hand on Julianne's shoulder. "Folks, it gives this old man great pleasure to hear that Dr. Julianne Chu—"

"Julianne, dammit!" Julianne said, smiling. Everyone laughed.

"—will be joining me as a partner. She's forgot more about horses than I'm ever gonna know—"

"Not likely," Julianne whispered.

"—and she's a damn fine vet all around. All the animals in these mountains, including y'all and me, are lucky to have her." Hap held up his glass. "Julianne, welcome to Hunter County!"

Applause and cheers went around the room. Everyone toasted Julianne, and circulated to shake her hand.

When the applause began to fade, one single handclap persisted until everyone turned to see who continued to applaud alone. On the raised edge of the room near the hallway stood Karin Steiger, now dressed in a visually commanding ankle-length dress of an east Indian pattern, mostly maroon in color. Every shining strawberry-blond hair was in place, her make-up was flawless, and she did look stunning. The passion, tears, and disarray of an hour ago were nowhere evident, though she looked tired.

Having captured all the attention, as always, Karin stepped down into the room, halted a passing waitress, and took a glass of the champagne. She downed it in a single draw, dropped it back on the tray, and took another, which she carried to the group of us. Elsewhere in the room, conversation resumed, but most eyes followed Karin.

"The . . . animals of Hunter County are indeed fortunate," Karin said, joining the group by the piano. "Perhaps some animals more than others," she said, leaning heavily against me and attempting to kiss me on the lips. I turned my head slightly so her kiss tagged my cheek. I certainly wasn't averse to Karin's kiss, but I didn't wish to become a tool in her attack on Julianne. To my surprise, Karin suddenly looked not angry, as I expected, but genuinely hurt. The pained look vanished and she turned to Julianne, lifting her glass. "Congratulations . . . *Doctor* Chu," Karin said dryly. She loosely aimed her glass at the near group, glancing at me again in the process. "I'm sure you will all . . . live . . . happily ever after."

Julianne replied, "Thank you, Karin. Now, if you'll all excuse me, I need to make some phone calls." Julianne walked away along the path of evacuation Meriah had taken some thirty minutes previously. That gave me cause to wonder how Meriah was feeling.

"Aren't you lucky?" Karin said to me as the others drifted into private conversations near us. "Now your little dogs and cats and horses and . . . God only knows what else of yours . . . will receive lots of tender loving care."

"Everybody likes a little ass, Karin," I said with an edge. "But nobody likes a smart ass. You could have passed on slamming Julianne long enough to let her enjoy her announcement."

Karin looked me in the eyes over her glass as she sucked it dry. She snapped her fingers at the waitress, who brought the tray. Karin dropped the empty glass on the tray so suddenly it bounced onto the floor. She snatched another full glass from the tray and left the empty to the waitress to retrieve.

"Oh, how gallant," Karin sneered. "Sir Lancelot rides to rescue of the little Chinese-American princess."

"Karin—"

"Oh, the romance, the chival—"

"—what the hell is the matter with you?"

"Nothing. I'm fine. I'm wonderful. Have you seen my beloved fiancé?" Karin asked acidly. "He disappeared during the hunt."

"Nope, but I'd sure like to."

"He's probably in his room, sulking," Karin said. "His precious male German ego—oh, and that's as macho as they come, believe me—is still stinging from your arrest of him last night. He swears he's going to kill you, incidentally. Eicher is relatively harmless without his henchman, but I would be cautious all the same, if I were you. He can get more henchmen."

"I'll bear that in mind." I suffered a mental image of a wicked wire going through my neck like a cheese cutter. I looked up to notice Meriah Reinholdt reenter the room, composed but changed from her riding clothes to casual wear. She saw Karin and me, and joined us.

"Karin, dear, you look flushed. Do you feel all—"

"Yes, Meriah, I feel fine! Why must everyone keep—? I am fine. There is nothing *wrong* with me! What about you? You look like you've been crying."

Meriah paused, examining Karin. "You'd cry too, dear, if you loved Eicher. His life is ruined."

Karin laughed. "Oh, please. Eicher loves Eicher enough for all of us. And he has escaped worse calamities than this."

Meriah stared out the tall windows at the steadily pouring rain.

I became aware of a motion at the corner of my eye and I turned toward the hall leading to the foyer. There, Mitch Whitley was discreetly trying to get my attention. Then, from behind him, came a woman's shriek, which pretty much put discretion to the wind. There were several gasps, and everyone turned to face Mitch. The cry had sounded to me like Christine Whitley. I set my champagne on the piano, hurried across the room, and jumped to the foyer floor level. Mitch took me by the arm and led me to the foyer, beneath the ornate chandelier, where Christine wept in her mother's arms. Mitch's land manager, Houston Devar, stood in his huge Stetson and cracked-wax Australian raincoat, dripping water everywhere. People hurried into the big stone-floored foyer behind us.

Houston's weathered brow was furrowed. Water dripped from his mustache. "Me and the boys was walking the barns, Sheriff, like the professor told us, you know, when we . . . when we seen it."

"What?"

Houston Devar swept his tall hat from his head and combed wet hair back with the other hand. "That crazy man, Sheriff, what's been cutting up them horses! He's *been* here! He's done tied up and cut up Miss Steiger's horse. He's—"

"Bitter *Stone?*" Karin cried from behind me. I turned to see her holding both quivering hands by her face. "Is . . . is Stone hurt bad?" Meriah appeared behind Karin, distress also in her face.

Houston Devar looked sick. "Bad as it gits, ma'am. I'm sorry. And that ain't—"

"*Damn!*" I exclaimed, clapping my hunt cap on my head for rain protection. *Damn that evil fucking troll,* I raged silently. Right under my goddamned *nose!* Karin's Olympic-bound champion!

"Sheriff." Houston gripped my arm. "That ain't all, Sheriff."

I looked at Houston Devar.

"That crazy som-bitch has done killed Doc Dietrich, too."

34
●●●●●●●●

Personal

Meriah Reinholdt went down like she was turned off with a switch. One of the women squealed. Karin barely noticed. She ran immediately out into the rain.

Hap and Bev Morgan moved in to roll Meriah onto her back and check her. "Breathing okay. Fainted, near's I can tell," Hap said.

I sent Helen Whitley to call my office. "Tell them to send everybody, and get an ambulance for Meriah!" I yelled. Julianne and I ran down the broad stone steps into the pouring rain and across the descending slope toward the stables. Ahead of us, Karin ran wildly, having shed her shoes, her hair now in wet strands. Behind us, Mitch, Houston, and others hurried.

We entered the larger of the barns, ran its length, crossed the rainy gap between them, and rushed down the aisle of the smaller stable. Ahead, I could see Karin screaming and thrashing to escape the restraint of two of Houston Devar's men, who were attempting to keep her out of Bitter Stone's stall. She was soaked and barefooted except for muddy pantyhose. I pushed the struggling trio aside. Julianne tried to calm Karin.

Houston's people had turned on the lights. The German Equestrian Team horse blanket was wadded in a corner. The horse lay on its right side, its head hung awkwardly from a series of heavy nylon halter ropes hooked to the horse's halter and secured to rings or posts. Its hind feet were closely hobbled by twisted cords of twine scrap cut from hay bales. Blood was vivid against the shiny black hide and the woodchip bedding of the stall. Bitter Stone had been severely sliced about the throat, the exposed left side, and flank. Blood discharge from the neck was extensive.

No trauma surgeon was required to pronounce Eicher Dietrich dead. He lay on his back in his riding coat, tan trousers, and tall, muddy boots, scowling fiercely, except that his eyes were half closed in a sleepy way. His color was already pale, for most of it had run out of him through multiple stab wounds of the chest and stomach, and now trickled through the chips, pooling in depressions. Dietrich's arms lay out from his sides and his hands were heavily smeared with blood. It wasn't hard to imagine him, a physician knowing he was multiply and mortally wounded, growing weaker by the second, but struggling to plug the leaks with his hands.

No weapon was in sight.

Karin shrieked again and wrenched herself loose from the two men. She pushed past Julianne, leaped into the stall, and froze, soaked and gaping. Houston's men made for her, but I waved them off. Julianne entered the stall behind Karin and stopped when she saw me.

Karin looked first at the still horse to her right, then at Dietrich, who lay to her left. She was at once beholding the violent death of her fiancé and the brutal torture-slaying of Bitter Stone, her twenty-year eventing horse. She must've also seen the utter ruin of any victory in the coming Atlanta games. I expected she would shortly pass out as well. I might have.

Karin trembled and her face contorted from all the inevitable agony. She looked again at Bitter Stone, and then she did—as Karin always did—the last thing I expected her to do. She walked slowly to the gray corpse of Dr. Eicher Dietrich, fell to her knees, cradled his head to her breast, and wept wretchedly. I studied the sight, memorizing the details of a crime scene I was somewhat unprofessionally allowing Karin to disturb.

Julianne went immediately to Bitter Stone and began to

examine the slain animal. She looked over her shoulder and locked eyes with me. I knew what she was trying to tell me. I already knew.

Meriah Reinholdt appeared in the stall door, heaving for breath. She surveyed the grisly stall, leaned against the door edge, and moaned deep in her throat. Mitch and Helen, Hap and Bev, and many of the other guests clustered in the aisle, some struggling to see through the slats of the upper stall wall.

Meriah walked, halting every couple of steps, to Dietrich and the sobbing Karin. She extended her shaking hands, retracted them, and extended them still again. She knelt, placed her face against the back of Karin's wet head, held Karin's face, and Meriah, too, cried.

I double-checked the entire stall for the weapon, including beneath the horse blanket, but found nothing. I stepped into the aisle, and was followed quickly by Julianne. Most of the peripheral people had drawn back from the horrid scene. Merlin Sowers trudged up, gasping like a beached whale. He looked over the stall wall, blanched, and staggered back. He gaped at me with wide eyes.

"Ah! That lunatic! That maniac!" Merlin croaked. He looked back into the stall. "Good God, look what he has *done!* You should have *caught* that crazy son of a bitch this morning, Lewis! You should have shot *him* instead of his goddamn *mother!* Then this wouldn't . . . Oh, good God. When the press gets—when the news of this killer gets out, we'll never attract any big horse money! Oh, good God! Two people dead, Lewis! Two *people!* Old Henry Tucker and now the most famous equestrian champion in the—! We're ruined! Destroyed!"

Julianne seized me by the arm and towed me ten feet down the aisle. Her face was red. "Lewis!" she hissed urgently, "the butcher didn't *do* this! It wasn't *him!*"

"I know!" I whispered. "The whole thing isn't his signature. The style of the wounds, the method of restraint, it's all wrong."

"The butcher would never have just stabbed Doctor Dietrich, he—"

"—would have slashed him seven ways from hell. The butcher's a slasher. I know."

"There's no bucket; nothing to stand on," Julianne added.

"And there is no tying of the tail, no visible semen trace, no inserted devices, no genital slashing."

"All because of the patently obvious!" Julianne said. "Because—"

"Bitter Stone is a *stallion!*" we acknowledged together.

"It's a sexual thing for the butcher," I said. "A mares-only perversion. He didn't *do* this."

Julianne whispered, "Lewis . . . who *did?*"

"I don't know," I answered, but I had a real bad feeling.

I turned back to the crowd outside the stall of horrors. "Houston!" I called to Devar. He and his men came close with Mitch. "Yes, sir, Sheriff?"

"Houston, exactly what did you guys see?"

"Well, just what we done said, Sheriff. We was walking the barns on Professor Whitley's orders, and we come in here from the other end. When we come this far, Richard saw it first. He said, 'Holy shit, Houston, look at this!' I run up and seen everthang, an' I says to Richard and Lonny, 'You boys wait here and don't let nobody in 'til I git the sheriff and the perfesser.' That's it, ain't it, boys?" Houston queried Richard and Lonny.

"Yeah, Sheriff," the short, scruffy Lonny agreed, "that's what we saw!"

"That's it, Sheriff!" Richard nodded, water dripping from his droopy hat.

"All right, guys, you did good. If you think of any—"

"O' course," Lonny mumbled, rubbing his chin and squinting at me, "they *was* that dude a drivin' like a fool."

"*What* dude?" I demanded.

"Oh, yeah!" Richard said.

Houston answered, "I remember now, sheriff, but I don't know as it has anything to do with—"

"Tell me exactly what you saw, guys."

Lonny spoke agonizingly slow. I leaned close to hear him over the rain noise. "Well, Sheriff," he said elaborately, "about maybe ten minutes before we come in here—"

"Hell, no!" Richard corrected him. "Five! Maybe seven minutes, max!"

"Seven minutes *what*, guys?" I asked, running a little short on patience. "We're looking at a warm murder here."

Lonny continued. "Five or six minutes before we come in this barn, Sheriff, we seen somebody a rippin' up the drive toward the highway. You know, a-drivin' like a fool, swervin' and throwin' gravels and mud everwhur. We just took notice of it, you know?"

Sirens howled up outside and car doors slammed. Pierce, Haskel, and Billy ran down the aisle toward us.

"What kind of car was it? Did you get a tag number, or see who was driving?"

"Didn't get no tag," Lonny said, disappointed. "Too far away!"

"Dark!" Richard confirmed.

I waved Pierce toward the stall. "Let the women grieve," I told him. He nodded, parted the crowd, and entered with the two deputies.

"Couldn't make out who was drivin', neither," Houston said. "And I ain't sure what kind of car it was."

"One of them fancy Jap jeeps!" Lonny declared.

Oh no, I thought.

"Yeah," Richard chimed. "Like a Blazer, you know? Only one o' them Japanese four-wheel-drives with chrome wheels and all."

Oh, Christ. "What color was it?" I asked, feeling sick.

"Black."

"Black."

"Black."

I rubbed my eyes.

Pierce came out of the stall, posting Billy at the gate. He strode over to us, wearing his long orange raincoat and narrow-brimmed Stetson. "You want a dog, Lewis? Ain't much chance of trackin' Horrow in this rain."

"No," I replied. "It . . . I'm pretty certain this wasn't Caleb Horrow, Pierce." Pierce registered surprise.

"Roadkill!" Merlin shouted, pointing a fat finger at me. "I knew it! I knew it all along! It's that crazy Roadkill! You should never have—"

"Shut up, Merlin!" I yelled, losing my cool. "Just shut the fuck up and stay out of this." Merlin stared, shocked.

"Pierce," I said, tired, "get on the radio. Put out a BOLO for Trooper Boyce Calder and his POV. Get the tag for his black Nissan Pathfinder from State, and let's get him. He's got maybe twenty minutes' head start."

"Shhhit," Pierce said, looking down and shaking his big head.

"Tell the night desk deputy to put us on maximum staffing, back-to-back twelve-hour shifts until further notice. Tell the units we don't need anyone else here. You and Haskel and I can handle the scene. Put Billy back on the road. Get everybody looking for Boyce."

Pierce nodded and walked swiftly away, snapping his fingers at the deputies.

"Pierce," I called. They stopped and turned. I sighed, drawing my hand across my face. "Put it out as armed and dangerous. The charge is murder."

Torrents of rain sluiced through the blue glow cast by the street lights outside the dungeon. Milly looked up when I slammed through the doors into the otherwise empty booking room. She had evidently come in to work and had put the night desk deputy on the road to help look for the butcher and Corporal Boyce Calder. I shucked the wet riding jacket as I strode into my office and threw it by the fireplace. I struggled to tug the long boots off, tossed them after the coat, and began peeling off my other clothes. Milly waddled in, threw a towel to me, and went to my office closet. She got out a spare complete uniform, some dry socks, and a pair of rubber barn boots, and set them on the couch. She looked out the window at the pouring rain while I dressed.

"Whatchu think, Lewis?" Milly asked. "You think Boyce went over the edge, stabbed Dietrich, and then cut up the horse to make it look like the butcher man?"

"It plays in Peoria," I said, zipping up my pants.

"Say what?"

"It sounds right. The scene is all wrong for it being Caleb Horrow, who had no motive unless Dietrich happened on him doing Bitter Stone, and Stone is a stallion, which makes it highly unlikely Horrow was doing Stone. Boyce sure had a motive; he threatened to kill Dietrich several times, and it's damn near certain he was at the scene only minutes before the murder. As for the means, Boyce is quite capable of killing tougher men than Dietrich with a lot less than a knife. Also, Boyce wouldn't have known that Horrow's victims are always mares, because nobody outside us knows about the sex angle except Rev Hodges, and he's keeping quiet. Yeah. It makes me sick to my core, but I think Boyce did Dietrich and Bitter Stone."

"My Lord." Milly shook her head sadly. "That poor boy. He was a happy kid, a damn fine cop, until that drunk Dietrich kill his little Cathy and his baby. Now Boyce got to go down for murder. Ain't no justice in this damn world."

In silence, Milly built a fire in my fireplace and exited, closing my door behind her.

I called Pete Floyd at the paper, to fill him in. "Jesus," Pete said. "When it rains, it pours."

I put the phone in its cradle and propped my head in my hands, massaging my temples. My intercom buzzed, and I tagged the button.

"Lewis," Milly said, 'little Elizabeth on line one."

"Hi, sweetheart," I said, glad for the diversion. "You about ready for bed? It's after eight."

"Me and Gruesome are in my bed, Uncle Lewis. Polly gave us some hot chocolate." I knew Polly had given Elizabeth a mug of hot chocolate, of which she no doubt alternated sips with the shameless Gruesome.

"Gruesome and I, darlin', not me and Gruesome."

"Gruesome and I are in bed. It's raining out, Uncle Lewis. Polly has gone over to her apartment above the garage. Me and Gruesome . . . Gruesome and I . . . are kind of . . . lonesome, you know? When are you coming home, Uncle Lewis?"

I decided an eleven-year-old girl alone in a big house on a rainy night could wait a day to hear about the murders of a man and a horse. "Soon as I can, darlin'. There's a lot going on tonight, but I'll probably be home in an hour or so. Don't wait up. Turn the light out at nine and go to sleep. The security alarm is set. Polly is across the drive, and Arthur is in his place above the stable. If you need them, all you have to do is press the intercom button by your bed. I'll be home as soon as I can, and I'll come in to give you a good-night kiss."

"Okay, Uncle Lewis. Promise?"

"I promise." Something in Elizabeth's tone worried me. "Are you okay, Elizabeth?"

"Yeah . . . yeah. I'm okay, Uncle Lewis. I . . . sometimes I just miss Daddy and Momma, you know?" My heart broke to hear her sniff and cry softly. I cursed the circumstances that demanded I be in my office instead of home, holding a little girl who deserved more in a guardian that I was sometimes able to provide her.

"I know, sweetheart. That's perfectly all right. It's healthy to miss your dad and mom. It's part of the healing process, darlin' girl."

Elizabeth cried miserably. "But it hurts so *much*, Uncle Lewis!"

I cried, but I choked to keep Elizabeth from hearing it.

"I know, love. I know. It hurts me, too."

"Why did they have to *die*, Uncle Lewis?" Elizabeth wailed.

"I don't know that, Elizabeth. Don't make yourself crazy looking for reasons, child. Sometimes there just are no reasons. Sometimes we have to suffer unfair things that hurt us. In the end, we have only one choice in our lives, and that is to make the very best of all of it that remains for us. That's a long life for you, sweetheart, and you mustn't spend it suffering. Your mom and dad would be very unhappy if they knew you were crying for them. They would not want you to cry for them. You know that. They would want you to put the bad memories behind you and live a happy life."

"I love you, Uncle Lewis!" The child wept.

"I love you, too, sweet child. You are the most important little girl in all the world for your uncle Lewis. Listen to me. It's time to stop crying now, okay?"

I could hear her sniff and honk her nose in a tissue. "Okay, Uncle Lewis."

"You can cry again another time, darlin', but that's enough for now. Now it's time to be strong, and think about happy things. That's what your mom and dad would want."

"I will, Uncle Lewis."

"I know you will, sweetheart. I know I can depend on you. You're tough and you're strong. I've always been so proud of you for that. Now put a Keno Reeves movie—"

"Keanu!"

"—on the VCR, turn the sound down low, and watch the movie 'til you go to sleep. Okay?"

"I will! Thanks, Uncle Lewis! I love you!"

"Sleep tight, sweetheart."

I was leaning back in the faded old cracked-leather judge's chair, wiping my eyes and having my own suffering session for Coleby Butler, when there came a tap at the window behind me. I jumped and whirled about in the swivel chair, reaching for my gun.

I sprang from the chair, stunned to see the face that looked through the rain-streaked glass at me, for it was the most wretched face I'd ever seen. It was saturated, exhausted, and light years beyond care.

I bolted into the booking room, gun in hand, startling Milly, who stood suddenly. I clapped my hat on, hurrying to the tall, oaken front doors.

"What the hell the matter with you, boy?" Milly asked, surprised.

I shrugged into an orange police raincoat and charged out into the cold, rainy night, sighting over my pistol. I rushed to the edge of the building and peered carefully around it.

Boyce Calder was there under the building corner lights, drenched, his head bowed. His hands were empty and he held them out from his sides, palms toward me. The figure he cut in the driving rain reminded me of Jesus Christ. *Forgive them, Father, for they know not what they do.*

I hurried to Boyce, gun still ready; I turned him and searched him. I holstered my pistol and handcuffed Boyce's thick arms behind him. He was compliant—catatonic, in fact. Milly scrambled around the corner in a raincoat, a shotgun at port arms.

"It's all right!" I called to her over the hissing rain. "He's under control!" Milly took Boyce by his other arm and we led him inside.

Before Milly, I said, "Boyce, listen to me." Boyce stared straight ahead, water dripping from his nose and lips. I pulled his arm. "Boyce! Listen up!" He rotated his head toward me, but he was still not in this world. "Boyce," I continued slowly, "you have the right to remain silent, and I encourage you to do so. Anything you say may be used against you in a court of law. You have the right to have an attorney present before answering any questions. You —"

The lights came on in Boyce's eyes. "I . . . I know Miranda . . . Sheriff Cody. I waive my right to counsel. I'm guilty."

"Boyce, you should remain si—"

"I wanted to kill him," Boyce whispered, infinitely weary. "I wanted to kill him, and I went there to kill him, and now he's dead. I'm guilty. That's it."

35
• • • • • • • •
Guilt

With Boyce Calder in custody, things were settling down slowly. Pierce and Milly put the department back on standard hours. Milly went home. Pierce coordinated the alert for Caleb Horrow with the night desk deputy. The men on the road would pay special attention to stables and other assemblages of horses; would visit all the county sources of cigarettes, alcohol, and gasoline; and would scour the county for Horrow's old Camaro. Pierce stuck his head in my office. "Lewis, we got Boyce dried out and outfitted in some jailhouse dungarees. He's in holding block eight, but he ain't sayin' shit."

"Okay Pierce. It's been a long few days. Go home and get some rest. Say hello to Brenda for me. And thanks. I'd be lost without you."

"Uh, Lewis, what do you think they'll do to Boyce?"

I leaned back in my chair. "I don't know, Pierce. Given Boyce's confession, his threats, and the witnesses, I think the best we can hope for is a temporary-insanity verdict, but it's a long shot. Boyce's attorneys will have to convince a jury that he was so stressed he didn't know right from wrong. That'll be a tough since Boyce is a cop, schooled and experienced in determining legal right and wrong under stress. Plus, every time a cop goes on trial, he gets held to a higher standard by judges and jurors. It doesn't look good to me."

Pierce shook his head for the hundredth time in the evening. "Damn shame. What a shit thing to happen to a good kid."

For a long time after Pierce left, I stewed over Boyce and the Dietrich killing. We hadn't questioned Boyce yet; I had hoped he would ask for an attorney, but he had clearly given up on living. Still, it seemed open and shut, especially given Boyce's profession of guilt, his witnessed threats, his pronounced motive, and his witnessed opportunity. I stared at the ceiling, rolling everything over and over in my mind. Then I went to holding cell number eight.

Boyce Calder lay slouched on the bunk in jail jeans, denim shirt, and sock feet. His face was darkened with beard stubble. He was staring blankly at the graffiti-scratched stone wall and he didn't even blink when I came in. "Come on, Boyce," I said. "Let's go in my office and talk." He ignored me. "On your feet, Boyce," I repeated.

Boyce slowly rolled onto his side, facing the wall. "Go away, Sheriff Cody. You got what you want. I'm guilty. Leave me alone."

I crossed the cell in two strides, grabbed Boyce by the hair and right arm, and spun him out of the bunk, face down on the floor. I knelt on his back and pulled one arm back. He glared at me when I hauled him to his feet, but he didn't resist, and he said nothing as I propelled him along the corridor, across the booking room, past the perplexed night desk deputy, and into my office. I kicked my door shut and shoved Boyce backward onto the old leather couch. "Have a seat," I said. I flopped in my chair.

"What do you want from me?" Boyce asked listlessly. He looked at me with bloodshot, baggy eyes, rubbing his wrist. "I told you, I'm —"

"Yeah, yeah. You're guilty, I know. *Talk* to me, guilty man; tell me how you killed Dr. Eicher Dietrich."

Boyce just sulked and stared at the orange flames in the fireplace.

"Because you know what really gets me about all this, guilty man? You know what I just can't find a nice, warm place in my mind for?" I rose, threw another chunk of wood on the fire, and sat back down. "Boyce, I can believe you killed Dietrich. If he hurt me the way he hurt you, I'd probably have killed him myself. So I'll believe you killed Dietrich, but you know what I can't bring myself to believe? I can't accept that you cut up a helpless animal just to cover the killing. You're a tough mountain redneck. You hunt deer and other game all year long, but you kill clean and quick, and you don't shoot what you don't eat. Real hunters respect animals and despise killing just to spill blood. That's how your daddy raised you." I sat forward. "You'd kill a guilty man in a heartbeat if you believed he needed killing, but you'd *never* kill a nonthreatening, *innocent* creature! Especially not a horse, and especially not to cover up a crime you march in here two hours later and *confess* to! Stop *shittin'* me, Boyce! Right goddamn *now!*"

"I wanted to kill him!" Boyce shouted, sitting up. His voice was raw from hoarseness. "I hated him! I went there to find that blueblood bastard and kill him! And now he's dead! I'm guilty!"

I kicked my chair back and walked around it to stand before Boyce, who looked up at me, his face radiating misery.

"Bullshit! I know you wanted Dietrich dead and I know you were there. But that's when things start falling apart! Where's the weapon? What was Dietrich doing in that stall with Bitter Stone? Why a knife? And why stab him twelve times? A guy like you could kill him easily with one! And why brutally torture a horse to make it look like this fucking freak did it, then pop in here barely two hours later and try so goddamn hard to make me think you're guilty? Hanh? *Answer* me, boy!"

Boyce's jaw tightened, then began to quiver. He lowered his head and began to dry weep. His huge shoulders shook.

"I don't think so, Boyce! I don't think you killed him!"

Boyce lay back on the couch, covering his eyes with an arm, weeping quietly. "Sheriff Cody . . ." Boyce sobbed wretchedly. "I went to Laurel Ridge Farm to commit murder. I'm a cop . . . I *was* a cop . . . and I was prepared to take the law in my own hands and kill a man! And now he's dead. Isn't that guilt?"

"Hell, no! Not for several reasons! So you wanted to kill Dietrich; so you even went there intending to do so. A, you *didn't* kill him, and B, do you think you're the only cop who ever felt enough hate for a perpetrator, felt enough remorse for a victim, to want to kill somebody for it? And C, goddamn it, Boyce, if you didn't kill Dietrich, then I still have to find out who *did!*"

"Oh God!" Boyce cried with the open-mouthed, stricken expression of a man who has just been shot in the back. Through the heart. "Oh God . . . I just want to die, Sheriff Cody. I just want to *die!*" Boyce was wracked with soundless sobs.

I knelt on the worn hook rug before Boyce Calder, seized him by the hair of his head, and yanked his ear near my mouth. "Years ago," I whispered hotly in his ear, "years ago my marriage was coming apart! Rather than make our daughter listen to the two of us tear each other up, I put her on a plane in Washington to spend a couple of weeks with her grandmother until we sorted things out!" I was shouting now. Boyce jerked his head, but I yanked it back. "That night that goddamned airliner hit a fucking mountain and *smashed my little girl into a million wet pieces, goddamn it!*"

Boyce sobbed out of control. I released him and stood. He placed his hands at the sides of his head and shook, now past even crying. "Just last year, I promised a fifteen-year-old child I wouldn't let her black-hearted father hurt her anymore! Ten minutes later, he took her right away from me, and ten minutes after that, he shot her in the head right before my *fucking eyes!* You were there! You are *not* talking to a man who doesn't understand your grief or your guilt, boy! *I know it hurts!*"

Boyce wailed high and long, like a mourning wolf.

I went to my desk, snatched up a copy of the *Roanoke Times,* pulled out the regional news section, and threw the rest in the fireplace. I folded it back to an obituary photograph of a smiling and beautiful young Cathy Calder. I grabbed Boyce by his hair again and forced him to look at the photograph. By now he was wasted, drained.

"Look at her, Boyce! She's dead, son, and so is Steven, and they're not coming back. The same happens to be true about the man who killed them. Now you can waste yourself in suffering and guilt, or you can *pick your ass up and march on!"*

"I can't," Boyce barely rasped. "I can't. I just want to die."

"Listen to me, son. You *look* at this picture and you *ask* yourself what she would have you do!" I drew my pistol, seized Boyce's hand, and slapped the gun into it. "Grief is one thing, Boyce. Self-pity is something else! Men like you and me don't get to whine, Boyce! It's the one emotion we aren't allowed! Now you make a *choice,* and you make it now!"

I stepped back, offering a prayer to any gods that might have been listening that I hadn't misread Boyce Calder's character, because the gun was loaded.

Boyce stared at the gun. He looked up at me, his mouth agape, trying to weep, but drained. He hung his head for what seemed like a very long time. The picture of his Cathy lay on the floor between his feet. When he raised his head again, I was so weak with relief I sat down in my chair.

"You're a hard man . . . Sheriff Cody," Boyce whispered calmly. He sniffed on last time and sighed. "Thank God for that." He stood, handed me my pistol, and looked at me with his head up and with life back in his eyes. "Thank God for that, sir."

Amen.

I took a statement from Boyce about how he went to Laurel Ridge Farm with the vague, agonized intent of killing Eicher Dietrich. He had sat in his car in the rain at some distance, watching the Laurel Ridge complex, as he had no precise knowledge of where Dietrich was or how he would kill him. While he watched, he spotted Dietrich walking from the house to the larger of the two stables and disappearing inside. Seeing Dietrich's arrogant, confident swagger rekindled the rage that drove Boyce, and he bubbled at a slow boil, torn between his rage and the sure knowledge that what he was about to do was wrong, wrong, wrong. As he stewed, he was assaulted by images of the lovely girl with whom he had made love under warm Shenandoah night skies, with whom he had pledged a future and created a son. He saw the plump, smiling baby boy who worshipped him, who never threatened a soul, and who asked only to eat, sleep, and love. Boyce had studied the pistol in his lap and considered killing himself for the millionth time. Occasionally, he had lain his head on the steering wheel and wept. But then came more images: hideous mindflashes of a brutally distorted, toothless, scarlet mess where the love of his life once dwelt. Dead. After a time that Boyce swore was about forty minutes, he kicked open his car door and walked slowly through pouring rain with murder in his heart. To his surprise, he found that the large barn contained several stalled horses, but Dietrich was not present. For a moment, he considered it possible that Dietrich might have gone back to the house during one of the extended periods while he'd had his head down. But then the lights went out in the smaller adjacent barn. He drew his gun, crossed between the two barns, and crept down the aisle to the far end, hoping to find Dietrich alone in the rain, outside, on his way back to the mansion. Boyce had been unable, as I had been, to hear anything for the incessant rain roar on the roof. When he drew even with the last dark stall on the left, he became aware of strange, dank, evil odors that made the skin of his back crawl. He found the light switch on a nearby post and threw it, and then he cried out.

The sudden impact of the scarlet carnage in the stall panicked even Boyce. The butchered horse was completely unexpected, and when Boyce saw the blank-eyed Eicher Dietrich sprawled in the opposite corner, blood oozing from a dozen holes in him, Boyce was suddenly sickened. Dead, Eicher Dietrich looked like so many deer kills had seemed to Boyce Calder. Pitiful. There was no threat, no arrogance in a corpse. You couldn't hate a corpse. The stress and shock of the last few days of Boyce Calder's young life had overcome him. He still ached for Cathy and Stevie, but his hate for Dietrich had become replaced by a revulsion born of beholding still more unnecessary, ghastly death. And something else. Boyce saw what he had become: a murderer. Not a killer, because there is a difference. Boyce Calder knew he had become a murderer in all but deed.

Boyce fled headlong through the rain to his vehicle, and

was seen by Houston Devar and his men as he recklessly careened out the long Laurel Ridge drive toward the highway.

"You're right, Sheriff Cody," Boyce croaked, exhausted but back in command of himself, "I didn't kill Dietrich. But I went there to kill him, and if I had found him alive, I would have. I'm no better than whoever did kill him. ' "Revenge is mine," saith the Lord.' "

I squinted at Boyce for several seconds. " 'Bullshit,' saith Lewis Cody," I said. "Religious bullshit."

Boyce stared back at me.

" 'Revenge is a healthy thing,' saith Lewis Cody. Revenge at the hands of the victimized, or their agent, is part of the price an asshole pays for being an asshole, and that's as it should be. I know you were raised under the standard Christian dogma, Boyce, but all that forgiveness voodoo is part of the reason crime is as rampant in America as it is and is getting worse. We, as civilized citizens who respect the rights of others, are too busy forgiving or wallowing in righteousness, when we should be killing or imprisoning our enemies, as the law allows, because that's what criminals are as long as they choose to remain criminals: enemies. In the meantime, the criminals are murdering us because they aren't hung up on trying to kiss a fictitious deity on the ass so they can get to some heaven place they've been brainwashed since childhood to think really exists. 'Thou shalt not kill,' the anti–capital punishment demonstrators chant while they carry their little candles outside prisons when the lights dim. Oh yes, thou shalt, because if thou don't, then the murderers keep murdering and more innocent die. Sure, in a practical sense, it all has to be consistent and governed by law. But don't lose any more sleep because you felt the need for revenge, Boyce. That 'revenge is mine' crap is the rhetoric of preachers, and it isn't preachers who have to go after the murderers; it's men like you and me."

Boyce stared out my office window at the wet darkness beyond. "Doesn't that make us as bad as the bad guys?" he asked.

I gazed into the fire. "Certainly not," I answered. "That's more religious bullshit. The critical difference is that the criminal murders the innocent for profit or rage or drunken carelessness or sometimes just for fun. We kill criminals, where the law allows, to protect the innocent. It makes for poor sermons, but so do a lot of brutal moral truths."

Boyce continued to stare through the wavy old water-streaked glass. In a minute, he pulled in a long, deep breath, held it, and let it out slowly. "Will it always hurt like this?" he asked, softly.

I thought. "The healing process is slow, and feeling your grief is an integral part of it, but in time it will become manageable. You're two seconds closer to getting there than you were two seconds ago. Some nights, you'll pay the ghost tax, but you'll cope. Look at me, Boyce."

He turned to me with his devastated gaze. "You'll cope, and you'll do it for two reasons. The first is that Cathy loved you, and she would want you to heal and live a good life. And the second is that you don't have any choice, son, because men like your daddy and mine, and you and me, we don't fold and we don't quit. Suicide is not an option for us."

I was immensely relieved that Boyce had, in my judgment, hit bottom emotionally and was now on the long journey back up. I was even more relieved that he had not killed Eicher Dietrich, but now I was stuck with two other sticky problems. The first was that I could not release Boyce based solely on my personal belief in his story. He had confessed, he had made threats on Dietrich before witnesses, he did have a motive, and he had been there. He was still the prime suspect under the law. I sent him back to the holding cell with a cold beer and one of Milly's sleeping pills.

I checked out with the night desk deputy, walked through the cold rain to my cruiser behind the dungeon, and started for Mountain Harbor. On the way, staring through the silent swish of the windshield wipers, I churned with troubling thoughts.

The second sticky problem was, of course, who *did* kill Eicher Dietrich? Julianne and I had reflexively ruled out Caleb Horrow for sexual reasons, but was that valid? How do you attach rationale and logic to a lunatic? Maybe Horrow had killed horses so often that just killing them gave him some sort of sexual gratification, regardless of their sex. Maybe he killed Karin's high-profile Bitter Stone as some perverse move to get even with her for his faceful of hot coffee. Maybe he killed Stone to embarrass me. And maybe while he was busy slicing and dicing Bitter Stone, Dietrich showed up and Horrow gutted him to eliminate the only witness.

Which brought up still another question. What was Dietrich doing at Bitter Stone's stall? It was reasonable to assume he might have gone to the stables to check on Grand Teuton. These expensive, carefully bred high-performance animals were the essential keys to success for competition riders; equine sickness or injury could destroy an Olympic competitor's one window to fame forever. Fanatic fussing over prime horses was legend in world-class riding circles, but Grand Teuton had been in the larger barn, not in the smaller, where Bitter Stone was stalled alone. Did Dietrich just swing by Stone's stall as a courtesy to Karin? It was conceivable, if out of character for him. And did he come upon Caleb Horrow?

Reluctantly, I opened the squeaky door to Pandora's box. Who else might have wanted Dietrich dead? A man like him made battalions of enemies. Who else might have benefited from his death? Karin? Not likely; they weren't married yet, so it was unlikely she would stand to inherit any of his estate. Moreover, in her peculiar way, Karin actually loved Eicher for being one of the few men she had not wholly dominated and for being the one rider that posed a real threat to her at Atlanta in the summer. She would want him alive and in top form at Atlanta so that, when she won, the world would know she was the best. Further, Karin would never destroy Bitter Stone, a horse she had lovingly and painstakingly trained for years, the vital cornerstone of any victory for her at Atlanta. Julianne? Absurd. Why? Meriah Reinholdt? Maybe. Dietrich apparently had left her for Karin; gentle people had murdered for less. Was Klaus still in Roanoke Hospital under guard? That could easily be confirmed, and besides, under law, he had to be released back to me even if he had sufficiently recovered from his injuries. Why would Klaus want to kill Dietrich, anyway? He had tried to kill Julianne and me to protect Dietrich.

Could the killer have been someone not yet introduced? But didn't it have to be someone who knew about the horse killings, presuming it wasn't Horrow? Otherwise, why cut up Bitter Stone to make it look like Horrow had committed both killings?

Dietrich's body was in Roanoke for autopsy. A forensic pathologist would fix the time of Dietrich's death within an hour or so. I would have to reconstruct Mitch Whitley's post-hunt party to pin down the times that Meriah, Karin, Julianne, and others were present and absent during the time Dietrich could have been killed. Meriah Reinholdt would have to be questioned, a task I didn't look forward to, as I admired her very much.

Julianne. Absurd, I had thought. But the first rule of investigation is you never put anything past anybody. Anyone under enough pressure would do anything. What could have driven Julianne to kill Dietrich? To get even with Karin for driving Julianne's husband to suicide? But was it even within the pale of reason that Julianne would butcher Stone to cover—no, of course not—the deed was almost certainly beyond her, even if she were not the one possible suspect other than Horrow who knew the sexual aspects of the horse killings. She would have known Horrow slew only mares. She would have known intimately Horrow's different style of butchery. Julianne would have known the killing of Stone wouldn't steer the blame for the killing of Dietrich to Horrow. It was Julianne herself who had pointed that out.

I knew only one thing for certain. I was crushingly tired. As I pulled off the highway at Mountain Harbor between the gray stone gate pillars and accelerated up the long, winding, rain-shiny drive, I could barely hold my eyes open.

I parked in the garage beneath Polly's apartment, pulled my raincoat about me, and secured the drawstring to my hat. I tilted my head against the blowing rain and crossed the footbridge to the stable over what was now a coursing creek.

I disabled the infrared alarm system with the keypad code and went down the broad, cold aisle under Arthur's quarters. Moose stuck her huge head out and her ears rotated forward when she saw me. Dublin was in her stall, asleep on the straw, her sides slowly rising and sinking with her breathing. I got an apple from the old refrigerator in the barn office, along with a cold bottle of Norwegian. I fed Moose the apple and stroked her snoot while she ate it. Then I re-armed the alarm system and sipped the beer while clumping back across the bridge to the house in the rain. Unavoidably, I scanned the dark woods beyond the yard lights, but I saw nothing but rain-wet pines.

As I topped the long, curved stairway to the second floor, Gruesome in trail and thrilled to see me, I noted a blue glow emitting from Elizabeth's bedroom. Elizabeth lay asleep, huddled in a ball in her pajamas, having kicked her quilt onto the floor again. I covered her and kissed her. Before I staggered out, I turned off her VCR and TV.

While I was soaking in a womblike hot jacuzzi bath, the roiling considerations of who killed Eicher Dietrich gave way to fatigue. I barely heard a clink when Gruesome tipped my beer over and lapped up the spillage from the tiles. I dried and got into the big bed on its elevated platform. I was only dimly aware of Gruesome licking my face as sleep closed me down.

At first, I ignored him. It was not unusual for Gruesome to growl during the night. He had nightmares of his own from time to time, and he was eternally hearing sounds that set him off. But it was unusual for him to bark, and his sharp cries cracked through my deep sleep. I squinted blearily at Gruesome as he jumped up and down in the bay window, barking and looking through the rain-spattered glass. "Gruesome, goddamnit . . ." I mumbled.

Then I heard it, too, though it was muffled by the closed, tight house and the falling rain.

The alarm horn at the stable was shrieking.

36
•••••••••

Suffer the Little Children

The VCR clock read 3:18. I threw back the quilt, raced to the bay window, and peered through the rain at the stable across the creek. The view was partially blocked by tall pines, but I could see nothing out of the ordinary. I grabbed the phone and dialed the intercom line to Arthur's apartment over the stable. I hooked the receiver in the crook of my neck as I struggled into my uniform, which still lay on the floor by the bed. The phone rang and rang and rang.

I tossed the phone down, and pulled on my boots, hat, and leather coat. I grabbed my raincoat, then threw it down, not wanting to risk being encumbered by a voluminous coat in a fight with Caleb Horrow. I gripped my pistol and bolted for the stairs, with Gruesome in hot pursuit. Downstairs, I ran across the den and burst into the rain through the French doors. I studied the stable from behind a tree before exposing myself to the open ground of the bridge and the approach to the stable. Seeing nothing, I raced across the bridge to the edge of the barn doorway, gun in hand, and peered in. The alarm pierced the rain's roar: *Tweeee! Tweeee! Tweeee! Tweeee!*

Only a slight light from the staircase leading up to Arthur's apartment illuminated the otherwise dark barn, but it was enough. I could see Arthur collapsed in his plaid bathrobe on the dusty dirt floor of the barn near the stairway, his old shotgun laying nearby. He moved just slightly.

"Shit!" I hissed. "Arthur!" I shouted over the wailing alarm system. "Where is he?" Arthur did not stir. I jumped quickly to the master light panel, threw up all the switches, and keyed off the alarm horn, which resulted in a deafening sudden silence. I pulled back to the cover of a support post. Even in the brilliant fluorescent lighting, I saw nothing but Arthur's prone body. I cursed myself for rushing out without bringing my portable radio, with which I could have called for help. I crept slowly down the aisle, fighting the urge to rush to Arthur's aid, clearing each stall as I went, nakedly aware that Caleb Horrow could spring out of anywhere at any moment, his gleaming knife in hand, and be on me in an instant. As I neared Arthur, Moose stuck her head out of her stall, to my immense relief, but she was clearly nervous, snorting and stamping. Dublin, who could not possibly be still asleep, I could not see.

The back of Arthur's bathrobe was wet with blood. He lay face down in the dirt, with his mouth open and his eyes half closed, breathing in a bubbly gurgle. I fought off the shock. Arthur had been stabbed in the back near—if indeed not in—his heart. Gruesome whined and sniffed at Arthur. Briefly, I wondered why Gruesome was not on Horrow's scent. Probably the blood in the dust had him boggled. I glanced around for Horrow, then put my hand in Arthur's sparse, brittle silver hair. "Arthur," I said.

"Lewis!" Arthur heaved, blowing the dust near his mouth. "Lewis! I never saw him!" Arthur choked.

"Easy, old man," I said softly. I continued to scan around me.

"Lewis! Dublin!" Arthur wheezed. "Dub—aaaaaah."

"Hang tough, old friend; I'll get you help as soon as I can."

I stood, extended my gun before me with both hands, and slowly approached Dublin's stall, very much dreading what I knew I would find. Gruesome barked maniacally. I leaped to the stall half-door and thrust the weapon over it, only to be astonished at what I saw. Dublin stood perfectly healthy in the rear corner of her stall, swinging her head and stirring nervously about.

Then it hit me and I nearly screamed.

"Elizabeth," I whispered in horror as I spun about. "Oh God, no."

As I sprinted wildly down the barn aisle, Polly appeared near the end, hunched in her robe beneath a large umbrella, carrying a small revolver I had taught her to use. "Lewis!" Polly called. "What is—what's the matter with Arthur?"

"Polly!" I shouted on a dead run, "get up to your place! Lock the door and call my office!" I rushed past Polly into the rain. "Tell them we need Rescue for Arthur, and tell 'em to send the whole damn cavalry! Tell 'em Caleb Horrow's *here!*"

"Well," Polly said, confused and frightened, "what about Arthur, Lewis?"

My boots pounded hollowly over the foot bridge. Gruesome's claws scratched close behind. "Do what I told you, Polly! Now! *Move!*" As I glanced over my shoulder, I could see her hustling for the garage. I rushed into the house, caution thrown to the wind, scrambled up the curved staircase two steps at a time, and charged to Elizabeth's room, my heart thundering. I kicked back the door, flipped on the light, and swept the room with my aim. My worst imagined horrors were now real. On the now-lit carpet, I could see large, wet, muddy footprints that weren't my own.

The quilt was on the floor, but Elizabeth Butler was gone.

Gruesome began barking from somewhere back near the staircase, which his old bones were having difficulty climbing. Then I heard a shrill, terrified child's voice scream, "Uncle *Lew—!*" before being abruptly shut off. It came from downstairs near the main front door.

I was running too fast, and I fell on the carpeted stairs, tumbling down several of them before regaining my feet. The big oaken front door to Mountain Harbor stood open to the blowing rain, and Gruesome was outside still barking.

I ran through the door onto the pillared stone porch in time to see a single automobile taillight fading down the pine-bordered driveway.

You bastard! I screamed at myself as I bolted through the house and out the den doors to the garage. *You* fucking *idiot!* I railed. *You* stupid *fool!* I bailed into the cruiser, fumbled with the key for an eternity and lit the big engine. The tires whirred in the wet gravel as the silver cruiser clawed back from its garage spot, rocked to a halt, and lunged forward.

I almost lost the cruiser into the big trees bordering the drive before I got a grip and convinced myself that I couldn't help Elizabeth by crashing my car. I settled down and drove fast but controlled—almost controlled. At the gate to Mountain Harbor, I slid the car out into the highway to a stop, and was unbelievably grateful to see the single taillight disappear around a bend to my right. I crammed the cruiser in reverse, backed ten feet, slapped it into drive, and stood on it as much as possible without spinning the wheels on the slick road. It accelerated rapidly.

"Sheriff One, emergency!" I said into my radio microphone.

"Sheriff One, County!" the night desk deputy replied, and then he shut up, which was how he was trained.

"Sheriff One, Leonard, I'm in pursuit south on 621 from Mountain Harbor. I don't know what I'm chasing yet but it's got only one taillight on the right side. I think it's going to be the Horrow subject, because he's taken my—he's abducted Elizabeth Butler. Also, he's stabbed Arthur Harmon, my stable hand. Get Rescue out here. I want everybody, and I want 'em fast!"

I remembered to switch on my flashers and siren.

"Sheriff Six, I'm en route!" a voice said over the radio.

"Sheriff Eight, responding!" said another.

"Yes sir, Sheriff One!" Leonard the night desk deputy answered. "Miss Polly called us. I've done called Cap'n Arroe and Sergeant Stanford. They on they way in."

"Sheriff Five, I'm coming from north county!" another deputy called.

"Leonard," I continued, struggling to talk on the radio and negotiate the wet mountain turns. "We're still south on 621. I can still only see one taillight, but it's compatible with the '89 Camaro that Double-Parked got a hit on belonging to Horrow; repeat the description and tag to all units. Call State and tell 'em we need a helicopter. Call Corrections and start us a K-9."

"Ten-four, Sheriff!"

Not again, I whispered to myself, swerving left and right

through the sharp banked turns in the rain. *Not again. No. No. No. Not again. Not again. It can't happen again. If Elizabeth dies, I die.*

I drew closer to the single bouncing, swerving red light in the rainy fog ahead. I didn't want to get too close and cause him to push his limited driving skills and wreck the car, possibly injuring Elizabeth. Yet I could not, would not lose him.

At almost four in the morning, there was no traffic, which was a blessing, but the rain and darkness made an already dangerous chase treacherous. When both cars soared past Abe Slayer's general store, leaving rooster tails of mist, the porch light presented a brief silhouette in the car ahead of a shaggy-headed large man in the driver's seat pushing and striking at whatever was in the passenger seat. Elizabeth. *I'll kill you, Horrow,* I swore. *I'll kill you for touching that child. I swear to God, I'll kill you.*

Horrow's car's single taillight brightened and the rear of the old Camaro rose under hard braking. The car slid, and I prayed he wouldn't wreck it, but he got it under control in time to hook off the road to the left into the woods. I hauled the big Chevy down hard, and dived it into the same hole in the forest.

"Sheriff One," I broadcast, struggling to steer on mud and rock. "We've left 621 to the east, a little south of Abe Slayer's store. I don't know the road; it's some kind of unmarked jeep trail." The car bounced and heaved and debris clattered against the underside. Horrow was barely forty yards ahead, his spinning tires spewing mud. Pine needles peppered my windshield, becoming lodged beneath the wiper blades, causing them to clear the glass poorly, leaving it streaked and hard to see through. I flipped the wipers to the top speed and pressed hard on the washer fluid button, but it only further clouded my view.

"Ten-four, Sheriff One! Attention all units, Sheriff One has turned east off highway 621 south of Slayer's General Store. Sheriff One, be advised Corrections is starting a dog, but State says they helicopter cain't fly fer the weather."

Damn! "All right, Leonard, get everybody down here as soon as possible. Look for an unmarked hole in the woods on the east side of the road. It's muddy and it's barely one lane wide. I don't know how much farther either of us is going to get. Get me some *help* up here!"

"Ten-four, Sheriff!"

"Sheriff Two in service!" Pierce Arroe called over the radio. "Where are they?"

Leonard repeated the vague location information.

"He's got Elizabeth, Pierce!" I said into my microphone.

"We're comin', Lewis!" I could hear Pierce's siren whooping in the background of his transmission.

Horrow's rusty old Camaro topped a ridge and hurtled down the opposite side, slewing, swerving, and bounding. I followed. Pine boughs swept the vehicles like an automated carwash, making wet slapping sounds against my car. The road was viciously rutted, and the cars bounced violently, their headlights sweeping the trees. Suddenly, the trees fell back, but then my entire vision was obliterated by flying water. I yanked the cruiser to the left of the only thing I could still see, the taillight, and then the cruiser hit something, the airbag exploded in my face, and the car smashed to a halt.

The headlights were knocked out. The air inside the car was obscured with white dust from the airbag, and water coated the outside of the windshield. I grabbed my long six-cell police flashlight from between the seats. I released the seatbelt, kicked open my door, and got out, only to be instantly swept from my feet by a two-foot-deep raging current. I was immersed in freezing, fast-moving water. I thrashed for balance, got footing, stood, and wiped water from my eyes. I shined the light through the rain.

The two cars had come to what was normally a shallow creek ford, but the rains had turned it to a car-stopping torrent. Horrow's battered old Camaro lay in the water just upstream of my cruiser, its headlights still on, reflecting off the surging creek through the falling rain drops into the wet pines beyond.

"Uncle *Lewis!*" Elizabeth screamed hysterically from the upstream side of Horrow's car. I could barely hear her for the rain and the roar of the creek. In the dim reflected light from the headlights, I could see Horrow, his eyes wide and his teeth bared, pulling Elizabeth from the passenger door with one arm. In the other hand, he held that horrible knife.

He effortlessly gathered Elizabeth under one arm and clambered from the creek onto the muddy jeep trail ahead. I clawed for my pistol, but then Horrow turned and gripped Elizabeth before him, her terror glowing in the beams of car headlights. I raised the weapon, but there was no safe shot with Elizabeth held up as a shield. Horrow grinned and placed the gleaming knife against Elizabeth's neck beneath her ear. Elizabeth screamed and I died and died and died.

"Nooooooo!" I shouted. "Don't hurt her!" I holstered my gun and held up an empty hand, palm forward. "Don't hurt her!"

Still grinning, eyes bulging, still clutching my little girl, Horrow backed out of the light and disappeared. I could only barely hear still another high, shrill squeal of terror from the darkness.

I fought the powerful, knee-deep current around to the trunk of my cruiser. With my spare key, I opened the trunk and uncased my old M-14 rifle. I crammed a loaded magazine into it, chambered a round, and stuffed two other magazines into my water-logged jacket pockets. Scrambling over the uneven, rocky creek bottom against the relentless tug of the water, I fell to my knees, submerging the rifle and flashlight briefly. I hoped my ammunition was watertight. The flashlight still worked. Thank Christ for good equipment.

The old jeep trail was awash in water and was gooey with mud. My boots were so filled with water I could barely move. Hating the delay, I paused long enough to lift my feet and let the water drain from the boots. I was soaked but so amped I was unaware of the cold. My heart seemed to be tearing out through my chest. My hat was long since downstream and rain trickled into my eyes.

Horrow's tracks were filling with water in my flashlight beam. I staggered up the steep trail, slipping in the mud. I slipped and crashed to my knees again, rose, and struggled on.

About fifty yards higher up the rutted, tree-shrouded trail, I oddly came to give thanks to the world's largest drug cartel, the American tobacco industry. A lifetime of sucking cancerous stinkweeds had taken its toll on Caleb Horrow by robbing him of his wind. He lay in the muddy road thirty feet ahead of me, squinting into my flashlight, heaving, fighting to breathe, exhausted. He wore the same jeans and heavy overshirt he'd had on in Adeline Horrow's little house, except that the left sleeve was dark brown, probably dried blood from the hit he took running from me at Adeline's. He still clamped Elizabeth to him with one long arm and held the knife to her right eye. Her flannel pajamas were soaked and she was crying, clearly terrified. She flinched from the point of the knife, but Horrow only squeezed her more tightly. Horrow glowered at me, his voluminous shaggy hair saturated, laying heavy about his shoulders, strands of it over his face.

"That's far *enough,* motherfucker!" Horrow croaked hoarsely, gasping for air. "You come another step . . . and I'll eat this little bitch's fucking eyeballs . . . right in front of you! I swear to God!"

I stopped. I dropped to my right knee and propped my left elbow on my left knee. Gripping the flashlight together with the forestock of the M-14, I sighted on Caleb Horrow's squinting, narrowed eyes. He heaved Elizabeth up and peered around her head.

"Drop it!" Horrow yelled. "You drop that fucking gun or I'll kill her! I'll cut her fucking throat, man!"

"Uncle Lewis! Uncle Lewis, help meeeeee!"

"Caleb Horroooow!" I shouted over the hissing rain. "Come on dowwwwnn! Let's make a deal!"

"What? I said lose the fucking guns, man! Or I'll—"

"No chance!"

"I'll make you *think* no chance, motherfucker! I'll kill this little cunt right here! *Drop the fuckin' guns!*"

"That little girl alive and healthy is all you got between you and twenty rounds of 190-grain silver-tip slugs, you sick savage."

"Drop the fucking guns or I swear to God I'll kill her!" Horrow squawled, now holding the knife to Elizabeth's neck and shaking her.

"You watched too many cop shows on prison TV, Horrow!" I replied. "This is reality! If I drop my weapons, you'll kill me and then you'll kill her anyway. I'm not dropping shit. You turn her loose unharmed and you escape! That's the deal. Do it!"

"*Fuck* you, man! How do I know you'll let me go?"

"We're alone up here right now, Horrow, and she's freezing to death. I won't leave her in the rain and the dark to chase you! You know that! It's your only prayer, asshole, and you better do it fast, because my people are on the way in force and they want your head!"

What I saw next was not a good sign. Horrow sneered and grinned again. He was getting his wind and his confidence back.

"*Fuck* you Cody! I'm taking your little girl with me for insurance, man! Fuck you *and* your people!" Horrow lifted himself to one knee, holding Elizabeth in front of him.

"Uncle Lewisssss!" Elizabeth wailed. My heart cried.

I sighted down the rifle and through the flashlight beam. "You're too big to cover all of you with that child, Horrow," I said. "You make another move without releasing her and I'll blow a leg right out from under you. Turn her loose!"

Horrow wrenched Elizabeth higher before him and repositioned the knife to her throat. Her bare, wet feet shone in the flashlight. "All right, tough guy, kiss this little bitch good-bye! I ain't going back to prison!"

"You move and you're a wounded man."

"And your little bitch is *dead,* motherfucker!"

"Sawmill," I said.

Horrow paused on that one. "What?"

"Sawmill," I repeated. "I just figured out where we are, Horrow. Do you know?"

"I know you put that fucking rifle down or there's gonna be one dead little girl in the mud, *that's* what I know!"

"We're about a quarter-mile from Abner Tull's old sawmill."

"*Fuck* sawmills, you crazy son of a bitch! I'm outta here! And when I'm gone, I'll have your kid for fucking breakfast and I'll leave her greasy bones on your doorstep, motherfucker!"

"You know what's in every sawmill in the world, Horrow?" I asked, still sighting down the rifle at Caleb Horrow's exposed thigh.

Horrow wasn't communicating with me and it frustrated him.

"What the *fuck* are—"

"Acetylene torches," I said.

"What—?" Horrow rasped, but he was beginning to receive a signal.

"Every sawmill has tons of steel machinery and racks and conveyor frames, and they keep acetylene cutting torches around to work on it." Horrow whipped his head from side to side, as though he could see the sawmill that lay a few hundred yards up the mountain.

"So what! That ain't gonna save this—"

"I know you aren't afraid of dying, Horrow. I know you'll die before you'll go back inside, where you can't practice your twisted little thrills."

"What the fuck do you know about my 'thrills,' Sheriff? All you fuckin' doctors and laws and your bullshit! What do you know about what my old man done to me? What about them homo guards in the juvie centers?" Horrow snorted in amusement. "Shit. What about my crazy fuckin' *momma?* Huh? What about—"

"Save it, Horrow! What do I look like, some cloistered sociology professor? Sexual abuse and flawed parents and poverty and all the other excuses are tough shit, but they *cannot* be tolerated as a rationale for crime. Either the law is the law and we have civilization, or everybody has a private excuse to break the law and we have *no* civilization. Turn that child *loose!*"

"You don't understand, man! You—"

"I understand you got a knife to my girl's throat! I also know that *you* understand what pain is, Horrow. You know pain real well, because it turns you on, doesn't it? As long as it's some other creature's misery! Writhing, screaming agony really cheers you right up, doesn't it, you freak? Well, try this idea on, big boy. You harm that child or you try to run with her, and I'll put a bullet through your leg. You won't die, but you won't run either."

"I'll kill her, man!"

"And then I'll drag your crippled ass to that sawmill and I'll handcuff you to something that won't move."

"*Fuck* you, you crazy son of a bitch!"

"And then I'll light that torch and, Caleb Horrow, I swear to you on my love for this child that I will cut pieces off of you, beginning with your toes. You'll smell your own flesh burning and you will know pain you haven't seen in your juiciest wet dreams."

"You are fucking *nuts,* man!"

"The sawmill is closed for the season, Horrow. Nobody will know where we are. Nobody will hear your screams. The torch will cauterize the amputated veins, Horrow. You'll beg for death for at least three days."

"You're fucking *crazy!* You can't do that! I got *rights,* man!"

"You left every civil right you ever hoped to have at the gate to Mountain Harbor, Horrow; you're fresh out of rights."

Horrow tossed his head to fling wet strands of hair from his face. "You're bluffing, man! They'd put *you* in the fucking psycho ward for that!"

"No, they won't!" I spat, angrily. "Because, Horrow, if you kill that little girl, as soon as your limbless, faceless, barbecued torso finally caves in from the shock, I'll be following you to hell. You kill that child, and the only thing that'll matter to me is how long I can make you scream."

"Jesus fucking *Christ,* man!" Horrow whispered, shading his eyes from the light with his knife hand, removing it briefly from Elizabeth. My finger twitched to shoot him, but I wasn't confident I could kill him fast enough to keep him from cutting Elizabeth's pale throat. "You're as fucked up as I am!" Horrow said in shock. "Shit, you are . . . *sick,* man! You're sicker than *me!"*

"Truer words were never spoken, Horrow," I said, looking him in the eye over a gunsight. "I'm worse than you know. Turn her loose and run. It's your only prayer."

The message had reached Horrow. For possibly the first time in his adult life, he was afraid. The malevolence in his face had disappeared, replaced with fear. Not fear of me, but with genuine fear of something he knew only too well. Pain. He wiped his eyes with the back of the wrist that held the knife.

Horrow's evil returned to his face. He scowled, squinting against the light. His lip curled up from his teeth. "I'll be back, Cody," he snarled hoarsely, spitting glistening spray in the flashlight beam. "You'll be hearing from me! One day, this little bitch will just disappear! You won't know what happened to her 'til I leave her panties and her heart in your *fucking mailbox!* I'll be *back!"*

Horrow suddenly propelled Elizabeth violently at me. She sprawled to her face and slid down the steep trail in the mud. When I could pull my eyes from her, all I could see was rebounding pine boughs. As poor Elizabeth screamed and covered her ears, I unloaded the entire twenty-round magazine into the quivering branches.

I lay in the cold rain, covered in mud, holding Elizabeth as she clung to my neck, sobbing. I could not cover enough of her with my arms, as I slipped and slid, carrying her down the trail toward the creek, the rifle slung over my shoulder. Pierce met us near the creek. He whipped his raincoat from his massive shoulders and I wrapped Elizabeth in it. We waded the now even deeper creek to a host of cruisers flashing in the rain. I handed Elizabeth over to the warm bosom of Sergeant Milly Stanford, who took her to a car.

Pierce threw a blanket over me as I sat in his cruiser, the heater running full blast. He slid in behind the wheel and looked at me dolefully. "Arthur's dead, Lewis," was all he said.

We found no body in the pines at dawn. And we found no blood.

Arthur's body had been prepared during the night and lay in his casket beneath the big glass chandelier in the foyer at Mountain Harbor amid flowers arriving by the minute. Elizabeth rested under sedation in her room, and shotgun-armed deputies walked in the fog outside. The rain had finally ceased.

As I collapsed into my wondrously warm, dry bed, distressing visions haunted me. I saw the hate in the hideous face of Caleb Horrow, but more troubling were his last statements. No, not his vow to "be back," frightening though it was; what kept burning into the center of my weary mind were his words: ". . . *sick,* man . . . sicker than *me!"*

I knew who killed Eicher Dietrich. And Bitter Stone.

37

· · · · · · · ·

Sick

I woke up a little after noon. I hadn't slept very long, but it had been deep, because I woke up with both Gruesome and Elizabeth snuggled tightly against me, both asleep. Gruesome was snoring louder than a B-29.

Elizabeth's face was puffy and red, with a few minor bruises and scratches on it. I hoped the emotional damage was no worse.

I eased out from between them, wearing the sweatsuit pants I slept in, and went to the window in the guest room across the hall, which looked out onto the front drive. Fog had moved in to enshroud Mountain Harbor; nature in her mourning veil. I was not surprised to see several cars belonging to citizens of Hunter County who had known Arthur, come to pay their respects. One elderly woman held a casserole dish of some no-doubt delicious food. It was like the mountain women, to bring food to a home in its time of grief.

I looked until I saw what I knew would be there; one of my deputies stood unobtrusively in the trees nearby, sipping coffee, his shotgun cradled in his arm. Through the steam rising from his coffee, Billy stared into the fog for Caleb Horrow.

I felt a cold, wet nose on my ankle. I bent and picked

Gruesome up and stroked his wrinkled head. He lapped at my cheek.

"Uncle *Lewis?*" I heard Elizabeth call from the master bedroom, just a trace of panic at the edge of her voice.

"Right here, sweetheart," I answered, trotting quickly back to the room, carrying Gruesome. I dropped him on the bed and he hopped into Elizabeth's embrace. I sat down, put my arm on her shoulder and hugged her. "How're you doing, darlin'?"

Elizabeth hung her head and nuzzled Gruesome. "Sergeant Milly says Arthur is dead."

I sighed. "Yes." A silent pause passed.

"Will he come back?" she asked.

"No. Arthur . . . has died, love. He won't—"

Elizabeth looked up at me with frightened eyes. "No! I mean that . . . that *guy!* Will he come *back?*"

"We haven't caught him yet, sweetheart. But we will. In the meantime, I will have deputies watching this house and with you everywhere you go, if I am not with you myself. I know last night was a terrible time for you, but I want you to try not to worry about that man. He won't get near you again."

Elizabeth released Gruesome, and squeezed my waist. "I tried to bite him, Uncle Lewis."

"What? Last night, you mean?"

"Yes. When he woke me up, I didn't know who he was or why he was carrying me. But when he was driving near Mr. Slayer's store I knew he was the bad guy who hurt . . . Tara Hodges's little pony. I told him to stop the car and let me go, but he just said a nasty to me and pushed me against the door. So I tried to bite him, but he hit me."

"Jesus. Baddest dude in Hunter County and my little woman tries to bite him. You're a tough little brat, aren't you?" That got just a twitch of a smile from her.

"Uncle Lewis, you remember how you said you'd teach me to shoot if I ever wanted, like you taught Polly? Well, I want to learn."

I hugged her. "I'll teach you soon, sweetheart, but for now, try not to worry. You'll be guarded securely until we get him, I promise." God, how I hated to promise.

After sending Elizabeth to her room to dress, I showered

and put on a clean uniform. When we descended the steps to the foyer, I smelled death's perfume, the fragrance from dozens of floral tributes propped on wire stands about the foyer and living room. I saw several of Arthur's elderly fishing buddies and a few women sitting or standing near the casket and in the living room. Polly was wearing her church dress and was carrying a tray of coffee to the mourners. Arthur's death showed in Polly's face when she glanced at us, but I knew the kindest thing to do for her was to allow her to busy herself with serving the guests.

Elizabeth and I stood silently by the casket in the marble-floored foyer beneath the huge crystal chandelier. People watched but seemed to know to leave us undisturbed. Lawrence the undertaker had done Arthur proud. He was attired in his favorite fishing duds, instead of a suit, which Arthur truly would not have been caught dead in. His old fedora with the fly-fishing lures hooked to it rested over his hands, which were crossed at his chest. I watched Elizabeth, but though obviously sad, she seemed to take what she saw in stride. She didn't cry. Elizabeth would either grow up to be a tough, adaptable woman or she'd become a worm can of neuroses. I squeezed her and kissed the top of her head.

Polly handed the empty tray to another woman and hurried to us. "Lord, child, look at your face! Now, you ain't buttoned that dress straight! Ain't I taught you to turn you collar down all around? My sakes!" She led Elizabeth away to the kitchen, where I knew she would try like hell to pack her full of good food.

Pierce loomed up at my side. "Ole Lawrence knows how to send a man out, don't he?"

"Yeah," I agreed. "The clothes are perfect."

We walked into the unoccupied sunken den. Polly brought me a steaming mug of hot chocolate. When she left, Pierce spoke. "Lewis, we got Stout's Texaco to hook the cars outta the creek. We impounded Horrow's junk heap, of course. Hauled your cruiser to the Chevy place. Hallman Vaughn says it ain't hurt that bad; they'll have it road ready in a couple of days. He's bumped it ahead of the other jobs in his body shop. I know you're gonna ask me; ain't nobody seen hide nor hair of Horrow, but we're looking everywhere. You saw last night the dog couldn't track a bitch in heat in that rain. Colonel Clair sent us four troopers to help with manpower. Said he'd send a helicopter if this damn fog ever lifts. Speakin' of troopers, what do you want to do with Boyce? Understand he retracted his confession?"

"Yeah, Pierce; Boyce didn't kill Dietrich. We'll get him released on bond, and when I've had time to discuss the case with the county attorney, she'll agree not to charge him."

"If Boyce is innocent, Lewis, what do we do about the Dietrich killing?"

I sighed and stared at the rug. "I'll handle it," I told Pierce.

"You know something we don't, Lewis?"

"Horrow said something to me last night that opened up a line of thought we haven't considered. Let me run it down some more. If there's anything to it, I'll let you know."

"Lewis?" a sweet voice called from the hall. We turned to see Julianne Chu in a shapely, dark gray dress with a covered dish in her hands. Her eyes were beautiful, but they looked as tired as mine. Behind her, I could see Hap and Bev Morgan handing their coats to one of the women. Polly hurried from the kitchen to take the dish.

Pierce excused himself and strode out, leaving Julianne and me alone, looking into each other's eyes.

"Dr. Chu," I said. "I have to ask you some questions."

Julianne looked calmly down at the rug for a moment, then she looked back up at me. She nodded.

Two hours later, I drove the big Ford dually into the drive to Laurel Ridge Farm, towing the long gooseneck with Moose in it. Rain was oozing out of the fog again, though not as heavily as the previous night, and the sky pressed cold and gray against the hills. Houston Devar and his sidekicks met me at the stables; they offloaded Moose and tacked her up. They asked about "the som-bitch that killed Arthur." I said we were still looking for him. That sounded pretty lame even to me.

"Like I tole you on the phone, Sheriff," Houston said, blowing rain from his mouth, "the perfesser and the ladies is out ridin' Miss Meriah's new property."

Richard sniffed and squinted at the rain. "Goddamn if I know why anybody would want to ride in this shit."

I heard horses' slow hoofbeats and turned to see Mitch Whitley and Meriah Reinholdt ride out of the mist, the horses blowing vapor in the cold November air. The riders wore long, expensive riding raincoats of green and brown, and rubber boots to their knees. They rode in under the barn and dismounted. Houston and his men took the horses.

Meriah studied me with a drawn face. Professor Whitley had water droplets finely coating his beard. He offered his hand. "Lewis! Good to see you looking well! I heard you had an atrocious night. How is Elizabeth?"

"She's as good as can be expected, Mitch; thanks."

Meriah looked very weary. "Lewis," she said, "we've just ridden up to the property one last time before I go back to Washington. I need to coordinate with Eicher's family, of course, to arrange for . . ."—she sighed and smiled very tightly—". . . for Eicher's body to be moved to New York when . . . whenever you're . . . done with it."

"The boy who killed Dr. Dietrich, Lewis," Mitch said, "the young trooper; I understand he gave himself up?"

"He turned himself in, Mitch, but . . . I don't think he killed Dr. Dietrich."

"You're kidding! I'm told the boy made several threats to kill Dr. Dietrich, and Houston and the men saw—"

"There's more to this than you know, Mitch. When I sort it all out, I'll fill you in. Right now, I need to talk to Meriah alone."

Meriah looked up at me suddenly, even as Mitch looked at her with surprise. "Ah . . . of course, Sheriff. I . . . I'll be at the house if you need me, Meriah." She nodded.

Meriah Reinholdt and I walked slowly along the aisle as the rain roar on the roof picked up.

Rain ran in rivulets off my Stetson and pattered against the long, yellow police rubber-ducky I wore. Moose walked along briskly, the parts of her hide that were not covered by my raincoat gleaming wet. She snorted and sighed as though resigned to the incredible stupidity of humans who made them ride in winter rain. We rode along the path of the fox hunt, but in the reverse direction.

Clawmark Gorge was about twelve feet wide. The chasm descended twenty feet to where the rain-gorged Buffalo Run roared between rock walls. The water frothed from where it cascaded over Clawmark Fall to the pit below, and it gushed through the narrow gorge to the flatter, broader rocky river downstream. The water blasted through the gorge with the speed and force of the sea exploding through a torpedo gash in a ship, roaring furiously as it sped.

I rode Moose on the flat west precipice near the edge, along but opposite the path on which the wily old fox had led the hunters a day before. The east precipice was bare or mossy rock that rose from the wall of the gorge, angling steeply upward to the woodline some fifty feet upslope. As we neared the deeper thrum of Clawmark Fall, I heard a sound that penetrated the roar of falling and rushing torrents. I halted Moose and cocked my head to hear, then I was sure: the distinct clack of iron horseshoes on rock.

I reined Moose to my left, and walked her thirty yards away from the howling gorge, through the few tall pines that could grow on the rocky ground. I turned the big horse and waited.

Karin Steiger was probably the only woman in the world who could look sensual even in a caped raincoat with the collar turned up beneath her rider's helmet. The coat flowed over the golden sides of a prancing Grand Teuton to cover the tops of Karin's boots.

Grand Teuton must've scented Moose, because he started suddenly and cocked his ears toward Moose and me. Expert at reading her mount, Karin followed the horse's gaze to us.

"Lewis!" Karin called faintly over the water noise. Her smile was incredible even from twenty yards away in the rain. She trotted Grand Teuton quickly to join us. She gave me that sly, I-know-what-you're-thinking look. "What a pleasant surprise! How did you know where to find me?"

"Meriah said you had gone to ride Dietrich's horse along the track of yesterday's hunt."

Karin assumed a sober expression suddenly. "Yes. I didn't care to ride with Mitch and Meriah up to the new property again. I wanted to be alone. And Eicher would have wanted his favorite horse ridden." She leaned forward and patted Grand Teuton on his neck with wet slaps of her gloved hand. She gazed toward the yawning trough of Clawmark Gorge thirty yards away. "Professor Whitley said at lunch that . . . policeman . . . who stabbed Eicher . . . surrendered himself?"

Karin had tied her hair back in a short pony tail beneath her helmet. Grand Teuton steamed and shifted nervously; he had been ridden with vigor, and he was unprepared for the sudden stop. Karin controlled him effortlessly without even appearing to be aware of the fine, hot-blooded horse.

"I have Trooper Calder in custody, Karin." I took a deep breath and let it ease out slowly. "But we both know he didn't kill Eicher, don't we?"

Karin turned her head slowly, her eyes down. Then she looked up at me and smiled with those pretty white teeth and saucy lips, wholly unconcerned. Karin laughed easily. "Mitch said the young man confessed."

"You killed Eicher, Karin. You stabbed him with Klaus's bayonet."

Karin looked at me as though I were an amusing child. "Lewis, I realize I am a bit . . . different, shall we say . . . from the Julianne Chus and the other . . . country women in your experience. Certainly, I fit no molds and make my own rules, but that doesn't make me a murderess. It is true that I hated Eicher in ways, and it's true that I would have castrated him at Atlanta. But Eicher is . . . was . . . one of only two men I've ever known, other than my father, who had any spine. I admired him, Lewis. I hated him, but I loved him also. Why would I have killed him so crassly when I could have killed him so exquisitely at the games next summer?"

Moose shifted her massive weight and settled down. "Ho," I said to the horse. I looked at Karin. "You would have lost in Atlanta."

Karin laughed again. "Lewis, if you understood international three-day eventing, you would know what the whole equestrian world knows, that Eicher's star was setting, and there is no one else even close to me."

"I do know that, Karin. But I know something more that no one else except you knows. You're sick."

Karin's smile dissolved instantly.

"I don't know what it is," I went on, "but you're bad sick with something. It's interfering with the motor control in your hands, it's making you dizzy, it's affecting your vision, and it's affecting your bladder control. That's why you jumped too soon yesterday and made Bitter Stone fall. It's why you fell in my bedroom and in the barn. It's why you couldn't pick up your helmet with your left hand. It's why you urinated on yourself in the barn."

Karin's eyes watered. "Nonsense!" she snapped angrily. Grand Teuton stirred. "You are grasping, rather pathetically!"

"I wish. I talked to Meriah. Your mother. You've always been a driven woman, but even you didn't try to fanatically squeeze so much out of life until the last few months. She noticed the change in you and so did Julianne. They wrote it off to competitive jitters about the coming Olympic games, but, looking back, it fits a pattern. It's why you're so recklessly sexual; it's why you're so bitter. And now I know it's why you are so obsessed with gouging as much out of your life as you can. Sometime in the last year, Karin, you learned you're sick. You knew that by next summer your muscle control and your vision, even your equilibrium, would degrade to where you wouldn't even place, let alone defeat the master. What is it, Karin? Cancer?"

Karin gave me her patented look of amused contempt, that crazy, entrancing smile a little higher at one corner than the other. "Really, Lewis. I never made you for a frustrated Hercule Poirot. You're hallucinating. Even if I had killed Eicher, do you think I could have . . ."—Karin's face distorted with pain—"could have . . . tortured—butchered!—so noble an animal as Bitter Stone? I was present when that stallion was born! I *raised* that horse, and trained him by hand for *seven years!* He was absolutely essential to my success at Atlanta! I loved Bitter Stone like no mere *man* ever deserved! Can you possibly be so stupid as to think I would have harmed that horse for *any* reason? That I would do so just to divert suspicion when this entire community knew about the policeman who so publicly threatened Eicher with death? You disappoint me, Lewis!"

Both horses sensed the tension between Karin and me, and they grew restless.

"No," I answered, reining Moose and watching Karin carefully. "You certainly would never have cut up Bitter Stone—"

"At last! A trace of intelligence!"

"—but Eicher Dietrich would have, Karin! And you would have killed him for that in a heartbeat!"

"You're insane!"

"Eicher didn't know you were sick! Nobody did but you and whatever doctors are involved. He was terrified that you would decimate him in Atlanta, that you would rob him of the most important thing in his life, his eminence, his title! When I arrested him for killing the Calders, he knew the chances were strong that when the games in Atlanta opened, he'd be in a prison cell, where he'd certainly have no chance to win, and Eicher was one of those guys who doesn't lose, no matter what. Most especially, Eicher Dietrich could not lose to you, because he hated and loved you! He knew when I nailed him for drunk-murder that he'd lost the games, and he couldn't live with that. With this lunatic Caleb Horrow killing horses in Hunter County, Eicher saw a perfect chance to cover killing Bitter Stone, and thus ensure *you* wouldn't win in Atlanta, either! Dietrich himself sliced up Bitter Stone, didn't he? Somehow you caught him, and in a rage, you stabbed him to death. Where's the bayonet, Karin?"

Karin backed Grand Teuton a step and halted him. The beautiful smile was gone now, probably forever. Karin's lower lip trembled and I saw something in her face that had probably never dwelt there before. Fear.

"Lewis . . ." Karin whispered.

"What is it, Karin? Tell me. What has moved in on that amazingly passionate, beautiful body and begun to destroy it?"

Karin began to cry, though she held her head high. "It's multiple sclerosis . . . if you must know . . . Lewis. MS, you Americans call it." Karin lowered her head. "I've known since January. It's . . . it's incurable."

"Karin, I am so very sorry."

"It is so *unfair!*" Karin suddenly shouted, startling both horses and me. "It's taking me apart in the cruelest ways! It's diabolically cutting away at the one thing I love to do! The one thing I'm good at! You were *right,* damn you! I couldn't win at Atlanta if the games were tomorrow instead of six months away! I might not even qualify! I can't *see,* Lewis! I can't grip the reins!" Karin began to weep. "I can't even . . . control my . . . body functions, for God's sake."

"Karin—"

"Bitter Stone has . . . had . . . a respiratory condition. It wasn't enough to affect his performance if he was watched carefully and he got the right drugs on time. I put him in the small barn after the hunt, because that's where Helen Whitley's foaling monitor was installed. There was a monitor screen in Professor Whitley's library. I could keep an eye on Stone while I was at the party without having to go to the barn in the rain."

"You saw Dietrich go to Bitter Stone's stall."

"After . . . after you left me in the barn by Bitter Stone, I went to my room at the house to bathe and dress. When I passed through the library, I switched on the foaling monitor at Professor Whitley's desk, and I couldn't believe what I saw! Eicher was tying my beautiful stallion up like some rodeo stock horse! Suddenly it struck me what Eicher intended to do! I ran to my room, took Klaus's bayonet, and ran through the rain to the barn, but I was too *late,* Lewis! That heartless bastard was . . . cutting Bitter Stone! *Butchering* him with a *scalpel!* There was blood everywhere!"

"So you—"

"I stabbed him! I stabbed him and stabbed him and stabbed him! 'You *bastard!*' I screamed in German. 'You could never defeat me at the games, so you *killed my horse!* You bastard!'"

Karin was breathing hard now. Grand Teuton whipped his head up and down, as though anxious to leave this terrible scene and run.

"Karin, listen to me. You—" I halted, so immensely saddened at the resignation, the defeat, in Karin's tear-filled eyes.

"I suppose you . . . you must arrest me," she said.

"I can't arrest you, Karin. You have diplomatic immunity; you know that. I can and I must detain you until you can be turned over to the embassy, but then you can go home to Germany."

"Go home to *what,* Lewis?" Karin cried, misery in her eyes. "To never ride, never compete again? To an obscure, painful, debilitating, slow death from the disease?"

"You have to come with me, Karin."

The lovely, proud woman gigged Dietrich's horse gently and walked him alongside Moose and me. Tears ran down her cheeks, but she held her head up, and bore herself with grace. "Kiss me, Lewis," Karin whispered to me, "then I will go." She sidestepped Grand Teuton expertly until our stirrups touched, then she leaned toward me and raised her face, that beautiful, beautiful face. I bent and covered her lips with mine. She placed her hand at the base of my neck and we kissed slowly, gently. With love.

We kissed for nearly a minute, and when we parted, she smiled once again, though tears trickled into the corners of her lips. I can taste her and feel her womanly heat even now. Her eyes looked inside mine. She frowned, as though very, very sad. "Good-bye, Lewis," she whispered. I knew instantly, but even then it was too late.

"Nooooo! *Karin!*" I shouted. I grabbed at her arm, but Karin had already reined Grand Teuton about. She dug with her short, chromed spurs and lashed the sleek, wet animal across its withers with the reins. The horse squatted and churned mossy sod in big arcing clumps as he scrambled to accelerate.

Straight for the torrential gorge.

Moose gathered herself and launched in pursuit, uncommanded, as one horse is prone to do when another bolts.

Karin had leaned forward and raised on her stirrups, still whipping Grand Teuton. As the horse closed on the gorge, Karin made no effort to steer him to parallel it until she and he went way beyond the point of no return, beyond a range and a headlong speed to stop or turn. Even as I galloped after her, I knew what she intended and I knew she would never make it. I believe she knew it too.

"Karin!" I yelled again. If she heard me over the roaring water, she gave no sign.

Grand Teuton was an experienced, highly trained, cross-country jumper; he was quite used to being ridden up to precarious obstacles and being jumped over them, often unable to see the other side. He'd been charged into many a water hazard and jumped over many a ditch onto upward and downward grades; he was a world-class eventing horse schooled from birth to trust and obey his rider. He would not falter. He did not.

Karin timed her last jump perfectly and Grand Teuton launched from the last foot of the edge of the gorge. I hauled down hard on the excited Moose, who dropped her haunches and skidded on the slick, smooth rocks welling through the mossy earth.

Karin and Grand Teuton hit above the east precipice and the horse dug frantically for footing on the steep mossy slope. For a brief moment, it appeared he would gain purchase as desperately he lunged upward several feet. Karin threw her weight forward and shouted to him, though I could not hear her for the roar of the water coursing the gorge below.

The noble creature gave all he had, but it wasn't enough. The embankment was a smooth, rocky surface carpeted by deep, rich moss and wet brown leaves. The emerald carpet tore loose from the wet rock beneath the sharp, clawing hooves of the horse. It gave, and Grand Teuton's flailing shod hooves sparked on the exposed stone.

The high nasal scream of the struggling horse penetrated the crescendo of water as it came to know what Karin must already have known.

Grand Teuton pitched and thrashed to get his balance as

he slid rearward over the edge. Karin fought to the last second to drive the horse against the impossible, then she seemed to lie over his neck and cradle him in her arms. As Grand Teuton tumbled backward into the raging gorge, Karin still astride him, I caught one last view of that achingly beautiful face. It was calm. Her eyes were closed.

Grand Teuton impacted the surging water on his back, his eyes bulging, his hooves flailing, Karin beneath him. Both disappeared in the frothing white torrent gushing through the gorge.

I heeled Moose and rode her as fast as I dared downstream, close along the gorge. In the few places where the terrain permitted a view, I saw nothing but spewing, bounding water.

The trail along the gorge came to a steep descent that demanded slow negotiation by switchback. I forced myself to calm and I pulled Moose down to a careful step over the descending rock.

Ten minutes later, I cantered Moose through the towering pines along a flat, broad rapid of the Buffalo Run, possibly a third of a mile downstream of Clawmark Gorge. Ahead, I saw him, belly deep in the fast flowing brown water, trembling, struggling weakly to free himself from the rocks among which he was wedged. He was bloody and exhausted. I could not see Karin.

Here the water still moved swiftly among the rocks, but it was at the most four feet deep, and was nowhere near as consumptively fierce as when traversing the gorge. I gigged Moose into the racing water up to her belly and she lunged to keep her footing on the rocky river bottom.

We got close enough for me to be able to reach Grand Teuton's reins, which trailed downstream on the current. I backed Moose and called to the fading gelding. Bravely, he staggered clumsily over and around the slippery rocks, but when we made the shallows, what I saw overcame me.

Grand Teuton's right rear leg was broken above the hoof, which was hideously cocked ninety degrees to the trembling leg. Just as tragic, bound by the left stirrup to the horse was the battered, pale body of Karin Steiger. The helmet remained on her head, but given the angle of her neck to her torso, there was no question of her death.

It tore my heart out, but I forced Grand Teuton to stagger onto the mossy river bank among the trees, dragging Karin's corpse behind him. I dismounted Moose and let her back away in horror from the dead human and the wretched, heaving gelding.

With my knife, I cut the strap of the stirrup that encircled Karin's clearly broken left leg. Her body slumped into a heap. Grand Teuton was spent and he swayed on wobbly, destroyed legs, wheezing with agony at each breath.

"Christ," I said.

Grand Teuton's head hung low and he looked up at me, shivering, struggling to breathe.

"Ah . . . shit," I whispered, rubbing my face.

I grasped the collar of Karin's raincoat and dragged her body away from the suffering horse.

I stood by Grand Teuton, stroking the side of his muzzle and whispering sounds of approval in his ear. "Good boy," I said. "You've done good, old boy." Then I stepped before him, sighted my pistol just above the eyeline, and I shot him.

I turned away even as the animal crashed to the earth and the crack of the shot echoed down the river. Moose jumped rearward a few steps, then stopped.

I holstered the weapon and sat on a boulder near Karin's lifeless, pitiful remains. For a time, I wept, looking at the wet moss between my feet. Then I raised my head and my cries also echoed among the mist-shrouded hills.

"Aaaaaaaaaahh!" I screamed. *"Aaaaaaaaaaaaaaaaaaaaa aahh!"*

38

•••••••

Hemlock

It was dark when I rode out of the fog at Laurel Ridge Farm, with Karin's body draped over the saddle before me. Houston Devar hurried to hold Moose. "Gimme a hand here, Lonny!" Houston called to his men, running through the rain. "Richard, go git the perfesser!"

Meriah Reinholdt ran out of the barn, stopped suddenly, put her hand to her mouth, and began to weep. She stumbled forward, one hand extended before her. "Oh no," she whispered, "oh no."

By the time we completed the formalities on the Buffalo Run and I put Moose away in her stall at Mountain Harbor, I felt like the walking dead. I just left the truck and trailer hitched and parked in the stableyard. I stumbled over the footbridge, unsure if I was asleep or just having a bad dream, but I had enough energy remaining to jump at a movement I sighted near the garage. Otis Clark walked out of the shadows, the house corner lights glinting on his badge, his shotgun laid back over his shoulder. "Evenin' Loo," Otis said.

"Hi, Otis," I replied. "You guys okay out here? Need some coffee?"

"Naw, thanks, Loo. Haskel's watchin' the front. Miss

Polly brung us some food and coffee 'bout a hour ago. We all right." Otis squinted at me. "Don't mind me sayin' so, Sheriff, you look like shit."

I breathed deeply. "Otis . . . does it *all* turn to shit . . . in the end?"

Otis shifted the shotgun to his other shoulder and looked into the darkness across the creek, beyond the stable. He sighed. "You tired, Loo. Carry you ass on upstairs and git some sleep. Me an' Haskel will keep watch 'til mornin'."

"I *need* to know, Otis," I persisted, staring at the swollen creek. *"Does* it all turn to shit in the end?"

Otis squinted at me with concern. "Ain't much on philosophy, Sheriff. Closest to a philosopher I ever knowed was ole Grandma Hattie. Ole Hattie lost two soldier sons she loved and a navy husband she worshipped in one year of World War II, and her country still called her a nigger. But I never knowed her to complain about nothin'. She used to tell me, 'just live and laugh and love much as you can, boy. Don't look for life to make no sense. Doin' that just make a body weary.' I reckon that's all the philosophy I know, Loo."

I patted Otis on the shoulder and headed for the door. "It'll do, Otis," I said, "it'll do."

"Git some sleep, Sheriff."

Upstairs, I groaned as I bent to pick up Elizabeth's quilt from the floor and spread it over her. I lifted Gruesome back onto her bed. He lay his ugly wrinkled muzzle on Elizabeth's waist and sighed.

I don't even remember showering or hitting the mattress.

I slept solid for about two hours, then fitfully for another two or so. This night had become a ghost reunion, as had so many before it and as would so many after.

The blue VCR numbers said 4:18 when I heard Gruesome growl low in his throat and bound off Elizabeth's bed. While I stuck my feet into moccasins and seized my gun, I could hear him making his clumsy way down the staircase. By the time I got to the foot of the stairs, carefully without turning on any lights, Gruesome was near the French doors that opened from the sunken den onto the brick veranda.

366

Oddly, I thought, he wasn't barking, but he was whining like he did when he wanted to go out.

When I opened the doors and peered around the edge, Gruesome ran out onto the brick and looked about, still whimpering as though frustrated.

To my left, near the garage, I saw Otis, walking slowly away from me along the brown gravel drive, still carrying his shotgun. I stepped out and started as my foot hit against something soft on the brick. I hopped in surprise, and flipped on the outside lights. The floods blinded me briefly, but then I could see. At my feet lay a common black plastic garbage bag containing something roughly the dimensions of a small couch cushion. I picked it up while a realization suddenly soaked into me. My deputies notwithstanding, I'd had a visitor.

"Loo!" Otis shouted, running down the drive with the shotgun in both hands. "Jesus! Damn lights comin' on scared the shit outta me."

"Sorry, Otis," I said, tucking the package under my arm. "Just taking a breath of fresh air."

"No sweat, Sheriff. How you doin'? Cain't sleep?"

"Off and on. Can't get all those dead folks out of my bedroom. See you at daylight, Otis."

"G'night, Sheriff."

In my bedroom, Gruesome sniffed at the black plastic bag and licked the raindrops from its surface. I opened it and slid the contents out onto the bed.

Neatly folded was a small ankle-length dress splendidly hand-made of tanned doeskin, soft as chamois. It was finely and decoratively stitched with thin leather thong and fitted with buttons of carved deer antler artfully engraved with the initials EB. I was certain beyond question would fit Elizabeth perfectly.

On the beautiful dress were two other items. One was a small, galloping Irish pony, exquisitely carved of black walnut and in all respects identical to Dublin, strung on a strand of silver.

Elizabeth would be thrilled, and so would her granddaughters in their time.

The other item was a fresh, wet sprig of fragrant hemlock.

* * *

At dawn, I retrieved the quilt and covered Elizabeth still again. I placed the doeskin dress and the necklace at the foot of her bed.

With obvious puzzled expressions, Otis and Haskel waved at me as I rolled down the Mountain Harbor drive in the fog, driving the truck and pulling the trailer. The rig rocked as Moose shifted in the trailer, no doubt shaking her huge head at the lunacy of her master.

Mounted, it took only a little under an hour to make the hemlock cathedral near the ancient Indian caves. I dismounted Moose, and walked slowly along the rushing creek to the site of my campfire three nights earlier. Nothing but blackened wet sticks remained in the stones, but next to them rested the answer to several questions.

Caleb Horrow's long body lay wet and gray against a boulder. It was stiff and beginning to bloat. Both his hands, palms out, one on top of the other, were neatly skewered by a deer arrow, which nailed them to the left eye socket, through which the arrow had passed before stopping, protruding twelve inches out both sides of his skull. Horrow must have known he was about to die, and thus had thrown up both hands in a futile effort to stop the long feather-ended carbon shaft with its razor point. Black, caked rivulets of blood extended from the eye socket down his face and neck.

I suspect he was killed somewhere else and his body was brought to the cathedral of towering hemlocks. I also suspect he lived long enough after the arrow hit to understand the price for being an inconsiderate asshole.

I fished some items I brought with me from a saddle bag. I sat down and wrote a note, which I left at the hemlock grove, sealed in a sandwich bag, anchored to the boulder by a small rock. The note said:

The war has been over for twenty years. That good woman paid such a terrible price for fourteen of them. Hasn't she earned some happy years? Haven't you?

Butcher of the Noble

I fired nine shots into the mountainside, three short, three long, and three short. I picked up the hulls and I climbed into Moose's saddle.

I knew the note would be gone by the time a recovery party arrived to claim what remained of the butcher of the noble.

EPILOGUE

•••••••••

The sun shone at last, the day we buried Arthur near the Captain in the little plot overlooking the valley. Anne came in from UVA for the funeral, and it was good to have both my girls home again. Elizabeth wore the doeskin dress and the carved pony on the silver chain. I figured it would be at least a week before I could talk her into wearing anything else. It was.

We found a wet dress, a surgical scalpel, and a German army bayonet in Karin Steiger's room, at Laurel Ridge farm, all bloodstained. The evening after the morning we put Arthur to rest, we also buried Karin near the lake that would become part of Meriah Reinholdt's new Shenandoah Equestrian Center. Ambassador Goss Steiger agreed with Meriah that Karin would have wanted it. We buried Bitter Stone and Grand Teuton nearby. Meriah and the ambassador are seeing each other occasionally. Construction has begun on the stable. Already, the horse journals are calling it "the future of American equestrian excellence!"

I ride alone to Karin's grave sometimes, not to cry, but to sit in the peaceful meadow among wildflowers and remember a beautiful woman of immense passion, for they are few. Once, I found Meriah standing by the stone with Goss Steiger. He held her. I did not disturb them.

Merlin Sowers holds forth ad nauseam to all who will

listen about how his "vision of new vistas of greatness for Hunter County has resulted in a redefinition of the great horselands of America!" In the meantime, he steals about, trying to buy land short from uninformed farmers. I've managed to slip a word to the wise to most of the land-owners.

The day we released him, Boyce Calder voluntarily re-lated his transgressions to VSP Internal Affairs, who did an investigation and, given the mitigating circumstances, rec-ommended to Colonel Able Clair that Corporal Boyce Calder receive a letter of reprimand for conduct unbecom-ing a police officer. Clair overruled the recommendation and ordered it removed from Boyce's personnel file. Boyce was offered a month's bereavement leave, but he declined it. Wisely, in my judgment, Boyce went back on the road and immersed himself in his work. I offered him a low-rent arrangement on Arthur's apartment over the stable in exchange for part-time horse care and groundskeeping. He was pleased to accept. The grief is still in his eyes, but it is beginning to fade from his smile.

Julianne Chu bought into Hap Morgan's practice, and she's becoming popular far beyond the county's horse owners. "That little chink broad is the *best* goddamn vet *they is!*" Arnold the fire chief declared to the gentry, when his prize beagle got hit by a school bus and was saved by Julianne. She bought a little home on Bram's Ridge. Julianne and I ride together a lot, and have dinner occasion-ally. A rich friendship has grown; she says that in time there will be more. Who knows? The only sure thing about love is there's nothing sure about it.

Hap Morgan sticks pretty much to his small-animal patients, and fishes more these days.

In the "cause" blank of the death report on Caleb Horrow, the words *hunting accident* were written.

Six weeks later, on a snowy, lonely Christmas Eve at Cynthia Haas's little house, Garvin "Roadkill" Rudesill came in from the woods to stay. In February, Garvin and Cynthia Haas were married in a five-person ceremony in the hemlock cathedral. I was proud to be best man. Cynthia's little shop flourishes now. Customers drive in from as far away as Richmond; the *Roanoke Times* even did a style-section special on her. Awed by their beauty, customers and wholesalers alike ask Cynthia where she gets the exceptional leathercrafts and silver-inlaid, carved antler figurines she recently added to her line. She just smiles and glows.

Moose and Gruesome and I ride the Blue Ridge at sunset and look out on the Shenandoah. Sometimes I think maybe the scar-faced old dump-truck driver was wrong. Maybe it doesn't all turn to shit in the end.

AUDREY PETERSON

SHROUD
FOR A
SCHOLAR

A Claire
Camden
Mystery

"Audrey Peterson's mysteries are delightful,
engrossing and thoroughly enjoyable."
—Mary Higgins Clark

POCKET
B O O K S

1164